As he undressed her, Emma told him about her discoveries, that the pulse of the world beat in every object and that love and prayer were the same. When they were both naked, he pushed her down on the bed and lowered himself on top of her. His mouth covered hers, stopping the breathless flow of her words. When at last they found their rhythm and moved together, the pulse of the universe crashed in her ears like a tide.

After they made love for the first time, they slept, and awakened refreshed. Love came again and again, a promise which renewed itself every time it was fulfilled. She received his instructions humbly and obeyed his commands without question, because his desires were her desires. She felt no shyness, no awkwardness, only a willingness to yield.

The night went on forever . . .

WILD NIGHTS

NATASHA PETERS

FAWCETT COLUMBINE · NEW YORK

1

SEPTEMBER 8, 1952 (Postcard)

Dear Mom and Aunt Louise,

WOW! I finally made it to Cambodia! Trip up the Mekong River was beautiful but scary—boats travel in convoys as protection against pirates on water and guerrillas on land. After I explore Phnom Penh, I'm going to find a way to get to Angkor Wat. This has already been the most fantastic experience of my entire life! Can't wait to see what happens next!

Love, Emma

Alan Hazen lay as still as a dead man. Under his body, the hard earth smelled of rotting vegetation, baked clay, and his own sweat. Although the pistol in his belt dug painfully into his hip, he dared not shift his weight. The slightest shiver in the grass would alert the sniper, whose aim had already proved accurate and deadly. Just twelve feet away, flies were buzzing over the corpse of a Buddhist monk.

The sniper had stationed himself in the top gallery of the highest tower, a vine-encrusted pyramid of crumbling stones surmounted by lushly growing trees. From his prospect one hundred and fifty feet above the ground, the gunner commanded a panoramic view of the moat, the entrance, the overgrown courtyard, and the ruined temples.

The French archaeologists who had cleared and restored the ancient capital of Angkor Thom and the spectacular temple complex at Angkor Wat had ignored Ta Prouhm, a crumbling monastery in the jungle east of the abandoned city. Nowadays the ruins were nearly as wild and overgrown as they had been when the explorer Henri Mouhot had stumbled upon these lost enclaves a century earlier. After the fall of the Khmer empire in the fifteenth century, the jungle had moved in to embrace the ruins, throwing a lacy pall of roots and vines over every tower and gallery. Here in Ta Prouhm, floors tilted crazily, roofs opened to the sky, walls buckled, and doorways listed. Enormous stone faces peered through nets of roots and greenery as their great sightless eyes strained for a glimpse of the past.

Hazen's heart swelled and pounded within the cavity of his chest. To his left, across the corner of a courtyard, an immense silk-cotton tree had burst through the northern wall. Behind its roots he could find safety, shelter, and shade. But first he needed to cross twenty feet of open space, in full view of the sniper. He would have to wait to make his move until the sun swung around to the west, covering him with the shadow of the enclosing wall.

Hearing a noise, Hazen opened one wary eye. Someone had just entered the compound. Through the strands of grass at eye level, he saw tanned slender legs, a flash of white skirt, and a camera hanging in front of a small waist. A female tourist. He opened his mouth to shout a warning, but clamped it shut again. To call out now would be disastrous for both of them.

The woman seemed to be alone. She picked her way through the tall grass and halted halfway between Hazen and the beckoning shelter of the silk-cotton tree. From her oversized shoulder bag, she removed a small red-bound guidebook and opened it to a marked page in the middle. "Jayavarman," she said aloud. She was reading about the Khmer king under whose direction this temple had been constructed nearly eight hundred years ago. "Prajnaparamita, the Perfection of Wisdom." Slowly, she pronounced the name of the king's mother, whose image was enshrined at Ta Prouhm.

Hazen braced himself, expecting to hear the crack of a rifle and to see her crumple. Incredibly, the sniper held his fire. Curious, Hazen lifted his head half an inch to peer through the weeds and grass.

Blonde, fair, dressed in white, the woman seemed to glow with a ghostly radiance in the leafy gloom of the courtyard. Her golden hair was parted in the center, and it fell to her shoulders in smooth waves. As she gazed at the intricate facade of the temple, enmeshed in a web of roots and the tendrils of ancient trees, her lovely face opened into an expression of wonder and delight. No wonder the sniper hesitated to fire. Looking at her, Hazen realized that he had stopped breathing himself. Shifting his feet slightly, he gripped the earth with his toes and tensed every muscle in his body.

The girl put away her book and lifted her camera. Except for the erratic chatter of the birds and the distant shrill cry of a monkey, the courtyard remained silent.

Hazen sprang into action. The sniper's reflexes may have been dulled by the afternoon heat, for he did not begin firing until Hazen had nearly reached the girl. Grabbing her arm, Hazen dragged her along a zigzag course toward the shelter of the silk-cotton tree. Bullets whizzed around them. A blow on his right shoulder staggered him, but he forced his legs to keep moving. Reaching the tree, he pulled the girl down behind a mass of tangled roots between the trunk and the high wall, into a pocket that was not much larger than a packing crate.

The crackle of gunfire ceased. In the silence that followed, Hazen and the girl extricated themselves from a jumble of elbows and knees and sat up, arranging themselves side by side like two young birds in a nest.

Hazen was the first to catch his breath. "Who are you and what in hell are you doing here?"

Anger deepened the flush that exertion had brought to the girl's cheeks. "I might ask you the same question. What gives you the right to go manhandling perfectly innocent people—"

"Don't you know this whole area has been off limits for the past twelve hours?" Hazen winced as a bullet smacked into the tree trunk above their heads. The girl didn't seem to notice. "Didn't anybody warn you?"

"No, they didn't. Well, I guess the man at the guesthouse near Siem Reap did say something as I was leaving this morning." With a brisk motion, she brushed out her skirt, smoothing it down over her thighs. "But I don't speak French. I thought he was telling me to watch out for crocodiles in the moats. I walked around some barricades on the road near Angkor Wat, but— anyway, I had to see these temples. Aren't they incredible? The Khmer civilization was even more advanced than—"

Hazen expelled his breath. "You can't ignore warnings— Stop!" Seeing the girl lean forward to peer around the tree trunk, Hazen jerked her back. "For God's sake, keep down. That sniper's got us in his sights."

"But my camera. I dropped it when you attacked me."

"Camera? Is that all you can think about?"

"It wasn't just any camera. The Lincoln Rotary Club gave it to me. When I was chosen to be Miss Nebraska."

"Miss—" Hazen recoiled at the idea. The movement was slight, but the girl noticed it. Her chin went up.

"That's right, you heard correctly. I was Miss Nebraska of 1947, and I'm proud of it. Oh, I know what you're thinking. I can see it in your eyes. You think that beauty queens are brainless bimbos who don't have anything better to do than parade around in bathing suits and smile for the judges. Well, am I right?"

"I can't understand why any decent young lady would want to display her body to strangers," Hazen said stiffly.

"Well, I'll tell you why, Mr. Whatever-Your-Name-Is. I happen to have a pretty face and I look sensational in a bathing suit. My mother and I worked very hard so I could capitalize on those assets. By winning that title, I earned enough money to pay for four years of college at the University of Nebraska. As for being decent—oh, my goodness! You're bleeding!"

Hazen glanced down at his right shoulder, which he had kept turned away from his companion. Blood was flowing down his arm to his wrist. Flies had already alighted on the wound. Probing with his fingertips, he found torn tissue and some chips of bone. His right hand felt numb, but he could still move his fingers. At least the bullet had not damaged any vital nerves.

The color had drained out of the girl's cheeks. "Does it—does it hurt?"

Hazen took a handkerchief out of the pocket of his khaki trousers. "What do you think?" he growled. "Of course it hurts. Bind it up. Come on, hurry. What's the matter, are you afraid of blood?"

The girl tossed her golden curls. "Why didn't you say something sooner? When I was in high school during the war, I worked as a nurse's aide in the VA hospital in Lincoln." She lifted up her skirt and pulled a white cotton half-slip down around her hips over her knees. "I have yards of fabric here." A faint expression of regret crossed her face; then she began tearing strips off the bottom. Using Hazen's large handkerchief as a pad to staunch the bleeding, she bound the arm. Wriggling back into the remains of the slip, she announced, "That's the best I can do right now. You really ought to see a doctor."

"Thank you. Maybe the nice man with the rifle will write me an excuse." Hazen pulled his pistol out of his belt and flicked off the safety catch. The girl's eyes widened. They were clear and green, like the water in some tropical lagoon. "Looks like we're going to be stuck here for a while, Miss Nebraska."

"My name is Emma Louise Vaughan."

Her white skirt was stained and wilted. Through her sweat-soaked blouse, Hazen could see the outlines of her brassiere. Her breasts were a healthy size, swelling generously above her small waist. She probably did look sensational in a bathing suit. He swallowed hard and looked away.

Emma Vaughan endured his scrutiny without flinching. She was accustomed to men assaying her proportions. "And what's your name?" she asked.

"Hazen. Alan Hazen." With his left hand, Hazen groped clumsily in his shirt pocket for his cigarettes. He found them—squashed, broken, and soaked with perspiration and blood—and tossed them away. He should have had the wits to bring his pipe. "You're a long way from home, Miss Nebraska. I mean, Emmy Lou."

"My name is Emma," she corrected him. "The last person who called me Emmy Lou met a horrible fate."

"I'll bet he did."

Emma studied her companion. Alan Hazen was older than the boys she had dated back home, but a good deal younger than the men she saw at church and family gatherings, other people's uncles and fathers and grandfathers. This man fell somewhere in between, into that vast stretch of years between thirty and fifty. Everything about him was long, brown, and weathered like a lone prairie tree: long hands, long face, long nose. A hank of long brown hair fell over his high forehead. His eyes, a brilliant shade of blue, were a striking exception.

"That man," Emma said, "the one who's shooting at us. Is he a Viet Minh?"

Hazen shook his head. "An Issarak, more likely. From the Nekhum Issarak Khmer, the Cambodian Khmer Freedom Front. They've formed an alliance with the Viet Minh and the Pathet Lao in Laos. They're all Reds masquerading under fancy names."

"Golly." Emma opened her purse and took out a small notebook. She flipped to a blank page. "How do you spell Issarak?" Hazen told her, and she scribbled busily. "And your name, Mr. Hazen? Do you spell that with an *a* or an *e*?"

Hazen supplied the correct vowel. "What's that, your diary?"

Emma smiled. Her teeth were white and even. She looked like the sort of fresh-faced girl who should have been advertising soda pop or tooth whiteners. "No, I'm a journalist. A foreign correspondent. That's why I have to see everything right away. This is my first job outside the United States."

Hazen snorted. "I can't believe any editor worth his salt would turn a greenhorn like you loose in Southeast Asia in the middle of a war."

"For your information, Mr. Hazen, I turned myself loose

here," Emma said. "I'm free-lancing until I get some experience. I spent three dismal years working for the *Lincoln Sentinel*, reporting on meetings of the Ladies' Methodist Auxiliary and fashion shows at the local department stores and reunions of the university cheerleaders, the sort of thing women reporters have always been stuck with. I kept asking for a better job, but my editor was a lot like you: stubborn and prejudiced and small-minded."

"Now wait—" Hazen began.

"No, you wait a minute." Her green eyes grew dark. "It's time somebody told you what the world is all about, Mr. Hazen. This is 1952, not 1852. We women don't have to wait for permission from you men before we do something exciting and worthwhile. That's what I told Edward. He's my fiancé, or at least he was until I decided to become a foreign correspondent. 'You go to Indochina and we're finished,' he said. That was on the Fourth of July. I handed his ring back and I said, 'Then I guess we're finished.' He was so shocked he told me I could keep the ring. I did, too, for a whole week, and then I sold it to help pay for my passage. I also sold my car and my stamp collection. Then I borrowed some money from my mother and my Aunt Louise, and here I am."

Hazen groaned aloud. He could hardly believe his bad luck: trapped under a sniper's sights with a useless arm and a mindless ex-beauty queen yakking in his ear.

Emma assumed a professional attitude, her pencil poised over the page. "And what about you, Mr. Hazen? If this area is sealed off, what are you doing here?"

"Miss Vaughan, I am in no mood to be interviewed right now. I have a lot on my mind—namely, how I'm going to get us out of here alive."

"That's not so hard. Why can't we wait until after the sun goes down and then walk away?"

"I might have done that if I were alone. But now I've got you to worry about. The moon is on the wane, but it will still be plenty bright tonight, and in this white dress of yours, you'll shine like the Hope diamond. He would have to be a pretty bad shot to miss us, and he's not. He's damned good. Besides, he's not alone. His friends have an arsenal in one of the inner chambers of the temple."

"Really? How do you know that?"

"See that pile of yellow-orange cloth in the grass over there?" He indicated a spot slightly to the right of the central tower. "That is—or was—a *bonze*, a Buddhist monk. Before the sniper shot him, he told me that the Issaraks have been active in this area for some time. The French didn't seem to know about it, or if they did, they took no action. At this moment, the rebels control the entire area around Angkor Wat. They've killed several tourists, as well as a few monks."

"Golly." Emma chewed the end of her pencil while she absorbed this information. "Angkor Wat is the most famous spot in Cambodia, isn't it? If they've stored up enough food and ammunition, they could stay here for days, even weeks. By that time, the whole world will have taken notice." She bent her head over her notebook and scribbled madly for half a minute. "Who's their leader?" she demanded.

Hazen shrugged. "I'd like to know that myself. Maybe I could persuade him to let us go. We are neutrals."

Emma looked thoughtful. "On the other hand, if they find out we're American, they might try even harder to kill us. After all, they're trying to make a political statement, aren't they? You know what happens any time an American is killed abroad: The press picks it up, pretty soon the whole country's talking; then Congress takes notice and demands that something be done to protect our nationals in foreign lands. It's just the kind of publicity these people want. Of course, I'm nobody. I mean, I'm not even officially employed by the *Lincoln Sentinel* anymore. But you might be important. Just what do you do for a living, Mr. Hazen?"

Hazen polished the barrel of his pistol against his thigh. "I'm a geologist for Chrome Petroleum of Fort Worth."

"Really?" Emma sat up straighter. "You don't sound like you're from Texas."

"These days people go where their work takes them."

Emma looked interested. "So you're searching for oil here?"

"We're doing preliminary studies of the terrain," Hazen said vaguely. "The French government would like to keep the rest of the world out of Indochina. But we at Chrome Petroleum would like to make our own leasing arrangements in Laos and Cambodia, which are supposedly independent states."

"Those French make me so mad," Emma fumed. "What are they doing in this part of the world, anyway?"

Hazen cupped his left hand under the opposite elbow. The blood from the wound in his arm was stiffening as it dried on the bandages. "The French have a lot at stake here. Why shouldn't they try to take back their plantations and factories? The government at home is nearly bankrupt. The mines and plantations in Vietnam have made a lot of Frenchmen very rich."

"But it's not fair!" Emma protested. "France lived under Nazi domination for five years, and the French hated it. Now they're turning right around and trying to subjugate someone else."

"Baloney. The rest of the world should be thankful the French are here." The shock had worn off, and the onset of pain was beginning to make Hazen feel dizzy and nauseated. "They're doing our job for us, checking the spread of communism, which is the greatest spread of evil in the world today."

"War is the greatest evil in the world today," Emma sniffed. "What does it matter to the people of Southeast Asia whether the guns that kill and maim them are Chinese or French, communist or capitalist?"

Sweat trickled down Hazen's cheeks. "You will find that the situation here is not as simple—"

His tongue felt furry and thick. A loud rushing noise filled his ears. "Mr. Hazen!" He forced himself to open his eyes. A small sunburned nose and a pair of concerned green eyes hovered very close to his face. "Are you all right?"

A spasm of pain wracked his body. Hazen clamped his teeth down on his lower lip. The moment passed, leaving him white-faced and shaken. "I've come through worse than this. Where's my pistol?" Finding it, he cradled the big .45 in his lap. "They'll try something before it gets dark. Got to keep awake. Don't let me fall asleep. Talk to me. Keep talking."

"Well, that's easy. I've never had any trouble talking." Emma Vaughan fanned him with her notebook. "Let's see, where shall I start? How about my itinerary? I took the train from Lincoln to San Francisco; then I found a freighter that was going to Honolulu, Manila, and Singapore. Hawaii was dreamy, but I didn't think too much of Singapore. Too dirty. Anyway, from there I took a cargo steamer to Phnom Penh. I never get seasick, even though broad bodies of water are not easy to come by in Nebraska. I've always loved the water. But I can't stand heights, which is why I never went in for diving. I climbed to the high board once and then I couldn't get down. It was awful."

She waved the notebook gently in front of his face. From time to time she mopped his forehead and cheeks with a leftover strip of fabric from her slip. Her voice was pleasant, high and clear but not shrill. Hazen's eyelids began to droop.

"I visited Angkor Thom this morning, before I came here. I couldn't believe that I was actually walking through the Imperial City of the Khmers. I don't know how I'm going to describe it to Mom and Aunt Louise—I think I'll tell Aunt Louise to get a book from the library. She's a librarian. Anyway, I saw the Elephant Terrace and the Terrace of the Leper King—do you know about him, Mr. Hazen? Yoo-hoo, are you still awake?"

"Legend," Hazen said in a sluggish murmur. "Cambodians are very superstitious. They have all sorts of myths—"

"Oh, I don't think it was a myth. The man in the statue had a kind face, very serene and thoughtful. I read about him in my guidebook. The king had conquered his enemies, and he was leading his army into the city in a victory parade. The people were cheering, throwing flowers, celebrating wildly. All of a sudden a woman dashed out from the crowd, right in front of the king's horse. The horse reared up and threw him, and the woman rushed over and embraced the king and kissed him. The crowd was horrified and everyone ran away, even the king's bodyguards, because the woman was a leper. The king lost his throne and was locked up in a cell. But his wives dug a tunnel to reach him, and they stayed with him until he died."

Alan Hazen's chin touched his chest. Emma wondered if she should awaken him, and decided to let him sleep. He was clearly exhausted, and the wound in his arm must have been painful.

The heavy pistol slipped out of Hazen's fingers. Moving slowly so as not to awaken him, Emma picked up the weapon and hefted it. A chill ran up her arm. The gun was weighty, cold, and lethal, an iron embodiment of death. But it was all the protection they had from the Issaraks. Emma curled her fingers around the grip, lifted the gun with both hands, and sighted along the barrel. Her forefinger rested on the curve of the trigger. The gunfighters she had seen in the movies always handled these weapons easily as if they were made of balsa wood. Long ago, in one of her wilder adolescent fantasies, Emma had imagined herself as a girl gunslinger, a sort of Calamity Jane who could outride and outshoot any man in the Nebraska Territory. She wondered if she could bring herself to aim this weapon at another human being and pull the trigger.

Hazen moaned softly in his sleep. Emma felt her own eyes growing heavy in the heat of the afternoon. Prodding herself to stay awake, she studied the section of wall through which the tree had erupted. It was covered with a frieze of *apsarases*, barebreasted dancing girls, in various graceful postures. Emma could imagine the women of Lincoln, Nebraska, confronted with these lovelies: Their prudish pioneer souls would shrink from this display of insouciant paganism. She smiled to herself.

The shadows of the trees and the temple buildings lengthened. A flicker of gold brightened the gloom. Emma caught her breath: A flight of yellow butterflies, thousands of them, drifted under the dark canopy of leaves that hung over the corner of the courtyard. They danced and swirled in soft silence, like petals of sunlight. Emma thought longingly of her camera, lying just out of reach in the grass. To capture this moment, she would have to rely on her skill with words.

Suddenly the lazy, swirling pattern of the golden flight altered.

The butterflies dispersed raggedly and then vanished. Emma heard a rustle in the grass on the other side of the tree. Her bowels contracted and her mouth went dry. The pleasurable shivers of fear that the ghost stories of her childhood had evoked were nothing like this cold terror, this paralysis that knotted her insides and froze her legs. The gun in her hands felt as cumbersome and useless as a plumber's wrench.

"Mr. Hazen." She tried to speak, but produced a barely audible squeak. Panic had closed her throat. "Mr. Hazen, wake up."

Then a figure appeared about twenty feet in front of her. The man's hair and eyes and clothes were black. His skin was the color of burnished copper. With a hoarse cry of *"Bâtards américains!"* he hurled something into the nook in which Hazen and Emma had found shelter. Emma screamed and squeezed the trigger of the .45. The gun went off with a deafening report. The brown man disappeared.

Instantly awake, Hazen saw the object the man had thrown at them: a grenade the size of an orange. Without thinking, he hurled it into the center of the courtyard and threw himself on top of Emma. The explosion opened a crater in the moldy earth and showered them with bits of grass, pebbles, and clods of dirt.

Emma had never heard anything so loud as the noise of that explosion. It filled her mouth with a metallic taste and reverberated through all the cells in her body. Oh, God, she thought, I don't want to die. Not yet. Let me live a little longer, just a little longer. Hazen's pistol fired over her head—once, twice, a third time.

Finally Hazen eased himself off her. He was furious. "I told you not to let me fall asleep."

"I kept talking, but you wouldn't stay awake." Emma sat up. She felt hot, shaken, and sick.

Awkwardly, with his numbed hand, Hazen shoved fresh bullets into the chambers of the pistol. "Crazy women, no brains at all, just cotton wool stuffed between their ears. Didn't you think that sniper was for real?"

"Yes, of course I did, but—"

"Next time follow orders." Hazen snapped the revolving cylinder back into place.

Emma studied him through narrowed eyes. "That man said something before he threw the grenade. In French. He called us American bastards. My French is pretty terrible, but I understood that much. He knew that you—that we were Americans."

"That's ridiculous." Hazen looked up from the pistol. His gaze was steady. "To him, all white men are foreigners and therefore they're bastards. French or American, it makes no difference. We all look the same to him."

Emma remembered some advice given her by a veteran political reporter at the *Sentinel*: If they don't blink, they're lying. If they do blink, they're lying.

She retrieved her fallen notebook and pencil. She wanted to write about the experience, but it was too fresh and she was too rattled. Instead, she tried to describe the butterflies, but her joy at seeing them had been swept away by the orgy of noise and violence. She managed to jot down, "Swarm yellow b-flies, like autumn leaves," before closing the notebook.

Hazen rested his elbows on his knees and gripped the pistol with both hands. Emma asked him if the assassin would return. He shook his head. "He knows we're armed. He might try something after dark, but not before then." His gaze was fixed on the middle distance, like a sailor scanning the horizon. His attitude suggested that he would not be caught napping again.

"You don't like women, do you, Mr. Hazen?" Emma asked after a while.

"They have their place."

"In the kitchen and the nursery, you mean. Are you married?"

"I was." The corner of Hazen's mouth twitched, not with amusement. "Let me give you some advice, Miss Vaughan. Go home and marry Edgar or Edward or whatever his name was. Have six kids and join the Methodist Ladies' Auxiliary, and forget you ever saw Cambodia. This is no place for a green kid from Lincoln, Nebraska."

"Let me tell you, Mr. Hazen, this green kid has no intention of going back to Lincoln." With a furious gesture, Emma shoved her notebook into her purse. "Do you have any idea what life in the Midwest is like? Your neighbors make your business their own, and if you dare suggest something radical or revolutionary, they treat you like some kind of Red Menace. No, Mr. Hazen, I am not going to take your advice. I would rather die here, right now, than go back home and become Mrs. Edward Adams, or Mrs. Anybody Else, and bake cookies and mend shirts and wash diapers. For the first time in my life, I feel like I'm really living." Crossing her arms in front of her waist, she glared at the soft-edged shadows.

"This country isn't very hospitable to foreigners," Hazen told her. "Many of the people here are godless, corrupt, utterly without moral principles. I knew a man in Saigon who worked for the American embassy. His name was Morton, Alexander Morton. He shot himself in the head, in a stinking opium den in Cholon. That's the kind of glamour you'll find in Indochina, Miss Vaughan. Not a couple of movie stars hacking their way through a Hollywood jungle, and then making love while somebody plays a violin in the background. You don't know what it's like here—"

"I doubt very much if I will hear the truth from you." Emma inched away from him and drew her skirt tighter around her knees. "I know what I want, and I'm going to find it here."

Darkness descended with tropical swiftness. No twilight, no long red sunset, no dreamy onset of evening. As if on cue, birds ceased their songs and monkeys their chatter. Insects awoke from their daytime torpor and began to saw and rattle and chirp. Hazen struggled to stay awake. At his side, Emma Louise Vaughan sat erect, smiling slightly as her imagination soared.

2

SEPTEMBER 12, 1952

Dear Mom and Aunt Louise,

You won't believe the things that have happened to
me since the last time I wrote! I've been menaced
by guerrilla soldiers, pinned down by sniper fire,
rescued by a handsome captain of the French
Foreign Legion, and made a mascot by an entire
regiment of paratroopers. Really, could Hollywood
do any better? . . .

The moon had risen, filling the courtyard with a pale, smoky
light.

Emma shifted her weight onto her right hip. No matter what
position she tried, she could not make herself comfortable in
their cramped quarters. Beside her, Hazen seemed sunk in contemplation. He reminded her of a stone Buddha, able to sit for
hours without moving or even blinking his eyes. Watching him,
her natural curiosity reasserted itself.

"You said you were married once, Mr. Hazen. Does that mean
you're not anymore?"

Although Hazen made no movement, Emma felt him grow
tense. "We're divorced," he said after a moment.

"Oh. Was she pretty?"

"I suppose so. I really can't remember. She was blonde, like
you."

"Where did you live?"

"In a house somewhere."

"What do you mean, somewhere? Where, exactly?"

"What does it matter? It all happened a long time ago."

"So that's how you want to play, is it?" Emma was pleased. This little excursion into her companion's private life was proving unexpectedly stimulating. "All right, I don't mind. We have a long night ahead of us and I can be very persistent."

Hazen, who had known many journalists, was appalled that one so young had all the right inquisitive instincts. She asked more questions: Where had he grown up? What did his father do? Had he gone to college? Hazen continued to feign ignorance and loss of memory. Momentarily defeated, Emma lapsed into a sullen silence.

Hazen watched the play of the moon and the shadows on the wall friezes. The lovely bare-bosomed *apsarases* seemed to be moving, gliding, turning slowly. If he listened hard enough, would he hear them laughing, singing, chattering to each other in the ancient Khmer language?

"I can't stand much more of this." Emma gave an angry flounce. "Those guys in the temple have gone to sleep. Why don't we just walk out of here?"

"Because I am weak from loss of blood, and I can't depend on my reflexes," Hazen explained with elaborate patience. "My right hand is useless, and I cannot shoot accurately with my left. I don't need to remind you that you can't shoot at all. We'll just have to wait here until we're rescued."

"I might as well be in a cave with a big black bear," Emma grumbled. "He'd be better company."

Hours passed. Emma seemed to melt with heat and fatigue, sinking gradually lower until her head came to rest on Hazen's lap. She slept soundly, breathing with a deep, peaceful rhythm that reminded Hazen of the child he had fathered long ago. He glanced down at her. In the moonlight, her golden hair gleamed like priceless treasure. Her ivory arms had fallen into a pose as graceful as any of those assumed by the stone dancing girls who kept watch over them from the wall.

Hazen wondered what fate had appointed him to guard this beautiful innocent. He had lost his own innocence of the world when he was about her age. A pair of gray-flanneled visitors had come to his office at the university one day. Britain's war with Germany had just begun and America stood firm behind a policy of isolationism. But certain people in Washington were worried about the enemy's long-range military capability. America had needed Alan Hazen.

The rattle of insects was accompanied by the high-pitched squeaks of bats, hundreds of them. All the old temples around Angkor Wat were full of them, especially Ta Prouhm. From time to time, Hazen saw one swoop low over their hiding place to snatch an insect out of the air.

He felt uneasy. At night, the jungle was a different world, one in which men had no place. Only at night did he find himself believing in the ghosts and demons and evil spirits who ruled the lives of the natives of Southeast Asia.

He scolded himself for discarding his damaged cigarettes. He could have salvaged the tobacco and rolled it into a piaster note or a page from the girl's notebook. God knows, he needed something to distract him, and to fend off the memories that lurked in the shadows, waiting to pounce on him. Emma Vaughan, with her all-American smile and stunning naïveté, had brought them with her, like infant-demons clinging to her skirts. They waited, murmuring in faint whispers among themselves, laughing softly, taunting him. A sharp-faced blonde woman, a towheaded little girl with silken hair and smooth, warm cheeks. A small house on a shaded street. Sunday mornings in church. Chalk dust on a blackboard. The fog of cigarette smoke and gossip in the faculty lounge. He had given them all up so readily, so eagerly.

The pain in his shoulder was like an auger boring into his flesh, persistent and sharp-toothed. He was grateful to it for keeping him awake. On the other side of the crumbling walls, the jungle breathed like a sleeping giant. Hazen listened for changes in the rhythm, the first bird calls that would precede the dawn, the low growl of a tiger, the splash of a fish or a turtle in the moat.

He did not know what the day would bring, but he was eager for the night to end. He tightened his fingers around the grip of his pistol.

In the moments just before dawn, Hazen was aroused from a near doze by the drone of an airplane. Through a break in the leaves of the silk-cotton tree, he saw a flower blossoming in the sky, blazing like a crimson poppy as it caught the light of the rising sun. Another parachute burst into bloom, and then another. He sighed. Their ordeal was almost over.

A short spurt of gunfire on the other side of the wall shattered the quiet. Emma sat up, instantly awake. Hazen, who had allowed his left arm to fall over her waist as she slept, kept his hand on her shoulder as insurance. He didn't want her to do anything stupid.

"What is it? What's happening?" She seemed not to be aware of his touch.

"Comb your hair and freshen up your lipstick." Her flesh was cool and firm. She felt different from the Vietnamese girls he had known, stronger and more substantial. It had been a long time since he had held an American girl in his arms. "We're being liberated."

The sounds of battle came closer. Three men wearing camouflage fatigues ran into the center of the courtyard. They fell, one after another, clutching their middles, as if their whole purpose in entering the temple grounds were to receive death. From the great crumbling tower of the temple, the sniper raked the courtyard with machine-gun fire.

"Those soldiers will never get near him." Emma strained against the pressure of Hazen's hand. "He's too well placed. And you said he had a cache of arms—"

Someone vaulted over the crumbling stone wall about ten yards from where Hazen and Emma sat. Hazen hailed him, and he ran toward the sheltering embrace of the silk-cotton tree. In one hand he carried a pistol, in the other a knife with a curving blade. Reaching them, he threw himself down behind the root mass.

"*Bonjour, madame. Monsieur.*"

Hazen spoke rapid French to the soldier, who listened, nodding, not taking his eyes off Emma. He looked like an Arab, with black eyes, close-cut black hair, and smooth olive-toned features. He wore his red beret at a rakish tilt. Where Hazen was long and lean, this soldier was compact, powerful, and well muscled. Emma thought he was the handsomest man she had ever seen. She wanted to ask his name, but the words dried in her throat.

The deadly voice from the tower stopped momentarily while the gunman changed ammo belts. Seizing his opportunity, the paratrooper vaulted lightly over the hummock of roots and sprinted toward the temple.

"But he'll be killed!" Emma attempted to peer around the solid trunk of the silk-cotton tree. Hazen grabbed her arm and pulled her back to safety.

"He knows what he's doing. His men can't move until somebody wipes out that sniper."

The crass, nerve-shattering din of the sniper's gun seemed to last forever. Emma pictured each shot as a period hammered out on a gigantic typewriter, an endless string of black dots, noisy and evenly spaced and too numerous to count. For the first time she was afraid to leave her shelter and look around the tree, afraid that she would see the mad, brave soldier lying on the ground outside the temple while bullets shredded his body.

The barking of the sniper's gun was silenced. Closing her eyes, Emma breathed a prayer of thanks. With a shout, the red-bereted paratrooper appeared on the top gallery of the tower. More soldiers poured through the gate. They were slowed by sporadic fire from the area behind the temple, but they fanned out and surrounded the structure. After fifteen minutes, all was quiet again. The battle for Ta Prouhm was over.

A warm glow surged through Emma's body. Looking down, she saw that her hands had been clenched so tightly that her fingernails had pierced the flesh. For a few minutes, the life of that brave paratrooper meant more to her than her own life, her job, her title as Miss Nebraska, more than anything that had ever happened to her. She tried to stand up and almost fell. After a night on the ground, her limbs were numb, wobbly and unreliable.

"Wait until you're sure it's safe," Hazen warned.

She ignored him. Out in the courtyard, two men were attending to the wounded. Overhead, the leaves of the silk-cotten tree rattled as a monkey swung through the branches. Looking up, Emma gazed straight into a beam of sunlight.

"You are not hurt?"

Emma blinked and tried to readjust her focus. The brave soldier stood in front of her. She shook her head, then realized that he had spoken to her in English. "No, thanks to you," she said warmly. "I didn't think we'd ever get out from behind that tree."

Hazen came up behind her. "Good work, Captain. We were getting desperate."

"The area is secure now," the captain assured them. "But you are wounded, my friend. The beast got you, eh?" Hazen introduced himself. The soldier did not ask what an employee of Chrome Petroleum was doing in a restricted area in Cambodia. "We have taken a few prisoners," he told Hazen. "We will move them to our base at Baray for interrogation."

"Can you fellows give me a lift?" Hazen asked. "I can catch a plane at Baray for Saigon."

"Of course. Everyone wants to go to Saigon, yes?" A dimple appeared on the captain's left cheek. "We will get there ourselves eventually. The journey by road through the jungle may be delayed by these Issaraks."

Emma spoke up. "May I come with you, too? I'm heading for Saigon myself—that is, if it wouldn't be too much trouble."

The captain smiled, and glanced at Hazen. "Your wife, monsieur?"

Emma answered quickly. "Not at all. We met purely by accident. My name is Emma Louise Vaughan, Captain. I'm a foreign correspondent, from America," With dazzling swiftness, Emma produced her credentials, a notebook and pencil. "May I have your name, and the name of your—ah, your unit?"

"Certainly, mademoiselle. I am Captain Robert Janvier of the Premier Bataillon Étranger Parachutiste, that is, the First Paratroop Battalion of the French Foreign Legion. Everyone calls it the First BEP."

"You're really a Legionnaire!"

Hazen smirked inwardly. On Emma's lips, the word sounded almost reverential. Meanwhile, Emma was struggling to pronounce Janvier's name correctly: "Row-BEAR Zhan-vee-AY. Is that like the month?"

"Yes, the same thing. I joined the Legion in the month of January. The name seemed appropriate."

"Then it's not your real—"

"A nom de guerre, mademoiselle. The Legionnaire does not use his real name. It is traditional." Janvier watched a group of his men emerge from the bowels of the temple carrying crates of arms. Emma's gaze traveled to the bodies of several French soldiers being loaded into a truck at the main gate. Then she followed the captain over to the bloodied corpses of four Issaraks lying at the foot of the temple.

"Japanese," Janvier declared when he had examined their guns, "left over from the last war. The Viet Minh use the same weapons."

Simultaneously with the parachute drop, Legion jeeps and personnel carriers had arrived from the garrison at Phnom Penh. They were waiting on the main road between Siem Reap and the great temple of Angkor Wat, a couple of miles away. Now the captured weapons and a handful of prisoners were loaded into the backs of two of the jeeps. Janvier sent one of his men to fetch Emma's suitcases and portable typewriter from the guesthouse near Siem Reap where she had been staying. Emma found her camera, miraculously undamaged, and then with Hazen she climbed into the first jeep, behind Janvier and his driver. A Legion medical officer had changed the bandages on Hazen's arm and had given him a shot of penicillin to ward off infection, but he felt fatigued from lack of sleep and dizzy from the hard red wine Janvier's driver had given him.

As they passed the great temple at Angkor Wat, Emma twisted around in her seat and gazed at the five immense towers rising out of the jungle. Hazen watched her face. She could not have looked more rapt and enchanted if she had emerged from a fairy tale.

A few minutes after leaving Siem Reap, the convoy of jeeps and trucks left the main road. Janvier turned to Emma. "That way is too dangerous. The jungle is very close, and makes it easy for the enemy to ambush us."

They passed through the marshland surrounding Tonle Sap, the immense lake that lay at the heart of Cambodia. Almost fifty miles wide and a hundred miles long, the lake was really an inland sea that supplied the marsh dwellers with quantities of fish. Centuries ago, Khmer engineers had crisscrossed the country with canals, ponds, and reservoirs, as well as an irrigation system that still made it possible for farmers to raise three rice crops a year.

Images passed too swiftly for Emma to record them in her notebook. At the edge of the marshland, the jungle thinned to clumps of greenery rising out of plains of golden grass. Small villages built on stilts huddled at the edges of the lake. Children played on narrow verandas above the gound, or in narrow skiffs tethered to the posts that supported their dwellings. Water buffalo wallowed in the shallows. Fishnets and strings of colorful laundry flapped in the breeze. Life here was no struggle to survive, but a simple matter of harvesting the bounty that nature provided.

Children as well as adults wore cone-shaped bamboo hats to ward off the burning rays of the sun. Janvier purchased one from an old woman and presented it to Emma along with a stern lecture on the folly of exposing one's head to the midday sun.

As they rode, he offered commentary on the passing scene, pointing out to Emma a blue heron wading in the shallows, a soaring eagle, a king cobra coiled at the side of the road.

"The most deadly snake of all," he told her, "but the only one of the species to care for her offspring. If you find a small nest of cobra eggs, be on guard. The mother will not be far away."

The road through the marshes was only a narrow track, barely wide enough to accommodate the chunky personnel carriers that followed Janvier's jeep. They bounced along, pitching in and out of potholes, meeting an occasional boy driving a water buffalo or a few women carrying baskets slung from poles on their shoulders. Janvier ordered no stop for lunch, but instead shared candy bars and cigarettes with his driver and two passengers. Emma wondered if she would ever eat a real meal again. Beside her, Hazen was wrapped in impregnable silence.

Late that afternoon, they reached the Legion outpost at Baray. The dismal-looking village was surrounded by a barbed wire fence that was broken by four guard towers. Except for a cluster of raised huts, a clump of ragged palm trees in the center of the compound provided the only scrap of shade.

"We try never to be on the road after dark," Janvier told Emma as he helped her out of the jeep. "At night, the jungles and the swamps belong to the guerrillas. They are welcome to them. You will be staying with Lieutenant Burton, in that hut over there." He motioned to a young officer climbing out of the jeep behind them. "The lieutenant will show you to your quarters. If you need anything, she will do her best to supply it."

Emma gave the officer a closer look. The hips were definitely broader that Janvier's, and the chest hinted at unmasculine contours under the wrinkled uniform blouse. The woman approached them, nodded to Janvier, and greeted Hazen and Emma in French.

"Our guests are both American," Janvier told her. "This will give you a chance to use your English, Constance." He turned to Emma. "Lieutenant Burton might interest you, since you are a writer. She is the only woman in the history of the Legion ever to hold rank. If her next promotion goes through, I will be able to salute her and address her as 'Ma Capitaine,' a rare privilege in any army. Go along, you will find her quarters quite comfortable. At least she keeps her mosquito netting mended and in good repair, isn't that right, Constance?" He laughed pleasantly, then gave Emma a casual but friendly salute. "We shall meet again at dinner, mademoiselle. Your hostess will escort you to the mess hall at the proper time."

Lieutenant Burton turned on her heel and swung off in a manly stride toward her hut. Emma followed reluctantly, with a backward glance at Janvier. They climbed a rustic ladder to the veranda, the lieutenant scrambling up with agile grace in her heavy boots while Emma tried to keep her thin-soled sandals from slipping on the rungs.

Inside, the hut was airy and clean, with bamboo mats on the floor, a cot draped with mosquito netting, and a pitcher and basin on a washstand. Lieutenant Burton scooped up an armful of the netting from a pile in the corner and carried it out to the veranda. She dumped it on a second cot, actually a small straw-filled mattress on a bamboo frame.

The woman spoke to Emma in rapid French, indicating the hooks on the ceiling from which to hang the netting, instructing Emma to make sure it was tucked in on all sides of the mattress.

"I'm sorry, but I don't speak French." Emma quailed inwardly at the hard expression in Lieutenant Burton's blue eyes. What was the matter with her? Couldn't she at least be friendly? "Is there someplace where I can take a bath? And I really need to go to the bathroom. I didn't want to make the convoy stop—"

Pushing her way past Emma into the hut's single room, the lieutenant pulled out a chamber pot from under her cot, then jerked her head at the pitcher and basin.

"There's plenty of water in there," she said in perfect English. "If you want more, ring the bell at the corner of the veranda. One of the servants will come." She crossed the room and the veranda, swung herself down the ladder, and disappeared.

Emma stood still in the middle of the floor and wiped her eyes with the hem of her soiled skirt. Captain Janvier's kindness, his easy acceptance of her, had not prepared her to expect such rudeness from one of his fellow officers. Odd, she felt more hostility from this woman than she had from the sniper last night. She wondered how dour, dependable Alan Hazen would deal with a formidable person like Lietutenant Burton.

Emma was just fluffing her damp hair when she heard a familiar voice on the veranda.

"Are you well, mademoiselle? Our dinner is half over and you have not appeared. Constance said you wanted to stay in your room."

"No, I'm coming." Emma clenched her teeth. That bitch Burton— She wished she had a mirror larger than the small disc in her compact. Her blouse was clean but wrinkled. She tucked it neatly into the waistband of her summer-weight trousers and went out to greet her host. He, too, had bathed, and had put on fresh fatigues. "I'm sorry to be late. I guess I lost track of the time."

The woman hadn't even sent a servant to fetch her. She might have starved waiting for something to eat.

"Come. My fellow officers are eager to drink a toast to you."

Janvier led the way down the ladder and stood at the bottom to give Emma his hand as she descended. They went to the officers' mess, located in a shabby bungalow just inside the fence. To Emma's surprise, the table was set with white linen and china, glass tumblers, and bottles of mineral water and white wine. The officers had dined on baked fish fillets, fried plantain, and rice pudding.

Janvier introduced Emma to his superior officers, Colonel Clermont and Major Bernhard, and then to the junior officers. All of the men rose and bowed to the new arrival. Only Lieutenant Burton remained seated near the end of the table, idly crushing out a cigarette on her empty plate. Janvier told Emma that Alan Hazen felt too ill to come to dinner. A steward had taken a tray to his room.

A Cambodian servant wearing black trousers and a white tunic appeared at Emma's left elbow and noiselessly placed a steaming platter on the table in front of her.

"Our cook is excellent," Janvier said, "but here he lacks the ingredients to create a truly brilliant meal. And so we must make do, as you Americans say."

"Have you been to America, Captain?"

Janvier filled her wineglass, and then his own. "In my youth, I passed many hours in dark cinemas watching American films. My friends and I considered it vital to our education."

"Where did you grow up?"

From the few sharp intakes of breath that greeted her question, Emma realized that she had committed a gaffe. Colonel Clermont and Major Bernhard lifted their eyebrows. Burton glanced up briefly, smirked, and then looked away again.

Janvier smiled. "That is a question you must never ask a Legionnaire, mademoiselle. When we join, we leave our pasts and our real names and nationalities outside the recruiting office. We become Legionnaires. That is our nationality."

"I'm sorry." Emma felt her cheeks turn pink. "I didn't know."

"How could you? But you ought to be cognizant of these things before you interview any of my men. You do not wish to embarrass yourself."

The conversation around the table resumed. Emma ate hastily, aware that she was the last one to be served and that all the others had finished long ago. Colonel Clermont and Major Bernhard excused themselves, wished Mademoiselle Vaughan good night, and departed. The atmosphere in the room eased instantly. Burton made a wry remark in French, which made the men laugh.

"She said that Bernhard wears the ring in his nose better than the one on his finger," Janvier translated for Emma. "She means that he is more faithful to Clermont than he is to his wife."

"We are all married, Robert," Lieutenant Burton said in crisp, upper-class English. "The Legion is our bride—or in my case, the groom."

"With a wife like that, any man is a fool not to take many mistresses," Janvier replied. The meal ended on a chorus of laughter and a toast to the Legion.

Walking back to her quarters with Janvier, Emma heard singing coming from one of the bunkhouses near the gates. "That song—they're not singing in French or English, are they?"

"No, that is the '*Horst Wessel*' song. Many of our men are German. Young soldiers and sons of the Reich who had no place to go when the war ended; men who had no skill but fighting, no talent but killing."

"You mean they're Nazis!" Emma gasped.

"They are not Nazis," Janvier corrected her. "They are Legionnaires."

"But that's terrible! I mean, some of those men may have committed terrible crimes. And you're harboring them! Worse than that, you're paying them and feeding them and telling them that what they did no longer matters."

"Why not, mademoiselle? That particular war has been over for seven years. The dead do not come back to haunt the living, Miss Vaughan, despite what religious and superstitious people would have us believe. Besides, for some of our soldiers, serving in the Legion is worse than going to jail. We have our prisons, too. And also our tortures. Ways of breaking a man's spirit, of forcing him to obey, of making him fit into the mold. Do you want to know a punishment for insubordination? They call it *le crapaud*, the toad. You lie on your belly for three days with your hands tied to your ankles, behind your back. When they finally cut you loose and the blood returns to your extremities, the pain is so terrible that you think you will die. And that is just one of our milder treatments. The Legion is a haven for the soul, where a man can forget everything that has gone before. But for the body it is pain, hardship, denial. Many of the Germans adapt very well to life in Indochina. Now and then a few desert to the other side, to the Viets. Sometimes on the night patrols they call back and forth to each other: 'Come over to this side, it is better here.' 'No, come over here.' But of course, those who desert can never return."

"Why not?"

"Because they will be shot," Janvier said simply. "That is the

Legion's way of teaching her errant husbands a lesson. Here is your hut. I hope you have everything you need for comfort?"

"Yes, Lieutenant Burton has been very kind." Emma wasn't sure why she was lying. Perhaps she feared that Janvier would regard any criticism of a fellow officer as an insult to the Legion he seemed to cherish. "And so have you, Captain Janvier."

Janvier lifted his shoulders. Emma recognized the gesture as pure Hollywood Gallic—the weary bon vivant, the jaded boule-vardier—but it suited Janvier down to the ground.

"It is easy to be kind to so charming a lady. Sleep well, mademoiselle. We will protect you from the enemy, I promise you."

He waited at the foot of the ladder until she had reached the top. They reiterated their good-nights, and Emma ducked inside. Lieutenant Burton had not yet come in, but a kerosene lantern lit up the little room, and the mosquito netting had been arranged over the lieutenant's bed and also over the cot on the veranda.

Emma brushed her teeth and changed into her pajamas quickly, in order to get out of her hostess's way. Lying on the floor mats by the lamp, she wrote a lengthy description of her day's adventures in her diary; then she went outside and tucked herself into her cot.

Despite having spent the previous night on hard ground, in the steely embrace of a tree, and then having ridden over rough ground for six hours in Janvier's jeep, Emma could not sleep. She lay awake, listening to the sounds of the army post battening down for the night. The Germans continued to sing for another hour; then they stopped abruptly. Emma suspected they had been given an order to cease and desist. The guard in the nearby watchtower greeted his relief. The two men laughed together and talked for a few minutes; then their voices were silent. Far away, another guard whistled as he confronted the night. Whistling in the dark, her mother used to say. Letting the lurking spirits know that you're ready for them.

Finally, long after midnight, Lieutenant Burton returned. She made no attempt to be quiet, stumping around noisily, dropping one boot from the greatest height she could achieve, then the other, splashing water, muttering to herself. When she came out onto the veranda to dump the wash basin, gin fumes wafted through Emma's netting. Apparently the Legion's wife was a hard drinker. At last she extinguished the fire in the lantern. She moaned softly as she lay down, expressing infinite weariness.

I don't know what she's complaining about, Emma thought. After all, she's used to it.

But still the images continued to march through her head: the sodden, inhuman heap on the ground in front of the temple; Captain Janvier crouched behind their tree; Alan Hazen holding his wounded arm during the jarring ride to Baray; children looking like animated mushrooms with their pyramidical hats and brown, sticklike legs. You could walk around Lincoln, Nebraska, for an entire day, Emma thought, and never see one remarkable thing. Here everything is remarkable. I'll never get bored with it all. I'll never want to leave. Maybe Mom and Aunt Louise can come and visit me after I'm established. I'll send them the money. Won't take too long, if my stories sell. They will sell. They've got to.

Emma slid gently toward sleep. Just as she reached the edge of sweet oblivion, something tickled her foot. A snake. A cobra. That crazy, vicious woman had planted a cobra under her bunk, and the creature had managed to find a hole in the mosquito netting. Emma sat in a tight huddle at the head of the bed, clutched her arms to her waist, and screamed.

Lieutenant Constance Burton stumped across the veranda, flashlight in hand, and demanded what the hell was going on. Emma, thinking she detected movement under her sheet, leaped out from behind her veiling and screamed even louder. All around the camp, lights came on. The little house shook as someone scrambled up the ladder. Captain Janvier appeared in T-shirt and khaki trousers.

"What is it? What has happened?"

Emma pointed to the cot and said something shrill and incoherent about cobras. Janvier whipped the mosquito netting aside and poked at the bedding with the tip of his knife.

"Nothing. There is nothing there."

"Of course there's nothing." Lieutenant Burton sounded scornful. "She was dreaming, the silly child."

"I was not dreaming. I wasn't even asleep. I did feel something," Emma insisted. "And she put it there." She pointed at Constance Burton, who looked surprisingly feminine in a lacy nightgown with sheer panels over the breasts through which her nipples showed like brown shadows. Emma was conscious of the dowdy appearance she must have presented in her pajamas, highest quality one hundred percent cotton, purchased by her mother at Seltzer's Department Store in Lincoln, two sets for five dollars.

"That's absurd." Lieutenant Burton's disdainful sniff would have done justice to royalty. "I've never heard such nonsense."

Janvier tried to persuade Emma to forget the incident and return to bed, but she refused to spend another minute under the other woman's roof. Grinning at Lieutenant Burton, Janvier shrugged. "Very well, you may sleep in my bed. I shall be right outside, with my knife and my gun. You will be perfectly safe."

"Good." Swiftly, Emma gathered up her belongings. "I certainly don't want to inflict myself on anyone who doesn't want me." As she moved toward the ladder, she saw Hazen standing in the shadow cast by the overhang of the roof. "Did you enjoy that little scene, Mr. Hazen? That ought to provide further confirmation that women are dim-witted, fluff-brained idiots."

"Good night, Miss Vaughan," he replied. "I hope you will sleep better in your new quarters."

Seething, Emma hurled herself down the ladder and crossed the field at the center of the compound. Janvier ran to catch up with her.

"You forgot to put these on." He handed her the sandals she had left under the cot. "It is very bad to go without shoes in this country. The worms."

"Bother the worms." Emma took the sandals but did not put

them on. "You don't believe me, do you? But I felt something in the bed with me, I'm sure I did."

"Sometimes dreams have a way of seeming very real." Janvier spoke seriously, without smiling. "I know. I have heard men scream in the night, seen them wake up with sweat covering their bodies. Whether the thing actually existed in reality or not, to you it was real. Come along, you have only six more hours before your plane leaves in the morning."

Emma pulled herself up. "I don't want to take the plane."

"But Monsieur Hazen said—"

"I don't care what Monsieur Hazen said. He has nothing to do with me. Can't I travel to Saigon with you? Please, Captain. It would really give me something exciting to write about, a whole different perspective. And don't tell me that you can't take me because I'm a woman. Lieutenant Burton is a woman, too. Although I may not have proved it tonight, I'm every bit as tough as she is."

"No, it is too dangerous," Janvier told her. "Convoys through the jungle are easy targets for ambush and attack. I cannot be responsible if any harm comes to you, mademoiselle."

"You don't have to be responsible. I'm responsible. I'll put it in writing if you like. I'll even give you a letter to send to my mother if I'm killed: 'Dear Mom, I am going on this expedition because I want to, and because it's the best thing for my career.' Please, Captain. I won't be a nuisance, I promise. I'll carry my own luggage and cook my own food. I didn't take up very much room in the jeep today, did I?"

"My God, how you talk." Janvier picked up her suitcases and started walking.

Emma trotted after him. "I'll keep talking until you say yes. You won't get a minute's sleep."

"Then I must say yes. I like to hear you talk, mademoiselle, but another time. In the daylight, yes? You may talk as much as you wish after the sun rises."

"Thank you, Captain. Oh, Captain, I wish you'd call me Emma."

"And you may call me Robert." Janvier smiled wearily. They climbed the ladder to his hut. "Your bed is in there." He pointed. "Now perhaps we can sleep, eh?"

"I'll try. I don't know, though. I feel very keyed up."

Emma fell asleep almost as soon as she closed her eyes.

Janvier was gone by the time she awakened. The sun rode high in the sky. Emma checked her watch. Nearly nine o'clock, and already the heat of the day had closed in. As she splashed water on her face, she wondered why these little bamboo and grass huts didn't just combust spontaneously.

A soldier arrived to collect her suitcases and typewriter. He greeted her with a bow and a grin. She received the same reception as she crossed the field toward the waiting trucks. Men smiled and hailed her with friendly waves and poked each other as she passed.

Janvier was checking supplies. He bade her good morning, then handed her a sandwich wrapped in a cloth napkin. "You missed your breakfast. I did not want to wake you. As a heroine, you deserve to sleep as long as you wish."

"What do you mean, a heroine?"

"Some Issaraks cut the wire and came into the camp last night. They killed two guards. They might have killed more and also raided our supply of arms if you had not screamed and awakened everyone. However, they got away with empty hands. The men say you are a lucky charm. They are delighted that you are traveling with us."

A few minutes before the convoy pulled out, Alan Hazen approached Emma. He looked tired and pale and clearly had not yet recovered from the ordeal at Ta Prouhm. His right arm was freshly bandaged and looped up in a black sling.

"I thought your plane had already left," Emma said.

"They had some trouble with the engine. We won't be taking off until after noon. I hear you're going to rough it with the boys."

"Why not? It will make a good story."

Hazen sighed. "If you live to write about it."

"Oh, I will." Emma saw Janvier signaling to her. "I've got to leave now. So long, Mr. Hazen."

Hazen watched the convoy pull out through the open barbed wire gates and turn sharply onto the road that led south. Just before Janvier's jeep disappeared into a cloud of humidity and dust, he saw a slender white arm come up in a jaunty wave, then clamp itself down on the crown of a wide hat woven of native straw. Hazen shook his head. Emma Vaughan was still a beautiful child: reckless, naïve, and trusting. He could not begin to hope that she would emerge from her adventures unscathed. He just wanted her to survive.

3

SEPTEMBER 12, 1952 (Continued)

. . . war was terribly glamorous. Now that I've seen
it up close, I think it's just terrible. . . . Even so, I
admire the men who do the fighting. Yes, and the
women, too. I told you how nasty Lieutenant
Burton was to me at Baray—I will go to my grave
believing she put something in my bed. Well, I
hate to admit this, but she's as tough and
courageous as any of the men. I don't think the
men all like her, but they seem to respect her. I
wish I could find out what made her want to
become a soldier, but I don't suppose I ever will.

The truck rocked violently as its front wheels hit a rut. Emma's
pencil slashed across the page of her notebook, defacing what
she had already written and ripping the paper. She could hear the
driver grinding the gears and spinning the wheels.

To her annoyance, Captain Janvier had assigned her to one of
the personnel carriers in the middle of the convoy as soon as they
left the marshy plains and entered jungle again. He explained
that the position of the leader was too exposed and too dangerous.
As point man and lookout, he himself had been badly hurt once
when the jeep in which he had been riding had driven over a
mine. The three other men riding with him had been killed.

"But I don't want to go back there, with men I don't even
know," Emma protested.

"You have no reason to be afraid," Janvier assured her. "They
will care for you as if you were their little sister."

During a brief midmorning halt, he came back to check on her. "It's so boring," Emma complained.

Janvier laughed. "You have learned one of the essential truths of army life, Emma. The soldier's greatest enemy is boredom."

Emma found herself wedged between the back of the cab and the substantial bulk of a corporal known as Lucky Pierre. She suspected that her situation was not accidental; Janvier and the corporal seemed to be on good terms, with much jostling of elbows and slapping of backs when they were together, and she silently accused the captain of placing her in the care of this amiable oaf.

At least the corporal spoke English. He entertained Emma with stories of the Legion, some that he had experienced, others that to Emma sounded apocryphal. He had known Janvier since his own enlistment at the Legion's recruiting office in Sidi-bel-Abbès, Algeria.

"He is only an adjutant then, but he shows me how to be a good Legionnaire. I help him, he helps me, that is the best way to be in the Legion. I am his *copain*. That is like a buddy, you understand? The captain and I, we are good buddies."

Emma decided to ferret some information out of Lucky Pierre. "Your English sounds like home," she said disarmingly. "You must be an American, like me."

Lucky Pierre roared with laughter. "Oh, no, lady. Everybody knows I am Canadian. It is no secret. I am the only Canuck in the First BEP. If you ask them, the boys will say that is enough, right? They don't like the way I talk French. I talk better than some of those Belgians, you betcha."

Emma homed in on the main object of her interest. "Then the captain is French?"

"Sure, he is French. From Paris, maybe. He doesn't talk about it much. But they say his whole family was killed by the Germans—mama, papa, his little brother, all of them. The Gestapo."

"I see. That's very sad. Was he—the captain—ever married?"

"The captain? Hah! Who knows? Maybe he has a hundred wives. Maybe none."

The truck lurched into motion again. A few minutes later, they were climbing, turning, negotiating a narrow mountain road.

"We are crossing the border between Cambodia and Vietnam. We are in Cochin-China now," Lucky Pierre told her. "The mountain we are climbing is called Phu Khuong. This part of the road is very bad. Lots of ambushes, plenty of men killed. Hey, I remember one fellow, sitting right where you are now, he gets hit by a bullet right through the heart. One minute we are talking about the girls in Saigon; then I turn around and look at him and he is deader than a stump."

Emma closed her eyes and rested her head against the metal frame that supported the moldy canvas cover that was drawn over the truck bed to shield the soldiers from the burning sun. The air in the compartment was stale, fouled with cigarette smoke, and unbearably close. So far, the trip from Baray to Saigon had been singularly devoid of excitement. Penned in with fifteen stalwart Legionnaires, she couldn't even see the passing scene, much less admire it. She thought about Constance Burton riding along in an open-topped jeep, the wind ruffling her mannishly short hair. Captain Janvier didn't pad her in cotton wool and stow her safely out of harm's way. Emma had asked for no special privileges; only to be treated as the captain would treat any of his men. Even so, she had to admit that Burton outranked her. As a hanger-on, she had to settle for the least comfortable accommodations.

Lucky Pierre jostled her arm and offered her some chewing gum. She accepted, and was fumbling with the wrapper when the truck halted again. Hearing shouts from the front of the line, the sergeant who sat near the tailgate jumped down and went off to investigate. Pierre made an observation. His tone was light, but no one laughed. The other soldiers stirred restively and checked their weapons. Emma's heart began to pound. Perhaps they had driven into an ambush. A trap.

She heard an explosion, then scattered gunfire. The men scrambled out of the truck, with Lucky Pierre the last to leave. Seeing Emma about to follow him, he spun around, grabbed her shoulders, and pushed her down on the floor of the truck bed.

"Stay here," he told her. "Lie down flat, okay?" Then he launched himself lightly off the back of the truck, using the tailgate as a springboard, and disappeared.

The firing was coming closer. Suddenly Emma heard a reverberating bang against the metal side of the truck. Lifting her head slightly, she saw a small round hole just inches from her face. She was just wondering if she should seek out safer quarters when Janvier appeared.

"Come on, get out," he ordered. "Get under the truck. It is the safest place. Hurry up. Do not move until I come for you, understand?"

"What is it? What's happening?"

But Janvier had no time to answer questions. He dragged her off the tailgate and shoved her under the belly of the truck. Emma lay facedown under the exhaust pipe, which radiated such intense heat that she could feel the skin on her arms begin to blister. Even if she wasn't shot, she would be burned to a crisp. She could see very little; the truck's massive tires obscured most of her field of vision. Occasionally a pair of feet in heavy black jump boots ran past, but she could not distinguish one set from another. Janvier? Lucky Pierre? From the knees down, they all looked the same.

A mighty explosion shook the ground and sent a wave of heat from one end of the convoy to the other. More feet ran past. Shouts mingled with the spatter of gunfire and the crackle of flames. Emma supposed that a bullet had caused a gas tank to ignite. If the truck under which she was hiding had been the target, she would be a cinder herself now. Despite the heat, she felt cold with terror, frozen stiff to her marrow with fear.

They had been waylaid and attacked not by a small band of guerrillas but by a larger contingent of well-equipped Viet Minh soldiers whose leaders had seized this opportunity to try to exterminate forty-five Legionnaires. Hidden by the thick undergrowth on either side of the road, sheltered by the trunks and roots of palm and banyan and silk-cotton trees, the Viet Minh were in control of the situation. Emma assumed that the road ahead was solidly blocked, otherwise Janvier might have attempted to outrun the enemy.

How did the Viet Minh know that they would be passing that way, and on that day? Foolish question. Any guerrilla group worth its salt has an efficient network of spies. A sympathetic Issarak spy back in Baray, a servant or a villager, had probably passed the word along to the Viet Minh in Cochin-China.

Emma glanced at her watch. To her surprise, only fifteen minutes had passed since the attack began. She had never known time to pass so slowly, with each second bringing some new dread. She had not written to her mother, as she had promised Janvier. In the brightness of morning, she had felt young, invincible, indestructible. She wished she hadn't been so cocky.

Inching closer to the rear tires, she peeked out and saw several of the men and Constance Burton lying on their bellies thirty feet away firing calmly into the brush. Emma wished she had some of the other woman's courage. Or madness. A couple of other Legionnaires had set up machine guns on tripods and were raking the undergrowth with waves of bullets.

The intensity of enemy fire lessened. At an order from Janvier, the Legionnaires plunged into the jungle, in pursuit of an enemy who had decided to retreat when they saw that victory was impossible. Emma lay still, her head buried in her arms. She wanted the nightmare to end, the noise and the stink and the heat to vanish. No story was worth this, no mere collection of words and phrases that would be wadded up and hurled into the trash the following day.

Today was September 11. If she had been at all sensible, she and Edward would be sitting in her mother's living room, planning their May wedding while the wind carried the falling leaves across the prairie. Yes, she would like to keep working for a few months after the honeymoon, or until she got pregnant. After that, she would confine her writing to Christmas cards and notes to her friends, and entries in *Baby's First Book*. Scrubbing toilets?

Ironing Edward's shirts? Oh, yes, even that. Anything was better than this.

The silence, when it came, had a dead quality. Emma wondered if the noise had deafened her temporarily. The jungle itself looked like a painted backdrop, with color and shape but no dimension, no life. In this place, on the side of Mount Phu Khuong, all life had ceased momentarily.

When Janvier came for her, he had to call her twice, and even then she left her shelter reluctantly. He asked if she was all right. She nodded, but discovered that she had no voice to reply. The front of her trousers and blouse were filthy, coated with a thin paste made of dust and sweat. She made no move to brush herself off. Seeing that she was unharmed, Janvier warned her not to stray too far, then he ran off to assess the damage.

The barricade the guerrillas had erected in the middle of the road needed to be removed and the twisted ruins of the incinerated truck shoved to one side so that the remaining vehicles could squeeze past. Bullets had punctured tires. Patches were needed, and pumps. Glass had to be cleared off seats and dashboards. A cracked engine block required makeshift repairs. A jeep, which had been overturned and used as a barricade, needed to be righted.

Most of all, the wounded needed attention. Men lay sprawled or huddled on the ground. A soldier returning from the jungle carried a body over his shoulder like a stag brought in by a returning hunter. Seven men had been killed, twelve more wounded, two critically. A medic was busy applying tourniquets, knotting bandages, injecting morphine.

Emma felt that she should have offered to help. She was not a certified nurse, but at least she could sponge away blood, offer sips of water from her canteen, murmur words of comfort to the poor men who lay writhing with pain. But she did not move. She could not.

The men she had known at the VA hospital had been severely maimed, some of them horribly disfigured. But at least they had been clean, their wounds bound and bandaged, their mangled limbs straightened out or amputated or at least concealed. When a man died, he vanished from his bed and another well-scrubbed invalid took his place. Some mornings, walking through the wards with a load of magazines or water pitchers, Emma had pictured herself as a youthful Florence Nightingale, dispensing healing balm as easily as a smile. She had never experienced anything like this before: blood seeping into the sand, men groaning, weeping.

She turned away and stared into the tangled undergrowth. It looked cool and inviting and peaceful. The jungle gave no sign of the nightmare of horror and violence it had just witnessed.

The sun was dipping toward the Phu Khuong peak behind them by the time the wounded had received rudimentary attention and they were ready to proceed. Janvier had radioed for help and had received instructions to proceed to Saigon, only fifty miles away, with all possible haste. A helicopter unit would meet them at Dau Tieng, a village ten miles down the road, to airlift the casualties the rest of the way.

Janvier found Emma leaning against the side of a truck. Lucky Pierre had wedged a lighted cigarette between her fingers, even though she had told him earlier that she did not smoke. She stood watching the paper and tobacco burn down toward her fingers.

"What are you doing?" Janvier took the butt from her hand and smeared it into the ground with the toe of his boot. "We are almost ready to go. You can ride in front with me. Pierre, too. We need the space in back for the wounded." Taking her elbow, he pulled her gently away from the truck. They stopped at the side of the road. A Vietnamese lay on his back, his arms flung out, his sightless eyes staring up at them. He wore the uniform of a peasant, black trousers and a black shirt. A small pouch at his waist held his rice ration for a week, little over a half a pound. Janvier picked up a battered and scratched automatic weapon, another remnant from the Second World War. "We will leave their dead," he said. "They always take them away—we never find a trace of them a few hours after a battle."

Emma nodded and started to move on, but Janvier jerked her back. His voice was harsh. "Is that all you can do, nod your head? What is the matter, Emma, does the sight of a dead boy mean nothing to you? Look at him. Look! He is only sixteen years old, perhaps younger. He has a mother, a father, brothers. When he was small, he used to play in the paddy fields and fly kites and tease his sisters. Perhaps his parents have arranged for him to marry a pretty girl from the next village. Why do you walk past without seeing him? Are you too good to cry for a dead foreigner, Emma Vaughan? Have you lost your heart as well as your tongue?"

"No. I didn't mean—"

"Then cry." Janvier slapped her. The blow was light but stinging. Emma looked at him, amazed and hurt that her new friend would treat her so brutally. "Cry!"

"I—I can't, Captain Janvier. I've forgotten how." Emma caught a glimpse of Lieutenant Burton standing a few yards away, calmly polishing the stock of her rifle. "What about her? She's not crying. Why should I?"

"You do not want to be like her," Janvier said. "She is dead inside, like all us Legionnaires. She has forgotten what it means to be human, to be a woman." He hit her again, twice. "Cry. Show me that you feel something, Emma. Show me!"

Tears rolled down her cheeks. She began to sob, and all her pent-up horror and anguish came spilling out. Janvier watched her for a moment and then held her close while she wept.

"That is better," he said, rocking her gently. "If you do not let it out, it eats at you like a monster, and after a while you forget how to feel anything, joy or sorrow. Cry now. Yes, that is good, very good. You are human after all, little Emma. Only humans weep for the dead."

*　　*　　*

They reached the Saigon headquarters of the First BEP at eight o'clock, after a brief stop at Dau Tieng to transfer the wounded to waiting helicopters. Stupid with exhaustion, Emma stumbled through the door of the guesthouse to which Janvier led her. To her surprise, a servant was waiting inside, a small Vietnamese woman whose tired eyes and wrinkled hands reminded Emma vaguely of her own grandmother. Gratefully, Emma gave herself up to the woman's ministrations. A hot bath, a bowl of soup, a soft bed, someone to tuck in the netting properly: following the horrors she had experienced that day, it all seemed singularly inappropriate. But she welcomed it nonetheless.

At ten o'clock the following morning, Emma put on her white skirt and blouse, which the servant had washed and ironed, and ventured out into the Legion compound. The place was nothing like the Spartan outpost at Baray. Here the houses and barracks and office buildings were freshly stuccoed, painted dazzling white and roofed with red tile, faced with roofed colonnades and windows with louvered shutters. The fence that surrounded the grassy compound was wrought iron, eight feet tall and topped by loops of barbed wire. Groves of palm and flowering jacaranda and banana trees provided ample shade. Emma found a seat on a bench near a bamboo grove. Her notebook lay closed on her lap, and she absentmindedly chewed her pencil.

"Lieutenant-Colonel Jacques André Grenelle presents his compliments." Captain Janvier bowed to her, then seated himself beside her and lit a cigarette. "He wishes you to join us for lunch, and asks me to tell you that you are welcome to stay with us for as long as you wish. This is an excellent opportunity for you, Emma. He is always at his best at mealtimes. He will give you a good interview."

"Interview?" Emma scuffed the earth with the heel of her sandal. "I don't intend to interview anybody. I think I had better go back home. I have saved some extra money that was supposed to tide me over while I found a place to live and until I started selling my stories. I'll buy a ticket to San Francisco right away, before I spend any more of it."

"I do not understand. Why leave, when you have only just arrived?"

"You saw the way I behaved yesterday. I didn't know it would be like this. I didn't realize it would be so bloody and noisy and horrible—and final. I don't think this is the way I want to spend my life."

"What did you expect?" Janvier looked amused. "A civilized game like tennis, in which the winner and loser shake hands after the match and the loser gracefully retires from the court? You were naïve, true. But the best cure for that is experience. So far you have been very lucky, no? Journalists are seldom permitted to accompany Legion patrols. You have an inside story, a scoop. Your editor will be very impressed."

"I don't have an editor. Either he fired me or I quit—I can't even remember now. I don't even have an assignment, at least nothing official. I'm doing this all on my own. I thought I could impress Mr. Bailey and the others, make a name for myself as a reporter, but now I don't want—"

"Impress them, Emma," Janvier interrupted. "To begin, you can ask our esteemed lieutenant-colonel this afternoon how long he expects this war will go on. You could say something like this: 'Surely with the support of a nation like the United States, which is giving the bankrupt government of France over three million dollars a year for arms, the officers of the French army should be able to bring the fighting to a quick end.'"

"That sounds thrilling. And what will he say?"

Janvier grinned. "He will tell you that we are gaining ground every week, and that it is only a matter of months before our superior might overwhelms the enemy."

Emma shook her head. "I didn't need to come halfway around the world to find a story like that. Honestly, it's the same wherever you go—the statehouse, the church, even the PTA. People are afraid to tell the truth, to give anything but the standard response to questions. No, the government isn't any more corrupt than it used to be. Yes, the church has compassion for the poor and the underfed. Of course our children are smarter and better educated than in any other country in the world. Newspapermen soon learn that there is no such thing as an honest man, just people trying for all they're worth to protect their own positions and to preserve the status quo. I suppose you can't blame them. If your Lieutenant-Colonel Grenelle gave the press an accurate appraisal of the situation here, he would probably be demoted to captain and sent back to Paris."

"Oh, not to Paris," Janvier said with a smile. "To Algeria and a desolate outpost on the Moroccan border."

"Why did I ever think I wanted to be a reporter?" Emma moaned. "The whole world is corrupt and violent, and so is everybody in it. I can't change anything by being here. I want to go home and marry Edward. He's so gutless that he'll probably forget our quarrel and take me back."

"You can marry him if you wish, but you would be turning your back on an excellent opportunity." Having tossed away his spent cigarette, Janvier extracted a fresh one from the pack. Instead of lighting it, he rolled it between his thumb and forefinger. "How many journalists in Saigon have a source close to headquarters—that is, an officer privileged to hear the latest rumors and the latest facts? Very few, I promise you. You are in an excellent position to outstrip them all."

"What do you mean? How can I do that?"

"I am offering to help you gather information, Mademoiselle Emma. As I say, I am well placed in the French Expeditionary Forces in Indochina. I can gain information about the progress of the war in every part of the country. As a young officer who has risen from the ranks, I have the confidence of the enlisted men. They know exactly how many of their mates have died, where the enemy is strongest, where we are weak. When you attend press conferences at military headquarters in Saigon or Hanoi, you will hear different statistics. I can give you the truth. My superior officers also have confidence in me. When we play bridge in the evenings, they speak freely to me of their worries and concerns. We discuss shortages of manpower and equipment. I am privy to intelligence reports. Yes, I know a lot about this war."

"But why?" Emma looked troubled. "Why would you want to risk everything to help me?"

Janvier smiled and touched her cheek. When he spoke his voice was soft and caressing. "Because you are not yet cynical, like so many journalists I know. I can trust you to tell the world the truth."

"That's all very well." Emma turned her head aside, out of his reach. Her heart was racing. Her engagement to Edward had not prepared her for this, to be reduced to a quivering mass of flesh by a single harmless caress. "You realize, I can't even guarantee that my stories will be published."

"They will, in time." Janvier sounded confident. "You are very aggressive, and quite talented. I suspect you will have no trouble getting what you want."

"I don't understand, Robert. You love the Legion. But what you're offering—to reveal their secrets, to pass on facts that aren't normally available to the press—" She hesitated.

Janvier nodded. "You are suggesting that I am a disloyal son. Quite the opposite, I think. I believe that my parent is engaging in erroneous behavior. If he persists, he will die, and all his family will perish with him. But if I alert the world to his mistakes, perhaps I can persuade him to change his methods and thus save all our lives.

"The war here is changing, Emma," he went on. "In 1946, the enemy was weak, scattered, armed with the most primitive weapons. Now, after six years of fighting, they are growing stronger instead of weaker. And yet we have attacked them with the most sophisticated armaments. We bomb their strongholds and destroy their hiding places with napalm, a sort of jellied gasoline. We chase them in our armed tanks and boats and personnel carriers. But instead of conquering them, we are losing. Modern weapons are useless against guerrilla warriors who have been trained not to fight unless they have the advantage. And they are gaining that advantage."

Grateful for this diversion, Emma opened her notebook. "What about the attack yesterday afternoon? Your men survived a well-planned ambush. They performed brilliantly under impossible circumstances."

"Yes," Janvier replied, "but I lost seven men, and for every seven of my men, the Viet Minh can recruit seven hundred or seven thousand. Next time, the situation may be wholly different. A convoy will be stopped by a barricade in the road and attacked by mortar and small artillery fire. After the vehicles are destroyed, a horde of Viet Minh infantrymen will rush in and finish off the survivors. Attacks like that have already taken place in the north—again and again."

Captain Janvier glanced over his shoulder at the gleaming white Legion command building. "So far, the Viets have not been able to fight offensively in the Mekong Delta. They are too far from their sources of supply. And so they content themselves with these hit-and-run tactics. But they will continue to gain strength. The tide of war in the south will soon turn in their favor. In the north, we have already lost."

"Are you saying that France can't win this war?"

"Never. The French government is like an ostrich with its head buried in the sand. It must give these people back their honor, even their independence, and find a native Vietnamese leader around whom the common people in both the north and south can rally, someone better than that corrupt and dissolute relic from the imperial past, Emperor Bao Dai. In order to fight off the Viet Minh, who have the support of Russian and Chinese communists, we must change tactics. We must become guerrilla warriors ourselves. Abandon our heavy equipment, which holds us back. Move through the jungle like tigers instead of elephants. Track the enemy to his lair and destroy him. Like that, we can win the war in the jungle."

Emma studied this dark, handsome Legionnaire. He was not only a fine warrior but a convincing talker. He would be an invaluable source to a foreign correspondent. A shiver of pleasure ran up the backs of her legs and spread through her middle. If she went home now, she would never see this man again.

"I think you want to reform the entire French army," she said in her best reporter's voice.

"That is so." Janvier looked grave. "The Viet Minh have vowed never to give up so long as one foreign soldier remains on their soil. I believe them. They have nothing to lose if this war continues for many more years, while we have everything. They will win. In the end they will conquer us. I have not the slightest doubt of that."

Emma looked puzzled. "Why don't you leave the army, then?"

Rising, Janvier offered her his hand. "Mademoiselle, I am a soldier. I love the battle if not the war. Come, let me show you around the post. By the way, today is also General de Mornay's birthday. He was General de Lattre's chief adviser before our good commander in chief became ill and returned to France. Some say that de Mornay wanted very badly to take de Lattre's place. I am happy that the French high command was not so foolish as to let him. Anyway, we must go to luncheon with Lieutenant-Colonel Grenelle right now, but tonight we are invited to a celebration in honor of General de Mornay."

"What sort of celebration?"

"Ah, you will have to see that for yourself. The general's birthday party is one of Saigon's most elegant social occasions. Every year de Mornay's wife, Eliane, throws a huge party at the Hotel Majestic. Perhaps this is her way of making up for all her infidelities and indiscretions the rest of the time. She always invites a few officers of the Legion in order to lend excitement and glamour to the occasion, and besides, she and I are old friends. I spoke to her this morning on the telephone. She insisted that I bring you. I hope you like to dance."

"But I have nothing to wear," Emma protested.

"Not so. The Legion prides itself on being able to satisfy a guest's every need. We have gowns in our stores. You don't believe me? Our quartermaster will show you designer fashions, straight from Paris, with the couturiers' labels still in them. Some of the senior officers' wives get homesick for the Champs-Élysées, you see. We must keep them happy so that their husbands will be able to fight, isn't that so? I hope they have something in your size by Dior—his styles are very feminine."

"Dior!"

"Why not? We also have the finest selection of wines and spirits in Saigon. They are guarded even more closely than the gowns, let me tell you."

Emma laughed. "This isn't what I expected of the Foreign Legion."

Her mental image of a typical Legionnaire had been formed by Hollywood. A strapping, hard-nosed defender of some isolated desert fortress, his eyes pressed perpetually into a squint against the glare of the sun, his head adorned with the distinctive flat-topped kepi to which a white neckcloth had been attached. Instead she found herself with a suave and charming gentleman in a milieu of society balls, fine wines, and fashions by Dior.

Janvier seemed to read her mind. "Those old romances are all very well, but the Legion today is a modern army, the best in the world. It wasn't always that way, you know. In the beginning, the Legion was a repository for human refuse collected in the streets of Paris."

They passed the gymnasium, where the officers kept themselves fit, and poked their heads into the smoke-filled billiard room. Behind the mess hall was a large swimming pool. Janvier told her that the French Foreign Legion had been formed in 1831 in an attempt to rid Paris of undesirable elements: mercenary soldiers without wars to fight, hardened criminals, chronic troublemakers. Those men were recruited and sent to Algeria, where they were molded into units of crack desert fighters. Over the years, this body of mercenary soldiers became an elite fighting force, distinguishing itself in both world wars as well as in campaigns in Mexico, Algeria, and Indochina.

They stopped and entered the post chapel, which was as large as the Methodist church Emma had attended since childhood. Now, on a Saturday morning, it was empty except for a few soldiers waiting to confess their sins to the chaplain, and an old

Vietnamese woman praying to the statue of the Blessed Virgin. Two banks of flickering votive candles flanked the altar. A trace of incense lingered in the air.

"General Negrier, who directed one of the first Legion campaigns in Indochina, in the 1890s, said, 'You Legionnaires are soldier in order to die, and I am sending you where you can die.'" Janvier's voice was hushed. "For anyone to look beyond tomorrow is useless. For a Legionnaire it is folly."

"I don't understand you at all." Emma shivered. "How can you live each day with the thought that you're going to die?"

"Because I am a pragmatist," Janvier replied. "Death comes to all of us sooner or later, does it not? I would rather die as a soldier than grow old and rot and wait for death to find me in my rocking chair."

The officers' mess had tiled floors and pale green walls. Narrow wands of sunlight filtered through the slats of the louvered shutters. Captain Janvier's fellow officers made Emma feel welcome, overwhelming her with compliments and admiring gazes. Before they sat down, servant girls passed plates loaded with hors d'oeuvres, small tarts filled with a mixture of egg, cheese, and mushrooms. The champagne and vermouth that accompanied this course were well iced. Then the officers and their guests seated themselves at the table. Vietnamese stewards poured more wine. The post's commanding officer, Lieutenant-Colonel Grenelle, proposed a toast: "To our brothers in the sands." He drank, then slammed down his glass on the table. Each officer did the same.

"Part of Legion tradition," Janvier whispered to Emma, seated at his right.

Before the meal commenced, songs were sung, including the Legion's most famous anthem, *"Le Boudin,"* "Blood Sausage," a marching tune whose dirgelike tempo had marked the slow pace of trudging through the deserts of Morocco and Algeria. Janvier translated the chorus and verses:

> "Hey, here is the *boudin,*
> Plenty of blood sausage

For Alsatians and Swiss and the boys from Lorraine.
No more for the Belgians, those backside warriors.

In Tonkin, the immortal Legion
Covered our flag with glory at Tuyen-Quang.
Heroes of Cameroon, ideal brothers,
Sleep peacefully in your graves.

In the course of our faraway campaigns,
Facing fevers and gunfire,
Let us forget, along with our sorrows,
Death, who never forgets us."

The youngest officer, a sublieutenant whom Emma guessed to be no older than eighteen, read the birthdays of the day and offered congratulations to those officers; then he announced the day's menu, cried, "Long live the Legion!" and sat down. The stewards began to serve a clear soup with crispy toasted croutons, fish lightly sauced and sprinkled with fresh herbs, veal cutlet and tiny potatoes, and an array of cheese and fruit.

Lieutenant-Colonel Grenelle was small of stature, slender and gray-haired, with keen black eyes that flashed appreciatively every time he glanced at Emma. He asked about her background, and she made the most of her ten years of experience as a journalist—without revealing that most of this experience had been gleaned in the service of the North Lincoln High School *Bugle* and the University of Nebraska *Star*. As Janvier had predicted, Grenelle evaded her questions about the war.

"You see," Janvier murmured as they left the table, "I told you he would wriggle away from you. They are all like that. Now you shall select a dress for this evening, and when you have done that, you must rest. Eliane de Mornay's parties never end before dawn, and she frowns on anyone who tries to leave earlier."

"You're such a thoughtful host," Emma burbled as they crossed the green. "You think of everything."

"Only because you are such a delightful guest," Janvier responded with smooth gallantry. "You see, I have gone to extraordinary lengths to keep you in Indochina. I hope I have succeeded?"

Emma's head was swimming. She was not accustomed to drinking wine with her noonday meal. "I—I think you have."

"Excellent." They had reached the quartermaster's station. Janvier placed his hand on her waist to steady her on the two steps up to the door. "You see, General de Mornay is not the only officer who has reason to celebrate tonight. You are staying in Saigon. If I were the mayor of the city, I would order a display of fireworks."

"But since you're not—"

"I shall have to think of something else."

As he smiled into her eyes, Emma felt her legs turn to water. Edward had never made her feel like this, light-headed and silly. She wanted to sing, to dance, to float. What was happening to her?

4

SEPTEMBER 20, 1952 (Postcard)

Dear Aunt Louise,

Saigon is the most glorious, the most beautiful city
in the world. At night it shines like a jewel. I love
being here, even if my stories don't sell!

Love, Emma

"Ah, regard our esteemed General Salan and his wife." Eliane
de Mornay's lips brushed Alan Hazen's ear. "Observe the
healthful color of his complexion and the keen light of satisfac-
tion in his eyes. Quite amazing, the effect that promotion to
commander in chief has on a general's appearance, even if the
position is only temporary. Who will be De Lattre's true suc-
cessor? That is what we would all like to know, particularly my
husband. Poor Lucien. I will have to work especially hard to get
him what he wants this time. Ah, my dear General Salan, and
madame, how thrilling that you could come! Lucien, darling,
look who's here. Just look at that husband of mine"—Eliane
dropped her voice again—"the perfect toady. Getting a bit senile,
too. Do you know, I have to check his uniform before he leaves
the house in the morning, just to make sure he's properly turned
out? That valet of his is worthless, always sneaking out to spend

more time with his Vietnamese whore, paying no attention at all to my Lucien. Oh, so few people appreciate the difficulties of being the wife of an officer in the French high command—"

"I'm sure the life has its compensations." Alan Hazen looked over her head. A waiter was coming toward them with a tray of drinks. He tried to catch the man's eye so that he could ask for a ginger ale. "Particularly for a clever woman like yourself, Eliane."

General de Mornay's wife waggled a little ivory fan under her chin. The theatrical gesture suited her perfectly. "As you well know, my dear Alan. Your friendship is one of them. I should have died of boredom if you had not come to Saigon. I adore American men! Did I tell you, the American embassy has a new officer of communications, whatever that means—perhaps he will command the typing pool. He only arrived this morning. I insisted that Bunny bring him along tonight. I want to take a look at him." Bunny was the American ambassador, a white-haired, pink-fleshed career diplomat whose real name was Arthur Bunning. "I hope he is a better tennis player than his predecessor— what was his name, the poor man who shot himself?"

"Morton. Don't you remember? You were sleeping with him." Hazen surveyed the guests assembled in the ballroom of the Hotel Majestic without much enthusiasm. Occasionally he picked up some useful information at these society affairs, but he had met most of the assembled guests and found them uninteresting. The military men tended to clump together in one corner of the room; civilian men did likewise. Their wives segregated themselves along similar lines. "How did you hear about his replacement? Do you have a microphone planted under the ambassador's pillow?"

"I have something just as good. His wife. She and I have become quite good friends lately. Dear Judith. She is so relieved to find someone who speaks English in this awful country. She called this morning to give me a recipe for that salad she served at luncheon last week. It was made out of some horrid quivering orange stuff she called Gel-lo or Jelly-O. Of course I made a great fuss over it, although it started to melt all over my plate the minute it was served. I am afraid Judith thought I was sincere. She says she will have her daughter send me some of the powder from which it is made. I suppose I can sprinkle it around the garden. I hope it doesn't kill Lucien's roses."

A Filipino band played "In the Mood" as if they weren't. A few couples were dancing; the rest sipped champagne, snatched hors d'oeuvres from passing trays, and waited for the buffet supper to be served. Eliane de Mornay's parties were loud, lavish, and lively, like the lady herself. Hazen sighed inaudibly. Eliane blazed like a searchlight in a roomful of flickering candles, but one couldn't stand too close to her without getting scorched. Vital energy, a quick brain and sharp tongue, a passion for gossip, a talent for organization and command—which surpassed considerably her general-husband's: This was Eliane, a formidable personality packaged in a body no larger than an adolescent girl's. Her friends called her vibrant and colorful; her enemies, cheap and vulgar. With her crimson lips and ash blonde curls—the shade varied from week to week depending on her own whim and her hairdresser's stock of bleaches and dyes—she reminded Hazen of an old patent medicine advertisement that purported to have bottled the waters of the Fountain of Youth. Eliane must have bought out the company.

A few more guests drifted in, a colonel in parade dress and his lady in pink chiffon. Hazen wanted to escape, but Eliane insisted that he stay and help her greet her guests. "I refuse to stand next to Lucien," she hissed. "I must have someone interesting to talk to, or I shall go mad. I shall tell everyone that you helped me plan this party. They will think you are sleeping with me, but what of it? Perhaps it will inspire you, dear Alan."

"You can have your pick of the men in Saigon," Hazen replied. "Why bother with me?"

"Because you are my most conspicuous failure, my dear. What can a woman think? Ah, two weeks ago, I really thought I would triumph. I arranged a lovely dinner for the two of us in a private dining room at the Palais de Jade, with lovely wine and candlelight. But you refused the wine and complained that the light was too dim for you to see the food. Afterward, you wouldn't even escort me home. That very same night, you decamped to Laos or Thailand or some other dreadful place! No woman ever had such an undependable lover."

Hazen stifled a yawn as the new arrivals approached them. He and the colonel exchanged a couple of lame remarks about the heat and humidity while the ladies exclaimed over each other's gowns. With a sigh of relief, the colonel moved on to greet General de Mornay. Medals vibrated as the two men shook hands.

"I can hardly believe that the silly cow would have the nerve to wear pink," Eliane murmured when the couple had passed. "It makes her look like a strawberry bombe. Don't laugh, Alan, it is very rude. Boy, bring some of that champagne over here. Who do you think is paying for this party, anyway? Honestly, the servant class here is getting more impossible every year. I shall never understand why France wants to hang on to this country. Completely worthless as a colony. Who's this coming in the door? Ah, that devilish young Legionnaire, Janvier. I telephoned him this morning and insisted that he come. Haven't seen him in ages. And my God! Who is this new conquest of his? What a gorgeous animal. And where did she get that dress? Pale blue satin, white trim—my God, a new Dior! It must be. Robert," she trumpeted, "come over here at once. Where have you been keeping yourself, you wicked boy? And who is this charming young lady?"

Speaking English, Janvier introduced Emma Vaughan to Madame de Mornay.

"A journalist! How exciting!" Eliane made a smooth transition from French to strongly accented but idiomatic English. "I told you I adore Americans, didn't I, Alan? My dears, this is my old friend Mr. Hazen."

Hazen's eyebrows inched up. Emma's shoulders and back were bare except for two small wired rings of fluffy white tulle that encircled her upper arms and kept the vertically shirred blue satin bodice from slipping off her bosom. More white tulle formed a bow at her waist and trailed away in two cloudlike strands. Her natural corn-silk-colored hair was arranged in a triple-tiered flip.

Noting the disapproving arch of Hazen's eyebrows, Emma almost wished she had chosen a more modest gown. But Janvier, teasing her, had urged her to be more daring, to select something that she would never wear at home.

"Hello, Mr. Hazen." Emma did not offer her hand or cheek to him. Nearby, Madame de Mornay was greeting Captain Janvier warmly, kissing both his cheeks. "How's your arm?"

"Stiff. How was the trip from Baray? I heard you had some trouble on the road."

"Some small excitement," Janvier put in. "Seven of the finest soldiers in the French Foreign Legion gave up their lives to protect Mademoiselle Vaughan—and their comrades, of course."

"But this must be the young lady you were telling me about, Alan!" Eliane clasped her hands in front of her bosom. Her own gown was black, tightly fitted to the hips, where it flared away into a blossom of rustling satin. "Alan says you saved his life, my dear. He was pretending to be dead, and the horrid sniper was about to shoot him at any moment, and then you came along and distracted him. Alan is sure the man would have killed him otherwise."

"Oh?" Emma was pleased to see Hazen shifting uncomfortably. "Any time, Mr. Hazen. Glad I could be of service."

"So then he rescued you, and Robert rescued you both. I am sure I could never have survived such excitement." Eliane fanned herself briskly. "My heart would never have stood it."

"Your heart is as strong as an army tank," Hazen said. "But we shouldn't detain our guests. I'm sure they're eager to wish the general many happy returns."

As Robert and Emma moved on, Emma looked over her bare shoulder and gave Hazen a wide smile.

"I've had enough of this." Hazen started to move away.

"No, no, just a few more minutes." Eliane's small hand on his arm held him back. "Look, here are Bunny and Judith. Who is that with them? It must be the new boy. My God, but he's ugly. And I thought all Americans were handsome, like you."

W. Powers Brewster had a morbidly pale complexion and thinning red-blonde hair combed back from a high domed forehead. Eliane welcomed him to Saigon, and cautioned the ambassador and his wife to be sure to instruct the newcomer in the fine art of surviving in the tropics.

"Not too much exercise, enough alcohol to ensure rest and to thin the blood but not enough to damage the liver. Do not forget your mosquito netting and quinine tablets. And only play tennis in the early morning or after five o'clock in the evening. You do play tennis, don't you? Mr. Hazen is my favorite partner, but he has hurt his arm and now he is no good to me at all." Eliane gave Hazen a meaningful nudge, which he ignored.

Brewster admitted that he had tried tennis in college but had never gotten the hang of it. "These days I prefer ping-pong."

"Ping-pong! But that is a game for children!" Eliane, seeing that Captain Janvier and Emma Vaughan were still conversing with the general, called them back. "Come and meet your ambassador, child, and his new chief of communications. What exactly does that mean, Mr. Brewster? Do you answer telephones and send wires, or are your duties more complicated than that? I am afraid your title sounds rather vague."

"I will be monitoring any official statements that go out of the embassy, to the press and so on, and making sure they're in line with government policy." Brewster's bland voice barely escaped being a monotone. "You can't always depend on secretaries to pick up on nuances, and the ambassador is a busy man."

"Preserving the purity of the party line, eh, Mr. Brewster?" Emma remarked. She and Janvier had joined the group in time to hear Brewster's explanation of his duties.

Ambassador Bunning beamed at Emma. "Our government seeks always to be consistent and evenhanded in its attitudes toward other countries." He and Judith shook hands with Emma and Captain Janvier before moving on to greet General de Mornay.

W. Powers Brewster lowered his voice confidentially. "Few of us realize that every utterance, no matter how casual, has the potential of influencing public opinion negatively. We want to keep official lanuguage clear, plain, and subject to no erroneous interpretation."

"Sounds to me like you're succeeding very well so far," Hazen said with a straight face.

Brewster looked at him curiously. "You know, Mr. Hazen, I think I've seen you someplace before."

"That's possible. I've been lots of places."

"Are you any relation to the Doctor Hazen who discovered Hazen's law of relative numerals?"

"That's me."

"No kidding? Say, I was in one of your classes, at the University of Chicago. Before I switched my major to history. What happened to you, anyway? Nobody seemed to know. Sometime before Pearl Harbor, you just dropped out of sight. Sabbatical, it was supposed to be, but some of the guys heard you were involved in a hush-hush project for the government. What are you doing out here, if you don't mind my asking?"

"Going native, making a living." Briefly, Hazen described his job with Chrome Petroleum. "I move every few years, see a different part of the world. It suits me."

"Alan, you never told me you made a law." Eliane's fan created a welcome breeze within the tight little circle. "What are these relative numerals Mr. Brewster is talking about?"

"Theoretical mathematics." Hazen sounded bored. "They have very little practical application outside the classroom. I won't bother to explain because you wouldn't understand it. I doubt if I still understand it myself after all this time. Let's just say that some mathematicians play with numbers the way philosophers play with theories about the nature of existence. As a way of passing the time."

"People were very excited about it," Brewster recalled. "You got your picture on the cover of *Time*, didn't you? The University of Chicago's Whiz Kid. You had a lot of great offers from big corporations, but turned them all down. I guess you've changed your mind since then."

"What's a former whiz kid doing negotiating oil leases in French Indochina?" Emma unsheathed her reporter's probe.

"Looking for a change of climate." Hazen turned to Eliane. "Madame, you promised I might be excused if I behaved myself for an hour. My time is just about up." He wandered away toward the bar, where he ordered a Coke with plenty of ice.

"Say, I hope I didn't embarrass you back there." W. Powers Brewster had followed Hazen to the bar. "They didn't give me too much background on you in Washington. I think we ought to get together, talk things over. What are you doing tomorrow?"

"Tomorrow?" They moved over to a quiet corner behind a sofa occupied by three women chattering in French. Hazen took a long sip of Coke. "After a late breakfast or early lunch, I will catch up on my reading for a few hours. Later, I may stroll over to the Cercle Sportif for a sauna and a massage, try to get this arm loosened up a little. Work. Dinner. Diversion. And then to bed."

"How about the afternoon?"

"How about never? After tonight, Powers, I don't want to be seen talking to you. I don't want you anywhere near me. In case Bunny hasn't told you, I communicate directly with my superiors in Washington. Your job, as I understand it, is to translate my reports into code and send them on, and then to pass instructions back to me in such a way that no one—I repeat, no one—will have any cause to connect me with the embassy in any way. Morton and I had our own special procedure, but I've decided to change it. Let me explain the new one to you."

"Now really, this is hardly the place, Hazen—"

"Why not? Listen carefully because I'm not going to repeat myself. This is how I want it done: Anytime I want to send a message, I'll give you a call and ask if you want to play tennis at nine o'clock in the morning. During the monsoon season it's squash. Okay so far? You say sorry, but you can't make it until after lunch. I leave my message in the right tennis shoe in my locker at the Cercle Sportif. Got that, Brewster, the right shoe? When you arrive for your afternoon swim, you open my locker with your special key—I will give it to Bunny—and remove the message. Anytime you want to leave something, you reverse the procedure. Simple, isn't it? And Powers, you will send my messages as written, without editing, without comment, without changing so much as a comma. Is that clear?"

Brewster flushed to the roots of his ginger-colored hair. "Look here, I don't intend to go fishing around inside your old tennis shoes, Hazen. I'm not your lackey."

"Oh, but you are, Powers. I work alone, independent of the embassy, and you are at my service whether you like it or not." Hazen moved away. Meeting the Ambassador coming toward the bar, he said, "I just gave your new boy a tongue-lashing."

The ambassador sighed. "He's going to be a bit of a problem, that lad. His father is undersecretary of state for foreign affairs. Powers thinks he knows everything."

"I don't want him touching my dispatches. Give them to someone else to encode, or do them yourself."

"You know I can't do that, Alan. That's his job, and I can't encroach on his territory."

"Afraid his father the undersecretary will get you sent back to Timor or Mombasa? All right, I'll give him a chance. But keep him away from me."

"Poor Morton." The ambassador's shoulders sagged. "He was so dependable. I warned him not to get mixed up with that de Mornay woman, but he didn't believe me. They never do."

"At least Brewster won't give you any problems that way. He's too ugly for Eliane's taste."

Heading from the bar to the terrace a few moments later, Hazen was intercepted by Eliane, who wore a satisfied smile.

"Ah, things are finally beginning to pick up. I was getting quite desperate. I wondered if I should set off my firecrackers."

"Firecrackers?"

"I always keep a box in case of emergencies. If things get dull, I can set one off in the middle of the ballroom. Bang! Everyone will think it is a grenade, and by the time they find out it was only a joke, they will have lost their inhibitions and will begin to laugh and drink." She stroked the back of Hazen's hand and said in a throaty whisper, "Sometimes I wish I could set off a firecracker under you, *chéri*. Do you really find me so unattractive?"

Hazen remained stony-faced. "I prefer not to involve myself with married women."

"Bah. If everyone felt as you did, the world would be even drearier than it is. Dance with me, darling."

"Later."

"Oh, you are impossible," Eliane declared. "The rudest man I have ever met."

The party really was getting livelier. The band, refreshed by quantities of champagne and some top-quality marijuana from Vietnam's central highlands, played with more passion and verve. Hazen still remembered the year Eliane pushed one of her husband's junior officers into the swimming pool at the Cercle Nautique and then jumped in on top of him. The scandal was quickly hushed up, and the officer transferred to Hanoi.

Oddly, General de Mornay's career had not suffered because of his wife's periodic excesses. Quite the opposite, in fact. A widower with two grown children, he had spent the war years with De Gaulle in London, a dogged and unimaginative colonel who had risen slowly and steadily through the ranks, content to do his duty so long as someone told him what that duty was. He had met Eliane in Paris after Liberation. Her own father had served in Algeria and died in Morocco. Some said that Eliane's mother had been a Moor, which explained her dark skin and eyes. Marriage to this vital young woman had galvanized the old soldier and shaken him out of his torpor. Eliane lobbied hard for promotions, transfers, choice assignments. She cultivated the general's friends—some said in bed—and undermined his enemies—probably also in bed and with the intention of blackmailing them. War in Indochina meant further possibility of promotion; she persuaded him to ask for an assignment there. One year after arriving in Saigon, Lucien de Mornay received his first star.

When Hazen arrived in Cochin-China in 1949, the first person he met was Eliane. She sought him out, as she sought out all newcomers, and even though he clearly could do nothing to further her husband's career, they had remained friends.

"They are charming, are they not?" Eliane murmured.

"Who?"

"Captain Janvier and your young lady, the pretty American." Eliane waved as the couple glided past. Janvier nodded but Emma did not see her. "Ah, for her the rest of the world has already ceased to exist. Poor thing. She is finished."

"Finished? What do you mean?" Hazen sipped his drink.

"Really, Alan, are you so blind? She is an innocent, still a virgin. And he—you know what soldiers are like, but he is one of the worst. The stories I have heard about him! He has dangerous friends, and an interest in some very shady businesses."

"What do you mean? What sort of businesses?"

Eliane shrugged. "Stolen weapons, drugs—what does it matter? He will never love that poor child. He will destroy her. He is an evil man. Ah, you see how she looks at him. She has fallen in love with him already. How could she not? All she sees is a man who is exceedingly handsome, a figure of romance and mystery. A Legionnaire. Vital. Someone who takes risks, who laughs at danger. But he will break her heart and worse, that one."

Hazen turned away abruptly. "I need some air." Out on the terrace, he surprised a pair of lovers who had been embracing in the shadows. Giggling, they scurried back to the ballroom.

"There you are." Emma Vaughan appeared in a swirl of satin and tulle. "I'm looking for somebody who speaks English, and Madame de Mornay has just appropriated my escort. I certainly don't want to talk to that horrible Brewster man. I realize that having a friend inside the embassy can be a valuable asset to a reporter, but there are limits to how far I'll go to get a story. The ambassador's wife seems nice enough. Maybe I'll cultivate her instead."

Hazen set his empty glass down on the balustrade. "And Captain Janvier, has he turned out to be a valuable asset?"

"Oh, yes! He's wonderful!" Emma looked out over the Saigon

River to the dark marshy land on the opposite shore. Lights floated in the water like drowned stars. The air was sweet and warm, perfumed with the fragance of honeysuckle and sweet olive. "I never expected Saigon to be this beautiful."

"It isn't. This is make-believe, one of the islands of civilization the French colonials have cultivated in a hostile and barbaric land. After a glass or two of wine, they can pretend they're in Paris."

"A pretty expensive illusion. I'm sure Paris never gets this hot." Emma pushed a damp strand of hair away from her forehead. "I feel a little like Alice in Wonderland tonight. One day I'm dodging bullets in the jungle; the next I'm attending the premier event of the Saigon social season. From fatigues to a Paris gown. Aren't you going to tell me how beautiful I look?"

"You're absolutely stunning, Miss Vaughan, although you look more like a box of candy than a reporter."

Emma laughed. "I should have known better than to try and beg a compliment from you. Tell me, does your wife still live in Chicago?"

Hazen pulled himself away from the railing. "I don't think my personal life is any of your business."

"Don't be annoyed. I'm only exercising my prerogatives as a professional snoop. You know, you're a very fascinating character, Mr. Hazen. University whiz kid, loner, adventurer." She picked up his empty glass and sniffed. "And a teetotaler as well. You do surprise me."

"I don't need alcohol in order to enjoy life."

Emma cocked her head. "No? But everybody needs something. Just how do you extract enjoyment from life? By making the rest of us feel intellectually inferior, I guess. What did you say to Brewster? He's been looking daggers at you all night."

"I told him to mind his own business." Hazen crossed his arms over his chest. "I suggested that if he persisted in prying into my private life, he would find himself swimming in a crocodile-infested river in Cambodia, with leeches sticking to whatever pieces of flesh remained after the crocodiles had finished with him."

Emma's eyes gleamed. "Well, I can't say I haven't been warned."

The band began playing "Sentimental Journey."

"I have an idea. Why don't we go in and dance?"

"I'd rather stay outside," Hazen said. "It's cooler."

"Then we'll do our dancing right here." Emma moved into his arms. Even though Hazen's right arm was still weak, he provided a firm lead. "You're not bad." Her smile was mischievous. "As a dancer, I mean. As a person, I find you irksome, irascible, and extremely annoying."

Hazen whirled her slowly around. "You're not the first one to think so."

"You seem determined to dislike me, Mr. Hazen."

"Not at all." Hazen spoke slowly, choosing his words with care. "I think perhaps this Far East escapade of yours was not wise, Miss Vaughan. Do you know what you reminded me of when you walked into that ballroom? A lost sheep wandering into a den of wolves. If you're not careful, the people in this city will eat you alive. Then they'll burp, spit out a few bones, and look around for the next victim. Nice girls like you don't belong in places like Saigon."

"Perhaps, Mr. Hazen, I am tired of being a nice girl. Maybe the people of Lincoln, Nebraska, consider themselves alive, but I think they're the biggest bunch of deadheads on the face of the earth. I am not interested in their petty problems. I don't care if the Cornhuskers never win another game. I had to get away from there so that I could grow up."

"You can grow up without endangering your health and your sanity and your immortal soul," Hazen said sharply. "Try developing a few mature attitudes for a start. You've been in Saigon for one day, and you've already made a big mistake."

"Oh?" The tulle wings of Emma's gown quivered. "And what mistake is that?"

"Your Captain Janvier is well known in this part of the world, and not well liked. He is a bad man, a dangerous man. Take some advice from an old Indochina hand, Miss Vaughan. Pack your bags and leave town first thing tomorrow morning. If you're broke, I'll lend you the fare. But don't think that guy is going to be the big romance of your life. He'll take what he wants and then he'll destroy you. Get out before you disgrace your mom, your profession, and the good old American flag."

Emma pulled away from him. Her cheeks were burning. "Mr. Hazen, you can take your advice and — and stick it up your nose. What gives you the right to preach to me? If you're trying to take credit for saving my life back at Ta Prouhm, forget it. As I understand it, I did you the favor."

"I suggest you pay attention to what I'm saying, Miss Vaughan—"

"Ah, here they are, the two American refugees, enjoying a private tête-à-tête while I slave over my duties as a hostess." Eliane emerged from the ballroom with Captain Janvier. Leaving him, she pranced toward Emma and Hazen, her hands fluttering. "We will be dining very soon. The general is unaccustomed to these late hours. Ordinarily, he likes his supper at seven so he can be in bed by nine at the very latest. I hope he manages to stay awake through the toasts and the speeches. I will stand very close to him and stick him with a pin. I have done it before. Tell me, my dear, where are you staying in Saigon?"

"In a guesthouse at Legion headquarters, madame." Emma's voice sounded flat and brittle. "Until I can find a room or an apartment."

"Let me think." Eliane did this charmingly, casting her eyes skyward while she rested her forefinger on the tip of her chin. "I know, that wicked old man, the artist. What was his name, Alan? You remember, he has a villa on Avenue Jean Jacques Rousseau, up on the Plateau. A good neighborhood. The house itself is not in the best repair, as I recall, but at least it is fairly clean. It should be, with all those women around."

"Women?" Janvier looked interested.

"Wives, daughters, mistresses—who knows? But he is good-hearted and he will look after Emma as if she were his own child."

"Really, madame," Emma ventured to protest, "you don't need to trouble yourself on my account."

"Oh, but I want to trouble myself. I could not sleep thinking of you living someplace unsuitable, with no one to protect you. De Chesnay, that's it! André de Chesnay. I will give you his address. Go and see him tomorrow first thing. Tell him I sent you, and that I said not to overcharge you. Refuse to pay more than twenty-five hundred piasters a month."

"Thirty dollars?" Hazen laughed. "You can't expect the man to give his rooms away."

"Why not? I have quite a few of his wretched paintings hanging in my closets, for which I paid exorbitant amounts of money. It is time he returned the favor. And now that we have solved all the problems of the world, let us dine. Poor Lucien gets so cross when he's hungry."

By three in the morning, the older soldiers and civilians had all taken their wives home. General de Mornay had departed at one, suppressing his yawns with difficulty. Even so, the dance floor was still crowded with couples clearly intent on partying until the sleepy hotel staff served breakfast on the terrace.

"I think I must be getting old." Eliane joined Hazen on a brocaded sofa near the doors to the terrace. "Only three o'clock, and I feel exhausted."

"Maybe the boys in the band will give you a couple of their fancy cigarettes."

"I cannot smoke those things. They make me very silly. After all, as the wife of a general, I have a certain decorum to maintain."

"Remind me not to go near any swimming pools when you're around."

"You wicked man." Eliane rapped Hazen's knuckles with her ivory fan. "Everyone else in Saigon has forgotten that incident. Only you have the bad taste to bring it up again and again."

"At least your enemies can't fault you for being stingy. Although some of them might be wondering where you get the money to pay for all this."

"Where do they think? I have some very good friends at the

Crédit National and in the customs department. They do me a few favors now and then."

The French government had fixed the official rate of exchange between the currencies of France and Indochina. This meant that everyone in Saigon was trying to amass quantities of fairly worthless piasters that they could then, with the right connections, exchange for French francs. The scheme was easy and profitable. Hazen was not surprised that Eliane took advantage of her friendships in the banking world to enrich herself and her husband. Eliane took advantage of most things that came her way.

Hazen yawned broadly and stretched out his legs. "I suppose Captain Janvier is on your long list of conquests?"

"What does that matter? If you care about that girl, you will rescue her from him."

"Well, I don't care for her, and as for rescuing her, I wouldn't know how to go about it."

"Make her fall in love with you instead. It is not so difficult. You can be very charming, Alan. You don't need to behave like a cross old bear all the time. And later, when Janvier is out of sight, you can detach yourself from her very gently."

"I find this conversation extremely boring."

"What, one of my guests is bored? I cannot have this." Eliane jumped up. She shouted to the orchestra to play a conga, then ordered all the guests to line up behind her and Hazen and to follow them wherever they went. The party wound its way onto the terrace and down to the street, around the block, through the front doors of the hotel and across the main lobby, up the main staircase to the rooms on the second floor, and up and up until they had reached the rooftop bar. To those guests who appeared, sleepy-eyed, at the doors of their rooms, Eliane shouted an invitation to join the fun. Early on, Hazen was aware of a flash of yellow and white near the end of the line: Emma and Janvier. But when the conga line reached the ballroom again, they had vanished.

* * *

"I thought we were supposed to stay until dawn." Emma glanced over her shoulder through the rear window of the taxi. She expected to see Madame de Mornay come hurtling after them, screaming like a fishwife whose customers have cheated her.

"I tire of Eliane's nonsense very quickly these days. And you, did you enjoy yourself at her party?"

"I had a wonderful time, mostly because you were there. I love to dance." Emma thought of Alan Hazen's smug warnings, and her fury at him renewed itself. "I think diplomats and businessmen are the most boring people in the whole world. I wish I spoke French. The only people I could communicate with back there were you and Madame de Mornay and that awful Alan Hazen. As soon as I find a place to live, I'm going to hire a tutor and learn the language."

"I will teach you," Janvier offered. "It is not difficult."

"Not difficult for you. You're French."

He stiffened. "Do you not know that Frenchmen are not permitted to enlist in the Legion?"

"But French is the Legion's official language. That's all I meant." Emma congratulated herself for remembering that fact. She did not want to tell Janvier that Lucky Pierre had been gossiping about him. "No, you have your own work to do, Robert. I'll find someone else to teach me. Do you think Madame de Mornay would be interested?"

Janvier laughed, and his tension eased. "Eliane would fill your ears with a lot of useless gossip. You would learn much about the private lives of the leading citizens of Saigon, but very little French." He took Emma's hand and tucked it under the curve of his arm. "You are the most beautiful woman in Saigon tonight, Emma. Everyone at Eliane's party thought so. Even your tall American."

"My tall American is the most infuriating man I've ever met. He thinks I should pack my bags and go home."

"You yourself had similar thoughts this morning. I am pleased that you disagree with him now."

"So am I."

She waited for him to kiss her. She knew before it even happened that his kisses would be very different from Edward's mushy, moist attempts. The taxi rounded a corner too quickly, throwing their bodies together. Janvier slid his arm around her shoulder and tilted her face up to his. The kiss was surprisingly gentle and straightforward, with none of Edward's straining and nervous breathing, but it pierced Emma to her core. When it was over, she rested her head against his chest and closed her eyes. Her escapade, as Hazen called it, had produced an unexpected dividend. She had fallen in love.

5

OCTOBER 15, 1952

. . . into a Buddhist temple near the Jardins Botaniques. It was so pleasant and peaceful I felt as if I had wandered into another country. I bought a stick of incense and lit it—the smoke is supposed to be like a prayer. Maybe Mr. Bailey will get a whiff of it! . . . You asked about "my" Legion captain. Yes, I still see him from time to time. He has been very courteous and helpful, showing me around town, taking me to places that as a woman and a foreigner I might not otherwise see.

Emma dropped her pen and rested her chin on her folded hands. From the other side of the garden wall came the music of a world more exciting than anything she had created in her dreams: tramcar bells and pagoda bells, car horns and police sirens, the hawking of peddlers and the shouts of the men who pedaled trishaws, those hooded conveyances that reminded Emma of oversized baby strollers, with the driver seated behind the single passenger.

The capital of Cochin-China was more cosmopolitan than any city Emma had ever visited in America. Certainly her hometown had nothing that could match Saigon's splendid opera house, its baroque public buildings, its posh department stores and elegant shops.

But it was more than architecture. Life in America was a crude scramble for wealth. Here, the citizens—both French and Vietnamese—seemed to savor the richness of their surroundings, the pleasure of drinking aperitifs at sunset or strolling along Rue Catinat, their city's main thoroughfare. They viewed money as the means of establishing a comfortable and civilized life, and not as an end in itself. How, Emma wondered, could she ever go back to Nebraska?

Having spent a month exploring her surroundings on foot, Emma was certain that she knew Saigon better than many people who had been born there. Her wanderings had taken her to tiny chapels and bizarre shops in obscure alleyways and hidden cul-de-sacs, to public wells where girls washed their long black hair and mothers drew water for cooking and laundry, to ramshackle docks and rat-infested warehouses, to the racetrack and the National Museum and the tree-shaded tennis courts at the Cercle Sportif.

In Saigon, everything she had always heard about the Far East came true. It was indeed a place filled with color and mystery, where an ancient civilization had bowed to accommodate the most up-to-date technology. Unlike Lincoln or Omaha or St. Louis, it wore its corruption with a raffish air and no hint of an apology. Sights that would have sent Lincoln's middle-class matrons scurrying to the nearest church were commonplace here: a pimp and prostitute arguing while a policeman turned his back on them; children begging on the steps of the Roman Catholic cathedral; a Chinese banker at the Grande Monde gambling club losing fifty thousand piasters on a single roll of the dice.

The wrought-iron gate in the wall around the villa banged shut. Monsieur de Chesnay had promised to give her a key, but he had been unable to locate one. The gate flapped open day and night, admitting a steady traffic of women, children of varying ages, old and new friends, and occasionally a buyer or a sitter for a portrait. From the balcony outside her room, Emma could always hear a cacophony of laughter and talk, music from the radio, an infant's cries, the rattle of bottles and glasses.

She wondered how her landlord ever managed to paint in such a turbulent environment, but he worked steadily, unperturbed by interruptions, turning out sketches, watercolors, portraits, silk screens, and lithographs. His studio occupied one end of the house on the ground floor. In earlier days, the room had been a ballroom or a grand salon. After dark, a few weak bulbs in the dirty crystal chandelier cast a watery light on the cracked plaster cornices, dingy flowered wallpaper, and stained marble floor.

When Emma first saw the house sitting in the center of its overgrown yard, with its fallen shutters and its cracked stucco, she wondered how a fastidious woman like Eliane de Mornay could possibly have recommended it as a suitable residence for her. Now she wouldn't move no matter what happened, even if she found a place for half the rent.

Monsieur de Chesnay had agreed readily to the terms she offered: twenty-five hundred piasters a month. He told her that he had little regard for money except as a means for giving pleasure to other people. He gave most of his paintings away. On her first day as his tenant, Emma had admired a watercolor of a tiger prowling around the crumbling walls of an abandoned temple in the jungle. De Chesnay had promptly presented it to her as a gesture of welcome.

"You see, the jungle always wins," he had told her in slow, careful English. "If all the people in this country were killed, the jungle would take over everything, and the tiger would be king once more."

Emma was never able to figure out, nor could anyone tell her, just how the various women in the household figured in the artist's life. Was the elderly wisp in the kitchen de Chesnay's number one wife or was she merely his cook and housekeeper? Were the four younger women, all of them sleek and fetching in their trousers and form-fitting *ao dais*, the Frenchman's daughters or his concubines? The children seemed to belong to the maidservants, who were more numerous than the daughters, but Emma noticed one small boy whose shock of black hair stood straight up over his forehead in a cockscomb just like Monsieur de Chesnay's.

In the 1930s, the French government had sent the young artist to Indochina to make a visual record of the region before modernization swept away the culture of centuries. De Chesnay stayed long after his assignment was complete, making a home in Saigon, venturing out to the countryside periodically to record a way of life that was soon to be destroyed, not by industry but by war. He lived through the uneasy truce between the French and the Japanese during the occupation, and he survived the savage coup of 1945, when the Japanese seized control of the government of Vietnam, imprisoned French officials, and executed thousands of French citizens. De Chesnay moved to one of the villages in which he had been a welcome guest in the past, and he stayed there until the Japanese had gone and the French had returned to power.

When Emma asked his opinion of the war, he lifted his shoulders. "The Viets will win, I suppose. They know how to be patient."

Another boarder occupied the room at the far end of the balcony, a bachelor civil servant in his early fifties whose rigid habits and strict adherence to routine were a household joke. Monsieur Varigny leaves for work? It must be seven-ten. Monsieur Varigny comes home again? Ah, one-twenty already. He has had his lunch, and he is ready for his siesta. He will close his shutters and rest until two-thirty, when he will arise, put on his white shirt and beige suit once more, and sally forth to his office, where he will stay until seven. After a leisurely dinner, which he always takes at the same restaurant on Rue Gambetta, he will come home. At eleven o'clock, his lights go out and he is in bed. On Sundays he goes to mass, and then to the Cinéma Catinat. On Wednesday evenings he attends a lecture at the Alliance Française.

Emma opened her notebook to a fresh page. She was working on a piece about her new landlord. Mr. Bailey probably wouldn't buy it, but someday she might be able to turn it into fiction or incorporate it into a novel. At six o'clock, she stopped writing and took a bath—her second of the day. How did anyone manage to stay beautiful in this climate? She applied her lipstick with a practiced hand, fluffed her pale golden curls around her face, and snapped a slim gold bracelet around her wrist. She was meeting Robert Janvier at the Café de la Paix at seven.

"Really, this heat is appalling." Eliane de Mornay waggled her fan under her chin. Suddenly her hand froze in midair. "Alan, I have just had the most marvelous idea! Lucien is away right now, in Hanoi. Why don't we fly to Hong Kong, just the two of us? He won't know. Even if he finds out, he won't care. What do you think of my plan?"

"Hong Kong is no cooler than here." Hazen sipped ginger ale. "Why don't you spend some of your precious piasters on air conditioning?"

"Because Lucien may be transferred out of this wretched country at any moment, and then my money would be wasted. I would rather spend it on pleasure, right now. What do you say *chéri*? A nice long weekend far away from this awful place, just the two of us."

"I'm busy."

"Pooh, you are so difficult, the most difficult lover I have ever had." Eliane lifted the small poodle sitting on her lap and kissed its black nose. "Thank God I have Mira to love me. He is never cross, never contrary. He always does just what I want. Oh, look, there is your little American girlfriend with her Captain Janvier. Over there, at the table with the blue umbrella. She is still a virgin, I see. I'm surprised."

Hazen glanced up. "You don't know that."

"Oh, but I do. You see the way she leans toward him as she speaks, but does not touch him? If they were lovers, she would cover his hand with hers, or touch his cheek. So far, they have not been intimate. What in God's name is Janvier waiting for? He is biding his time, I think, playing with her like a cat with a mouse. You doubt me? I will bet you five hundred piasters."

"I'm not a betting man." Hazen took a quick swallow of ginger ale. "Besides, we have no way of knowing, one way or the other."

Eliane smiled. "Oh, but we do. I will know at once, the day

after it happens. Just one look at her face. Not his—he's had too many women for one to make any difference."

"Now you're being a bitch."

"And you are jealous! Don't deny it. I know the signs. Not that I have observed any of them in Lucien—he doesn't care what I do so long as I keep his career moving ahead at a nice pace. But you, Alan. You are irritated, no? After all, you saw her first."

"That featherheaded young lady doesn't interest me."

"But you saved her life, or she saved yours. A meeting arranged by the Fates, if you ask me. Ah, they are arguing now. You see, he is shaking his head. He does not look pleased. Now she is begging. 'Please, Robert.' You see how she strokes his arm. And she is smiling. Yes, that's the way to do it, child. Smile at him like that—yes, it is working. He is weakening, even though he still shakes his head. Men are really so simple. Delightful creatures, like dogs. Yes, Mira, I am talking about you, my darling. They have simple, straightforward minds that do not deviate from the course they have chosen. A dog on the scent, a man with an idea—it is the same. Now women: We women are like cats. You pet one, it purrs, and the next moment it tears your hand with its claws." She laughed. "A nice simile, no? That is why we can never get along, not really. Men and women have what the newspapers would call an uneasy truce. All is calm and quiet for a while; then suddenly, poof! The battle rages. The man growls and barks, but if he is not careful, the woman will scratch his eyes out."

Hazen was watching the pair through narrowed eyes. "What do you suppose they're talking about?"

"I will tell you tomorrow. You see the woman at the table next to them, the one in the yellow dress? Marie Fournet. She worked with the BBC in London during the war and she understands English perfectly. She is surely listening to their conversation. If I meet her at noon tomorrow for tea, I can have a report for you by one o'clock."

"Brought to you by Radio Catinat, purveyors of gossip, slander, and character assassination." Having finished his drink, Hazen looked around for a waiter. "Don't you women have anything better to do?"

"Nothing," Eliane answered simply. "This city offers so little in the way of distractions—cultural or otherwise. We women must ease our boredom somehow. We talk on the telephone all morning, at noon we meet our friends in the cafés, we spend the rest of the day playing cards at the Cercle Sportif—talking more than playing, of course—and then we meet in the cafés again at seven. With a schedule like that, it is impossible for us not to know everything about everyone in Saigon. Like your young lady. She has been sending her stories to a newspaper in America, but so far she has received no response, even though her mother and aunt write to her at least twice a week. How do I know? My friend Babette's husband works at the post office."

"What kind of information do you have on me?" Hazen wondered irritably.

"Oh, you would be surprised by how much I know about you." With her fingernail, Eliane traced a random pattern on the back of Hazen's hand. "As a rule, you touch no liquor. But when you take one drink, you cannot stop. Then you find yourself a woman. The next morning, you are filled with remorse, and you never see that particular woman again. You should become a Catholic, my friend. The sacrament of confession is a wonderful release for troubled souls."

Hazen did not move his hand. "I suppose you've spread your tales about me to every woman in Saigon?"

"Not yet. But you can buy my silence," Eliane purred. "I will be at home tonight. I can guarantee absolute discretion. My servants are as reliable as mutes. Why not? I have sworn to cut out their tongues if they give away my secrets. They know I would do it."

"Not tonight. Reports to write."

"Bah, you work too much!" Eliane's gaze flickered past him. "Ah, they are leaving. You see how happy she is? She has won her argument. But what was it about? Yes, I would like to know myself."

* * *

Four days later, Hazen's telephone rang at a quarter to midnight. "Darling, this is Eliane. I do apologize, but my friend Marie Fournet ran off to Da Lat with her lover for a few days, and she just got back. Remember, she was sitting in the Café de la Paix when your little friend—"

"Yes, Eliane, I remember."

"Well, I have just heard from another of my spies that your little American and her handsome Legionnaire have been smoking opium for the last three nights down in Cholon. Yesterday they were there all afternoon as well. At this moment, they are in a brothel on Rue Pagode, that place where the high commissioner's chief assistant died of heart failure last year—or so the high commissioner would have us to believe. You know the place?"

"I've heard of it."

"You must go to Cholon at once and take her away from there. I cannot imagine what Janvier is thinking, letting the child even see a place like that. One of the worst. If she wanted to smoke opium, she could have borrowed my pipe, for heaven's sake. Well, are you going to rescue her?"

"No. Why should I? She wanted to see life in the raw, and she's seeing it. I don't care what happens to her."

"Oh, Alan, you are being silly. Even if you dislike her, which you don't, she is still your countrywoman. She has probably lost her virginity—that is inevitable—but you do not want her to lose her senses as well. Too many people have fallen under the spell of opium."

She rang off. Hazen hung up the receiver and leaned back in his chair. Dear God. Yes, he could imagine a hick like Emma Vaughan succumbing to the strange magic of opium. He himself had been initiated into the practice soon after arriving in Indochina, and one of the most difficult things he had ever done in his life was to quit it. His habit had been moderate, no more than six pipes in an evening, not an all-consuming and debilitating addiction. Some of the smokers he had met lived for opium, taking as many as sixty pipes a day. Nevertheless, Hazen knew that in deliberately quitting consciousness, in dropping worry and strain and the need for constant alertness, he was being delinquent and irresponsible. And so he stopped. He suffered through a painful period of withdrawal. For months afterward, he craved the sweet-smelling smoke and the forgetfulness it brought. He still thought of it often, with a mixture of disgust and longing.

The Vaughan girl was playing a dangerous game, sampling a vice whose delights were instant and real and extraordinarily seductive. Wearily, Hazen dragged himself out of his chair and gathered up the papers on his desk. When he had locked these into the safe in the wall, he rang for his houseboy.

"I'm going out, Pham. Bring the Buick around to the front."

Chrome Petroleum had provided its chief employee in Saigon with two cars, as well as a comfortable villa on the northern edge of the Plateau—an elevation so low it would have been unworthy of notice in most parts of the world—and a full complement of well-trained servants. Of these luxuries, Hazen appreciated the servants the most, particularly Pham, who anticipated his needs even before he knew them himself. Hazen slipped into the sports jacket he had hung over the back of his chair, turned off the lights in his study, and locked the door behind him.

Only two miles from Saigon, Cholon had been overtaken by the larger city's rapid, sprawling growth. Cochin-China's vast Chinese population congregated there. The streets looked no different from similar thoroughfares in Canton and Hong Kong and Shanghai: busy, noisy, crowded, with wares from a thousand shops spilling out into the open. Merchants offered lacquered ducks and exotic teas; spices and remedies for impotence; girls, guns, drugs, and engine parts. Hazen liked Cholon. In the smaller alleys and side streets, one could escape the glittering eyes of Saigon's gossip makers. Although in that respect, Emma Vaughan had been unlucky.

Hazen found Rue Pagode, a few blocks north of the Pont-en-Y, the Y-shaped bridge that spanned both the Saigon River and the Loop Canal. Here, below the piers and port facilities, sampans and houseboats were anchored so closely together that a man could walk for miles over the water without once touching land.

The entrance to the brothel in which the high commissioner's chief assistant had died was unmarked, but Hazen had been there himself on a couple of occasions, and he found the door tucked in between the facades of a restaurant and a laundry. He knocked, and a moment later was admitted by an aged Chinese who had the yellowed-parchment skin of the habitual opium smoker. Recognizing him, the man gestured toward the stairs, which were dirty, dimly lit, and quite steep. Stepping through another door, Hazen found himself in a small antechamber. An obese madame presided over her establishment from an ornately carved armchair, her weight supported by a pair of writhing dragons.

"The American girl," Hazen said. "Where is she?" The woman began to protest. "She is my niece," Hazen said in Chinese. "If you do not tell me where to find her, I will report you to the police. They will arrest you for kidnapping."

This was a meaningless threat since the police undoubtedly received a large percentage of each day's take, but Hazen made it anyway. The woman shrugged as if to say that his problems with his relatives were none of her concern. No matter, the foreigners had paid for their room in advance. Hazen was not aware that she had issued any command, but another man appeared, about twenty years younger than the first.

Hazen followed him through a beaded curtain. At the end of a long corridor, they halted in front of a closed door. Hazen pushed it open.

The low bubble of the pipe murmured a greeting, and the sweet smell of opium beckoned him inside. He fancied he could hear a whispered welcome: "Why have you stayed away so long?" The room was small, unbearably stuffy, and dark. The only light came from a tasseled lantern that hung over the bed, which was actually a broad, low couch piled with pillows. Hazen remembered the austere *fumeries* he had visited, with their hard board benches and bricklike pillows. The pleasures of opium needed no enhancement. This place obviously had been designed to impress the tourist and to seduce the novice.

A young Chinese woman knelt at a table near the bed. She wore a white silk tunic and trousers, and her hair was drawn into a chignon at the nape of her neck. She did not look up, although Hazen was sure she had heard him come into the room.

Seated cross-legged on the couch, Emma Vaughan watched the girl prepare a pipe of opium. She rolled a bit of brown gum into a ball and stuck it on the point of a needle. This she held over a candle flame for a few seconds, until it began to bubble and hiss; then she kneaded the ball between two needles until it had reached the proper consistency and dropped it into the bowl of a pipe, which she handed to Captain Janvier, who reclined on the cushions behind Emma. Taking the pipe, Janvier inhaled all the smoke in a single long intake of breath. Meanwhile, the girl prepared another pipe for Emma.

Hazen strode over to the bed and clamped his fingers around Emma's wrist.

"All right, you've had enough. Let's go."

She was relaxed from the opium and the heat and the quietude, so passive that she did not resist him until they had nearly reached the door. Then she pulled back, squawking in protest.

"What do you think you're doing? Let me go. Darn you, stop it! Robert!"

Janvier reached them in a single stride. He was not sleepy at all, but alert and watchful. Hazen knew the feeling. Sometimes the first pipes of the evening acted as a stimulant because they eliminated tiredness and anxiety and aches and pains. For a while, the smoker felt renewed, refreshed, rejuvenated.

"What are you doing? Leave her alone."

"I'm taking her out of here. I hold you responsible, Janvier. You have no right to expose her to crap like this. I ought to thrash you."

Janvier moved in closer. "You would regret it, Monsieur Hazen. You have no right to interfere. This is our business."

"It's my business to step in and do something when an American national is making herself and her country look foolish. This story is going to be all over Saigon tomorrow. How the hell do you think I found out about it? The two of you were seen coming in here. Recognized. Miss Vaughan, I give you fair warning. If you take one more whiff of opium, if you so much as come near a place like this again, I will know about it. First, I'll take you over my knee and give you the beating of your life. Then I will demand that the French revoke your visa. You'll be on the next plane out of here before you wake up from your opium dream."

The girl at the table watched the scene, her face betraying no emotion. Hazen knew the Chinese in opium dens. Their apparent remoteness came from a practiced lack of interest in other people's troubles. So long as she herself was well fed, able to support her mother or brothers or whoever else depended on her, she didn't care what happened to her customers.

"But I'm doing research!" Emma stamped her stockinged foot on the stained carpet. Her shoes, and Janvier's, stood by the side of the bed, neatly paired. "Robert didn't want to come along, but I made him. You are interfering with my work and my life and I won't stand for it, do you hear me, Alan Hazen? You don't own me. Now let me go!" With a single twist of her arm, she freed herself from his grasp. "I'm getting out of here."

Emma grabbed up her shoes and her purse and ran out into the hall. Hazen caught up with her at the street entrance. "I have my car," he said. "I'll give you a ride back."

She stopped in the middle of the sidewalk. "Mr. Hazen, I wouldn't take a ride from you if I were dying of thirst in the middle of the desert and your car was the only transport to water. Boy!" She hailed a passing trishaw with all the imperiousness of an old Indochina hand and climbed into the seat in front of the driver. As she rode away, she called, *"Maulen!"* in order to make her driver pedal faster.

"You are a fool." Hazen heard Janvier's voice behind him. "She smoked only three small pipes tonight. Hardly enough to harm a baby. If I had not brought her here, she would have come alone. Only God knows what would have happened to her then. She is like a child in a pastry shop. She wants to taste everything. A girl like that needs a friend, a protector. Not an adversary who will slap her hands and make her determined to indulge herself until she becomes sick."

Hazen strode away to his car without answering. More than anything else, he wanted to find a nice quiet *fumerie* where he could smoke a few pipes of opium himself and forget about Emma Vaughan and her kittenlike curiosity. Let her ruin her health, lose her virginity, endanger her soul. It was not his affair.

Instead, he stopped at the Bodega, a bar he knew near the waterfront, and ordered bourbon, a double.

An hour later he drove out to General de Mornay's villa on the northern edge of the city. He pulled up in front of the gate and blasted his horn. After a minute, a uniformed guard appeared, who recognized the car and admitted him. When Hazen entered the house, he saw Eliane coming down the stairs. The blue lace of her dressing gown swirled around her slim figure like sea foam.

"So you have come to me at last." Smiling, she stretched out her hand to him. "You won't be sorry, I promise you. Come, my darling."

Emma lay in a soft womb made of white bed sheets and yards of lacy mosquito netting. She was wide awake but curiously calm, and not a bit tired. The hands of the luminous dial of her alarm clock pointed east and north. Three o'clock. A generous slice of the night. At three A.M. in Lincoln, Nebraska, the whole city was sunk in a torpor that approximated death. Not here. The walls of the villa vibrated subtly, breathing as she breathed, slowly and evenly. Saigon was her true mother, the Far East her natural home. Perhaps her soul had been sent to Nebraska as punishment for some infraction. It must have been quite serious, to propel her to the outer crust of the civilized world. All aboard the Transmigration Express. She had been a jungle animal, a tigress, or perhaps she had been a peasant from the rice paddies. Her soul must be very old. How else could she have gained such wisdom?

Old and wise and quite wicked. Had she been the Dowager Empress of China?

She swept the netting aside and climbed out of bed. The secrets of the night belonged to her now. The gates of ignorance had been thrown open, and she was free to enter the world of light. But when the sun came up, and the city awakened, the gates would close again, and she would understand nothing. The time to penetrate these mysteries was now, while she was still in a liquid state, while her spirit still throbbed in harmony with this strange and wonderful land.

Emma dressed quickly and tiptoed along the balcony to the stairs. Monsieur Varigny was snoring. Somewhere in the house, a baby uttered a few anxious cries and was silent. Was he dreaming of his past life? A hidden memory, a secret revealed and then concealed, like a shell thrown up on shore and then reclaimed by the tide?

Streetlamps like surrogate moons bathed the sidewalks in a fine hard brightness like distilled sunlight. The other villas were quiet, breathing naturally along with everything else. Emma recalled that all matter is composed of molecules made of atoms that are eternally in motion. Even substances that most people consider dead, like ancient stones or modern concrete or stainless steel, hum with the same vitality as persons and animals and plants. The world was created out of a single breath. Everything lived. Emma touched a tree, then a lamppost, then an iron railing. Yes, she could feel the vibration as the object drew breath and expelled it again. Rhythm and harmony. The universal music.

She reached the square dominated by the huge red brick cathedral, whose spires illustrated man's conception of the shape of prayer. Why upward, and why pointed? Emma sighed at the limited capacity of the human mind. Didn't men know that prayer spread laterally, like fine soft mist, bathing everything in love?

Rue Catinat welcomed her with soft silence. The shops and cafés were closed and shuttered. A warm breeze stirred the leaves of the tamarind trees that lined the street. Emma had the sensation of floating rather than walking. The light wind carried her along, like a small boat skimming a calm sea. At the foot of Saigon's major shopping street lay the waterfront, an unsavory jumble of bars, flophouses, sailors' dives, cheap restaurants, and gambling establishments run by a small community of Corsicans.

Down here, on the banks of the Saigon River, the pulse of life felt stronger. Water slapped rhythmically against pilings blackened with creosote. A few yard away, coolies were loading a ship under the light of powerful arc lamps. Their bare feet slapped the gangplanks, which dipped and bounced under their weight. Bent nearly double under their loads—bales of cotton, sacks of rice and coffee beans, crates of tea and spices—they kept up a litany of sharp cries to warn people out of their way. Watching them from the dock, Emma smiled.

A knot of sailors stared at her from the doorway to a bar. A couple of them started to approach her. They were intercepted by an officer, a brawny Legionnaire who snarled at them in gutter French, "Get out of here. Go on, beat it. The bitch belongs to me." The sailors eyed the captain's pistol and the sheathed knife at his belt and vanished into the bar.

Coming up behind Emma, Janvier put both hands on her shoulders and turned her around. Her smile widened. "Robert, I've been waiting for you."

"I went to your room, but you were not there. Your door was open, your bed was rumpled, but you had flown away." He caressed her cheek and smoothed a lock of hair behind her ear. "I have been looking for you everywhere. Finally I saw you walking along Rue Catinat, and I followed you."

"I wanted to feel the breathing."

"It is not safe, Emma."

"Of course it's safe. Besides, I couldn't sleep."

"Neither could I. The opium has that effect."

Their arms entwined around each other's waists, they moved out of the light. The pulse was stronger, throbbing in Emma's ears. "Why did you go to my room?"

Janvier framed her face with his hands. "You are like a beautiful child, Emma. You want to learn all about war and opium, but as yet you know nothing about love."

His kiss was like a prayer whose lovely softness spread to every part of her body. The world folded around her and embraced her in loving warmth. This was light, this was life: to melt into another's body, to feel his heat and hear his heartbeat.

"Yes, I want to learn—"

"If I take you back to de Chesnay's house, all Saigon will know our secret in the morning. I know a little hotel near here. Shall we go there?"

"I don't care. I just want to be with you. I love you so much, Robert. Do you love me, too?"

"Of course I do, my dearest. Come."

His will was her will and the will of the universe. As he undressed her, she told him about her discoveries, that the pulse of the world beat in every object, whether animate or inanimate, and that love and prayer were the same. When they were both naked, he pushed her down on the bed and lowered himself on top of her. His mouth covered hers, stopping the breathless flow of her words.

She wondered what her mother and her aunt had meant when they taught her to beware of men and their savage hungers. His wants were her wants, nature's wants, honest and simple and beautiful. When at last they found their rhythm and moved together, the pulse of the universe crashed in her ears like a tide.

After they made love for the first time, they slept, and awakened refreshed to find that only ten minutes had passed. The opium, he said. Time has no meaning. Love came again and again, a promise that renewed itself every time it was fulfilled. She received his instructions humbly, and obeyed his commands without question, because his desires were her desires. She felt no shyness, no awkwardness, only a willingness to yield, to blend, to incorporate herself into the greater whole. To disappear.

The night went on forever, until he announced that it was dawn and he must leave her. Smiling, she closed her eyes and

listened to the music of her own heart singing its song of jubila-
tion.

"Good afternoon, Monsieur Alan." Eliane de Mornay came up
behind Hazen as he stood waiting for a white-clad traffic cop to
halt the waves of cars and bicycles that streamed along Boulevard
Charner. She slipped her hand under his elbow. "You might have
sent me flowers this morning, or a little note of thanks. After all,
I did you a kindness by taking you into my house in the middle of
the night, did I not? Instead, you took what you wanted from me
and went off without a word. I am glad I have no heart. You
would have broken it long ago." Mira, on his leash, yapped assent.

The cop waved his white-gloved hand at them and they
stepped off the curb. "Why don't you run along, Eliane?" Hazen
said wearily. "I'm in no mood for girlish chitchat today."

"I am not surprised." She did not release his arm. "You must
have drunk a lot of whisky last night. And now you are ashamed
of yourself, right? But why, my darling? I feel no shame. We had
a wonderful time. You cannot get away from me now. I will not
let you spurn me the way you have spurned those other girls. We
were good friends before, and now our friendship is even better.
To celebrate, I will buy you a nice Coca-Cola."

At an outdoor café, Eliane chose a table closest to the sidewalk. "Let me tell you about a little game I play with myself.
Whenever I go to a café, I always sit where I have a clear view of
all the people who pass by, and then I count how many of them I
know by name. You would be surprised. Some days that number
goes as high as fifty or sixty."

Eliane took out her compact and touched powder to her nose.
A waiter took their orders. Hazen, holding his lighter to a cigarette, paused with his hand in midair and gazed through a veil of
flame. Captain Robert Janvier and Emma Vaughan were strolling along the opposite side of the street. Emma was clinging to
Janvier's arm and smiling up into his face. They halted at the
intersection, and as they waited for the signal to cross, he stroked

her cheek with his fingertip. She caressed the back of his hand.

"You should be glad you did not take my bet," Eliane said softly. "She is his mistress now. My spies did not have to tell me that. I can tell by looking. And so can you, Alan."

6

MARCH 21, 1953

Dear Mom and Aunt Louise,

Sorry for the long dry spell. I've been busy with
French lessons every day, as well as press briefings
and interviews when I can get them. The war is
going badly—the French really took a beating at
Nasan. The high command is trying to make the
retreat sound like a brilliant piece of tactical
maneuvering, but no one here is fooled. . . .

Mr. Bailey clearly isn't interested in my pieces,
even the feature stories about life in Saigon and
Cochin-China. I'm not surprised. The other
reporters here . . .

"**D**amnedest female I ever saw." Walter Ashbourne took a sip of
whisky and propped his elbows on the bar of the Hotel Majestic. "At the briefing this morning, she pushes her way right to
the front of the mob and says, 'Excuse me, Major, but is it true
that some of the weapons taken from the Viet Minh near Nasan
were American-made seventy-five-millimeter recoilless rifles,
captured by the Chinese in Korea?' The guy was stunned. He
froze right there for thirty seconds, and then he issued the standard denial: 'We have had no information to that effect.' In
French. She got the message, though."

One of Ashbourne's colleagues laughed. "Every time somebody makes a statement at headquarters, she turns to me and asks
me to translate before she writes anything down."

"But she wouldn't drop it," Ashbourne went on. Assuming
what he considered a feminine pose, one hand on his hip, his lips

pursed into a pout, he lisped, "'But isn't it true that your forces
have only fifty-seven-millimeter weapons of the same type?
Doesn't the fact that your enemy is equipped with superior weap-
onry give them an edge in firepower as well as manpower?'
Whew, that guy was mad as hell. He didn't give her an answer; he
just turned around and walked out of the room. Got to hand it to
her, the kid's got guts."

"I don't know. If she keeps this up, she could get her credentials
revoked. They'll turn into clams at HQ, and none of us will get
any stories. Somebody ought to tell her to slow down, not push so
hard."

"I want to know where she gets her information and why the
rest of us can't get it. Hey, Al." Ashbourne noticed Alan Hazen
sitting near the end of the bar, a coffee cup at his elbow. "How's it
going, buddy? Your boss have any room on his payroll for a good
PR man? I could live very nicely on your salary: fancy house,
private plane, nice car. What do you say? I'm getting too old to be
covering wars in stinking sweatholes like Saigon." He gestured to
the big window that overlooked the city and the river. "Leave the
running around to the younger guys."

"And the girls." Hazen tossed a bank note down on the bar.

"Oh, you mean the Vaughan kid. You know her?"

"No, but it sounds like she's working harder than the rest of you."

"That may be, but she's not getting paid for it." He laughed.
"Waste of effort, if you ask me."

On Rue Gambetta later that afternoon, Hazen saw a familiar
figure approaching him. Emma Vaughan's head was lowered over
her pocket-sized notebook. She moved with the flow of pedestrians, occasionally glancing nervously ahead of her while her lips
moved soundlessly. Hazen planted himself squarely in her path
and caught her elbows when she barged into him. She murmured an apology in execrable French, then looked up. Her dark
glasses gave her the appearance of a startled insect. When she
recognized him, her words faded and her expression turned
wooden.

"Oh, it's you. I know you want to run me out of Saigon, but you don't have to run me down."

"My fault." Seeing her about to push past and hurry away, Hazen grabbed her arm. "Look, I want to apologize for that night in Cholon. You're right, it was none of my business. I only succeeded in embarrassing you, and making myself look like a fool."

"It certainly took you long enough to get around to saying something," Emma sniffed. "That happened five months ago."

"I've been out of town. An interesting trip; I'll tell you all about it sometime. Can I buy you a cup of coffee?"

"Sorry, I can't. I'm meeting someone."

Hazen knew without asking that the someone was Captain Janvier. "Is it really that urgent? A few minutes won't make any difference. And I do owe you a debt of gratitude, Miss Vaughan. I haven't forgotten that you distracted that sniper at Ta Prouhm and saved my life."

Emma glanced at her watch, then nodded. "All right. But I can't stay longer than half an hour. Can we find someplace air-conditioned?"

"The bar at the Majestic? If you don't mind rubbing the elbows of your esteemed colleagues, that is."

"No, thanks." She made a face. "Those middle-aged parasites. They're so full of opium and alcohol that they can't see what's going on in this country."

"Can you?"

"You bet I can. Look at the French high command, for example. They're operating autonomously, with no direction from their government. The only power the government has is economic: They're footing half the bills. The Americans pick up the rest."

"That's a considerable power." Hazen steered her around a pushcart loaded with long pieces of sugarcane. Not far from the large Central Market plaza, they turned onto a narrow side street lined with compartments, concrete structures having shops in the front, large living spaces in the center, and courtyards at the rear. The Viet Minh had created openings in the communal walls.

Fugitives from the police could disappear into the maze and, by darting from courtyard to courtyard, lose their pursuers among piles of crates and baskets and lines full of drying laundry.

"The government's not exercising any power." Emma walked determinedly through the clutter of merchandise spilling out onto the street: bolts of silk and printed cotton, woven baskets, urns of soup and caldrons of rice, sticks of incense and bouquets of paper flowers. Interspersed among these homelier artifacts were radios, new bicycles, automobile parts, Fench perfumes and cosmetics, cutlery from Germany, and hairbrushes from England. "The French army is running this country. There's no real ruling power here, no one group or organization willing to take responsibility for putting things back together after the fighting tears it all apart. The emperor is a playboy, his cabinet ministers are hand-in-glove with the most corrupt elements in the city, including that bunch of cutthroat gangsters that calls itself the Binh Xuyen. At home, the French government changes every six weeks, and despite rising public sentiment against the war, no one has the guts to call it off."

"They have a pretty big commitment to this country. You can't expect them to throw away a hundred years of investment and development."

"And exploitation. Do you know what the Legion did last week? They bombed a village in Tonkin, destroyed it, flattened it, because the Vietnamese villagers weren't showing them enough respect. Can you believe it? And they expect to win this war! That's what amazes me. The only solid Vietnamese support they have is in the cities, from people who are getting rich in the black market and in the currency exchanges."

"You seem to have caught on pretty quickly to the situation here." Hazen spoke cautiously. "But it's no different from anyplace else in the Far East. A backward country fighting for its independence, with powerful supporters on both sides—"

"And vultures like Chrome Petroleum just waiting to strike a bargain with the winner. Well, aren't you?"

"There's no crime in wanting to make a profit. The Vietnamese will get their fair share." Hazen stopped in front of a doorway curtained with beads. He looked down at her, his mouth bent into a quizzical smile. "Are you always so intense, Miss Vaughan?"

The question caught her off guard. "Intense? Well, I don't know. I'm always like this, if that's what you mean."

Hazen led her along a narrow corridor, then through another curtain. Emma gave a start of surprise. They were in a large courtyard. Slender tamarind trees shaded a flagstone-covered terrace on which small tables and chairs had been arranged. They sat at a table near a fountain. A silver trickle of water spilled over volcanic rock into a small pool in which swam a pair of brightly colored carp.

"This is lovely."

"The best I could do. No air conditioning, but at least it gives an illusion of coolness. What would you like?"

"A daiquiri, please."

Hazen ordered tea for himself. Their waitress, a slim girl in her late teens, wore a green *ao dai* over white trousers. The skirt of the tunic was slashed to the waist on both sides, and when the girl walked, the sheer panels of fabric flared out like butterfly wings. Emma watched her disappear into the house. "I feel like such an Amazon next to the women here," she sighed. "What can I say? I've got big bones."

"They're nice bones," Hazen said with unexpected warmth. He offered her a cigarette, which she declined. Her beauty really was astonishing, especially in this country where the standard of beauty had been set by women who were small and dark. "How's the writing going?"

"Fine. Selling what I've written, that's the problem. I've sent Mr. Bailey five full-length feature stories so far, and I haven't heard a word from him. My mother has telephoned him at least ten times. He said he hasn't had time to read them. The stinker. He told me when I quit that damned women's page that I would fall on my face, and now he's doing his best to make sure I fail. I could win a Pulitzer, and it still wouldn't make any difference to him."

"He's not the only editor in the country."

"No, thank God. I've asked my aunt and my mother to send the stories to other papers. Maybe somebody will notice me and offer me money. I'm not fussy. If I can't be a full-fledged foreign correspondent, then I'll do piecework as a stringer. I don't need an elaborate expense account to survive."

"From what I hear, you're way ahead of the rest of the pack when it comes to getting news."

"Them." Emma was scornful of her colleagues. "They're terrified that the government is going to take away their travel documents and their exit permits if they get too pushy. I don't know why they're worried. By the time the censors have finished with their stories, there's not much truth left in them anyway."

"They have a right to be concerned. You can't report a war like this from Hong Kong or Tokyo."

"Why not? I happen to know that some of them flew over Nasan, courtesy of the French Expeditionary Forces. They looked at the action from three thousand feet in the air, and then they wrote what the army told them to write."

"I gather you didn't go along on that jaunt."

"No. I can't leave Saigon without a travel permit, and I won't get one until I can prove to them that I am officially employed by an accredited newspaper. Anyway, what would be the point of my going? I can't afford to send telexes to an editor who doesn't even want them." Their drinks arrived. Emma removed her dark glasses. Her eyes were ringed with shadows.

"The heat in the tropics can really get you down," Hazen said sympathetically.

"Oh, I'm all right. I haven't been sleeping too well lately, though."

"You have to get used to the climate. Try to pace yourself, save all your strenuous work for the early morning or evening hours. What are you reading?" Hazen picked up the book Emma had laid on the table with her notebook.

"I'm studying French with a friend of Monsieur de Chesnay's. He told me today that he's never heard a worse accent than mine.

Honestly, I've tried and tried, and I am getting better, but I just don't have an ear for languages. '*Bawn joor, muhseeher.*' See what I mean? I still sound like a hick from the cornfields. It's disgusting."

"Your accent sounds as charming to French ears as a French accent does to our ears," Hazen assured her.

"Sure, like Madame de Mornay. 'But, *chéri*, you are so sharming, come and seet wiz me.' She sounds nearly as phony as I do."

Hazen laughed. It was a pleasant, relaxed sound. "That may be, but she happens to be the genuine article."

"I'm not so sure about that. Did you ever have the feeling that someone was too good to be true? She's a little too chic, a little too vivacious, a little too—everything. I bet you she's somebody's illegitimate kid from the Kasbah who's trying to claw her way to the top of French society."

"If that were true, she wouldn't be the wife of an army general, and she wouldn't be satisfied to be the Queen of Saigon. Only Paris would do."

Emma studied him over the rim of her glass. "Why are you being so nice to me, Mr. Hazen? If you're thinking of giving me some more fatherly advice, I advise you not to. I can take care of myself."

Hazen leaned back in his chair. "Actually, Miss Vaughan, besides wanting to apologize for my behavior last fall, I also wanted to discuss something with you. I am impressed by what I have seen and heard about your abilities as a reporter. You're not afraid to go after a story, and you're not afraid to write what you see. I'm going to Laos in a few weeks, just a weekend trip to visit a friend of mine, a medical missionary in Sop Pong, up near the Chinese border. I was wondering if you'd like to come along? Do a story about him, see more of the country? If you're looking for human interest, you'll find plenty of it there. Jack McGraw's doing incredible work among the mountain tribesmen."

Emma hesitated. "Can I think about it for a few days? I'm not sure I'll be able to get away."

Hazen watched her. She did not want to leave her Captain

Janvier, even for one night. He handed her a business card. "I have an office on Boulevard Charner. If I'm not there, my secretary will take a message. I'll be flying my own plane. It's not very big, and we stow medical supplies in any space not taken by passengers, so let me know as soon as you can."

"I will. Thanks." Emma fingered the card. "Frankly, the idea of flying doesn't appeal to me."

"Why? Have you ever been up in a plane?"

"God, no. Just thinking about flying terrifies me. It's stupid, I know, but I don't like heights. I never did."

"Well, if you want to see anything of this country outside of Saigon, you'll have to get over your fear. The roads are terrible, and they're open to convoys during the daylight hours only. The railroad lines between Saigon and Hanoi have been broken so many times that it would take you a week to get to the north from here, even without a war."

As they were leaving, Emma noticed Lieutenant Constance Burton sitting at a nearby table.

Hazen saw her too. "Hoping for an interview with the Legion's Iron Maiden? Good luck."

They stopped at Lieutenant Burton's table and Hazen greeted her cordially. The lieutenant peered up at them from under her red beret. She was wearing gray-and-green camouflage fatigues.

"Good Lord, the babe from Baray and her keeper. How did you manage to find this place? It's one of Saigon's best-kept secrets. No, that's not quite accurate. Saigon has no secrets." Constance Burton fixed Emma with a cold stare. "Tell me, how is your affair with Captain Janvier progressing?"

Emma blinked, but did not answer. The woman was drunk. She must be, to speak so bluntly.

"He's a bloody monster, you know." With a steady hand, Lieutenant Burton raised a coffee cup to her lips. "A fiend. But it's early days yet. I assume you haven't gotten beyond the gentle-words-and-soft-laughter phase. Well, he'll tire of you soon enough. Everyone in Saigon is waiting to see the black-and-blue badges of your shame on your cheeks and your eyes and your neck. But that won't stop you from crawling back to him every time he waves his cock in your direction. You'll hate yourself for doing it, but you won't be able to stop yourself. If I didn't dislike you so much, I would feel sorry for you."

"Why are you telling lies about him?" Emma gripped the edges of her book. "You're jealous, aren't you? You're jealous! You're in love with Robert Janvier yourself, and he doesn't care beans about you."

"Your nanny should have warned you never to fall in love with a soldier. All they understand is fighting and fucking." Lieutenant Burton refilled her cup with black coffee and added a slug of whisky from a silver hip flask. Her tone was as brittle as old glass. "They have no hearts. They have no souls. At least when two soulless individuals get together, they have nothing more to lose. Only life, and that doesn't count for tuppence."

"Let's go." Hazen pulled Emma away from the table and propelled her toward the exit. "I think you ought to listen to her," he said when they had reached the street.

Emma whirled on him. "Kindly keep your opinions to yourself, Mr. Hazen. I know what I'm doing."

"I have no opinions, Miss Vaughan. But I wouldn't want you to get hurt," Hazen persisted. "Men like Janvier are incapable of giving anything of themselves. They have nothing to give. They're dried up, burned out, barely human anymore. They're certainly not capable of falling in love."

"And how much of yourself have you given to anyone, Mr. Know-It-All God Almighty Hazen?" Emma pushed her freckled face close to Hazen's. "You had a wife yourself, as I recall, and you don't even know where she is now. A real loving husband. Don't preach to me about love, because I don't believe a word you say. And I don't believe her, either. You're a couple of bitter, lonely old people."

She ran back toward Rue Gambetta, leaving Hazen taut and flushed with irritation. Bitter and lonely, maybe. But old? Hardly.

* * *

Emma reached the little hotel at the foot of Rue Catinat half an hour late for her rendezvous with Janvier. He was not there. She railed at herself for allowing Hazen to seduce her with promises of air conditioning and cool drinks. Why hadn't she gotten here on time? Why wasn't Robert here? Had he already left? Where could he have gone? Why hadn't he left a message? Should she telephone Legion headquarters? Her limited French would never be equal to the task of locating him. No, she must wait here for him to find her.

The bars of golden light on the walls faded as the blazing rim of the sun sank behind the buildings across the street. Emma opened the louvered shutters. A breath of hot wind carried with it the fragrance of mimosa and frangipani, as well as automobile fumes and *nuoc mam*, the Vietnamese condiment made of salt and rotten fish.

Even in the mellow light of late afternoon, the room looked squalid and dismal. No doubt its threadbare carpets and sagging bed had witnessed many passion-filled afternoon encounters. Emma remembered the first time she had come here with Janvier, on the night Hazen had found them smoking opium together in Cholon. How magical these surroundings had seemed then, how welcoming and warm. Now she noticed that the loops of mosquito netting over the bed were soiled and gray, like heaps of cobwebs. The threadbare sheets were stained. The folding screen in the corner hid a sink and bidet that been old thirty years ago.

Emma sat on the hard-backed chair near the window and composed herself to wait. She smiled. Alan Hazen had worried that she might become addicted to opium, but since that first week she had only had a couple of pipes with Janvier. He did not seem much interested in the drug, and her own, mild addiction had somehow disappeared, consumed in the fires of a greater addiction: Janvier.

Closing her eyes, Emma recalled the hours she had spent exploring the terrain of his body: the ranges of smooth, hard muscle, the forests of dark hair, the mysterious scars and underground rivers of blue veins, and in the middle of it all, that sturdy monument to love, the shrine at which she worshiped.

Moaning softly, Emma doubled over and rested her head on her knees. Her engagement to Edward—how long ago that seemed!—had fooled her into thinking that men were easy to control. Her ignorance and arrogance amazed her. She compared herself to a weekend sailor who, skimming along the placid surface of a pond, fancies that he can handle his boat in all kinds of weather. Until he ventures out onto the ocean and is overwhelmed by fierce winds and crashing waves.

Gradually, as shadows filled the room, ugly fears crept into Emma's imagination. Perhaps Robert was injured, or even dead. A grenade had felled him, or a sniper's bullet had ripped through his chest. An accident with a jeep, perhaps. A bout of malaria or dysentery. What would happen to her if he didn't come back? If she never saw him again? She didn't think she could survive this time.

Janvier's battalion had been sent to Nasan before Christmas. Emma had never known such agony. For two months she had lived with acute fear and apprehension. She had haunted the offices of the French high command, hoping to learn how the battle was progressing. She wanted to believe the smooth assurances in the newspapers that the fighting was going well, but she had had enough experience as a reporter to doubt everything she read.

When Janvier returned in late February, he told her that the operation around Nasan had been a fiasco, a monument to double-talk and poor planning that had wasted lives and done nothing to secure the French hold on that part of Tonkin. The army had based its soldiers in an isolated mountain area near the Laotian border, far from conventional lines of supply. The Viet Minh, knowing that the base had to rely on air deliveries for fresh supplies and reinforcements, had attacked the landing strip and put it out of commission, leaving the base vulnerable to attack from the ground. Janvier's paratroop unit was one of several that had been dropped into Nasan to engage the enemy and relieve the pressure on the garrison. After weeks of bloody fighting, the French had decided to abandon the base. Those men who could not be evacuated by air had escaped through the jungle. Many perished.

Emma switched on the lamp on the bedside table. The light glared feebly through a tear in the grimy shade. The hole resembled a shaky sketch of a barbell, or the country of Vietnam, with Annam the narrow waist and Tonkin and Cochin-China the bulging weights at either end. As Emma spread her hand over the tear, her thumb touched Saigon and her little finger landed on Hanoi, the northern capital. The situation in the north was troublesome, growing worse by the day. Robert may well have been ordered to return there at once. He had not been able to reach her, to tell her.

Hearing footsteps in the corridor, Emma rushed to the door and looked out. A man in a tan business suit passed under the dangling bulb near the staircase. His arm was slung around the slender waist of a Vietnamese girl. Quickly, Emma retreated inside her own room. Outside, the bells in the cathedral tolled eight times. Janvier would not come now. She was a fool to keep waiting. She was hungry, sweaty, and tired, but she would not lie down on the bed alone.

Then a key scraped in the lock and the door swung open. Robert Janvier stepped into the room.

With a joyous cry, Emma hurled herself at him and clasped her arms around his neck. "I was so frightened, Robert. I've been waiting for hours. I thought you were hurt—"

"Hurt? Since yesterday? What nonsense." Janvier smiled. "Stop it, Emma, you are choking me, you silly girl. So you have missed me, eh?"

"Yes, oh, yes." She covered his face with kisses. "Why didn't you come sooner? I didn't know what had happened to you."

"I was detained on diplomatic business." He detached her

arms. "We had to escort a convoy of American officials to Tay Ninh, and then stand guard while they looked at the Cao Daist temple. A wasted afternoon, and a waste of paratroopers who should be out killing the enemy instead of impressing visitors. I didn't really think you would still be waiting." He grinned at her. "Well, what do you want to do now? Are you hungry? Shall we go out and get something to eat?"

"I'm hungry for you." Taking his hands, Emma led him to the bed. They lay in each other's arms, crushing their bodies and lips together. "Could I make it any plainer?"

Laughing, Janvier slid his hand along her thigh. "No, mademoiselle. You express yourself very well."

Emma adjusted her pillow against the headboard and sat up. "I discovered a wonderful little café this afternoon, not far from the Central Market," she said casually. She refrained from mentioning that Alan Hazen had taken her there. "I saw Lieutenant Burton. She said some very nasty things about you."

"That woman." Janvier yawned. "She always wants to be the center of attention."

"She suggested that you and she used to be—you know."

"Lovers?" Janvier chuckled. "I gave her a couple of rolls a long time ago, when our battalion first arrived in Vietnam. I tired of her very quickly. She was too selfish."

"I think she still loves you." Emma wound a coil of Janvier's hair around her forefinger. "She wouldn't have sounded so bitter otherwise. She hates me. Maybe I'll send a note to the police. At least if someone lobs a grenade into this room and blows us both up, they'll know who to blame."

Laughing, Janvier pulled down the sheet she had drawn up over her breasts. "Why do you frighten yourself with that bogeywoman? Don't you think I know how to protect you?"

"It—it's not that. I'm afraid of what will happen with us. She said you would grow tired of me, too." Emma gazed into his dark eyes, hoping to catch a glimpse of her future, but they were as hard to fathom as pools of ink. "I don't think I could live if that happened."

"You worry too much, *chérie*. You thought I would not survive Nasan, but I came back to you, didn't I? I will always come back to you, my little Emma. Don't you believe me?"

Grasping her waist, he pulled her down in the bed and covered her with his body. His thrust was hard and deep, and she whimpered with delight. They spoke no more.

"All right, all right, I understand. He's not here. Can you at least give him a note? *Donne—donnez-lui une lettre, s'il vous plaît?* It is *très* important."

The Legion guard on duty at the barracks studied the envelope Emma handed him. She was conscious of the taxi idling behind her, sucking thousands of piasters from her wallet with each passing minute, and of the soldier standing at the other side of the gate, his rifle at the ready. "*S'il vous plaît?*" she said pleadingly, and repeated that the matter was urgent and extremely important. The guard hefted the letter, decided that no bomb was enclosed, and shrugged. Emma expressed her thanks effusively, then returned to the taxi.

Fifteen minutes later, the cab dropped her in front of the high commissioner's palace. She walked down Rue Catinat to the Pagoda tearoom. Through the steel mesh over the window, she saw Alan Hazen sitting in one corner. He was reading a French-language newspaper. She retreated hastily and hurried back the way she had come, reaching her room in the de Chesnay villa at twenty minutes past one, just in time to meet her neighbor, Monsieur Varigny, returning home for his siesta. He gave her a puzzled smile, as if he did not recognize her. Not too surprising, considering how little time she spent in her room these days. Monsieur de Chesnay hailed her from the garden, where he had set up an easel in front of a spray of bougainvillea.

"How are your lessons progressing?" he asked in French.

"Very well, monsieur. Thank you very much." She fled to her

room before he could engage her further. Her bed, scored with
narrow bars of sunlight that gleamed through the louvered shutters on the windows, looked like an instrument of torture. Weeping, she collapsed onto her pillow.

At seven o'clock, Emma went to the room at the hotel and took
up her post in the hard-backed chair. A book lay open on her lap,
but she did not read it. At nine-twenty, Janvier walked in.

"Your note sounded somewhat hysterical." He tossed his red
beret onto the bed. "Is something wrong?"

"Yes, something's wrong. Where have you been for the past
week? I've been here every night, waiting for you. Couldn't you
at least have sent a message?"

"Ah, my Emma, I have had no time. I have been extremely
busy."

"Giving more diplomats the grand tour? I don't believe you.
You've been in Saigon all this time, haven't you? But you didn't
come here because you don't want to see me anymore. Well, if
that's the case, why don't you just be honest and say so?"

"Poor little Emma, why are you upsetting yourself in this fashion?" he crooned. "I have been on patrol in the countryside. We
have received reports that the Viet Minh were moving weapons
into the area around Chon Thanh. We searched everywhere and
found nothing, but we provided good meat for the guerrillas.
One of my men stepped on a mine. There was hardly enough left
of him to bury. We were all covered with pieces of his blood and
flesh. Two more were killed by snipers from the trees. In the end
we found no weapons. None at all. The report was false, intended to lure us away from Saigon. How else can they kill us
with such ease?"

Emma swiped at her eyes with her fist. "You might have let me
know you weren't going to be here. A phone call to Monsieur de
Chesnay, or a message. I feel like such a fool, keeping a vigil for a
man who doesn't care about me—"

"Emma, *petite chérie*, you are acting like a child." Janvier's voice sounded warm and comforting. "Of course I care about you."

For once, his smile did not reassure her. "Maybe all you care about is undermining the Legion and the army and the war. You think if you make me your whore, you'll be able to plant your own stories in the American press. Maybe you're just using me."

"I do want to help you in your work, Emma. And if I can bring the truth about this war to the people of America, that is a good thing. But I have explained all that."

"Oh, yes, you've explained so much. You can talk for hours about war and death and killing, but you never say one thing about yourself. I've been sleeping with you for half a year, Robert, and I still don't know one thing about you. I don't know if you're French or Belgian or Swiss. Where you grew up, where you went to school, what you studied, if you like sports or music or poetry or fast cars—things I could find out from any other person on the globe in six minutes. I haven't been able to find out anything about you in six months. What are you hiding? I don't believe you were ever anybody's son or brother. You've never loved another human being in your life. Why, if you treated your family the way you're treating me—"

The force of his slap caught her off-balance. She floundered and fell to one knee, and found herself staring stupidly at the wall behind her. He grabbed her shoulders and jerked her to her feet. His face was taut and waxen, like that of a corpse.

"Who has been talking about me?" he demanded. "Tell me! Who?" He shook her until her teeth rattled; then he hit her again, this time with his fist. She fell back against the dresser and slid to the floor.

"Robert! Robert!" she screamed. "I swear, nobody's—talking—about you!" Her voice was incoherent with sobbing.

"You lie. I am going to kill you, you snooping whore."

"Help! Somebody, please help! Robert!"

"Shut up." Standing over her, he struck her again and again. She tried to protect her head and face with her arms, but he wrenched them aside. "I am sick of people talking about me, telling lies. Don't you ever mention my name again, do you hear me? You know nothing about me. Nothing. Nothing." He accompanied each "nothing" with a blow.

Sobbing with terror, Emma lurched across the floor and crawled into the small space between the sink and the bidet. Janvier dragged her out by the hair and hauled her to her feet. She tried to scream again, to call for help, but the stream of blood and tears on her face was blinding her, and the blood in her mouth choked her so that she could neither swallow nor speak.

"Women make me sick," Janvier raged. "Lying gossips. Bitches. I'll teach you."

His fist slammed into her face. She fell heavily, as if she had been shot.

Like the porcelain vases on their rosewood pedestals, the oriental carpet on the floor, and the Chinese scrolls on the walls, the pretty Vietnamese secretary behind the desk seemed more decorative than functional. True, she was tapping out a letter when Emma walked into the offices of Chrome Petroleum at 47 Boulevard Charner. But she typed with exquisite slowness, using the pads of her fingers so as not to damage her two-inch-long nails.

Emma asked to speak to Alan Hazen.

"Mr. Hazen not in today," the girl responded automatically.

"Do you know where I can find him? It's important. My name is Emma Vaughan."

"Em-ma Vown? Will you write, please?" The long red talons pushed a pencil and a white file card across the desk. Emma printed her name. The girl nodded. "Mr. Hazen just come in through back door. You go inside now."

Emma entered the inner office without knocking. Hazen was standing sideways in the middle of the floor, one hand drawn back to his cheek as he aimed a feathered dart at a cork board behind his desk.

"Hard at work, I see." Emma hoped her voice didn't sound as

muffled and faraway to him as it did to her. The ringing in her ears almost deafened her.

"As a troubleshooter for Chrome Petroleum, I need to keep my reflexes sharp and my vision keen." The dart stabbed the center of the board. Hazen glanced over his shoulder. His visitor was wearing dark glasses and a straw hat with a brim so large that it obscured most of her face. At least she had enough sense to protect her fair skin from the sun. "How may I help you, Miss Vaughan?"

"If you're still flying up to Laos to see your missionary friend, I'd like to go along. If it's not too late."

"Oh, I think I can squeeze you in." Hazen felt a thrill of triumph. He had succeeded in luring her away from Janvier, however briefly. Perhaps her romance with the Legionnaire was cooling. She had come to her senses at last. "Be at Tan Son Nhut Airport at six tomorrow morning. We'll be loaded up and ready to go. If you leave your passport with Miss Nguyen outside, I'll take care of getting you a travel permit. I hope you don't mind if I tell the authorities that you're a temporary employee of Chrome."

"I don't care what you tell them. I just want to get out of this town for a while." Emma reached into her shoulder bag and pulled out her notebook. She kept her head bent over the page as she wrote. "Do I need to bring anything special?"

"Just the tools of your trade. Jack gives excellent interviews to reporters from the States. They help spur donations from the folks back home."

"Aren't you taking a chance by giving me this plum?" Emma made a few final scratches with her pencil. "Remember, I still haven't gotten any of my pieces published yet. If you really want to help your missionary, you'll find a bona fide expense-account foreign correspondent to do the interview."

"You won't have any trouble getting this article published," Hazen assured her. "Just send it to the *Chicago Tribune*. Francis Xavier McGraw, the managing editor, happens to be Jack's brother. If he likes your story, he may even sign you up. He's been relying on the wire services for news for the past couple of years, but things are warming up here. He might want a man—or a girl—on the spot." He waited for her exclamation of delight, or at least an excited smile. But she closed her book and put it away, then fiddled with the catch on her bag. She did not look up.

Hazen switched his remaining dart to his right hand and let it fly. It wobbled, sank, and stabbed the plaster wall four inches from the rim of the board. Without turning around, he said, "Don't be late tomorrow. I won't wait for you."

"I'll be there."

He crossed behind his desk and plucked the darts from the board. As Emma closed the door behind her, she heard the vicious thump of metal spikes burying themselves in cork.

7

MARCH 25, 1953 (Postcard)

Dear Mom,

Leaving tomorrow for Laos with Alan Hazen, the
geologist I met at Angkor Wat, to interview a
missionary whose brother is an ed. at the <u>Chicago
Trib</u>. This could be my lucky break. Shows how
desperate I am to get published—we'll be flying up!
Aside from periodic attacks of fear and trembling,
everything is great.

Love, Em

Very slowly, Emma turned her head and looked out the window. In the clear light of early morning, the ugly black sea of
jungle rolled endlessly beneath the belly of the plane, with only
an occasional bird raising a whitecap on its dark surface. Horrified, she snapped her head around and stared wild-eyed at the
wall of cardboard in front of her, ten paper cartons stamped with
the words "A Gift from the People of the U.S.A."

She tried to swallow her fear, but it met a hard lump that had
been lodged in her throat since she awakened that morning. Salty
tears stung her eyes. For the past three days, it seemed, she had
done nothing but cry. She didn't understand why. How could she
feel so scared and miserable when she didn't care whether she
lived or died?

The plane was a twin-engine Cessna from which all the passenger seats had been removed to accommodate the cargo of food and medicines Alan Hazen was taking to Laos. Upon boarding that morning, Emma had found herself seated on a case of penicillin next to a window, surrounded by cartons of vitamins and buckets of powdered protein supplement. As the plane had taxied down the runway at Tan Son Nhut Airport, she had felt little more than a flutter of nerves. Why, this was no worse than a ride on one of Lincoln's antiquated buses, she thought. Then the plane's nose had tipped upward and it had lifted itself into the sky. Watching the ground fall away, Emma had experienced a terror more profound and wrenching than anything she had ever known. Her limbs froze, her insides knotted, and the hard lump in her throat made it impossible to swallow or breathe.

A thought crossed her mind: She would endure a thousand beatings before submitting to torture like this again. She touched her dark glasses and adjusted the tilt of her straw hat. Robert Janvier's wildly flailing fists had smashed more than her face; they had smashed her hope, her joy, her enthusiasm for living.

She felt Janvier's betrayal in every cell of her body, every hair, every pore, every drop of her blood. How could his love turn so suddenly to rage? Every time she closed her eyes, she saw his face, grotesque and distorted and twisted with fury. She heard her own feeble cries for help even in her dreams. What had she done to provoke such a vicious attack? Yes, she was to blame. His treatment of her had only confirmed her deepest fear: She, Emma Louise Vaughan, was unworthy of love. Like a mythical Circe who could change men into swine, she had transformed Janvier from an ardent lover into a monster.

"We're flying north over the Annamese Cordillera," Hazen called back from the cockpit. "Picture Indochina as a huge dragon with Tonkin as the head. The Cordillera mountain range forms the spine of the dragon and separates Laos from northern Vietnam. Sometime I'll fly you all the way up the coast. If the sky were clearer, you could almost see the ocean on the horizon. The Along Bay near Haiphong is a great place. The wind and the waves have carved the limestone formations out there into fantastic shapes."

Emma was too sick and scared to respond. Every passing minute made her more and more certain that the plane was going to crash. She decided she would probably have a stroke and die of fright before impact. Vaguely, she wondered if the monstrous and red-eyed Indochinese dragon was salivating at the prospect of digesting Miss Nebraska of 1947.

"To the west are the plateaus of southern Laos," Hazen continued.

Dear God, why didn't he shut up and let her die in peace? The last thing she needed now was a guided tour.

"These mountains are the foothills of the Himalayas. Under the vegetation you'll find granite, metamorphic limestone, and even some oil-bearing shale. The coal fields in northeastern Tonkin are pretty extensive, but because transportation has been so poor, most of this region hasn't even been explored yet for mineral content. Whoever ends up with the power to exploit these natural resources will have control of all of Southeast Asia."

Emma rested her head against the crates stacked behind her. Through a fog of sickness and fright, she heard Hazen speaking to the third occupant of the plane. Hazen had introduced Pham to her as his mechanic, interpreter, valet, and indispensable ally. The young Vietnamese was seated in the cockpit beside Hazen, his body hidden from Emma by boxes of infant formula.

The morning passed accompanied by the drone of engines and desultory conversation. Emma kept her eyes closed and tried to pretend that she was traveling by bus or train across the prairie between Lincoln and Sioux City.

Then, sometime before noon, one of the engines coughed and missed. The reassuring duet of two motors ceased, leaving one to carry on solo. Emma's eyes flared open.

"What's happening?"

"A little trouble with the starboard engine," Hazen said. "Nothing to worry about. We'll find someplace to set her down so that Pham can take a look."

"Nothing to worry about? Are you crazy? You've got to do something! We'll all be killed! Stop the plane. We've got to get off!"

"Relax, Emma, everything's going to be fine."

"No, I don't believe you." Emma left her seat and crawled over bundles of blankets to crouch behind Hazen's seat. She grabbed his arm. "You've got to land this thing right away."

"Calm down, will you? It's probably just a little dirt in the fuel line. She'll start up in another minute."

"Oh, God," she wailed. "Oh, God!"

"Emma, sit down."

"No, I won't sit down. All the penicillin in the world isn't going to help us if we crash. Why did I come on this trip? We've got to go back. Take us back!" She jerked at his arm.

"Emma, let go. Sit down. Oh, hell. Pham, take over." Hazen left his seat and, turning, pushed Emma back to her packing case. Her hat fell off and her dark glasses slipped down her nose. Hazen's jaw sagged. "Dear God."

Emma's beauty had been obliterated. A huge purplish yellow bruise smeared the left side of her face. Her lips were swollen and covered with scabs. From the peak of her left eyebrow, a jagged cut crossed her forehead and disappeared into her hairline. The eye itself was swollen shut. Emma's right eye was also puffy and discolored, with a red mesh of broken blood vessels in one corner.

"Janvier! Oh, dear God, Emma. You let him do this to you." Hazen gripped her shoulders. "It was Janvier, wasn't it? Tell me."

"No. No one. No one did it." Emma turned her face to the side, trying to escape his piercing scrutiny. "It was an accident. I fell. On the stairs—"

"Don't lie to me! You let that maniac use you as a punching bag."

"It's not important," she cried. "We're going to die in this stupid plane—"

"Monsieur!" Pham called from the cockpit. "Vite!"

Hazen returned to his seat and pulled out his charts. Sobbing, Emma bent her head over her lap. After a moment, she felt the plane bank as Hazen changed course. They began to lose altitude.

The landing was rough, bouncing and bumpy. But the plane finally halted and Hazen switched off the remaining engine. Silence embraced them like a blessing.

Emma lifted her head and saw a green field bordered by palm and eucalyptus trees. Hazen and Pham had already left the plane. She clambered out of the cockpit, skittered along the wing, and hopped down to the ground. Hazen was standing under the engine with Pham. She started toward the Quonset hut at the edge of the airstrip, but Hazen caught up with her and whirled her around.

"You blind, stupid, empty-headed little fool." His cheeks were livid and his eyes were glazed over with anger. "I told you what would happen if you chased after that maniac. Well, didn't I? You've gotten just what you deserved. I hope you're happy."

"Don't you preach to me." Tears welled up in Emma's eyes. "Don't you dare preach to me!"

"Look at you." He snatched off her hat and her glasses. Emma winced at the harsh sunlight. "You look worse than the cheapest whore in Cholon. Well, why not? That's what you are, a soldier's whore. A gangster's slut. Here I thought I was doing you a favor by inviting you to come along on this trip. Instead I'm just providing taxi service so that you can get away from Saigon for a couple of days. Did you think I wouldn't notice, or that I wouldn't care? You tricked me, Emma. You came to my office, and you wouldn't even show your face because you knew that you'd been a fool and you knew I would tell you so."

"I don't want any favors from you, Mr. Hazen." Emma struggled to regain her composure. "If you think I'm getting back on this plane after the way you've treated me—"

Hazen's laughter was harsh. "You'll have a long walk back to your pretty boy in Saigon. We're about four hundred miles from anyplace, just a dot on the map called Huong Hoa. As far as I'm concerned, you're welcome to stay here until the next monsoon,

Miss Vaughan." He tossed the elements of her disguise on the ground at her feet. Weeping, Emma retrieved the dark glasses and set them on her nose. She clutched the hat in her hands. Her twitching fingers picked at the straw.

Hazen broke off his tirade as a French customs agent approached them from the Quonset hut. Nearby, a wind sock drooped at the top of a bamboo pole. Rumpled, sweat-stained, sallow-faced under an old pith helmet, the Frenchman informed them that only military planes were now permitted to land at Huong Hoa. They must leave at once. Hazen described their engine trouble and explained that they were on a humanitarian mission to Laos under the auspices of the French government. After some wrangling, the man agreed to let them stay long enough to perform repairs.

Then the customs official insisted on examining their cargo. Hazen produced documents that proved the cases had already been inspected and sealed in Saigon. The argument dragged on while Pham tinkered with the engine. Shading her eyes with her hand, Emma surveyed the airfield. At one end of the runway, a cluster of thatched huts hovered between the forest and the clearing. She walked down to take a closer look.

Hazen watched her go, a frail figure whose bright pink skirt and matching blouse looked incongruous against the clotted grays and greens of the jungle. Like molten metal, his anger was cooling into hard ingots of regret. He blamed her for her naïveté, but he also blamed himself. He knew what Janvier was like. He should have taken a stronger hand with her.

"Monsieur, this particular paper has not been properly signed by the officials in charge of exporting."

Grimly, Hazen gave his attention to the document the customs agent was waving under his nose.

Emma approached the huts. An old man squatted on the ground in front of the largest structure. He grinned at Emma and offered her a small object wrapped in a leaf, which she recognized from the Saigon markets as betel nut. It was actually a slice of the dried fruit of the areca palm wrapped in the leaf of the parasitic betel vine that was frequently found clinging to that tree. Why not? Emma thought. I couldn't feel any worse than I do now. She popped the betel nut into her mouth and bit down.

Immediately Emma's mouth began to pucker and swell. She was totally unprepared for its peppery, astringent taste. Chewing contentedly, the old man watched her. In desperation, she searched her bag for a handkerchief, then spat out the half-chewed betel nut.

She screamed. The handkerchief was full of blood. Looking up, she saw that the old man was laughing at her. A crimson stream dribbled down his chin. Betel juice.

A few yards away, a bare-breasted mother, hardly more than a child herself, watched Emma and the old man while she nursed a scrawny baby. A blue-eyed Eurasian boy of about two or three, his belly and limbs bloated with malnutrition, clung to her skirt. They stared listlessly at Emma while Hazen and the customs agent argued in the background. Emma ventured a few words of French, but the woman and the old man continued to gaze at her without expression.

For the first time since she had been in this country, Emma felt like an intruder. Like an alien from another planet, she had dropped into this valley, disturbed the lives of the people who lived here, spurned their offerings, and failed to make herself understood. Discouraged, she wandered back to the plane and sat in the shade of the wing.

The logo of Chrome Petroleum was painted on the fuselage above her head: A golden letter C framed an oil well that spurted a curl of some dark stuff in the shape of the letter P. Emma reached up and touched the metal, but it was so hot from baking in the sun that it burned her fingers.

By the time Pham announced that he had repaired the engine, the customs agent seemed satisfied that Hazen was not smuggling drugs or alcohol into Laos. Becoming suddenly warm and expansive, he invited them to drink an aperitif with him before taking off. Hazen refused. He explained that he wanted to reach the Laotian capital of Vientiane before nightfall. They would spend the night there and, after refueling and checking the plane over, leave for Sop Pong in the morning. The Frenchman made noises of polite regret.

Without glancing at Emma, Hazen said, "If you don't want to continue this journey, Miss Vaughan, this gentleman will make arrangements for you to travel to Saigon with the next convoy that comes through, in about six or eight weeks."

The customs agent spread his thick lips in a grotesque leer and looked at Emma with undisguised lust. She shuddered, and glanced back at the miserable little group huddled at the end of the runway. This man had fathered those children. They were starving to death, and yet he had offered his visitors aperitifs.

"I can't wait all day," Hazen snapped.

Emma turned to the Cessna. She had no choice. She could either spend the next two months rotting here in the middle of the jungle in the company of this lecherous old goat, or she could climb back into the plane. Without saying a word to Hazen, she mounted the wing and entered the cockpit. The familiar paralyzing terror returned, so that her legs were hardly able to carry her to her seat. She slumped down on the carton of penicillin and closed her eyes.

She could not go back to Saigon yet, not until her bruises had faded. Too many people in that city—Eliane, Constance Burton—had predicted how her affair with Janvier would end, and she didn't want them to know how right they had been. Neither could she go home, to Lincoln. Not after the way she had bragged to everyone about how she could become a foreign correspondent without the help of Mr. Bailey and the *Sentinel*. After quitting her job with a grand flourish, indebting herself to her mother and aunt, and breaking off her engagement to Edward, she could not slink home six months later and admit that she had failed.

She had to get that story about the mission. She had to sell it—and herself—to the *Chicago Tribune*. This was her only chance to succeed, and it all depended on Alan Hazen. He would certainly try to dump her at Vientiane. She could not let him do that.

The sun was riding low on the horizon by the time the plane dropped and circled over Vientiane. This time Hazen's landing was flawless.

Emma scrambled around collecting her possessions: notebook, camera, shoulder bag, and a canvas carryall containing the few items of clothing she would need for the weekend. By the time she reached the ground, she saw Hazen striding across the runway toward the low sheds that housed the Laotian customs and airport administration offices. She ran after him.

"Just a moment, Mr. Hazen."

He glanced at her out of the corner of his eye, but kept walking. "This is the end of the line for you, Miss Vaughan. Somebody else will take you back to Saigon from here. I'm sure you don't want to go the rest of the way with me."

"Just a second." She grabbed his arm and forced him to halt. "If I am not mistaken, you invited me along on this trip so that I could interview Dr. McGraw."

"Things have changed—"

"Why, because I have a couple of black eyes? How I got them is no business of yours. As far as I'm concerned, nothing has changed. If you want to treat me like the Whore of Babylon because I fell in love with a man and gave myself to him, then go right ahead. Cast as many stones as you please. I don't care. I'm not ashamed of what I did and I'm not sorry, and I certainly don't intend to grovel at your feet and beg your forgiveness. All I want to do is get a good story so that I can break into print in the *Chicago Tribune*. And if I have to fly that crate to hell with you in order to get it, then I will."

Hazen said nothing for a whole minute, but the set of his mouth was grim. Then he shrugged. "Do as you please. Pham and I will stay out here to guard the plane tonight. You can take a taxi into town and find yourself a hotel room. Just make sure you're back by six. I'm taking off at six-thirty, with or without you." He stalked off.

Emma, limp with relief, expelled her breath and murmured softly, "Thank you. Oh, thank you."

From the air, the landing field at Sop Pong looked small and dangerously short, wedged in between two mountains. The village was located in the heart of Laos' northernmost province, in a finger of land thrust into Red China on the west and north, and communist-dominated Tonkin on the east.

After circling the village once in order to check the direction of the wind, Hazen set the plane down swiftly and neatly, braking hard just a few yards short of a wall of vegetation. Emma sat frozen on her case of penicillin, stunned to be alive. Perhaps she had underrated these flying sardine cans. Nevertheless, she was quite certain that they could not fly out of here. The plane could not possibly pick up enough speed before the end of the runway to clear the towering jungle.

A dozen people ran toward the plane. One of them wore white trousers and a white smock. A stethoscope swung from his neck. Emma wondered if this was Dr. McGraw, but as the party drew nearer, she saw that the white-clad figure was a Laotian girl. Smiling and waving, the group welcomed the new arrivals.

Emma stayed out of the way while Hazen and Pham directed the unloading of the plane. A curious crowd gathered around her. Here, at least, the women seemed alert and the children were well fed and content. Their eyes were bright, and some of the bolder ones crept closer in order to touch Emma's white skin and blonde hair.

A parade of bearers, each carrying a crate or a bucket, started through the jungle toward the village where Dr. John McGraw had his clinic. Emma tagged along near the rear of the procession. Hazen had already vanished from the clearing, a couple of bottles of Dr. McGraw's favorite bourbon tucked under his arm. Emma wasn't surprised. Since their last quarrelsome exchange the previous evening, he had ignored her.

A wooden stockade fence surrounded the mission compound, a deterrent to roving water buffalo, wild boar, tigers, and the occasional stray elephant. Within the fence, Emma found simple structures made of teak and bamboo and roofed with thatch. In contrast to the other dwellings Emma had seen in the village outside the fence, all the buildings here were whitewashed and immaculate. She noticed that the gates stayed wide open during the day so that the life of the village merged with that of the clinic. Local children played in the yard while their mothers drew fresh water from McGraw's well, which saved them from hauling water from the river half a mile away.

Although the courtyard was bustling with activity, no one came forward to greet Emma or to show her around. Left to explore on her own, she entered the first building she came to, which was also the largest. Although she saw no beds inside and no white-clad nurses, she recognized instantly that this place was the mission's hospital. The patients lay on low pallets about six inches off the floor. The only nurses in evidence seemed to be members of their own families. These helpers fed and bathed their loved ones and changed their dressings. The large room reverberated with noise under the bamboo rafters. Although the arrangement was unorthodox by Western standards, the hospital was nevertheless spotlessly clean and fresh smelling. Large panels of netting over the doors and windows discouraged flies and mosquitoes.

Slowly, Emma walked down the broad aisle that divided the two halves of the room. In greeting, men and women pressed their palms together and touched their fingertips to their foreheads. Emma returned the gesture. Although she was a stranger here, a green-eyed foreigner and a woman, she felt no hostility or fear from these people.

She took a few pictures. On her way out, she stopped by the bedside of a small boy whose body was entirely swathed in bandages. He appeared to be sleeping, but as she leaned over him, he opened his eyes and gave her a warm, sweet smile. Emma's heart turned over. Kneeling down, she grasped his left hand, practically the only portion of his body except for his face that was uncovered. He regarded her without fear or even curiosity, but seemed content to have her near him, holding his hand and speaking softly to him in a strange language. She sat with him until his mother returned with a bowl of steaming broth; then she bade them both farewell and left the hospital.

Emma felt a rush of warmth and gratitude. It was worth coming a thousand miles, flying in an undependable plane with a grim-faced Alan Hazen at the controls, just to see that boy's beautiful smile. Nothing could diminish that pleasure, neither Janvier's violence nor Hazen's scorn. That boy had not judged her, he had not condemned her, and he had no desire to punish her. He had simply accepted her as his friend.

Hazen and another man emerged from one of the smaller buildings. Jack McGraw was nearly as tall as Hazen but shockingly thin. His cheekbones jutted out below tired blue eyes, and his dark hair was dull, graying at the sides, and limp with sweat.

"Alan said he'd brought a reporter," he growled. "I couldn't believe it when he said you were a girl."

"Smile." Emma snapped his picture, then stepped forward. "I wasn't aware that a person needed the strength of a linebacker to write a good story, Dr. McGraw. It was my understanding that Mr. Hazen wanted me to come along on this jaunt because I wasn't cynical and jaded like the soaks at the Saigon Press Club. You can cooperate with me or you can be rude to me, but I'm here now and I'm going to write my story."

They studied each other in silence while Hazen hovered in the background. Finally McGraw gave a weary nod. "All right, you can give me a hand in the outpatient clinic this afternoon. I just hope you have a strong stomach."

They lunched on fresh fruit and sticky boiled rice in McGraw's house. Emma noticed a crucifix hanging on the wall. She asked McGraw if he was a Catholic.

"I used to be a priest in the Maryknoll order," he said. "Somewhere along the line I decided that I could do more good for these people by healing their bodies than by trying to save their souls. Most of them were closer to God than I was."

After lunch, Emma accompanied her host to the hut that served as his outpatient clinic. They passed huge boiling caldrons in which bandages and linens were being sterilized. "Cleanliness is the first rule here, followed by decent nutrition and then medication. These people don't realize that the greatest evil in their villages is their own ignorance. They're enslaved by their demons. They can hardly make a move without offending one of them. I'm only a doctor part of the time. The rest of the time I'm a teacher."

Inside the clinic, Dr. McGraw introduced Emma to Tran, his assistant. Emma recognized the exuberant girl who had met the airplane. Dr. McGraw told her that Tran came from Vientiane.

"She's been with me for six years. I couldn't have done any of this without her." Jack McGraw dipped his hands into a solution of strong soap and water, rinsed them, then dried them on the towel Tran held for him. "All right, Miss Vaughan, if you're really going to help, wash your hands and pin the hair out of your eyes. People are waiting."

All the examinations and treatments were carried out in the noisy atmosphere of a public market, in a room crowded with waiting patients and the members of their families.

"They're less scared if they can see what I'm doing," McGraw told Emma.

Emma attended to minor wounds and dispensed vitamin pills and cups of protein supplement to mothers with babies while Dr. McGraw and Tran treated the more serious illnesses. Their first patient that afternoon was a leper whose ravaged hands and feet were becoming ulcerated and infected. Tran bathed the man's sores, and Dr. McGraw applied fresh antiseptic dressings. The putrescent stink of his infections nauseated Emma and made her long to breathe the purer air of the courtyard, but neither McGraw nor Tran seemed to notice.

At about three o'clock, a man brought in a child who had been horribly mauled by a bear. Emma held a tray of instruments while the doctor cleansed the boy's wounds and stitched the flaps of torn muscle and skin. The atmosphere in the room would have been stifling anyway, but with the heat of a few dozen sweating bodies, it was unbearable. But the doctor worked steadily, not even pausing while Tran blotted away the perspiration from his forehead.

The procession of suffering continued throughout the afternoon.

"I regularly treat diseases here that most American medical textbooks don't even mention." McGraw applied drops to the eyes of an old woman who was nearly blind from trachoma. "Yaws, plague, leprosy. We also treat elephantiasis, syphilis in various forms, worms, cholera, TB, and malaria. They're all part of life in this corner of the world."

Their last badly injured patient was a man with a shattered leg who had dragged himself across the mountains from a village some twenty miles distant. Dr. McGraw set the leg and splinted it, and the man was removed to the hospital.

At dusk, the room was finally empty of patients. For the fiftieth time that afternoon, Jack McGraw scrubbed his hands with strong soap and dried them on a clean towel. "You're pretty tough, Miss Vaughan. I've had strong men run out of here clutching their stomachs after seeing cases like we've had today. Now let me take a look at that eye of yours."

Emma hung back. "No, really, it's not necessary."

"Might as well. It's not every day that you get the best doctor in Laos to examine you. I suppose I should add that I'm the only doctor in Laos. The country has a handful of *médicins indochinois* who have had the equivalent of two years of high school plus a few months of medical training. But not one other certified physician. We have our French brothers to thank for the disgraceful level of medical care available in their former colonies. The brightest students, were denied a chance at formal education unless their parents happened to be rich enough to send them to French schools. Girls like Tran didn't have a prayer. And the French wonder why these people hate them."

He seated Emma on a stool, gently lifted her eyelid, and shone a small light into her pupil. "Without people like Alan dropping in periodically to restock our dispensary," he said, "we would be pretty helpless. The Laotian government doesn't want me here. They're convinced that I'm an American agent—OSS or CIA or whatever the people in Washington are calling it these days. They're not very cooperative, which means I have to arrange for my own supplies, my own mail delivery, and my own transportation. The minister of health also knows if he makes things too difficult for us, Tran and I will move across the border and set up shop in Tonkin. I guess he figures that a doctor who's a spy is better than no doctor at all."

Gently, he probed the bones around her eye socket. Emma winced. "When did this happen?" Emma told him. "Any dizziness, headaches?"

"Some."

"You should have gone to the hospital right after it happened. Concussion can be tricky. You're a lucky girl. You might have lost the sight in this eye. Whoever did this to you packs a mean punch."

"It was an accident," Emma said.

McGraw shrugged. "If you say so. I don't see many cases like yours here. In a Chicago hospital, I'd see twenty a week. So much for so-called civilization. He'll do it again, if you let him."

"No, he won't. I'm never going to see him again."

Dr. McGraw asked her to lean her head back while he put some drops in her eye. "What's the matter with Alan? He seems pretty annoyed about something."

Emma held a cotton ball against her swollen eye. "Mr. Hazen's annoyances are his business. I'm just here to do a job."

"He tells me you'll be working for my brother."

"That was the idea, to bring my talents to Mr. McGraw's attention." Emma watched Tran moving around the clinic. She sterilized tools, returned medicines and bandages to their shelves. "I haven't been able to persuade any other editors to buy my material."

"F. X. will buy whatever you send him about my work in Laos. He thinks I'm crazy to be doing this, but he's still my biggest booster. The readers of the *Chicago Tribune* paid for most of the stuff you brought in today. Who knows, after your article appears Frank's friends in the diocese might even kick in a few more bucks. And the pharmaceutical corporations are always happy to contribute samples to any cause that gets them a favorable mention in the newspapers." The doctor yawned, stretched, and rubbed his eyes. "Nice to talk English once in a while. Sometimes I forget how."

"Don't you ever get homesick?"

He shrugged. "I keep busy."

"How long are you going to stay?" Emma pulled out her notebook. Throughout the afternoon, whenever she had a moment to spare, she jotted down quick notes to remind her of the patients they had treated and the injuries she had seen. "Are you planning on going back to the States any time soon?"

Jack McGraw gazed at his assistant, moving with silent grace as she completed her chores. He shook his head. "Tran wouldn't fit in there. I couldn't do that to her."

"Then she's your—"

"Didn't Alan tell you? Tran is my wife."

Dr. McGraw's Laotian bride understood at least that much English. She turned to them with a shy peaceful smile.

Emma smiled back and then, after a moment, asked Dr. McGraw about the small boy she had seen in the hospital.

"Oh, you've fallen for Chai, have you?" McGraw's tension relaxed slightly. "He fell into a fire and received third-degree burns on over sixty percent of his body. I was able to harvest some skin from his legs and graft the tissues over the wounds on his chest. He might make it if we can ward off infection. It would be tricky enough in an urban hospital; here it's almost like asking for a miracle. But we've pulled off a few of those in our day."

As they were leaving the clinic, they saw an old man carrying a shrouded body to a waiting buffalo cart. He exchanged a few words with friends, then waved his hand in farewell and drove off.

"Don't let anyone tell you that Asians have no feelings, or that they don't care about their kids," Dr. McGraw said. "I know some Westerners find it chilling when they see how callously these people treat the death of someone they love. But it's not callousness. It's acceptance. Or sometimes they're just numb because they've suffered so much. Most of them are a hell of a lot braver about suffering and death than their civilized counterparts back home. Make sure you put that in your story, Miss Vaughan."

That night, the headman of the village of Sop Pong hosted a feast in honor of the doctor and his friends from Saigon. One of McGraw's boys had delivered to the village cooks two chickens that the doctor had received as payment for services that day, as well as a great fish one of his patients had caught in the river. Several of the dishes swam in a dark sea of *nuoc mam*, an odiferous sauce made from decayed fish that has been salted and fermented. This was Emma's first opportunity to sample one of the staples of the regional diet. She blanched, gagged, and took a long swallow of tea to flush the fishy taste from her mouth.

"You'll get used to the stuff," Dr. McGraw assured her. "It's very good for you. Loaded with minerals."

"So is cod-liver oil, but I wouldn't eat it with every meal."

At the other side of the table, Hazen was busy with his chopsticks. He and Pham had absented themselves from the village that afternoon on some errand of their own, and had barely returned in time for the feast. Emma wondered what he could possibly find to do in this remote spot. But she was still burning from his scornful rebuff of her the day before, and she refrained from asking him.

As the meal was ending, a young woman ran up to the table and bowed deeply to Dr. McGraw. She was dressed differently from the rest of the villagers, who wore simple sarongs topped by loose tunics. This woman's head was turbaned in a dull black cotton that matched her blouse. Around her neck she wore an array of heavy silver jewelry, hammered collars and necklaces that must have weighed twenty pounds.

"A woman from the Meo tribe," McGraw told Emma. "They don't trust regular currency, and so they turn everything they earn into silver. They wear their fortunes around their necks." After conferring with the Meo woman, McGraw stood up. "Maternity case. Sounds like a difficult birth. Tran, fetch my bag." But Tran had already vanished, having anticipated the doctor's request.

Emma put down her chopsticks. "Would you mind if I came along? I'll stay out of your way."

"You might as well. Meo births are fairly public occasions anyway. How about you, Alan? Do you remember Old Willie? She's the sorceress who rules that village. Ninety-nine if she's a day, only one eye, and not a tooth in her head. A real character."

They set off on foot for the village of Lao Meo Chai, four miles away on the northern side of the mountain. Puffing as she tried to keep up with the moving pool of light from Dr. McGraw's flashlight, Emma reminded herself that the trail would be downhill all the way home.

"The air is thin up here, which is why you're having trouble breathing," Jack McGraw told her. Ahead of them, Tran and the Meo woman set a brisk pace. Hazen brought up the rear with a second flashlight.

"Why don't these people build their villages someplace sensible, like the bottom of a nice, quiet valley?" Emma was glad she had packed a heavy sweater, although a woolen coat would not have been unwelcome. Nights in these mountains were crisp and cold.

"Centuries ago, a Chinese emperor rewarded his loyal followers in these hills by giving them the rights to all the land above the clouds, where dragons were reported to dwell. Some of these tribesmen actually become ill if they move to the valleys.

Their lungs have adapted to the clear air of these high altitudes."
He swung up the steep trail effortlessly, his long legs taking a
single stride to every two of Emma's steps.

"How did you meet Alan Hazen?" Emma asked him.

"Alan? I took a math course from him at the University of
Chicago while I was in the seminary, before the war. He wasn't
much older than most of us, but he was a fine teacher."

"Why did he quit? Was he really working on a secret project for
the government during the war?"

McGraw laughed. "You'd better ask him about that."

"Maybe you haven't noticed, but Mr. Hazen is not speaking to
me. He was offended by my carelessness in getting my face
bashed in."

McGraw grunted. "Alan was always pretty straightlaced. I
wasn't surprised when he entered the ministry after the war."

"The ministry? Alan Hazen?"

"It didn't last. Like a lot of guys, he had been through too
much. Settling down was a problem. I know it was for me. I was
a chaplain with the 5307th Provisional Regiment. You've heard
of Merrill's Marauders?"

"I certainly have. You guys really took a beating at Myitkyina.
Did Mr. Hazen serve in Burma, too?"

Dr. McGraw laughed. "You won't get any more out of me,
Miss Vaughan. In his day, my brother Frank was one of the hot-
test reporters around, which means that he was very skilled at
getting information out of people. I learned to tread warily if I
didn't want him to ferret out all my secrets. If you want to know
about Alan, you'd better go right to the source."

In a corner of the village's longhouse, the laboring woman squatted on her haunches while she clutched a rope suspended from
the rafters. She was naked, her brown belly grossly distended.
Sweat poured off her body, which looked like polished bronze in
the firelight. She was surrounded by the other women of the
village, who matched their groans and cries to hers. Old Willie,

the sorceress, circled the patient, sprinkling her breasts and belly with drops of pig blood and rubbing her forehead with a mixture of wood ash and earth.

The ancient crone greeted Dr. McGraw with a profound bow and a terrible smile that revealed blackened gums and a mouth stained crimson with betel juice. She was bent nearly double by the weight of silver around her neck. Her right eye was milky white, the color of old porcelain, but her left glistened and winked as she studied her visitors. Emma stood nervously while the woman dragged a clawlike hand through her golden hair. Before attending to his patient, Dr. McGraw solemnly presented his rival with two cigarettes. Cackling, Old Willie grabbed Emma's arm and dragged her to the side of the room, slightly apart from the other women and just outside the circle of firelight. They sat against the wall. Emma watched, fascinated, as the old woman popped Jack McGraw's cigarettes into her mouth and began to chew them.

At the other end of the room, the men of the community sucked on clay pipes and conversed in normal tones. They took little notice of the events attending the birth. A fire in the center of the house filled the space with a thick acrid smoke that made Emma cough and choke. Her eyes burned. She rubbed them with her fists, and when her vision cleared, she saw that Hazen had crouched down beside her, close enough that she could feel his warmth but not close enough for their arms to touch. Emma set aside her resentment long enough to wonder about him. In his own way, Hazen was as secretive and mysterious as the old sorceress, in whose single ancient eye flickered the timeless knowledge of her primitive ancestors.

The laboring woman screamed, and screamed again. Emma felt her hackles rising, exactly as if she were a frightened animal or a jungle savage terrified by the demons of the night. The murmuring of the men and the keening of the women grew louder. Beads of sweat popped out on Emma's forehead. Hot tears scalded her cheeks. She felt herself straining along with the woman in labor, as if by tensing her own body she could help the baby to be born. The screams of the mother were her own, the screams of every woman who finds herself twisted by unspeakable agony. Under the thin veneer of civilization, she and this Meo tribes-woman were the same. Old Willie, Emma, the new mother—they were sisters, children of the same darkness. These tribal women had their demons and Emma had hers: Robert Janvier, a smiling god who had tried to destroy her.

In a panic Emma reached out and, finding Hazen's hand, gripped it tightly.

"Do you want to leave?" he whispered.

She shook her head.

Tran mopped the sweat from Jack McGraw's forehead as the doctor struggled with what turned out to be a breech birth. The noise in the hut was deafening, the heat intense, the stink of sweating bodies overpowering. Emma, who had never fainted in her life, feared she might pass out.

Finally, Tran lifted a squalling baby boy and displayed him to the crowd. He was slick and shiny like a worm. The men nodded and the women sighed contentedly as Old Willy reminded them that she had predicted a son.

Looking at the baby, Emma wept silent tears of joy. She felt as if it had come from her own body. As a woman, she shared in the new mother's triumph.

After Tran had cleaned the baby, she brought it to the sor-ceress, who pronounced her own spells over the small squirming body. Old Willie brushed his head with ash, then severed the umbilical cord with sharpened bamboo knives and rubbed the end of the cord with a mixture of earth and blood.

"Jack has already tied it off," Hazen told Emma. "She can't infect the baby with that stuff now." He explained that Dr. McGraw made a point of cooperating with native practitioners. People like Old Willie could be powerful enemies.

When the baby had been given back to his mother, Old Willie turned to Emma and took her hands. She rubbed some ash in each palm, then pressed the palms together over Emma's belly, croaking all the while.

"She says that you will have a child of your own someday," Jack McGraw translated. Suddenly the old crone recoiled, muttering fiercely. McGraw looked confused. "I can't really make out— she's saying something about death and two children—two mothers—two fathers. But she promises you will be very happy with your husband, who is as tall as the giant bamboo."

"How does she know that my husband will be tall?" Emma wondered if Old Willie's blind eye, blue-white and rheumy, could really see into the future.

Jack laughed. "She thinks Alan is your husband. Why else would you sit close to him and grab his hand so tightly? You wouldn't behave that way with a stranger, would you?"

The old woman tied a white thread around Emma's wrist and another around Hazen's. As Hazen extended his arm, Emma noticed a glossy scar on the inside of his wrist.

"Those threads will keep the demons away," Jack explained. "You're not supposed to cut them off, but leave them there until they disintegrate."

They started down the mountainside. Amber wands of moonlight touched the path between the trees. Emma caught up to Hazen, who was following close behind the Meo woman. She had insisted on escorting them home.

"I noticed that scar on your wrist," she said. "I wouldn't have thought you were that kind of man."

"Really? What kind of man is that?"

"The kind who would want to kill himself."

Hazen threw back his head and laughed heartily. "You'd better switch from journalism to fiction, Miss Vaughan," he advised. "You could make a fortune selling the products of your fevered imagination."

Dr. McGraw's cottage was located just inside the gates of the mission compound. It was small, two rooms and a rude kitchen, and simply furnished with bamboo pallets covered with straw-filled mattresses, a few crude benches, and low Japanese-style tables.

Tran fixed a bed for Emma in the corner of the main living-dining room, behind a bamboo screen.

Her body was exhausted, but her mind was not ready to relax. She thought about the scene in the smoke-filled longhouse. Almost as soon as she had arrived in Cambodia, she had witnessed killing and death. Here in Laos, she had watched a birth. In Saigon, she had experienced a hundred different shades of passion, from brilliant ecstasy to dark despair, and she had suffered a brutal beating at the hands of the man to whom she had entrusted her heart.

She was not the same Emma Louise Vaughan who had left Lincoln, Nebraska, the previous autumn. Life, the master sculptor, was molding and shaping her into a new woman. Lying on her hard bed, Emma shivered. She had the feeling that Life hadn't finished with her yet.

8

APRIL 9, 1953 (Telegram)

TO
MRS ELIZABETH VAUGHAN
814 COTTONWOOD AVENUE
LINCOLN NEBRASKA
FROM
E L BAUGHAN HOTEL CARAVELLE
LUANG PRABANG LAOS
HAVE SURVIVED PLANE CRASH
STOP JOURNEY EMEMY TERRITORY
STOP AM OK STOP DETAILS
FOLLOW STOP

After breakfast the following day, Emma paid a farewell visit to young Chai, recovering from his burns in the hospital. She gave him a blue plastic comb and her gold compact. The boy was delighted with his gifts. When she left him, he had captured a ray of sunlight in the mirror of the compact and he was directing the beam to all parts of the room.

When Emma entered the clinic a few minutes later, she discovered Hazen and Jack McGraw bending over a large map that had been spread over the doctor's desk. The two men straightened up when she came in. Hazen hastily folded the map and stuffed it into the hip pocket of his trousers.

"Change in plans?" she inquired.

Hazen ignored Emma's question. He shook hands with Dr. McGraw. "I'll see you in a couple of months, Jack. It will take me at least that long to get everything on your new wish list." He turned to Emma. "We'll be taking off in fifteen minutes, Miss Vaughan. Don't hold us up." He went out.

Emma glared at his retreating back. "That man gets on my nerves."

McGraw shrugged. "Oh, Alan's all right. His divorce really shook him up. Sometimes it takes a while before a man feels like rejoining the human race after a trauma like that. I've always believed that the right woman could work wonders with him."

"Sure, provided she was a sorceress, like Old Willie." Emma thanked Dr. McGraw for his hospitality and wished him good luck. "I'll send you a copy of the story. If you can find the time to drop me a note, I'd appreciate an update on Chai."

"You're welcome to come and visit anytime."

Emma shook her head. "I doubt if your friend Mr. Hazen will want me as a passenger again."

"I told him to put in a good word for you next time he wrote to Frank."

"Alan Hazen is going to put in a good word for me? I might as well forget that job with the *Trib.*"

"No, Alan's fair-minded. And Frank is pretty good at recognizing talent. You won't have any trouble landing that job." McGraw looked up as Tran came into the room. "Wish I could escort you to the plane, but my patients are lining up outside. So long, Emma."

They shook hands; then Emma retrieved her knapsack and notebooks from McGraw's hut and ran along the trail to the airstrip. She had only gone halfway when she heard the roar of the engines. Hazen was going to leave her!

A crowd of villagers was waiting to watch the takeoff. Emma pushed through them and sprinted across the field to the plane. The propellers were whirling, scattering dust and leaves.

"Wait for me!"

Hazen poked his head out of the cockpit. "Hurry up, get in. I want to get off the ground before this wind picks up. The air currents in these valleys are tricky."

Emma mounted the wing, dove through the doorway, and sat

on a pile of parachutes near a side window just behind Pham. Hazen seated himself, revved up the engines, and opened the throttle. Relieved of its cargo, the plane skimmed along the runway and lifted off easily, clearing the trees at the end by a good ten feet. Glancing down, Emma saw the villagers waving. Feeling somewhat giddy, she waved back. Her departure had been so hasty that she'd barely had time to feel frightened. After they were aloft, the old feelings of desperation and panic asserted themselves, but somewhat less virulently than before.

The plane reached a cruising altitude and leveled off. Emma settled back with her notebook and started the first draft of her feature story about Dr. McGraw's work among the mountain people of northern Laos. She decided to begin with a description of the birth in the longhouse, with Old Willie and the chanting women in attendance. She scribbled busily for a few minutes and then paused for thought, tapping her lower lip with her eraser. Bending her head over her notebook again, she wrote:

"Then a tall slender man wearing a white T-shirt and white trousers steps into the room. He ducks his head slightly to clear the top of the doorway. The chanting women part as he makes his way toward the laboring mother in the corner, his old black medical bag in hand. He and the sorceress exchange greetings; then she retires into the shadows. Here in a mountain village in the heart of Laos, modern medicine and witchcraft have just met face-to-face. This encounter has been repeated scores of times in the past six years as Dr. John McGraw—Jack to his friends—brings new hope to a people oppressed by the demons of ignorance, hunger, and superstition. Little by little, the demons are losing."

Emma read her opening paragraphs. They needed some work, but the basic direction of the story was good.

She had been writing for over an hour when she noticed that the sun was on her right, in the east. Instead of flying south to Vientiane, they seemed to be heading north.

In the cockpit, Hazen handled the controls while Pham surveyed the countryside through high-powered binoculars. The two men conversed in low tones, in French. Below them, the mountains broke through the green carpet of the jungle. Limestone fingers, as gnarled and knobby as old bones, reached toward the belly of the airplane. Hazen was flying so low that Emma could make out the shapes of individual trees that clung to the sides of the mountains, resisting the gravitational pull toward the green ocean below.

Emma moved over to the left side of the plane. On the horizon, she saw a glimmer of white. The clouds parted briefly, revealing the summit of an immense mountain that even at this distance seemed to dominate the sky and tower over the airplane. Emma made her way forward, where she crouched behind Hazen's shoulder.

"Where are we? Shouldn't we be going south to get back to Vientiane?"

"Just doing a little exploring on behalf of Chrome Petroleum," Hazen said. "You can tell a lot about the mineral-bearing potential of a chain of mountains by observing certain geological patterns from above."

"That's crazy. You're flying straight into Red China. You can't negotiate mineral rights with Mao Tse-tung."

"We're still well within the borders of Vietnam," Hazen assured her. "That mountain you see is Phu Si Long on the Chinese border, ten thousand feet above sea level. It's farther away than it looks. We're just flying over the Black River now."

Emma tried to ignore the sinking feeling in her stomach. She looked down at the ribbon of water and across the smaller green peaks to Phu Si Long. "That means we're in the heart of enemy territory. Isn't this dangerous?"

"This part of the country is rich in minerals," Hazen said smoothly. "There are some wide veins of coal in these mountains, and, I would guess, some high-grade oil. I'd really like to get a drilling crew up here sometime, take a few core samples, but the French have declared the area off limits to travelers, and the Viet Minh aren't inclined to be too cooperative in that respect either. So I thought I'd do a little preliminary survey from the air."

At his side, Pham scanned the countryside with the binoculars.

"Pham's an old hand at this game," Hazen said. "He knows what formations I'm hoping to find. Having him search the ground while I fly the plane is a big advantage." Pham offered Emma the binoculars. "Want a look?"

Emma shuddered. "No, thanks."

"We'll do a little circling around and then head for Hanoi for the night. I have a little business to do there, and the hotels are better than the ones you'll find in Vientiane. Besides, the Press Club has a terrific chef."

Suddenly Pham pointed downward and spoke in rapid French. Hazen banked the plane so sharply that Emma had to clutch the back of his seat in order to keep herself from skittering into the bulkhead. While he leveled off and prepared to make another pass over whatever geological marvel Pham had spotted, Emma stumbled back to the belly of the plane and lashed herself down with the woven straps Hazen had used to secure his cargo.

She felt her terror welling up again. Surely airplanes were not made to turn so sharply. What if the wings fell off? She was already bruised and battered enough without being tossed around the inside of an empty plane like a bean in a tin can. What if we crash, she thought. I don't want to lose my arms and legs. I'd rather die than be a cripple for the rest of my life.

With an immense effort of will, Emma forced herself to think about her feature story. If she finished it by tomorrow morning, she could cable it to Mr. F. X. McGraw from Hanoi. The expense would be worthwhile if he hired her. She opened her notebook again and located a pencil, but her hand trembled so violently that she could not write.

After a few minutes, the plane dropped lower and banked so sharply that the sky disappeared and the trees seemed to brush the windows. A white puff of smoke appeared over the carapace of jungle below them. Hazen righted the plane and jerked it upward. Another plume of white blossomed over the greenery. The plane lurched violently as the right engine faltered and then quit.

"We've been hit," Hazen yelled. "The right propeller's gone—"

The little aircraft lurched again, then lifted. To her horror, Emma saw that the tip of the wing on her side of the plane had been sheared off. If a shell or a bullet hit the fuel tanks, the plane would burst into flames and hurtle to earth like a blazing comet. The plane's nose dropped sharply. They were whirling, spiraling into a nosedive.

A great sense of peacefulness enveloped Emma in its embrace. She knew with certainty that she was going to die within seconds. And she was not afraid. Calmly, she lay facedown and lashed her body to the belly of the plane at her waist. Then she wrapped her arms around her head.

Even with her eyes closed and her head covered, she felt Hazen pull the plane out of the spin. They began to climb once more. Then they received another jolt, this one in the tail section. The remaining engine coughed and faltered, and the plane began to lose altitude.

"I'm going to ditch her in the river," Hazen shouted. "Hang on."

Oh God I'm sorry sorry I've been so stupid about so many things but I didn't mean it I hope Mom and Aunt Louise don't cry too much—

With a roar of crunching metal and shattering glass, the plane collided with the surface of the Black River. The impact jolted Emma so fiercely that she blacked out for a few seconds. A flood of cold water into her mouth revived her. She gagged and coughed, and strained upward through the darkness and the rising water before she realized that she was still lashed to the belly of the plane. Fumbling with the knots while she held her breath, she loosened the straps and wriggled free. The tail section of the plane reared up at a crazy angle. It was still full of air, but the water was rising rapidly. Ripping off her skirt and kicking off her shoes, Emma filled her lungs, then dove down into the cockpit.

She reached Pham first. He was barely conscious, tangled up with the radio and wedged under the control panel. Emma struggled with the right door latch and managed to force the door open against the increasing pressure of the inrushing water. She pulled Pham free and hauled him out of the plane. He gave a feeble kick and struggled toward the surface.

Her lungs bursting, Emma returned to the tail. She took two quick gulps of air and dove again. She found Hazen slumped over the controls. His door would not open. She fumbled with his seatbelt for a full five seconds. Finally, just when she thought she would lose consciousness herself, she managed to free him and drag him over Pham's seat toward the exit. Gripping his collar, she lifted him up through the water.

Emma's head broke through the surface. Her chest was heaving and her heart pounded, and she gulped down great lungfuls of fresh air. Cupping her hand under Hazen's chin, she kept him from sinking while she treaded water and looked around. They were about twenty yards from the bank of a broad river. The current was pulling them downstream. Dragging Hazen, Emma swam toward the nearest shore, which seemed to offer a narrow strand of sand as well as a canopy of overhanging trees. As she got into shallow water she saw that Pham was already there, on his knees, retching.

Hazen's lungs were full of water and he was bleeding badly from a three-inch cut on his forehead. Emma rolled him onto his stomach and started pumping. She had just about decided that he was dead when he twitched, coughed, and doubled up with vomiting. Exhausted, Emma fell back on the sand and turned her face to the life-giving sun.

"Emma? Pham?"

Raising herself up on one elbow, Emma looked over at Hazen, who was attempting to stand. He swayed, then dropped to his knees.

"I'm here." She dragged herself to her feet and stumbled toward him. "Pham's okay, too."

Hazen touched the wound on his forehead, then winced. "God, that hurts. Must have a concussion. Can't stand up. Can't even see straight. Where are we?"

"How should I know? You were flying that plane, not me." Emma swept sodden strands of hair off her forehead. "As far as I can tell, we're in the middle of nowhere. There's jungle everywhere you look, the river looks filthy, and I'm being eaten alive by mosquitoes."

"The plane. What about the plane?"

Emma gazed dismally at the tailpiece jutting up from the rippling surface of the river like an abstract monument made of gleaming aluminum. "It's stuck in the middle of the river, about sixty feet out from shore."

"How much tail is showing?"

"I don't know. About five or six feet, I imagine. It's pretty mangled. I don't think you'll be able to fly us out of here."

He nodded. "We can use some of the stuff from that plane. How deep is the water?" Emma told him, and he grunted. "Can you swim?"

"I was good enough to qualify for the All-American swimming team in 1945 in three events. Also, I just saved two lives. Three, if you count my own. Why?"

"You've got to go back to that plane. But don't go inside unless you think the nose is securely dug into the bottom. If that wreck floats free while you're in there, you'll be in trouble." He told her where she could find the waterproof map case, a flashlight, the tool box. "Get the map case first. And my pistol. They're in the side pocket by the door. You'll find a couple of life jackets under the seats in the cockpit, and some nylon rope. Take Pham out with you in case anything happens."

"In case anything happens? What more could happen? We're stuck in the middle of Viet Minh country with no plane and no food and no way of getting out of here. This is your fault, Alan Hazen. Oil and mineral deposits, my eye! You were spying, weren't you? Taking us straight toward the Chinese border to see just how many Reds were infiltrating Tonkin. Who are you collecting this information for? The French? The CIA? Or maybe the highest bidder? How about the Russians?"

Hazen's dizziness worsened, and he lay back on the sand. "Accidents happen all the time in planes."

"Yes, but they happen more frequently when somebody shoots you down out of the sky. I will never forgive you for this, Alan Hazen. We are going to die of exposure and malaria and dysentery, if we aren't captured or killed by the Viet Minh first, and it's all your fault. If I had known what you were up to, I would have stayed at Sop Pong."

"You had a choice. You still do," he said quietly. "You can do your part in getting us out of here, or you can spend the rest of the afternoon bitching. I'm still too dizzy to see or I would go out to the plane myself." Hazen dragged his fingers through his wet hair. "We need that stuff right away before it all breaks loose and drifts downstream."

"The Viet Minh who shot us down are going to be looking for us. Americans are not exactly neutral in this war, you know. They'll imprison us and interrogate us and then they'll kill us."

"They won't kill us. It would be far more to their advantage to try and convert us. In any case, I do not intend to let them capture us," Hazen said, "which is why I suggest you fetch the map case and pistol from the plane at once. After we finish stripping the wreck, we'll figure out how to dismantle the wing."

"The wing?"

"That's right. We're going to build a canoe."

On her first dive, Emma brought out the rope and the pistol, an emergency first-aid kit and some waterproof flares, and the map case Hazen had requested. Pham swam out with her on her next trip and sat on the upended tailpiece with the loose end of the safety rope twisted around his hands. The other end was tied around Emma's waist. She located the parachutes, her own purse and canvas overnight bag, and Hazen's knapsack. She thought she felt her camera already settling into the silt in the cockpit, but she left it behind. At the last minute, she tried to lift the compass from its anchorage on the dashboard, but it was screwed down too tightly and she could not break it loose. Meanwhile, she was exhausted and chilled through, and the sun was dipping into the trees.

Hazen was sitting up when they got back to the beach this time. Emma shoved the map case into his hands and collapsed onto the sand. "Here you are."

"Good." Hazen fumbled with the catch on the flat metal box and opened the lid. "And now to figure out where we are." He crouched and opened a wet map on his knee. His long finger jabbed a blue strand that threaded through a maze of ripples. "The western shore of the Black River."

Emma looked over his shoulder. "Are there any French army outposts around here?"

"None until you get to Van Yen"—his finger slid along a crease—"and that's a good hundred miles downstream. The local tribesmen are Muongs, mountain people not known for their hospitality to foreigners. I don't speak their dialect, and neither does Pham."

After he put the map away, he took his pistol apart and began to clean it. "Can't you find anything better to do?" Emma snapped.

"We may need this," he replied calmly. "They're probably looking for us right now."

Emma stood up. "I'd better get back to the plane. It will be dark soon." She had stripped down to her bra and panties. Her limbs were straight and well muscled. The tops of her shoulders and the tip of her nose were beginning to turn pink.

"You should have worn a shirt." Hazen's voice showed concern. "The sun here is brutal."

"Mr. Hazen, I have just survived a plane crash," she said. "I'm not worried about a little sunburn."

Her back and arms were on fire and her head throbbed. The night had sucked all the heat out of the earth and the air, and the only covering she had was a white silk parachute folded—with difficulty—to blanket size. The clothes in her canvas bag were still too damp to be of any use. Hazen had given her the rubber ground sheet he carried in his knapsack. He had dug out a comfortable-looking depression for himself in the sand, and he slept soundly while Pham kept watch with the pistol.

Clouds obscured the moon and stars. Emma had never experienced such total blackness before, like sudden blindness. The smallest sounds coming from the river and the jungle seemed exaggerated and menacing. Every time she heard a splash or a ripple, she pictured a hungry crocodile or thirsty bear only inches away from where she lay. Bands of Viet Minh guerrillas and vicious tigers lurked in the trees. Shivering from cold and fright, Emma longed for her home. In the parks and streets of Lincoln, Nebraska, summer nights were gentle and friendly, full of dreams and sighs and the warm breath of the prairie wind. But here—no wonder the Meos and the Muongs and the Thais believed in demons. In the black heart of the jungle, she believed in them, too.

Although Hazen was still bothered by dizzy spells the next day, he helped Pham detach the undamaged wing. They used the tools from Pham's repair kit, which Emma had salvaged on her last dive the night before.

Emma watched the procedure from a bamboo grove on shore. She held Hazen's pistol in her lap. He had ordered her to stand guard while they worked.

Her stomach growled. She had gone fishing early that morning with a bamboo pole, a line made of sewing thread, a safety-pin hook, and a wad of chewing gum for bait. She had caught what must have been the stupidest fish in the river. Hazen had forbidden her to build a fire, and so the fish sat baking in the sun in an oven made of scraps of glass and aluminum from the plane. It would not be thoroughly cooked for hours. Pham had returned from the forest with a hatful of leaves, sprouts, berries, and roots that he had assured her were edible. Emma had eaten her share, but the stuff had not assuaged her hunger pangs. She wanted real food.

Finally, Pham and Hazen dragged the wing ashore. Using a screwdriver as a chisel and a rock as a hammer, they pounded off the tops of the rivets that held the pieces of metal together. Hazen was concerned about the noise, which was sharp and loud, but there was no way to muffle it, and so they worked with the greatest possible speed. He had announced at dawn that he hoped to shove off after moonrise that night.

Emma wandered down to the river. She splashed some water on her forehead and let it dribble down her neck. Her own hat had been lost, but Pham had fashioned a new one for her from reeds and leaves, so at least her face and neck were protected from the sun. Even in the shade the heat was blistering. Her clothes were soaked with perspiration, nearly as wet as they had been when she had dragged herself and Hazen out of the river the day before.

Hazen called her over. Pham had disappeared on another errand.

"Help me hold this down so I can square off the ends." He had stripped off a long rectangle of aluminum from the sheathing that covered the wing structure and the gas tanks. Now, pounding the stiff metal with rocks, he and Emma bent the sides up and brought the ends together to make a canoe shape. "I'll use these bolts to clamp the ends together fore and aft. Pham's gone to collect some pine pitch for caulking."

"What about food?" Emma asked. " Can we buy some when we reach a village?"

"Pham will gather as much as possible before we shove off tonight. We can't take a chance on stopping at villages."

"Why not? Can't you just pretend you're a French official dropping in to examine their rice crop?"

Hazen shook his head. "Tonkin is the birthplace of the nationalist movement, the home base of the Viet Minh. We wouldn't gain anything from the villagers by claiming to be

French. And if the Viet Minh find out we're headed down-stream, they'll rig an ambush. No, we'll seek shelter on shore during the day and travel by night. Pham might be able to buy food, but only Pham. A single Vietnamese traveling alone is not conspicuous. He can pass himself off as a Viet Minh cadre if necessary. But you and I will have to conceal ourselves at all times."

He began to pound the aluminum with a wrench from Pham's tool kit. Emma strolled along the beach. By the end of the dry season, the river was at its lowest ebb. The receding waters had dotted the shoreline with nothing more interesting than bits of driftwood and porous stones that Hazen said were lava rock. She reached the end of the strand, where the river curved and the beach vanished under a tangle of vines and brush, before she started back.

Hazen, busy hammering the boat into shape, did not hear the figures emerging from the jungle behind him. A scream died in Emma's throat. He would not hear her, either. Three men wearing helmets, shorts, and shirts stood behind him. Each held a rifle. With the sun in their eyes, they did not see Emma half-hidden by a fallen palm tree thirty feet away. Holding the pistol in both hands, she sighted along the barrel and squeezed the trigger. One of the men reeled backward and fell. The shot alerted Hazen, who whirled and threw his wrench at another soldier. It caught him in the face and he staggered and dropped his weapon. The third raised his rifle, but Emma fired again. Her shot went wide, but the man whirled and started to run away. He encountered Pham, returning to the campsite from the jungle at the northern edge of the clearing. Emma saw the glint of sunlight on steel, and in a moment a second man lay dead, stabbed in the gut by Pham's knife. The third, recovering from the blow of the wrench, plunged into the jungle and disappeared.

"Don't let him get away!" Emma shouted. Leaping over the trunk of the palm tree, she ran toward Pham and Hazen. Pham grabbed the pistol from her and took off into the jungle. Emma was about to follow, but Hazen called her back.

"Emma, no! Let Pham take care of it."

She dropped to her knees and huddled near the shining aluminum hull of the boat. Two minutes passed; then she heard a shot, so muffled by the heavy undergrowth that it sounded no more lethal than the popping of a balloon. Then Pham returned. Hazen snapped out a question in Vietnamese and he nodded.

"We've got to get rid of the bodies," Hazen said. "Emma, help Pham dig a hole—".

"I won't!" Emma cried. "I won't do it. I killed that man and now you expect me to bury him. It's horrible. Awful. We don't even know if they were Viet Minh or not. Maybe they were just simple farmers coming to investigate—"

"Simple farmers don't carry Russian-made weapons." Hazen stood over her. "All right, I'll help Pham. We'll stuff a few rocks into their clothes and sink them in the river. That way circling vultures won't give us away."

"How do we know there aren't fifty more of them looking for us?"

"We don't. Which is why we have to get out of here in a hurry. Here." He handed her his knife. "Cut some branches and take them out to the plane. Coat the metal with mud from the bottom and then drape the tailpiece with greenery. That way anyone passing on foot or flying overhead in a plane in the next couple of days will mistake it for a small island in the middle of the channel."

Emma gazed at the crumpled tail. In the coming weeks, the plane would sink lower and lower, working its way into the silt at the bottom of the river. Soon the monsoon rains would come and the rising water would submerge it completely.

"I shot that man," she said in a dazed voice. "I can't believe it. I killed another human being."

"Listen to me." Gripping her upper arms, Hazen lifted her to her feet. "You're in the middle of a war. You can either throw up your hands in despair, or else you can do whatever is necessary to survive. I don't like killing any more than you do, but I'll be damned if I'm going to let some wild-eyed communist carry my pelt back to Ho Chi Minh. Get moving." He gave her a little push toward the jungle. "I gave you a job to do, didn't I?"

By late afternoon, their rude craft was finished. Beaten into shape, strapped together by aluminum strips and rope, smeared with pine pitch from the forest and lined with banana leaves to keep the cargo and passengers from sticking to the pitch, it resembled no vessel Emma had ever seen. Pham had fashioned two crude oars out of bamboo.

They loaded the boat and then dragged it far up on the shore where overhanging branches would conceal it. Then they ate a meal of the baked fish, and some sticky rice they had taken from the pouches of the Viet Minh soldiers. Thinking of them lying in the shallow water a few yards away, Emma could not bring herself to swallow. She wrapped her portion in a banana leaf and stuffed it into her bag for later.

Hazen suggested that they try to rest until moonrise. He stationed himself in front of the boat, his pistol on his knee. Emma was sure she would be unable to sleep.

When Hazen shook her, she was amazed to see that night had fallen and that a brilliant half-moon like a lemon wedge had appeared over the tops of the black trees.

"Let's go," Hazen whispered. "No talking, You'll sit in the middle. Take this pole." He handed her a length of stout bamboo. "Use it to fend off rocks or anything else that gets too close. If we take on too much water, you may need to bail. Pham will be in front, paddling, and I'll be in back, steering."

He reminded her of the smartest kid in the school, isolated from the other students by his aloof manner and his superior intelligence.

"You're enjoying this, aren't you?" she charged.

He looked up, surprised. "Of course I am."

On most of the occasions when she and Hazen had been together, he had been bored, uncommunicative, almost sullen. Now, his dizzy spells were on the wane, and he fairly danced around the shallow skiff. Clearly, his boy-genius brain thrived on a regular diet of new challenges. The more precarious their situation, the happier he seemed.

They waded out into the shallows and climbed into the boat. The water around the sides rose alarmingly but did not swamp them. Hazen pushed them off and hopped in. They moved along swiftly with the current. To Emma's surprise, the boat rode well in the water. Twelve feet long and four feet wide at the center, with a flat bottom and high prow, it felt as stable as a barge. She sat in the middle, in front of the small pile of their luggage, which was swathed in rubber.

Pham, kneeling in the prow, paddled with the rhythm and ease of someone who had spent his life on water. With one arm he signaled silent directions to Hazen. Seated in the stern, Hazen used his bamboo oar as a rudder, keeping the craft in the deep central channel or jockeying back and forth around the rapids to avoid the roughest water. Because sound carries over water, they spoke softly, and then with the fewest possible words.

In the moonlight, the river became a ribbon of silver between the dark and hulking banks. Thousands of stars dotted the sky. Emma gazed at them, awestruck, until Hazen hissed a warning about a floating log coming up on the starboard side. She stabbed at it with the pole and it drifted away.

Emma longed for a decent meal. Thinking about the fish and gooey rice in her bag gave her small comfort. She remembered an evening in February. She and Janvier had dined at La Pagode, one of Saigon's most elegant restaurants. She pictured the snowy linen on their table, the gold-rimmed china, the single pink rose in a crystal vase, their meshed hands. They had feasted on roast duckling and small boiled potatoes, fresh asparagus tips and strawberries with cream. The bread had been fresh and crisp, the butter sweet, the wine delicious. They had toasted their love with champagne. Afterward they had gone to her room at the De Chesnay villa. She would never again know happiness like that.

Tears flooded her eyes. She had lost so much. If she had been more loving, more sensitive, less curious and complaining, Robert could not have stopped loving her.

They passed a village on the eastern shore. In the moonlight, with shadows obscuring their underpinings, the raised huts seemed almost to hover above the ground like the dwellings of some powerful magician. A dog barked but did not give chase along the riverbank.

Half a mile downstream, Hazen put into shore. "What is it?" Emma hissed. "Why are we stopping?"

"The map shows a waterfall coming up. Do you remember the drill for portage?"

Emma nodded. Hazen had explained the procedure before they shoved off. In silence, they unloaded the canoe completely. Emma carried most of their belongings bundled in the rubber groundsheet. Hazen and Pham wore the life jackets, so she did not have to contend with their bulk. The two men carried the inverted canoe along a narrow trail. Emma led the way with Hazen's waterproof flashlight, its glow softened by a square of parachute silk tied over the lens. The trail dropped sharply, and Hazen, at the rear, slipped and dropped his end of the boat with a resounding crash. In a matter of seconds, he was on his feet again and urging Pham and Emma to move faster. They passed the falls, which were unimpressive but high enough to wreck their small boat. Then Hazen and Pham put the canoe back in the water and Emma dumped her load into the center.

As the river broadened, the current became lazy and the boat lost speed. Emma allowed herself to relax a little. She had always loved swimming and boating, anything having to do with water. Hazen had said they might reach the French garrison at Van Yen in four days if they were lucky. And they would be lucky, she could feel it—

Suddenly she saw white foam ahead of them. "Rapids!" she cried.

In a moment they were shooting past rocks whose wide shoulders only hinted at the massive girth hidden beneath the spume. Then the canoe ran aground on a rock. They hung precariously for an instant while the current twisted them around; then Hazen jabbed his oar into another rock and pushed them free. They passed sideways between a pair of immense stones and found themselves floating in a placid pool.

Emma giggled. She had just been struck by the absurdity of

finding herself cruising down the Black River in a makeshift canoe. Slapping at mosquitoes. Watching for enemy soldiers. Shooting rapids. Her previous boating experience had consisted of Sunday afternoons pushing a rowboat around the pond in Lagoon Park. With Edward, that gentle exertion had usually been followed by a picnic and some tame necking under the cottonwood trees. Sometimes they attended a band concert, or sipped ice cream sodas—

"Emma, that's enough." Hazen's stern voice had the effect of ice water dashed in her face. "Take that helmet and bail."

With a dead soldier's helmet, Emma scooped water out of the bottom of the boat. When she had finished, she slapped the helmet on her head, then opened the bag, located the packet of food, which included part of a dead man's rice ration, and ate greedily.

9

APRIL 10, 1953
(From the <u>Chicago Tribune</u>)

> . . . clothes got looser, our tempers shorter, the innumerable mosquito welts on our arms and legs and faces guaranteed that we were as miserable as we could possibly be, the rains came. The river rose quickly, filling its banks and hurling us headlong toward our destination, the French garrison at Van Yen.

Hazen gave the signal to stop paddling and they ran the canoe onto a gravel shoal. After unloading their supplies, they dragged the boat to a spot high up on the riverbank, turned it upside down, and propped up one side on the oars. Pham camouflaged the makeshift shelter with palm branches while Hazen and Emma spread out the rubber groundsheet and brought their cargo under cover. Then, huddled together under a blanket of damp parachute silk, with life jackets for cushions and the inverted canoe over their heads, they slept.

Pham left them at noon to forage for food. When Emma awoke again a couple of hours later, Hazen was sitting staring out at the rain, his long arms wrapped around his updrawn knees. Postponing as long as possible a visit to a rain-drenched leafy toilet, Emma unwrapped her notebook and asked Hazen for his pocket knife.

"What do you want it for?"

"What do you think? To sharpen my pencil. Is there anything wrong with that?"

"Not a thing." He tossed the knife so that it landed close to her thigh. Emma glared at him. He didn't even have the good manners to hand it to her. In the three days that had passed since the crash, he had barely managed to be civil. She whittled her pencil to daggerlike sharpness and tossed the knife back in his direction.

"Thank you very much, I'm sure." Her exaggerated politeness failed to elicit any acknowledgment from Hazen.

Emma hunched over the precious notebook, one she had salvaged from her canvas bag and dried carefully on the sun-warmed bank near the wreckage of the plane. The pages were crinkled, stained blue from a blouse she had packed near them, but still usable. She had cut a square of rubber from Hazen's groundsheet and sewn it together to make a waterproof envelope for it. Inside the cover she had written: "Please return to Emma Louise Vaughan, 67 Avenue J. J. Rousseau, Saigon. In the event of her death or disappearance, Mrs. Elizabeth Vaughan of 814 Cottonwood Avenue, Lincoln, Nebraska, will pay the sum of fifty dollars U.S. ($50) to the person who delivers this book into her hands." Having done her best to preserve her thoughts for posterity, Emma had begun a journal of her adventures, starting with the crash of Hazen's plane.

Now she filled in the details of their previous night's progress down the river and their predawn landing. In the back of the notebook she reworded for the dozenth time her story about Jack McGraw's mission. Her original draft and all her notes had been washed away when the plane went down, but she thought she could patch together a story without them. She wondered if her effort was worthwhile: If they were captured or drowned, F. X. McGraw of the *Chicago Tribune* would never even know what he had lost.

When she glanced up from the page, she saw Hazen staring at her. He looked away quickly.

"Have I done something to offend Your Majesty?" Emma asked.

"No, not at all."

Emma studied him. At first glance, one might mistake him for a typical American in the Gary Cooper mold—tall, lean, and laconic. Like many Americans, he believed in his God, his country, and his own superior abilities. A man of principle, a man of faith, a loner who had adapted to life in the East but had never become part of it. So far as she could gather, Hazen's only friend in all of Southeast Asia was Jack McGraw.

While Saigon's gossips dismembered every important or mildly important personage in that city, Emma had never heard Hazen's name mentioned. If he kept a mistress, no one knew about it. His friendship with Eliane de Mornay was strictly platonic. If he gambled he did so privately and not in the noisy circus atmosphere of the Grand Monde. No one had ever seen him smoke marijuana or opium or heard about him making a killing on the piaster market. He didn't even take an occasional social drink. Emma had known him for six months, and she had been with him constantly for the past week, but he was still a blank page in her book.

"What are you really doing in Indochina, Mr. Hazen?"

"I've already told you, Miss Vaughan."

"Aerial surveys of the Tonkinese terrain?" Emma snorted. "I saw you and Jack McGraw with your heads together over that map. I sincerely doubt that he was showing you the most likely spots to find uranium in those hills. Sorry, Professor, but the evidence looks mighty fishy, even to someone who isn't a professional skeptic, which I am. I think you're working for the American government."

"Chrome does a lot of work for the government. Your guess about uranium was fairly close to the mark. But uranium is not the only strategic metal our people are interested in."

"Now you're being deliberately obscure, which means you're concealing something." Emma shifted closer to him so that she could scrutinize his eyes. "I've got to give your organization credit; the role of roving geologist is a great cover, even if it did literally land us in the soup. Tell me, just what does our government want here? What happens if the French lose this war and pull out? Who are you supporting in the war, anyway? Not Emperor Bao Dai, who is probably the most corrupt leader of men since Warren Harding. What's your plan?"

"You're wasting your time, Miss Vaughan. I admit I have a strong personal interest in the political and social forces that are shaping the future of Southeast Asia, but my interest is strictly extracurricular. At the moment, geology is my first love."

"You did some undercover work for Uncle Sam during the war, didn't you? That seems to be general knowledge among your friends."

"I won't deny it." Hazen kept his gaze fixed straight in front of him. "But that doesn't mean I'm doing that sort of work now. You can persist with your questioning if you want to, but you're wasting your time. All you'll get from me is the Chicago telephone directory: names, addresses, and phone numbers, correct to the last digit."

"You sound like you've been interrogated by experts." Emma pressed closer to him. "Who interrogated you? When?"

"The Gestapo." Turning, he let her look straight into his eyes. "Well, was I lying that time or not?"

"The big lie succeeds where little ones fail, isn't that right?" Emma sniffed. "Well, that one was a whopper, Mr. Hazen. The Gestapo, indeed."

She continued to write until both her ideas and her pencil tip gave out. A sidelong glance at Hazen showed that he had not budged at all in the past fifteen minutes. Only his thumb moved, gently rubbing the bowl of his cold briar pipe.

"What are you doing now?" she asked. "Inventing some new mathematical formula?"

"No, I was reading a poem."

Emma wrinkled her nose at him. "What do you mean, you were reading it?"

"Some years ago I was cooped up for a period of time with nothing to read but poetry. A lot of it just stuck in my brain. It's a great comfort when I have nothing else to think about." He had not taken his eyes off the surging river. "Does that satisfy your reporter's curiosity, Miss Vaughan?"

"Not quite. What were you reading?"

"Nothing you'd be interested in."

"That's not fair. How do you know I wouldn't be interested? Why won't you tell me? Why do you have to be so smug and superior all the time? I'm not asking you to reveal atomic secrets."

Sighing, Hazen stretched out his legs and leaned back on his elbows. "All right, if you insist. It was a poem by Emily Dickinson."

"Great. I like Emily Dickinson. Let's hear it."

Hazen took a breath and began to recite:

> "Wild Nights—Wild Nights!
> Were I with thee
> Wild Nights should be
> Our luxury!
>
> Futile—the Winds—
> To a Heart in port—
> Done with the Compass—
> Done with the Chart!
>
> Rowing in Eden—
> Ah, the Sea!
> Might I but moor—Tonight—
> In Thee!"

Hazen's voice grew and swelled, fraught with emotional intensity. Emma listened, astonished, to this passionate outpouring. When he was finished, she was silent for a full minute; then she said softly, "You filthy hypocrite."

Shocked, Hazen pulled himself up. "What did you say?"

"You heard me." Her cheeks were crimson. "After the things you said about me, the names you called me—whore and slut!

Oh, you've got a nerve, reciting love poetry to me. I've seen you looking at me, Alan Hazen. I'm not a child anymore. I know what you want. What do all men want? I suppose you think that because we're stuck on the equivalent of a desert island, I'll fall into your lap like a ripe plum. A little fun and games to pass the time."

"I assure you, Miss Vaughan, I have no intention—"

"Rowing in Eden! What does that make us, Adam and Eve?"

"You asked me to tell you what I was thinking—"

"That's right. And I don't like it. I don't like it one bit."

She unbuttoned her blouse and shorts and stripped down to her bra and panties.

Hazen looked alarmed. "What are you doing?"

"You needn't think I'm getting ready to seduce you. But I have to go to the bathroom and I am not going to spend the rest of the day sitting here in wet clothes."

Hazen set his jaw and resolved to say nothing that might aggravate her further.

"You're not such a saint after all, are you, Mr. Hazen?" Emma shoved her notebook into its rubber envelope. "I don't know why I'm so surprised. You're no better than Robert Janvier or any of the other men on this planet. But let me tell you something. I wouldn't let you touch me if you were the only male left on earth and I were the only woman and the human race were about to become extinct. I could never love you. I don't even like you. To me, you're about as attractive as a—a mongoose. So put that in your old pipe."

Too flabbergasted to speak, Hazen watched her duck out from under the boat and sprint along the riverbank. After she had disappeared from view, he remembered that he should have warned her to be careful.

Emma hadn't moved her limbs so freely for days, since the start of their journey downstream. Heedless of the needlelike darts of rain that pricked her flesh, she lifted her face to the sky and drank her fill of pure, untainted rainwater. She remembered reading somewhere that man could live indefinitely—thirty days? fifty?—on water alone. No doubt Alan Hazen, whiz kid and boy wonder, could tell her the exact number.

She halted abruptly. What had made her blow up at Hazen like that? Until this morning, he had not indicated by a single word or even the flicker of an eyelid that he felt anything for her but scorn and irritation. Then he had recited that absurd poem, a perfectly innocuous little verse by that New England spinster Emily Dickinson, for Pete's sake, in which the "Thee" probably referred to God, and Emma had snapped his head off. The memory of that scene would have been amusing if it weren't so embarrassing: Emma Vaughan warning Alan Hazen to stay away from her. As if he were capable of doing anything else.

Was she really so terrified of love? Not surprising, considering what Janvier had done to her. If she were wise, she would avoid entanglements with men in the future and concentrate on her work. Closing her eyes for a moment, Emma pictured herself lying in Hazen's arms while he kissed her lips and her eyelids and stroked her breasts with his long fingers. The image made her shiver, and she reminded herself not to stay out in the rain too long. She would take care of her business and get back to the boat.

Emma had just lowered herself into a squat when she heard movement in the brush in front of her. The blue-black barrel of a rifle brushed the ferns over her head. She caught a glimpse of bare feet and slender brown legs, green shorts, and net-covered helmets covered with leaves that exactly matched the surrounding forest. From a few feet away, the men would be invisible, perfectly camouflaged except for the small dabs of red on their collars.

Struck dumb with surprise and terror, Emma waited a full ten minutes before pulling herself together and lifting her head cautiously above the ferns. The path was clear. But she had counted forty-three pairs of legs. She jumped up and ran faster than she had ever run in her life.

She had nearly reached the shelter on the riverbank when she stumbled to a halt, her bare feet sinking into the mud. Perhaps the soldiers had already found their hiding place. She pictured Alan Hazen stumbling along a jungle trail between a pair of guards, his hands tied behind his back. Moving slowly, shivering from fear and the cool rain, she approached the upturned boat.

It was still there, nearly invisible under its covering of leaves and branches. Emma threw herself down beside Hazen, who was stretched out on the rubber sheet.

"Alan—oh, goodness, I can't catch my breath—Alan, there are Viet Minh soldiers out there. I saw them! Hundreds of them on the path. We're surrounded. They went right past me. We've got to get out of here right away, now. We can't wait for Pham. He'll understand why. They've probably found him already, and killed him or tortured him. Alan, please hurry, we've got to leave."

"Slow down, Emma." Hazen hitched himself up on one elbow. "Tell me what happened."

"No time—come on, Alan! They were carrying guns, nearly swatted me in the head. God, I was scared. I've never been so scared in my life. We've got to get out of here right away. We can't just sit here and wait for them to find us. Please!" She tugged at his arm.

"Emma, listen." Hazen, who was sitting up by now, gripped her elbows. "We are not leaving Pham. We'll have to wait here until dusk. That's the plan. If he isn't back by then, we'll shove off without him. But not before. Not before."

"No, no, Alan, you don't understand—" She could feel herself becoming hysterical, but she could not stop the momentum of her emotions. She was trembling all over from cold and fright and she was on the verge of tears. "We've got to get out of here. They're looking for us at this very moment. I know they are. They—they were looking for me. I think they must have seen me on the riverbank and followed me. They're like Indians, they can read signs and footprints on the ground—"

"Not in the pouring rain. Come on, Emma, control yourself. Calm down."

"You're asking me to calm down, after what I've just told you?" Her voice rose in volume and pitch. "I won't. I can't. It's just too crazy to sit here and do nothing and wait to be killed—"

Part of her mind was still working enough to know that her screaming was terribly dangerous. She wanted him to slap her. If their circumstances had been reversed, she would have done just that. Instead, he pulled her close and kissed her. She was so startled that when he broke off to gauge her reaction, she began to babble again. He kissed her once more. This time she fought him, straining against him and twisting her face out of his reach. Then her tension broke. She leaned against him, feeling grateful for his size and warmth and wisdom, drawing comfort from the kiss, letting it seep into her brain and her limbs, where it calmed and quieted her.

"All right now?"

Emma gulped and nodded. His arms felt wonderfully strong. Under her cheek, his heart was beating as rapidly as hers.

"Now tell me exactly what happened."

"They were wearing green uniforms and something red, a pin or a bar. I saw a flash of it as they went by. I remember their legs were bare. They must have been wearing shorts."

"Green uniforms. And what else?"

Hazen pressed her for details, but Emma could remember nothing more. She was sure that his camera-eye could have produced a description accurate to the last frayed buttonhole and the make of the weapon that had swept over her head, but her own recollections were exhausted. Hazen spread out his map of Tonkin. His finger hovered for a moment, then came to rest on a dot about a quarter of an inch from the line that represented the Black River.

"Muong Choi, a little village halfway up this mountain, about three miles from here. That's where they were heading. A likely place for a camp." He folded the map away. "You stay here. If I'm not back by the time Pham returns, go on without me." He crouched at the entrance to their hideaway and looked out.

"Go on? Are you out of your mind?" Emma was careful to

keep her voice down to a whisper. "I am not going anywhere without you, and you're not going anywhere without me. I refuse to stay here for sixty seconds by myself, is that clear? I absolutely refuse. Whatever happens to me, whether I'm raped or murdered or burned alive, I want you to be a witness so that at least my mother will know how it all ended. This is all your fault, anyway. You are responsible for my well-being, Alan Hazen. You're not leaving me here all by myself."

"The Viet Minh are fairly well disciplined." Hazen crawled out from under the boat. Emma scrambled after him. "They probably won't rape you, and they certainly won't murder you until you've told them all you know."

"Which in my case would take fifteen seconds. I don't have the Lincoln telephone directory committed to memory. And don't tell me about their honor and discipline. I heard about the massacre in Hanoi in 1946."

In a reprisal against those who had collaborated with the French, the Viet Minh had slaughtered over one thousand native women who had been married to, employed by, or living with Frenchmen. Their children had been killed, too. If the communists could punish their own women so viciously, what would they do to a foreigner?

They stood arguing in front of the shelter while the rain sluiced down, drenching them both. Finally Hazen agreed to let Emma accompany him, provided she followed his orders scrupulously and kept her mouth shut.

"I mean it, not one word. Not even a whisper. And put some clothes on. If we're caught, you'll wish you were wearing something more than underwear."

The path in the forest was awash with mud and the going was slow. Hazen moved cautiously and silently. Emma slogged after him. Her stout walking shoes were limp and moldy, of use only to protect her feet from sharp objects. She had grown accustomed to the feeling that her clothes were pasted to her skin, and that her hair was a sodden cap that directed small rivulets into her eyes, ears, and nose. Finding a dry place in this monsoon-lashed country was as fantastic a dream as finding water in the desert. Emma conjured up a mirage, a little farm in the middle of a Nebraska cornfield on a warm September day. Laundry snapping on the line. A windmill swirling smartly. The lane a ribbon of dust that rose into buff-colored clouds whenever a car approached. In a room upstairs a brass bed with plump feather pillows and crisp white sheets. And in that bed, a smiling man who looked remarkably like Alan Hazen.

The rain grew heavier as the leafy canopy over the path thinned. Suddenly Hazen grabbed Emma's arm and pulled her down behind a thicket. She had heard nothing, but after a moment soldiers began jogging past, their bare feet slapping the mud. This time she was in a better position to study their green uniforms. On their lapels they wore small red stars. Eighteen of them went by this time.

"Giap's elite," Hazen murmured when the men had passed. "There must be hundreds of them around here. I wonder what they're up to? Let's get back to the boat."

They reached the canoe and prepared to push off. With Pham helping, the procedure usually took no more than five minutes. Now Emma slipped and slid in the mud and dropped her end of the boat. It struck a rock with a reverberating shudder that sounded like stage thunder.

"Can't you even do a simple thing like balance an object on its natural center of gravity?" Hazen whispered furiously.

"No, I can't." Emma sank deeper into the mud, which rose around her ankles. Rich with decaying organisms and rotting vegetation, the mud of Indochina reminded her of a Nebraska pig yard. Same consistency, same smell. "I am not a genius like you, Mr. Hazen. Thank God. Smug, self-righteous, complacent boors—"

"Get those oars on board. And shut up, unless you want another kiss."

Blushing, Emma carried out the tasks he had given her. Having experienced one long kiss with Alan Hazen, she did not find the idea of being kissed by him again nearly so repellent as she might have once. He would need to find a more potent threat in order to intimidate her.

Hazen waited to launch the boat until the last possible minute, when the outlines of the trees were beginning to merge with the dark clouds overhead. Just as he was about to shove off, a figure came out of the jungle and waved at them. Emma screamed. It was a Viet Minh soldier, complete with rifle and leafy helmet. Hazen drew his pistol, then put it away again.

"It's Pham!"

The small man ran toward the boat and jumped in as Hazen and Emma used their oars to push it away from the shore. His uniform was complete, even to the small pouch on his belt in which the ordinary Vietnamese foot soldier carried his weekly ration of cold cooked rice.

Emma leaned forward. "Pham, where did you get those clothes?"

He turned around and gave her a broad smile. Just where he had found the uniform, Emma never learned. She suspected that he had killed a man for it.

"Everybody get down!" Hazen shouted from the stern. The current seized the boat and sucked it away from the shore. As she dove for cover, Emma glimpsed flashes of orange from the trees. At the same time she heard the crackle of gunfire.

Soon the sounds of the rain and the river overpowered the noise of the shooting. The current had swung them around so that they were in danger of capsizing. Water sloshed over the side. Sitting up, Hazen ordered Pham to paddle and Emma to bail. Looking back up the river toward the spot where they had spent the day, Emma saw only shadows.

Throughout the night, the river pulled them inexorably toward Van Yen, where the Troc and Black rivers joined. With the waters just a few feet below flood stage, the shallow boat was able to skim over dangerous shoals and rapids that might otherwise have wrecked it. Twice, Hazen's keen ear and his instinct for sensing changes in the current saved them from plunging over waterfalls that were not marked on the map. As on earlier occasions, they put into shore, unloaded their provisions, and carried the boat along a steep and slippery mountain trail.

Hazen warned Emma that Van Yen would probably turn out to be a squalid village whose normally rutted paths had turned into rivers of mud. But in her mind, it began to resemble the Promised Land. She knew what she would find at Van Yen: a warm, dry bed, quantities of wholesome French army food served with beer and wine and gallons of strong hot coffee. Perhaps even a hot shower, with fragrant soaps and shampoos, and at the end of it, a dry towel.

They drifted past the village just one hour before dawn, on the fourth day of their journey down the Black River. Hazen wanted to find a safe anchorage before sending Pham back to investigate. Emma was watchful, unusually alert for having been awake all night. Her senses were highly acute and she heard a slight buzzing in her ears. She decided she was suffering from fatigue. But the nightmare was nearly over now. Very soon, the government of France could take responsibility for their safety and well-being.

As they neared the shore, an object bumped against the side of the boat. An arm swung loosely out of the water, and a bloated hand flapped against the hull. Emma screamed.

They saw more bodies as they waited in a small cove about a mile dowstream from Van Yen, dozens of them, bloated, distorted monstrosities whose grotesque proportions mocked the human shapes they had once been. Hazen indentified most of the dead as old men, women, and children, with a few Viet Minh regulars and French paratroopers among them.

Emma stared horrified at a corpse snagged on a fallen tree just a few yards away from their anchorage. "What happened?" She had started to scratch a few notes in her book, but discovered that describing the scene on the river only made it more horrible. She had put the notebook away again. "What happened to them?"

"I don't know." Hazen gnawed the stem of his old briar pipe. He had had no tobacco since the crash, but he had not abandoned his pipe. "I have a feeling that Pham's news isn't going to be good."

It wasn't. Pham returned with a quantity of food he had bought from a peasant who had looted it from French stores after the army had pulled out: cans of rations, some moldy flour and rice, a container of Vinogel, an alcoholic grape concentrate issued to the sons of France, for whom a meal without wine, even in the jungle, was unthinkable. Emma sat at Hazen's elbow while he translated Pham's report.

"The French were routed two days ago. They were in such a hurry to get out that they left behind half a dozen mortars, cases of ammunition, and enough supplies to last for six months. They didn't really have a choice. One of General Giap's divisions is sitting just over the next ridge. The town came under heavy bombardment the night before last. That's where all these bodies came from. A dawn attack was imminent and apparently everyone knew it, and so they evacuated. The Viets moved in peacefully yesterday morning, with no resistance."

"But the soldiers? The soldiers? The soldiers?" Emma said through chattering teeth. "Where did all the soldiers go?"

"Into the jungle, apparently. They had been promised relief from Hanoi, but it never came."

"Like Nasan," Emma moaned. "They didn't have a chance. Just like Nasan. Robert was there. He told me about it. Oh, God." Her shivering gave way to a surge of weakness and profuse sweating. "Oh, God, it's all over—too late. We're too late."

"We couldn't be in a worse place." Hazen looked around anxiously. "This whole area is thick with Viets. Places, everybody. We're getting out of here."

Pham moved to the prow and untied the boat from the half-submerged log to which it had been moored. Hazen slid back to his seat in the stern.

"Not me." Emma stood up. The boat rocked precariously. "I can't go any further. I'll talk to them and tell them I'm a journalist. They'll be happy for a chance to indoctrinate an American woman. But I am not spending one more minute in this boat. I've had enough."

"Sit down, Emma."

"No. You and Pham can go ahead, but this kid is bailing out."

Before Hazen could stop her, Emma dove over the side of the boat and started to swim toward shore. Hazen shouted, "Pham!" At once the Vietnamese jumped into the river and swam after her. He grabbed her shoulder and pulled her around. Writhing together, they sank under the water. After a few seconds they surfaced, gasping, still locked in a desperate struggle. Finally Pham brought his fist up sharply under her chin. Emma went limp, and Pham dragged her back to the boat.

"She has a fever," Pham said in French as Hazen hauled her aboard. "Very sick."

Hazen's hand brushed Emma's forehead. "You're right. All right, let's go. Hurry." He jerked the rubber groundsheet over Emma to shelter her from the rain; then he returned to the stern of the boat. A floating corpse bumped against the hull, and he pushed it away with his oar.

"Robert!" Emma screamed suddenly. "Robert, no! Stop! Stop!"

Cursing, Hazen ordered Pham to paddle as hard as he could. The boat cut through the water, pulling away from the city of the dead. As Emma thrashed from side to side, the boat rocked dangerously. In the stern, Hazen stroked hard with his oar to keep them from capsizing. He was worried about Emma, deeply worried. Some of these tropical fevers struck with deadly swiftness. Unless he could get her to a warm shelter where he could nurse her, she would die. She screamed again, and a shiver traveled up his spine. Whatever she was seeing in her dreams, it was infinitely more terrible than the scene she had just witnessed at the watery hell of Van Yen.

"Be quiet, Emma," he pleaded. "You'll be all right, I promise. But you've got to be quiet. Pham, do something."

Pham crept back to the middle of the boat. He pinched Emma's nose and covered her mouth with his hand. Deprived of oxygen for a full minute, she passed out. He nodded to Hazen and returned to his place. Silently, they skimmed down the river until they reached the mouth of the stream for which Hazen had been searching. He shifted the oar he used as a rudder, and the little craft slid under an overhanging willow tree and vanished into the fog.

10

APRIL 10, 1953 (Continued)

The carnage at Van Yen overwhelmed me. I had been cold, wet, and undernourished for too many days, and I collapsed with a tropical fever. Mr. Hazen and his Vietnamese colleague Pham took me to the deserted village of Moc Lam, about twenty miles away from Van Yen on a small tributary called the Teune. We were only a few miles from Route Coloniale 6, the road that crosses the border from northern Vietnam into Laos. In Laos we would be safe. . . .

Hazen heard a low moan from the corner of the hut. Emma had kicked off her coverlet of parachute silk, and her nightgown had worked its way up around her waist. He pulled it down and readjusted the covers.

Her eyes were sunken and her lips were cracked and dry. Three days had passed since her collapse at Van Yen and the fever had not abated. If anything, it had climbed higher. Hazen held a bamboo cup of rainwater to her lips but she pushed it aside. He could not persuade her to drink.

He noticed that a trickle of rain had seeped through the thatch and was splashing near her shoulder. Lifting her gently, he shifted her to a drier spot; then he propped her head up on a life jacket.

Emma opened her eyes and looked at him. "Is it over?"

Her gaze was surprisingly clear and her voice sounded rational.

Hazen wondered if the fever had finally broken. But before he could reply, she started to rave again.

"Robert—sorry—so sorry. Please don't leave me—I'll die if you leave me. Die. Don't go!"

"I'm right here." Hazen tucked the silk shroud around her legs. "Don't worry, Emma."

"I didn't mean to make you angry." She was sobbing now, which made her cough. "My fault—my fault. Forgive me, Robert—won't do it again, I swear—I swear. Say—say you forgive me."

"I forgive you, Emma."

"You really forgive me?" Tears rolled down her cheeks. "You still love me?"

"Yes, I still love you."

"Hold me—hold me." She struggled to raise herself up. "Please, Robert."

"No, Emma." Hazen placed his hands on her shoulders. "Try and rest. You've been sick."

"You don't love me—you don't love me!" she wailed.

He pulled her into a tight embrace and rocked her gently. "It's all right, Emma, I'm here now. Don't worry. I won't let you go."

Her flesh was dry and wasted, and her heat welded them together. He knew he should leave her, but he couldn't move.

"I love you," she whispered urgently. "I love you."

"And I love you." His mouth was so dry he could hardly speak the words.

Sighing, she fell back on the cushion. "I'm only happy when I'm with you," she murmured. "Will you kiss me?"

She smiled up at him. Hazen knew she was seeing another man. Her fingertips played over his face and throat, but he knew she was touching someone else. When she spoke, it was to Captain Robert Janvier that her words were directed. She begged him again to kiss her. Quivering, Hazen leaned over her.

But the moment their lips touched, Emma twisted her face away. "Don't! Don't hit me! My face— Oh, dear God, he's destroying my face! Somebody help me, please help me! Stop him! Stop him! He's killing me! Killing me!"

Hazen staggered to the doorway of the hut. Emma continued to scream and rant. After a few minutes, her screams subsided into sobs. Finally, she was quiet. Hazen shuddered. He had come so close to the evil he loathed. He had been ready to take advantage of her weakness, her delirium, just so he could taste the passion she felt for someone else. Grabbing up a clay bowl, he crushed it between his hands, pulverizing it. Cuts appeared on his palms, and reddish brown dust fell at his feet.

Night had fallen when Emma awakened again. "Where are we?"

"We're in a Meo village called Moc Lam, about twenty miles from the Black River and Van Yen."

"Did the Viet Minh chase us here?"

"No. We needed to find someplace to stay while you were ill. You've had a fever. It might have been malaria or it might have been something else. Tropical fevers are unpredictable." Hazen gave the contents of the pot on the hearth a stir. He could not bring himself to look at her. "We've been here for three days. Do you remember anything about it? Anything at all?"

"Nothing. I must have been pretty far gone."

He sighed inwardly. She would never know how close he had come to violating her trust in him. "You were delirious."

Emma glanced down at herself. She was wearing a black silk nightgown Janvier had given her. "How did I get into this?"

"Your clothes were sopping. I found that in your bag. Can you sit up?" He approached her pallet carrying a wooden bowl and a spoon he had whittled from bamboo. Slipping his arm behind her back, he raised her into a sitting position and placed the other life jackets behind her for support. For the first time in days, her skin felt cool. The fever had broken at last. "Try and eat a little bit. You're very weak and dehydrated."

As Emma sipped her soup, Hazen described their situation. After unloading the boat, he and Pham had filled it with rocks and scuttled it in shallow water. If they needed it again, they could always raise it. They had plenty of food left from the supplies Pham had purchased in Van Yen.

"Now that your fever is gone, we can move on. I don't like staying in one place too long. So far we've been lucky."

He explained that Moc Lam was only thirty miles from the Laotian border. In just two or three days, they could reach eastern Laos and the airstrip at Ban Na Ha. But that would require a journey on foot over rugged mountain terrain.

"Pham has gone ahead to scout the trails and to check out the situation. He ought to be back by tonight or tomorrow morning. If you're still too weak to walk, we'll make a litter and carry you. It won't be an easy trip."

"I'll be well enough to walk on my own," Emma promised. "Just give me another day or two."

Except for a family of wild pigs and the usual assortment of reptiles and insects, Moc Lam was deserted, the villagers having fled from a recent plague of cholera. A few of the huts had been burned, but the longhouse remained, with its pile of water buffalo horns stacked outside to indicate how many beasts had been sacrificed on that spot to the gods of the harvest. For their shelter, Hazen had chosen a small hut on the perimeter of the village from which he and Emma could make a quick escape into the jungle if necessary.

"I decided that risking cholera was preferable to risking discovery," he said. "This village has only been empty for three or four weeks and the residents are still scared enough that they haven't bothered us. It's not the Ritz, but at least it keeps the rain out."

Near the raised platform on which she had been sleeping was a round hearth that Hazen told her had been built of the compact clay of termites' nests. There were no vents in the roof, and the whole room reeked of decades of stale wood smoke. The inhabitants had stored their grain in small enclosed cubicles, like closets. These granaries were swept clean; only a few rat droppings remained. Across the width of the room, Hazen had rigged a clothesline. Emma saw the shorts and the shirt she had worn for most of the trip downriver, and several stained bed sheets made of parachute silk.

A faint blush rose to her cheeks. "You seem to have been a pretty efficient nursemaid, Mr. Hazen."

"I did my best. After all, I'm responsible for getting you into this situation. I should have known better than to bring a woman along."

"Why did you?"

"I wish I knew. More soup?"

Emma shook her head. "It tasted good. I didn't know you could cook too. Do you have any more talents you haven't told me about?"

"Hundreds." He removed her bowl. "Take it easy now. Don't wear yourself out talking."

Warm, dry, well-fed, and confident that Hazen would take care of all her needs, Emma slept soundly that night.

Hazen spent the next morning performing household chores—laundry, sweeping, scrubbing. Emma slept fitfully throughout the day, but when evening came she was wide awake and clamoring to be entertained. "I'm bored," she complained. "Poetry, prose—I don't care. Read to me from the books in your brain."

Carefully avoiding anything she might construe as a love poem, Hazen recited Hamlet's soliloquies, the first part of Milton's *Paradise Lost*, and the Psalms. Halfway through the Nineteenth Psalm, Emma grew restive.

"I'm ready for something more exciting. Tell me a story. A true story. I want to know what you did in the war."

Hazen stirred their rice with a stick. "I was a spy. Not a very successful one. Did you ever hear about that man called Cicero? He was the valet of the British ambassador in—"

"I'm not interested in him. I want to know about you. Where did you do your spying? Here in Indochina?"

"No. In Germany. This rice is almost ready—"

"Come on, Alan, you can't hold out a tantalizing tidbit like that and then snatch it away again. Tell me what happened."

"This story is not as thrilling as you might think," Hazen warned. "Real-life spies are nothing like the ones you've read about."

But Emma pestered him, and finally he relented. "All right, you win. My story begins in 1941. I was married, living in a quiet neighborhood near the University of Chicago, where I was employed as a full professor in the Department of Mathematics. My wife, June, and I had one child, a daughter named Molly. We were happy together, content with our lives—or so I thought. Until a certain Wednesday in October. I had been teaching a graduate seminar in the afternoon. As the students were leaving the room, I noticed two men standing in the hall outside. When I started to walk back to my office, they stopped me and asked if they could talk to me for a few minutes."

The two men said they had come from Washington, but one of them was clearly British. They told Hazen that they wanted him to impersonate a young German physicist named Erich Von Stauffel, who had been on a sabbatical leave at Oxford University when the war broke out in Europe. In the next few weeks, Gestapo agents were going to make an attempt to smuggle Von Stauffel out of an English internment camp in Devonshire and take him back to Germany, where his help was needed on a top-secret project.

"At first I thought they were joking. To begin with, I was a mathematician, not a physicist. I had never even been to Germany. Surely this Von Stauffel person would have dozens of friends and colleagues who would know immediately that I was an imposter."

The men calmly refuted each objection. Although Hazen had only a general knowlege of physics, he was a quick study, and he could easily use his enormous strength in mathematics and his prodigious memory to compensate for any weaknesses in that subject. Secondly, Hazen's mother was German, a Berliner like

Von Stauffel. Her mother, Hazen's grandmother, had lived with the family since Hazen was a boy, and he had grown up speaking the language. After a week or so of intense study, he could pass for a native. Thirdly, the project was being undertaken in an isolated area of the Bavarian Alps, far from Von Stauffel's home. Workers were being drawn from industry as well as the far reaches of academe; only two of them could possibly have known Von Stauffel as a student, and then only as a young boy of high-school age. Von Stauffel's own education had been an international one that included years of study at the Sorbonne, Oxford, and MIT, where he had undertaken his first experiments with nuclear fission. He was known to be a loner who shunned the company of other scientists and preferred to carry out his experiments in his own private laboratory, assisted only by his students. He had a poor memory for faces and an even worse one for names. A confirmed bachelor, his antipathy toward women was almost pathological.

Perhaps most important, Hazen's physical resemblance to the man was astounding if not miraculous. Like Von Stauffel, he was tall, fair-skinned, and blue-eyed. He could easily cultivate a surly manner and brusque attitude that would keep his colleagues at bay.

"I told them I couldn't do it. I wasn't interested in being a spy, and I couldn't leave my family. My country was not involved in the war, and I believed it was my Christian duty to stay with my wife and child." Hazen paused for a moment. Emma noticed that the hand that held the stick over the stewpot was taut and white-knuckled. "When I got home that evening, no one was there. My wife and child had gone. Their closets and drawers were empty. I found a note from June on the table saying they had gone to her mother's. I drove down to Gary, Indiana, right away. June accused me of being arrogant, self-centered, and cold. She said she was tired of being the brilliant mathematician's handmaiden: washing, cooking, cleaning, raising our daughter, while I spent every spare minute with my slide rules and books and my friends from the university. I asked if someone had put her up to this, like those two men who had come to visit me at the university. She denied it. She said she had been planning to ask for a divorce for a long time. I still believe they persuaded her to leave me."

Hazen found a long strand of dried grass on the floor and fed it to the flames inch by inch. First it blackened, then it shriveled, then it vanished into smoke. Emma remained silent. When he spoke again, his voice was husky.

"I don't remember the drive back to Chicago. I don't remember the whole next week, but I was deeply depressed and I decided I was having a breakdown. I thought about committing suicide, but I prayed over it, and after a week I called the number the men had left me. They came over right away, and that same night we flew to Washington. They told me about the project Von Stauffel was supposed to be working on." Hazen's pupils reflected twin tongues of flame. "They seemed to know so much about it—clearly they already had an agent close to the source. The shorter of the two men, the Englishman, said they wanted me to sabotage the work the Nazis were doing on a new weapon, one whose capacity for destruction surpassed anything the British and Americans had in their arsenals. By 1941, the Luftwaffe had already dumped tons of bombs on London. The damage had been heavy, but not comprehensive, not total. Just one of those new bombs would destroy the city utterly, along with most of its inhabitants."

Von Stauffel was in a hospital outside London, suffering from a serious lung infection. The Gestapo agents would not want to jeopardize his health by moving him before he had regained his strength. Von Stauffel's physician had been instructed to keep him quiet for as long as possible, but with beds urgently needed for air-raid casualties, he could not refuse to release the patient indefinitely without arousing suspicion.

"They said to me, 'The man released from the hospital will be you, not Von Stauffel. You will not return to the camp in Devonshire, but to a new one in Hampshire. That's where their agents will find you. We won't make it easy for them to get you out, but when it's all over, they will congratulate themselves on a fantastic run of luck.'"

Hazen ladled some fish-and-rice stew into Emma's bowl. "That's enough talk for now. I don't want to tire you."

"I'm not tired." Emma cradled the rice bowl in her lap. "I feel fine, better every minute. You can't stop now. What happened next?"

He sighed. "Forty-eight hours after I made that phone call, I found myself in an English country house—I still have no idea where it was—being drilled by a middle-aged German couple whose names and occupations I never learned. They took turns working with me. My technical vocabulary was weakest. I spent ten hours a day with them. When I wasn't speaking German, I was studying nuclear physics, reading and memorizing Von Stauffel's published and unpublished papers, trying to learn all I could about the man and his work. It was hectic, and intense, and a little scary. But at some point I realized that I had never felt more alive. I was awakening from a coma that had lasted for the first twenty-five years of my life. Two weeks later, our people moved me to the hospital in the middle of the night. The next morning, I went to the Hampshire internment camp as Erich Von Stauffel. When my strength had supposedly returned, I was assigned to a crew digging a drainage ditch near the camp. One afternoon someone slipped me a note instructing me to be the last one in line on our way back to the barracks that evening. As we were walking along the road, under guard, a black car pulled up beside me. I jumped in and the car took off. A few shots were fired. I don't know if anyone was hurt." He broke off and glanced at Emma. "How's the stew?"

"Fine, fine. Go on!"

"I was taken to Liverpool by car, and then hustled aboard a fishing boat. Just before dawn, a German submarine picked me up off the coast of Ireland. I was allowed a few days' rest in Paris, and then taken to Bavaria in a small plane. A car met us at the airfield. As I was getting in, I managed to let the chauffeur close the door on my right hand. He broke two fingers. That would explain any shakiness in my handwriting for weeks, perhaps months, to come. I never saw the fellow after that. They probably sent him to a concentration camp."

"This is a hell of a story, Alan." Emma scraped the bottom of her bowl with her bamboo spoon and then lay back against her cushions. Her hair was tangled and her cheeks were pale, but Hazen thought she was still the most beautiful woman he had ever seen. "What happened next?"

"Not very much at first. We had a lot of brainstorming sessions in which the leader of the project tried to coordinate our various approaches. As Von Stauffel, I remained aloof and apart, growling at everyone who came near me. It was an easy part to play. Even before I left England, I knew that Von Stauffel had been working on an atomic bomb. Although I was still no genius in nuclear physics, I might have been able to fool them indefinitely if I hadn't come face-to-face with an old classmate of mine from Chicago, a young German mathematician named Bauer. He and I had spent a lot of time together when I was a junior, playing chess and working out the most fantastic equations. Of course, since I'd entered the university at thirteen, I was a good deal younger than he was. Nevertheless, he thought he recognized me, and like a good little Nazi he reported his suspicions to the project leader, who passed them on to the Gestapo. They located Von Stauffel's mother and flew her in to make a positive identification. She took one look at me and said, 'This is not my son,' and that was that."

Emma was sitting up again, her eyes wide. "Did they arrest you?"

"Yes, and charged me with espionage. I was tried and sentenced to hang. The execution was supposed to be carried out at Dachau, the concentration camp near Munich. When I got there, they shaved my head and threw me in with a lot of other political prisoners, all sentenced to death. I just had to wait my turn, apparently. One night I managed to short-circuit the electric fence and escape. I went to an address in Munich that the people in London had given me. It was the home of a family named Strauss, a Bavarian doctor with a wife and a couple of teenaged kids. They were brave people, devout Lutherans who detested the Nazis. Even though the dangers to them were immense, they hid me for two months, until my hair grew out a little and I no longer looked like a concentration camp inmate. Anyway, they helped me get to Switzerland. From there I went to London."

"So you escaped." Emma blew out her breath. "This is an incredible story, Alan."

"Lots of incredible things happen in wartime. Mine is just one of a million interesting stories."

"But what happened then? Did you go back to Chicago?"

"I'll tell you some other time. Get some rest now."

Emma pestered him to tell her more, but he clammed up and refused to say another word. He sat cross-legged near the fire in a meditative pose, his pipe cradled in his hand like a talisman. His expression was blank. Emma sensed that he was still wandering the landscape of his memory.

The next day, Emma took her first faltering steps around the hut, with Hazen's arm supporting her. Her fever did not rise again. Nourished by rice and fish soup, she felt her strength returning. That afternoon, she unwrapped her journal and brought it up to date. Five days had passed since her last rambling entry, written while she and Hazen had waited for Pham at Van Yen. Five days of which she had only the haziest recollection. She knew that she had been close to death, and that without Hazen's care she would have died.

After lunch, Hazen disappeared for several hours. When he returned near nightfall, he wore a worried expression.

"What is it? Where have you been?" Emma asked.

"I wanted to see if there was any sign of Pham. He should have been back by now. I got as far as RC 6. There's been a lot of traffic on that road recently. While I was there, a group of French planes went over. Bombers. I wish I knew where they were headed."

"You were gone a long time. I was getting worried."

"If I had wanted to abandon you, Miss Vaughan, I would have done it long ago."

"Don't you think we can drop the formality?" Emma said. "After all, you've been my nursemaid for five days and my boss for longer than that. We could hardly be more intimate if we were man and wife."

Hazen threw a handful of twigs onto the fire. "I'm glad you didn't let the fire go out while I was away," he said, ignoring Emma's comment. "The stew should be warm in no time."

"Okay, I'll be a good little girl and eat my stew, but only if you give me the next installment of your adventures. What happened after you got back to London?"

Hazen waited until the flames from the twigs had subsided and the coals were glowing; then he put the clay pot on the hearth. "Just before D Day, I was parachuted into Germany again. Berlin. This time I posed as a Gestapo agent, using papers the British had confiscated from a man they'd captured in Belgium. The disguise was a pretty good one. I was able to enter railroad yards and factories, and if anyone stopped me, I simply flashed my identification papers and told them to get lost. I lasted about two months, until the real Gestapo tracked down my radio transmitter. I spent the rest of the war quarrying stone at Mauthausen, near Vienna."

"Mauthausen!" Emma sat bolt upright. "But that was a death camp. Worse than Dachau!"

Hazen stirred the rice with a wand of bamboo. "Out of two hundred thousand prisoners, half died. Some of them starved, others perished from cold and disease. Most of them were murdered. Somehow I hung on. When Patton's army liberated the camp, I weighed one hundred and five pounds. Not exactly a sterling specimen of American manhood. But it was a good lesson. I learned that I could survive anything, as long as I kept my faith in God and didn't give up hope."

"Those scars on your wrist. You had your numbers removed."

He nodded. "I spent a few months in a sanitarium in England.

Eventually I went back to my job at the university. But the lecture room felt too much like a prison cell. Like a lot of veterans, I couldn't settle down. I decided to become a minister, but I left the seminary after six months. I knocked around, became interested in geology while I was living on an Indian reservation in Nevada, and worked as a consultant for a couple of industrial firms before Chrome hired me. It's been a good job. They sent me to South America for a couple of years before moving me here."

"What about your daughter? Molly? Have you seen her since then?"

Hazen shrugged. "Once or twice. I generally try and visit her when I'm home between jobs for Chrome. But she has a new father now, and two little brothers. Like most thirteen-year-olds, she's more interested in music and boys than she is in a man she hardly recognizes. Perhaps when she's older." He stood and stretched.

The little bed of coals in the hearth glowed cheerfully. Outside the hut, the night was black, rain-soaked, full of nameless terrors.

"I noticed some interesting gaps toward the end of your story," Emma said. "From spy to geologist is a fairly incredible leap."

"Not really. I enjoy working for Chrome. I can travel and pursue my interests in natural science, and I get just enough danger and excitement to keep life bearable."

Emma left her bed. She approached the fire and knelt down beside him. "One more question—just to satisfy a reporter's insatiable curiosity. Thanks to a combination of luck, brains, and skill, you got out of Germany alive the first time. You could have stayed in England, helping the war effort by cracking codes or interpreting intelligence information. But you went back. Why?"

"Because I love my country and we were at war, and because they asked me to. But mostly because it was fun." His eyes gleamed. "Living in Germany under the Nazis was like being part of an equation in which most of the factors were unknown, and those that were known kept changing. Even at Mauthausen.

The odds against my surviving that place were incredible. I wanted to see if I could beat them. And I did."

Emma took his hand and turned the palm to the firelight. Like her, he still wore Old Willie's white thread. "These certainly haven't brought us much luck."

"Sure they have. We could have died in that plane crash."

On the inside of his wrist, half-hidden by his watchband, Emma found the shiny scars where the tattooed numbers that had identified him as a prisoner at Dachau and Mauthausen had been removed. "What about other people?" she asked. "If you ask me, love is the most difficult equation of all. One plus one equals an infinite number of possibilities."

Hazen withdrew his hand. "That particular science has never appealed to me."

"Why not? Are you that much like Von Stauffel, a crusty old bachelor, a hater of women?"

"Women have always intrigued me," Hazen admitted, "but then so do tigers and cobras. I've learned not to get too close to any of them."

"You and I aren't so different." Emma looked up into his face. "I failed algebra twice and I have trouble balancing my checkbook, and you're the world's smartest man, but we're still just a couple of fugitives on the run from the inevitable. In your case, it was becoming an ivy-encrusted monument at the University of Chicago. With me it was Edward and all the things he represented: squalling babies and household chores and a circle of friends that could only talk about diapers and corn futures and the latest scandal." With the tip of her finger she traced the line of his jawbone and chin. "The winds of fate have blown us up on a riverbank in what must be one of the most remote places in the entire world. I realize that I don't look like a beauty-contest winner right now, and you could do with a shave and a haircut yourself. But the lights are low and the wind makes pretty nice music. Don't tell me this is going to be the kind of night I can write home to my mother about."

Hazen stood up. "Go back to bed, Emma. It's late." He ducked out of the hut and vanished into the darkness.

Emma followed him to the doorway. Pressing her arms against her waist, she gazed into the swirling blackness. The mystery of Hazen's past was solved. Odd how as the barriers of secrecy crumbled, she had felt herself drawing closer to him. Perhaps she simply craved the warmth and strength of a fellow human being on this cruel and storm-tossed night. No, more than that. She wanted to give him something precious in return for his honesty. Like for like. The gift of her self.

Hazen stood at the edge of the creek, just a few feet away from the spot where their boat lay submerged. The rain had stopped and a chilling wind blew down from the mountains like regret.

Lilli Strauss. He remembered she had been seventeen when he arrived at their big house in Munich, the only one in her family who showed no fear at his presence under their roof. He had spent two months living in a walled-off corner of their attic, an airless pocket that Lilli had jokingly called the priest's hole. She visited him every evening, bringing newspapers and books from the library downstairs, plates of food, cigarettes when she could get them, taking away his chamberpot, his laundry, the bowl of dirty water in which he had bathed and shaved. During the day the house was filled with maidservants, patients, friends. Only after everyone had left was she able to attend to his needs. The rest of the family stayed away from him, Dr. Strauss having decided that the best way for them to deal with the guest in the attic was to forget that he was even there. Lilli had wanted to practice speaking English, and so the care and feeding of the fugitive had fallen to her.

He had only been there a week when he woke up to find her lying naked beside him. He was appalled; he still considered himself married to June and he had never been unfaithful to her. In the darkest hours of his confinement, he still nursed the hope that his family could be reunited someday. But Lilli had overwhelmed him. To her, sex was as natural and necessary as eating and drinking. It would keep him from going crazy, she said, cooped up in that little attic.

Falling in love with her had been so easy. Hazen realized later what a mistake that had been; for his sake, because she loved him and wanted to please him, she had taken foolish risks. He had scolded her, but she had laughed at his fears. Leaving Lilli had been harder than leaving his own wife and child. He had returned to Germany determined to win the war for her.

After his release from Mauthausen and a prolonged stay in a London hospital, he had made his way back to Munich. Officers of the U.S. army of occupation had taken over the house. A neighbor told him, and the records confirmed, that the Strausses had been arrested soon after his departure for Switzerland. They had been gassed at Dachau, all four of them.

In the attic, he found some of the books she had brought him: Goethe, Heine, Shakespeare. Love poems that had gained new meaning when he was with her.

She had said to him once, as they lay on his narrow mattress under the eaves, "We are the only sensible people in Germany tonight. In the middle of this crazy war, we have made happiness for ourselves. I don't care if I die tomorrow. At least I will know what life is really about."

The moon emerged from the clouds. It looked hard and cold, like a golden platter. Hazen heard a noise and turned. Emma stood a few feet away from him.

She approached him silently. Placing the palms of her hands against his chest, she kissed him very softly on the mouth. Hazen stopped breathing. Her kisses were warm and vital, more life-giving than sun or rain. She slid her hands under his shirt.

With a low groan, Hazen crushed her to his chest and kissed the base of her throat. She whimpered and the strength left her legs. Hazen swept her up and carried her into the hut. They didn't get as far as the bed. He took her on the hard floor near the hearth.

* * *

After the fire went out, the darkness in the house was complete but no longer menacing. Emma stroked the arm that lay across her shoulders as she listened to the renewed pounding of the rain and to the quiet rhythm of Hazen's breathing.

Old Willie would have been proud of her. She had worked her magic well.

11

APRIL 15, 1953

To: Mom and Aunt Louise
From: Your correspondent in Luang Prabang

That's right, folks, I am finally, officially,
wonderfully employed as the Chicago Tribune's
man—I mean girl—on the spot in Indochina!
When F. X. McGraw read my story about his
brother, he responded with an immediate job offer.
And he's going to publish my diary of the Black
River trip! I guess Alan Hazen's plan worked after
all, although there were times when I doubted
whether I would survive long enough to enjoy the
fruits of my success. . . . Here in Luang Prabang,
an invasion seems imminent. My first experience as
a front-line reporter! I can hardly wait!

With the first gray light of dawn, Hazen opened his eyes. He
rarely slept more than three hours a night, four when he
was really exhausted. Beside him, Emma lay on her side, her
knees drawn up to her waist and her head pillowed on her curved
arm. Hazen captured a golden curl and lifted it to his lips. The
rightness of what had happened overwhelmed him.

Leaning over Emma, he kissed her thighs and belly and
breasts. She awakened slowly, and smiled at him.

"Don't you ever sleep?"

"Not when I have something more important to do."

She received him warmly, and they rose and fell on the same
tide of longing and desire. He had just about reached the peak of
his excitement when she dug her fingernails into his back and
cried out, "Robert! Robert!"

The words affected him like a sudden shock of cold water. He shrank inside of her and withdrew. Emma rolled away from him, her passion spent.

Hazen stood in the doorway of the hut, his old pipe nestled in the palm of his hand. He remembered the first time he had smoked a pipe. He had been seventeen, a candidate for his master's degree and a teaching assistant at the university. His adviser had encouraged him to do something to make himself appear older in the eyes of his students, most of whom were older than he. More recently, Eliane had remarked on how he often toyed with his pipe while talking to strangers. He was still using it to shield himself from hurt.

Emma sat up and wrapped her blanket of parachute silk around her middle like a sarong. Outside, it was morning. The rain had stopped and a thick fog had settled over the village. More than ever she had the feeling that she and Hazen were stranded in this remote spot, the only humans to survive after the rest of the world had evaporated into mist.

"I'm sorry about what happened just now."

He shrugged. "I realize I was only a convenient substitute. You don't need to apologize."

"I know what you're thinking." Emma sat back on her heels. "But you're wrong. I am not in love with Robert Janvier anymore. I do not intend to see him again, ever. But I did feel very strongly about him once, and that sort of love is hard to forget."

Hazen looked over his shoulder. "You're kidding yourself if you think you can forget him. Do you know that you're scared to death of him? When you were delirious, you mistook me for him, and you screamed and prayed for someone to save you."

"That's a lie!" Emma clutched the blanket between her breasts. "I was sick, out of my head. I'm not afraid of Robert. He has always been very kind to me."

Hazen laughed unpleasantly. "Is that what you call it when a man blackens your eye and almost blinds you? Kindness?"

"He never—"

"Now you're lying to yourself, Emma. Trying to persuade

yourself that it was all a stupid mistake. Don't do it. If you go back to him, it will happen again."

"No, it won't! I won't let it."

"Your captain makes his living killing people. Have you thought about that, Emma? He's a mercenary, a paid murderer."

"Don't you dare call him that!"

"What kind of life can you expect with a man like that? You'll share his bed, bear his children, endure his slaps and kicks, and then lose him to a sniper's bullet or a hand grenade. God, why are women so stupid?"

Emma grabbed her blouse and shorts from the clothesline and pulled them on. "Why does a man think he owns a woman just because he's made love to her?" she raged. "I don't have any proprietary feelings toward you at all, Alan Hazen. None. I don't want you to be my lover or my brother or my father. Who needs fathers? Mine never did a thing for me. When he died, it was like he hadn't even been there. I learned at a very young age that I couldn't depend on a man to make me happy. How I handle my affair with Captain Janvier is my business. Maybe I won't see him at all after I get back to Saigon and maybe I will. I don't know. But I don't need to defend my actions to you. We're even now, okay? You pulled me out of the path of a bullet in Ta Prouhm and I pulled you out of the Black River. No more credits, no more debits."

They avoided each other for the rest of the morning. Hazen cleaned and oiled his pistol while Emma washed her hair and brought her diary up-to-date. She was aware of so many things she could not include, in the event that the book eventually found its way back to her mother.

At noon a French army GMC truck toiled through the mud of the village square and pulled up in front of the longhouse. A party of eight soldiers jumped out and covered the area with Sten guns. Emma, coming up from the river, regarded them with a mixture of gratitude and fear.

Hazen came out of the house. The officer in charge saluted

him. "Sergeant Chevasson, at your service." Hazen shook the sergeant's hand and introduced himself and Emma. "Are you the Americans who came down the Black River in a canoe?" the sergeant asked. "We were afraid we were walking into a trap. This Vietnamese appeared at our encampment the day before yesterday with a wild story about a geologist and a woman journalist flying over Tonkin and being shot down by the Viet Minh."

As he spoke, a soldier pulled Pham out of the back of the truck and led him toward the house. He prodded Pham with the muzzle of a rifle. Pham's hands were tied behind his back, and he limped along trying to avoid putting his weight on his right leg. A purple bruise glowed on his forehead.

"This man is my friend and assistant," Hazen told the sergeant. "Please release him."

Emma walked over to Pham and asked him if he was okay. He grinned at her while the soldier untied his hands. "Of course, madame," the Vietnamese said. "It was nothing."

Sergeant Chevasson informed them that they were in the heart of a battle zone. The French army had just recaptured Route Coloniale 6 from the Viet Minh, who had crossed the Laotian border ten days ago. The Viets had taken Sampeua, thirty miles to the south, and were pressing toward Luang Prabang, Laos's spiritual capital, a city of shrines and temples and palaces and the royal residence of King Sisavang Vong.

"Two planes will arrive at the Ban Na Ha airstrip tomorrow to drop off some supplies on their way to Luang Prabang. They will take you there if you wish."

Hazen accepted. He and Emma went inside their hut to grab up their few possessions. Emma said, "Is this what you were praying for last night? A miracle rescue?"

Hazen fitted his pipe carefully into his battered knapsack. "This wasn't the miracle I had in mind."

The truck in which they rode smelled of mildewed canvas, cigarette smoke, diesel fuel, and the warm, sweetish odor of too many men packed too closely together for too many hours. Emma remembered her journey through Cambodia with the men of the First Legion Paratroop Battalion. Riding along with Lucky Pierre and listening to him talk about his *copain*, she had already been head over heels in love with the handsome Captain Janvier. Now she wondered how she could have been so reckless. She had learned her lesson. As the truck bounced along through the mountains on this one-lane highway, she felt wonderfully relaxed and free. Janvier no longer had any hold over her.

At her side, Hazen endured the jogging ride over rough terrain with placid equanimity. His eyes were closed and his pipe was clamped between his teeth. One of the soldiers had given him some tobacco, and the first puffs of his pipe had brought a blissful smile to his haggard face.

Sergeant Chevasson's unit had commandeered the home of a French coffee planter named Letroyer. The plantation was located about ten miles from the deserted village of Moc Lam, at the end of a winding mountain road.

Despite repeated threats by the Viet Minh and orders from the French government to leave the area, Letroyer and his wife had stayed. They had turned their homestead into a fortress. A high cement wall topped by barbed wire and shards of broken glass now encircled the estate. All the windows were screened against grenades, and a party of plantation workers regularly patrolled the compound. To their number were added Chevasson's troops, who were bivouacked on the grounds.

Emma was astounded when the sergeant told her that the arms and ammunition she saw inside the house belonged to the Letroyers rather than to the army.

The centerpiece on the dining room table was a bowl filled with cartridges for the rifles and pistols that lay on the windowsills. Photographs of the family, which included two half-grown children away at school in France, were scattered among boxes of hand grenades on the sideboard. In the midst of this arsenal, servants wearing the dark blouses of the Black Thai tribe calmly came and went with their trays of canapés and aperitifs.

Treating the new arrivals as honored guests, Monsieur Letroyer plied them with brandy, cigarettes, and wine from a supply as large as his stock of ammunition. Before dinner Emma indulged in a long soak in a steaming tub; then she put on a flowered silk frock that had belonged to the daughter of the house, whose room she was using. She was pleased to see that the bruises on her face were fading fast. Like the memories of her journey with Alan Hazen. Both seemed to belong to another time.

Sergeant Chevasson and two other noncommissioned officers joined them for dinner. They feasted on roast wild pig, freshly dug sweet potatoes, and canned white asparagus spears, and they enjoyed canned peaches topped with meringue for dessert. Emma, seated across the table from Hazen, gave him a cocky grin. The abrupt end of their adventure had left her feeling exhilarated and somewhat giddy. Her illness was completely gone and she felt ravenous after ten days of near starvation. Nonetheless, she was unable to eat very much of the rich food. She drank three glasses of wine and had eagerly accepted a fourth when she saw the disapproving set of Hazen's mouth. Hazen drank mineral water with his meal.

After dinner, they adjourned to the parlor to sip cordials and to sample some of Monsieur Letroyer's excellent coffee. In one corner, Madame Letroyer worked on a piece of tatting. The house was full of examples of her handiwork: lace antimacassars, place mats and doilies, knitted lap robes, crocheted curtains. She was small, thin and drab, so lifeless that the tropics seemed to have sucked all traces of animation from her face and every part of her body except her fingers. These moved ceaselessly, with a feverish, mesmerizing rhythm, as they wove a strand of fine thread into a destiny far more elaborate than the terrifying present.

Emma leaned forward and addressed a question to Monsieur Letroyer. After months of intensive study, her French vocabulary was adequate and her grammar was correct, but her American accent was still heavy. "Why do you stay here, monsieur, when the enemy is so near?"

"Why? Because every penny I have is invested in this plantation, that is why. Besides, where else could I live like this, almost like a king on my own land? I have servants to shine my shoes, to heat my bath water, to rake my gardens. And I pay them almost nothing. I am confident that France will win this war. But until they do, I must stay here and defend my property."

Emma glanced at his wife, but Madame Letroyer did not look up from her flashing needle.

Sergeant Chevasson predicted that the current Viet Minh push would run out of steam before it reached Luang Prabang. The enemy was overextending itself, moving too far from its supply bases.

"But the Viets don't have supply bases," Emma protested. She avoided looking at Hazen, seated in a chintz-covered armchair on the other side of the room. "They carry everything they need with them: food, weapons, ammunition. You French are so loaded down with heavy vehicles and massive artillery pieces and supplies that you can hardly move. When will you learn that you're not fighting a conventional war here?"

"I did not know that mademoiselle was an expert on military strategy," Chevasson said with a patronizing smile.

"I'm not. But I do know that nobody's going to win this war. Whatever happens, the Vietnamese people will be the losers."

"Emma, these men know what they're talking about," Hazen said.

"And so do I," Emma declared. "I know that this war only came about because a small nation wanted to throw off a colonial oppressor. I think the French ought to pull out right now and declare peace. Let the Vietnamese determine their own destiny."

"You're talking like a naïve kid." Hazen sipped coffee from a tiny demitasse cup. "This show is being run in Moscow and Peking. Things will be no better under the communists. In fact, they'll be worse."

"You sound like everybody else in Washington these days," Emma sniffed. "Scared stiff of the Red Menace."

"You're damned right I'm sacred. Let me tell you what life will be like with Ho Chi Minh as president. Every man, woman, and child in this country will undergo thorough political indoctrination. A network of neighborhood spies and Party cadres will establish files on all the citizens. Nothing will be secret: how many times a week a man makes love to his wife; how much money he has hoarded away in the coffee can under the bed; how often he attends education and self-criticism sessions; what he reads; what he says; what he thinks. Those files will be used by the secret police to keep the masses in their place. And anyone who complains about the system will end up in a human refuse bin, with numbers tattooed on his arm."

"Monsieur is right," Chevasson chimed in. "The leaders of the Viet Minh are prepared to sacrifice hundreds of thousands of soldiers in order to win this war. A single life means nothing to them. They are monsters, worse than the Nazis."

"They're just poor people trying to make a country for themselves," Emma insisted. "Why won't you give them a chance?"

"I think you'd better go to bed, Emma."

"Why?" she demanded. "Why do you want to get rid of me?"

"Because you're making a fool of yourself. You had too much to drink—"

"And now I'm drunk. Good." As she rose to her feet, she swayed unsteadily. "I would rather be a drunk with feelings than a pig-faced capitalist who thinks the people of this country were put here to be his servants. I would rather be a peaceful drunk than a soldier who uses his uniform as a license to torture innocent people like Pham. And I would rather be any kind of drunk than a heartless adding machine like yourself, Mr. Hazen. Don't bother to get up. I can find my way. Good night, ladies and gentlemen." She dropped an exaggerated curtsy, then lifted her chin and marched out of the room.

Emma sat down on the edge of her bed and rested her crossed arms on the footboard. It was rounded and carved and covered with a veneer of bird's-eye maple. The room, with its fluffy pink curtains and hand-crocheted lace bedspread over a pink satin liner, had belonged to the Letroyers' daughter. Emma wondered if the girl would ever see her childhood home again.

She lay down but, feeling the room begin to spin, got up again and stumbled to the window. She pushed her fingers through the bedroom window's iron mesh that kept the terrors of the night at bay. Alan Hazen was a perfectly loathsome man. The sooner they got to the airfield at Ban Na Ha, the better. She would fly around the world ten times just to get away from him.

Seeing a shadow flit along the garden wall about thirty feet from her window, Emma frowned. Surely she didn't need to be concerned. Sergeant Chevasson had stationed several men outside to guard the house. Something warned her—a rustle, a sharp movement, or a latent instinct for danger—and she threw herself down on the floor near the bed just as a bullet shattered the mirror over the dressing table.

Cold sober now, she crawled along the floor until she reached the light switch and turned it off. Than she opened the door to the hall. "Alan! Monsieur Letroyer!" she called. Just then a mighty explosion shook the house to its foundations and all the lights went out.

"Emma, where are you?"

The beam of a flashlight blinded her. Hazen reached her as another explosion shook the house. He pushed her down and threw himself on top of her. Emma heard the sound of glass shattering somewhere in the house.

Hazen helped her to stand. "The Viets are shelling us. We've got to get out of here."

They found Sergeant Chevasson at the front of the house. Two personnel carriers and three jeeps were revved up, ready to move out as soon as he had rounded up all of his men.

"The Viets have mortars in the hills," he shouted to Hazen. "This place is a trap. You see, some of the sheds are already on fire. If a shell hits the house, it will go up like an atom bomb. Get into that truck and wait for me. I will order monsieur and madame to come with us."

"My notebook!" Emma grabbed Hazen's flashlight and ran past

him into the house. She heard him call her name, but she ignored him. In her room, she scooped all her belongings back into her canvas carryall. She had paid too much for the stories in her notebook to leave it behind.

In the dining room, the Letroyers were working by the light of a lantern. Monsieur Letroyer was loading a pair of grenade launchers while his wife checked the action of all the rifles that were piled under the windows. Emma told them they must leave at once. The trucks would take them to safety. Eliciting no response from her host, she appealed to his wife.

"You cannot stay here. They will burn your house down around your ears. Come with us, madame, I implore you."

The woman shook her head. "I must stay here." The hard glint in her eye showed her close to madness. "Stay here."

Chevasson came in and began to argue with them. Then he turned to Emma. "It is no use, they won't listen. Go to the truck at once. We're getting out of here."

He had barely finished issuing that command when a shell landed in the garden outside. Flying stones shattered the windows. The house seemed to groan and list toward the crater. Emma followed the sergeant outside. Pham was waiting for her. He boosted her into the back of one of the trucks and jumped in after her. Hazen was already inside. Emma collapsed into the only remaining seat and hugged her canvas bag to her chest.

"They won't leave," she said. "The Letroyers. I don't understand it."

"They have nothing else to live for." Hazen shrugged. "We'll be lucky if we make it out of here ourselves."

At Chevasson's signal, the drivers engaged their gears and took off. The trucks and jeeps roared out of the compound and hurtled along a rutted lane toward the main road. A machine gunner mounted on the roof of the vehicle in front sprayed their path with bullets. From the darkness, the enemy fired on the length of the convoy as it passed. Hazen pushed Emma down on the floor and, leaning over her, protected her with his body.

"Get ready to jump out," he told her. "If we're stopped, we'll take off into the jungle."

After a few more stray shots the road was clear. As the convoy wound up the mountainside, Hazen said, "Look back."

In the east, they saw an orange glow. Even as they watched, an explosion shook the mountain and rattled the treetops. Then, as if a doorway from hell had opened, a huge column of fire and flame-colored smoke filled the sky above the plantation.

"Letroyer's arsenal," Hazen said. "Madame is probably crocheting wings for the two of them right now."

"Don't." Emma fingered the dress she was wearing. She had never thought to take it off. "They didn't need to die like that."

The following afternoon after the fog had lifted, Hazen, Emma, and Pham crammed themselves into a cargo plane filled with crates of Vinogel and cases of ammunition. As the propellers began to turn, Emma felt her old terror returning. Before takeoff she took her notebook out of her bag and held it in her lap in a fierce grip. Then she closed her eyes and did not open them again until the plane had landed safely at Luang Prabang forty minutes later.

As they stood under the wing, out of the way of the crew members, Hazen said stiffly, "Will you be flying back to Saigon with us?"

"No, I thought I'd stay here and cover the invasion."

"Do you have any money?"

"No, but—"

"I don't have any cash, but I can give you a letter of credit authorizing you to withdraw unlimited funds from Chrome's account. My signature is good in this part of the country. Do you have a piece of paper?"

With all her heart, Emma wanted to refuse his offer. But she was broke, and she had no choice. She ripped a page out of her notebook and handed it to Hazen with a pencil.

"I'll pay you back as soon as my stories start to sell," she said.

"Don't bother. I'll chalk it up to Chrome as a business expense."

"I would prefer to pay you," she insisted.

Shrugging, he made a few scratches with the pencil and handed over the paper. Emma thanked him and slipped it into her notebook.

Without another word of farewell, Hazen and Pham walked toward a C-47 transport plane scheduled to leave for Saigon within the next half hour. Emma watched them for a moment; then she hoisted her canvas bag up on her shoulder and walked toward the town.

When Emma saw the high mountains that surrounded Luang Prabang, she was glad she had had the sense to keep her eyes closed while their plane was landing. Rugged peaks embraced the city on all sides. In the softly diffused light of late afternoon, Laos' spiritual capital looked like a postcard of itself. Above the trees, towers and steeples and stupas of green and white and gold displayed themselves against the beige sky. At the summit of the steep hill known as the Phousi, a golden temple spire thrust its way skyward like a pointing finger or a spiritual directional. At the start of the rainy season, the Mekong River flowed strong and dark along the rim of the town.

Whereas Vientiane, the administrative capital of Laos, had two main streets, Luang Prabang, the country's royal capital, had only one, broad and rutted and filled with the slow-moving traffic of a poor country whose people had little to sell and not much money to buy.

Emma found the Post and Telegraph office in a shabby stuccoed building in the center of town. The Luang Prabang branch of the Crédit National adjoined the post office, and indeed the postmaster seemed ready to assume the task of teller when Emma told him that she could find no one in the bank to help her. She explained that she wanted to borrow some money from Chrome Petroleum using Hazen's letter of credit, and that she wanted to send two telegrams, one very short and one very long. After forty minutes of thinking and waiting, the old man took Hazen's letter, her passport, and her travel permit.

"Come back two days," he said. "No here tomorrow."

Across the street, Emma took a room at the Hotel Caravelle, whose lobby, with its lazily swirling ceiling fan and pots of half-dead palms, reminded her of a set from an old movie. The Chinese clerk at the desk spoke no English and only indifferent French. He treated Emma like an intruder rather than a guest.

Up in her room, Emma rinsed her face and brushed her teeth. Turning away from the sink, where the thin trickle of tepid water ran red with rust, she saw an enormous rat amble across the floor and disappear behind the dresser. Despair flooded over her. What was she doing in this place? She was waiting for a war that might never materialize, so that she could write about it for a newspaper that didn't even know her name. She sat on the edge of the bed and cried for ten minutes; then she marched down to the desk and demanded that the clerk either give her a new room or equip her with a baseball bat. He had no trouble understanding her.

Within four days, the Caravelle was crowded with journalists who had flown up from Saigon to cover the invasion. They were amazed to find Emma Vaughan already ensconced in the hotel's best room. She was full of information about the impending assault, and on friendly terms with the French infantrymen who were camped on the eastern edge of the city.

Best of all, Emma had mastered the use of the telegraph office. Two days after her wires had been sent, she received two messages from Chicago. One was a draft for five hundred dollars; the second said simply, "WELCOME ABOARD CABLE FULL DETAILS SIEGE LUANG PRABANG AIRMAIL OTHER STORIES SOONEST CONTRACT FOLLOWS F X"

The Viet Minh were rapidly closing in on the royal capital. To the east, the little village of Muongsung, thirty-five miles away, was now at the heart of the fighting. Refugees from the countryside streamed into the city, where they pitched camp in the parks, on the lawns, and in the temples. Every day the fighting moved closer. Soon the nights brought displays of fireworks on the eastern horizon. The sounds of warfare shattered the quietude of this sleepy capital: planes, bombs, hand grenades, machine guns.

One morning a week after her arrival in Luang Prabang, Emma awoke to see a squad of women and children filling sandbags outside the hotel. Hoping to hear the latest rumors about the invasion, she joined them. Down in the street, the women were saying that the enemy was only twelve miles away. Emma found herself working between a Laotian hotel maid and the wife of the British ambassador.

"The Viets have never come this close before," the English woman said. "Oh, they cross the border every year—it's a sort of rite of spring. The French have been bombing rebel positions since dawn. I don't know what they hope to accomplish, except to churn up the rice paddies and destroy the villages. Still, twelve miles away— So far, I haven't heard anyone talk about evacuating. Old King Sisavang Vong has absolutely refused to leave. He believes, like his people, that Buddha will protect his city."

But the other reporters from Saigon, who had gone straight from their beds to the bar of the Caravelle, were predicting that this was the year the Viet Minh would finally take Luang Prabang.

"God knows, the French aren't getting any kind of support from home," Emma heard one of them say when she stopped in at noon for a daiquiri to anesthetize her aching muscles. "They need more men, but Paris just ordered them to withdraw three divisions. I hear Ike is going to lend them a few Flying Boxcars. Transport planes aren't going to win this war."

"It's the communists, you know," a British correspondent said. "France came back in 'forty-six determined to reassert her rights over an old colony, and the Americans didn't lift a bloody finger to help. But now that the French have found themselves in a war against communism, the Yanks are backing them to the hilt."

After lunch, Emma strolled down to the marketplace. She

passed buckets of live eels and trays of fish, including one two-hundred pounder netted in the Mekong River that morning. Along the length of the street, the pepper merchants sat in a row in front of a long length of white cloth, on which were displayed clusters of ruby-colored pods and tin bowls filled with red powder that Emma knew from experience could set the mouth of an unsuspecting diner on fire.

None of the shoppers seemed disturbed by the prospect of a Viet Minh take-over. The women of the Meo tribe, with their black-turbaned heads and silver neck hoops, stood out from all the others. Emma had learned that the kingdom of Laos was actually a peaceful confederation of the Meos and dozens of other tribes, including tribes of the Kha and Thai peoples. Each group had its own customs, its own beliefs, its own legends. But the world was changing around them, thrusting twentieth-century ideas and weapons into their fifteenth-century lives. The demons and evil spirits who brought them poor harvests, sickness, and bad luck were being shoved aside by an even more destructive demon: modern warfare.

Leaving her shoes at the door, Emma entered the Temple of the Golden Buddha, not far from the royal palace where King Sisavang Vong was praying that his city would be spared in the fighting. Inside the temple, old women planted burning joss sticks in great bronze urns filled with sand. Bald-headed *bonzes* in orange robes sat frozen in meditative postures in front of the high altar, from which a seated Buddha cast his sleepy, benevolent gaze on his followers. Here all was peaceful. The rumble in the distance might have been thunder instead of the bombing of villages by French aircraft. The war had not intruded here.

That night Jean-Claude Berri, a young clerk from the French Ministry of Transport who had befriended Emma shortly after her arrival in Luang Prabang, joined her while she was having a cup of coffee in the hotel lounge. He suggested to her that they go for a stroll. They started off toward the temple, Jean-Claude casting furtive looks over his shoulder.

"What's the matter?" Emma asked.

"Hush! The walls have ears!"

Emma refrained from telling him that his efforts to be invisible could be seen a hundred yards away.

"A friend wants to meet you." Berri's eyes darted lizardlike from side to side as he looked for eavesdroppers. "He would not be welcome in a place like this."

They waited for nearly two hours in a park in front of the royal palace, on a bench under a dripping tamarind tree. Just as Emma was about to give up and go back to her hotel, Jean-Claude's friend arrived. He was a slender young Lao who had been educated at the University of Hanoi and had once been employed by the Ministry of Transport as a clerk, in the same office as Jean-Claude Berri.

"Ngoan is a member of the Pathet Lao," Berri explained. "They want you to tell their side of the war in your newspaper. I promised him that you would not betray him."

"Of course not." Emma turned to the young man and addressed him in her halting French. "Are the soldiers of the Pathet Lao supporting the Viet Minh?" They were. "I don't understand. You are helping foreigners who have invaded your country to expel foreigners who are already here. Don't you find that a strange contradiction?" The Viet Minh were friendly, Ngoan said. The French were the real enemy, and also the Americans, who were aiding them. His tribesmen had a saying: Better a tiger you can see than one you cannot see. When the revolution had succeeded and the French had gone, the Viet Minh would withdraw. "Do you wish to depose the king?" Emma asked. "To assassinate him?" Certainly not! Ngoan looked shocked. The king was their father and their friend. They simply wanted to purge all foreign influences from his court and his country.

Emma found the encounter disappointing. Ngoan, with his contradictions and elaborate system of apologetics, had been a most unsatisfactory source. Steeped in jargon and superstition, he had offered nothing in the way of hard facts—numbers of soldiers, amounts of war materiel, names of local Pathet Lao leaders. But he had been full of empty words—quotes from Ho and Mao, and declarations of hatred against the French. Ngoan was not as fanatical a communist as some, Jean-Claude Berri had informed her before they parted that night. But then, he was a Lao, and everyone knew the Laos didn't like to expend too much energy on any cause.

She met Ngoan two more times after that, without Jean-Claude. None of her interviews was more revealing than the first, but she began to feel that more was at stake than a simple exchange of information. Ngoan was testing her, weighing her trustworthiness. She was discouraged when, at the end of their third meeting, he did not reveal his plans, but merely suggested that she stand at the door of the Catholic church tomorrow evening at nine o'clock. Emma agreed and slogged back to her hotel through the rain.

Emma was crossing the Caravelle's veranda when she heard someone call her name. Icy prickles ran up and down her spine. Robert Janvier hobbled toward her. He was leaning on a cane. "Eliane de Mornay told me you were here."

Emma was shocked at the changes a few weeks had wrought in his appearance. He was gaunt and pale, with the smudged eyes and sunken cheeks of an invalid.

"You've been wounded!"

"A punji trap." Janvier shrugged and smiled. "I should have been more careful."

"How—how did you get here?"

"I got a ride on a plane from Saigon to Vientiane this morning; then some friends in the Second BEP brought me here."

"I didn't want—why did you? I didn't—I didn't think I would see you again," she finished lamely.

"I wanted to see you." His eyes were dark with longing. "A few minutes, that is all I ask."

"All right." Emma glanced at the night clerk, dozing under a month-old copy of *Paris Match*. "We can sit in the lounge. No one's in there now."

As they were seating themselves in a couple of sprung-out arm-chairs, Janvier extracted something from his pocket. "I have brought you a small gift."

Emma opened the little velvet box he handed her. A carved jade ring rested on a satin cushion. She had never seen anything so delicate or so fine. An intricate strand of green leaves and flowers encircled a fragile woody stem of gold filigree. At the heart of a small carved rose nestled a diamond.

"It's beautiful."

"I wanted to find you, to apologize, but I discovered that you had left Saigon with the American. Emma, what happened that night—I was not myself. I was not the man who loves you." Janvier took her right hand and raised it to his lips. "May God strike me dead if I touch you again in anger."

If she slipped the ring on her finger, he would know that she forgave him. She could not do it. She could not speak. Her mind had completely turned off. Time passed as she watched the tiny jade vines twisting around the sparkling rose. They seemed to be moving, growing, winding tighter and tighter until they were almost choking—

Janvier tapped his leg with his cane. "I have paid for my sin against you, Emma. This happened the day after you left Saigon. My leg was pierced in six places with bamboo arrows that had been smeared with excrement or rotten meat. The wounds became infected. In a matter of hours the leg was twice its normal size." He laughed. "But I have an excellent liver. It cleared all the poisons away. No wooden legs for me."

A tear fell on Emma's hand. Janvier left his chair and knelt stiffly beside her. He took the ring and placed it on her finger. She did not stop him. Rising, he drew her upward and kissed her. The kiss pierced through layers of anger and resolve and banished all her fears and misgivings. The old hunger for him returned, stronger and fiercer than ever.

Slowly, accompanied by the tapping of Janvier's cane, they walked out into the lobby and climbed the stairs.

* * *

"But why must you leave me?"

Emma slipped on her dress, buckled her sandals, and made sure her shoulder bag contained her notebooks and plenty of sharpened pencils. Janvier lounged on the bed, a bottle of beer in one hand and a cigarette in the other.

"I'm meeting a contact. I have the feeling something important is going to happen tonight."

"Ah ha, another man. I am very jealous."

Emma smiled at him. "You don't need to be. You know you're the only man in my life. I will never love anyone the way I love you." She gave him a hasty kiss, which he wanted to prolong, and then wriggled away from him. "I'll be back in an hour or two. Don't get too lonely."

She was five minutes late for her rendezvous with Ngoan at the Church of Saint Jerome. She hoped he hadn't given up on her. Twenty minutes later, he appeared at her elbow.

"Come," he said. "We must go at once."

"Go?" Emma was startled. "Where?"

"They want to meet you. Now. Tonight. We must go now. Right away!" Ngoan was insistent.

"Who are we meeting? How far is it?"

"You ask too many questions. Come, we have a long way to go."

They entered the dimly lighted church and walked along a side aisle to an exit near the sanctuary. As the door closed behind them, Emma saw that they were in a small walled graveyard. Ngoan hissed and beckoned to her. Hoping her sandals would survive a long journey, Emma followed. They left the churchyard through a rusty gate in the wall at the far end, passed along a narrow alley that reeked of rotting vegetables and cooking oil, and found themselves on a narrow jungle path.

They walked for three hours, with only a fitful moon lighting their way. Just when Emma was limp with fatigue and about to declare that she could not go any further, they arrived at a small clearing in the mountains high above Luang Prabang. A sentry challenged them, but he let them pass when Ngoan spoke to him. He and Emma approached the entrance of a limestone cave. Inside they found a half dozen men seated on matting woven of the same tough elephant grass the local tribesmen used to thatch their roofs. Ngoan went up to the man in the center of the group, a powerful-looking Lao with thick black hair, wide intelligent eyes, and the tanned complexion of one who has spent his life out of doors. Ngoan made a deep obeisance, then pressed his palms together and touched his fingertips to his forehead. The other man nodded impatiently and switched his glance to Emma.

"Welcome, Mademoiselle Vaughan." He spoke perfect French.

"Who are you?" she asked, unable to contain her curiosity a moment longer.

"I am Souphanouvong," he said simply.

Emma gasped. This was the notorious Red Prince, who had founded the communist-oriented Pathet Lao, or Land of the Lao, movement. Her patience with Ngoan had paid off. She was about to score a real journalistic coup, a scoop: an exclusive interview with Laos' renegade prince, whom the French regarded as a dangerous radical, a threat equal to Vietnam's Ho Chi Minh.

The prince invited her to sit down. Emma accepted a cup of tea; then Souphanouvong said, "Now we will talk." The other men rose and left the cave. Emma was surprised. Her experience in the Far East had led her to expect a long exchange of pleasantries before getting down to business.

The prince told her that he had studied road and bridge building in Paris. He and his two brothers were the only engineers in Laos. He described the Frenchmen he had met in Bordeaux and Le Havre, so different in their attitudes from the colonials he had met in his homeland. After returning home, the new engineer had been unable to find work in his own country and had taken his skills to Vietnam. There he had seen how French masters exploited the workers in the labor camps and rubber plantations. His hatred hardened into resolve. In 1946, he led his new Pathet Lao forces against the French. They were defeated by that nation's superior air and fire power. Seriously wounded, with a price on his head, Souphanouvong fled to Thailand. He returned in 1947 to lead resistance forces against the puppet government in Vientiane, headed by his half brother Souvanna Phouma. The king, Sissavang Vong, who resided in Luang Prabang, was old and rheumatic and served only as a figurehead.

"Your brother does not share your beliefs," Emma said. Souvanna Phouma, a moderate, had the support of the French and Americans.

The prince shrugged. "We both want peace and independence for our country, but he wants aid from foreigners to help us build. I say that to accept help puts us in debt to these other powers."

"But you have already accepted help from the Viet Minh." Emma looked back over her notes. "You said your first meeting with Ho Chi Minh took place in 1945."

He nodded. "The Viet Minh do not want to colonize and exploit Laos. They want to help us in our struggle against the imperialists. In 1949, I visited General Vo Nguyen Giap in his jungle camp. He taught me well. The French will not beat us again. We will wait to fight until we are certain we can win. That is the first rule of guerrilla warfare."

Emma's pencil flew over her notebook page. She was grateful for the hours she had spent drilling herself in shorthand in high school.

Finally the Red Prince stood up to signal an end to the interview. Emma thanked him. Ngoan reappeared and escorted her away from the mountaintop and back down the trail to Luang Prabang. He left her at the edge of the city.

At six in the morning, the streets of the capital were empty except for a few oxcarts bringing goods from the countryside. Emma could hardly wait to tell Janvier about her incredible luck. The hotel doors were open but the night clerk was nowhere in sight. She ran upstairs, entered her room quietly, and stripped off her clothes and shoes.

The light was dim, but as she lifted the mosquito netting she saw not one but two naked bodies sprawled on the bed. At first

Emma thought she had entered the wrong room. Then she noticed Janvier's cane and red beret sitting on the chair in the corner. Grasping the netting with both hands, she jerked it down from the ceiling.

"Get her out of here!" she shrieked. "How dare you bring a whore in here? This is my room! Get out of here, both of you!"

The girl, one of the hotel maids, leaped out of the bed and ran screaming into the hall without even stopping to grab her clothing.

Emma was shouting and crying hysterically. "I hate you—hate you, Robert. You can't even be faithful to me for a single night. How could you do this? Why? Making love to that woman—get out, get out, get out!"

Janvier wallowed through the fallen netting and bounded over to her. "Be quiet! Do you want to wake everyone in this place?"

"I don't care—hate you—get away from me!"

"Silence!" Janvier roared. As he shook her, her head snapped back and forth so violently that she feared it would break off. Weeping, keening, she broke free of him. She threw her dress on over her head and ran out of the room. Her bare feet slapped on the tiles in the hall.

The doors of the Church of Saint Jerome were open. Inside, Emma threw herself down on a prie-dieu, buried her head in her arms, and sobbed.

12

MAY 17, 1953

Dear Aunt Louise,

. . . since I got back to Saigon. The monsoon
season is here, and I guess I'm feeling low because
of the weather, which is unbelievably sticky and
hot. Some days I can hardly drag myself
around. . . . The rain never stops, it just pauses to
catch its breath and to refill its tanks, and then it
falls all the harder. This morning the sun was
shining, but it was just a cruel joke. Ten minutes
later, it was pouring again. This time of year, the
rain and the wind are as inevitable as fate.

Emma and the other journalists returned to Saigon in the middle of May, the attack on Luang Prabang having failed to materialize. When French forces stopped a Viet Minh battalion only nine miles from the capital, the enemy pulled back and vanished into the jungle, once again denying the French commanders the pitched battle for which they kept hoping. The king of Laos declared his city out of danger, and within a few days life in that sleepy capital was back to normal.

Back in Saigon, Monsieur de Chesnay was pleased to see his tenant. "An American gentleman, a Monsieur Hazen, came to see me a few weeks ago. He gave me an account of your adventures in the north. What courage! You told me before you left that you would only be gone for a few days, and here it is almost two months since I saw you last."

"Has anyone else called or left a message?" Emma asked.

Monsieur de Chesnay was not fooled. "You mean your Legion captain? No, mademoiselle. You have some mail, letters from your mother and aunt, and one from Chicago. The city of Al Capone, eh? Bang, bang, bang!" He postured with an invisible tommy gun and sprayed his paintings with imaginary bullets.

After cashing her second check from Chicago, Emma put together a bundle of piasters to tally with her withdrawals from Hazen's Chrome Petroleum account. She left it with the secretary in Hazen's office. Eventually she would thank Hazen in person for his assistance. But for the moment, she did not want to see him.

During the rainy season, the pace of the war in the countryside slowed. A good time, said the pundits, for the new commander of French forces in Indochina, General Navarre, to learn the ropes. An equally good time for correspondents to extend their network of contacts and to revitalize established relationships.

With his line to the inner workings of the military high command and the movements of the soldiers in the field, Captain Janvier had been invaluable to Emma. Well, she would have to rally her energies and search out new sources. In her new position as Indochina correspondent for a major American newspaper, she owed it to herself to meet as many people as possible, to cultivate a wide variety of friendships. And to stay away from involvements of the heart, which would only interfere with her work.

But she had no energy to enter into the fray again. Instead, she sat in her room hour after hour, doing nothing. She found herself returning repeatedly to her old haunts. She bought bouquets from the same flower seller from whom Janvier had purchased bunches of violets and lilies for her. At the Portail Bookstore, she bought the same magazines that Janvier had liked, and read them, she told herself, to improve her French. And after a few days, she started going to the Café de la Paix on Rue Catinat every evening between six and seven-thirty. She swore inwardly that she did not want to see him, but her feet took her again and again along the routes she had walked with Robert Janvier. She had dinner alone in Janvier's favorite restaurants, frequently at the Star of the East on Avenue Gallieni, where they had gone on numerous occasions.

And then, he came. Eleven days after her return to Saigon, she looked up from her table in the café and saw Janvier striding toward her with only a suggestion of a limp.

"My wounds are completely healed," he said after he had ordered a Pernod. "A good thing. I have finally received my orders, now that the doctors have decided that this leg of mine will hold up to a parachute jump again. I go to Hanoi on the first of July." He covered her hand with his. "What a time you gave me in Luang Prabang, eh?" He laughed. "I had no idea what had happened to you that night. And after such a happy reunion, no? I was devastated. And then to burst in on me at five in the morning. What a surprise! I was startled out of my senses."

Janvier stroked Emma's hand gently. His eyes filled with tears that miraculously did not fall. "Emma," he said, "you are not wearing my ring. Have you forgotten me?"

Without a word, Emma pulled a long golden chain out from under her blouse. Janvier's ring gleamed in her hand. It felt hot to the touch, burning with the captured warmth from her breasts. Slowly she unfastened the clasp and slipped the ring off the chain, then placed it on her finger.

Janvier smiled. "I love you, Emma. *Chérie.*"

"I love you, too, Robert."

Their fingers meshed. Emma's body came alive again. Energy flowed from Janvier's eyes into her own. It was like a powerful elixir, a stimulant. Her breathing quickened.

"You must come with me to Hanoi." Janvier's smile widened into a grin. "We will find a flat near the Petit Lac, and you will cook for me while I teach you all about love and war. In a few months, you will become a very important foreign correspondent, making lots of money. And then we can hire someone to cook for both of us." His laughter was like a blessing, a gift of rain to a parched field. She wondered how she could have imagined life without him. "We will spend the rest of our lives together, making love every morning and every evening." He stood up and held out his hand to her. "Walk with me, Emma. I want to put my arm around you. I won't disappoint you again, I swear it. You have nothing to fear from me."

They left the café without seeing Eliane de Mornay, who was seated with her back to them. By holding her compact a few inches from her nose, she could observe the other patrons in the room in the mirror. Her elegant eyebrows rose. "That Janvier is certainly persistent," she said. "I think that was their first meeting since she returned to Saigon. That man isn't satisfied until his women drown themselves in rivers of tears—or blood. He killed a woman, you know. Back in Algeria, a few years ago. Or so I have heard. Perhaps it is only a vicious rumor started by that ridiculous woman—you know, that British female Legionnaire who cannot make up her mind what sex she wants to be. Waiter, two more coffees, if you please. That reporter surprised him, you know, by running off with you. He didn't expect that. Is it true he almost beat her to death? She certainly looks ravishing now."

The newspaper Alan Hazen was pretending to read trembled slightly. "Yes," he said, "she was badly hurt." He folded the newspaper away and stared after the retreating pair.

"I hope you took advantage of your journey together to warn her about the dangers of continuing to see that man."

Hazen swallowed. "She said—she swore she wasn't going to see him again. I—she must have changed her mind."

"He will destroy her." Eliane's expression was unusually solemn. Then a smile tugged at the corners of her mouth. "Tell me, just between the two of us, did you take advantage of the situation in other ways as well?"

Hazen stood up and threw down a handful of piasters on the table. "See you later," he said, heading for the door.

Sheltered under Emma's tattered umbrella, she and Janvier walked down Rue Catinat to the waterfront. Their smiles and soft laughter recalled the nights they had smoked opium in Cholon, the night they had first made love.

"I'm so happy," Emma sighed. "I was terrified that you didn't want me anymore."

"Emma, *ma chérie*, I have always wanted you. Quickly, in here!" Janvier pulled her into the darkened entryway to a warehouse.

"Why?" Craning her neck so that she could peer over his shoulder, Emma scanned the street. She expected to see a sniper on the opposite roof or a bicyclist in the act of hurling a hand grenade.

"Because I want to make love to you." He pressed her back against the wall and dragged her skirt up around her hips.

Emma wondered vaguely if she should object, urge him to wait until they found a bed, either in her room or a hotel. Making love on the busiest street in Saigon, inches away from the rush of traffic and pedestrians— Then desire struck with the searing power of a lightning bolt. She moved with him on a crescendo of sighs until they were both gasping and laughing and sobbing with the deliciousness of it.

"You are mine," Janvier said in a hoarse whisper. "You belong to me, Emma. Never forget that. You belong to me."

The rest of May was a prolonged honeymoon. Janvier courted Emma like a French gentleman, bringing her exotic gowns, taking her to expensive restaurants, ordering the most extravagant dinners and the finest champagnes. She knew that his pay as a soldier must be meager, and she protested that she did not need to live in such an ostentatious manner. The whirl of their social activities ceased only when they spent an entire day in bed in an orgy of lovemaking. Perhaps, Emma reasoned, Janvier was getting rich by exchanging piasters for francs, as were many people in Saigon who had the right connections. Basking in the warmth of his attention, she could not think about anything or anyone else.

At the end of the month, General Navarre issued a statement blaming his armies' failure to contain the enemy on their lack of mobility. He promised to take the necessary measures to get the French army moving again.

"He must say something to appease the Americans, to make them think they are getting something for their millions." Janvier caressed Emma's shoulders and breasts while he looked over her head at the translation on her desk. "What does Navarre intend to do, build a Metro line between Hanoi and Saigon? The Viet Minh move on foot, and they transport their weapons and supplies on their backs or on bicycles. We have trucks, jeeps, tanks, amphibious vehicles, and planes, and we still can't catch them."

Emma paused over the cable she was drafting to send to Chicago. "Last week General Salan said that you would have defeated the Viet Minh long ago if the Chinese hadn't sent men and materiel of their own."

"And so the dirty war goes on. Our side makes excuses while the other side thinks up better ways of winning." Janvier ran his tongue up her spine and kissed the hairless patches behind her ears. "Have you finished yet? We haven't made love for two hours and now it's time for dinner."

"Almost. I could finish sooner if you would stop biting my neck."

"Your work, your work, I am jealous of your work," Janvier crooned. "Every second you spend writing takes time away from me."

"Robert." Emma laid her pencil down and smiled up at him. "I have something to tell you. We're going to have a baby."

He looked as if he had been shot: blank-faced, stunned, not comprehending at once what had happened. "What are you saying?"

"It's true. I missed in March, when I was in Laos, but I didn't think anything of it. But when nothing happened in April, I began to wonder. I had a test as soon as I got back." She grasped his hand and held it to her cheek. "I can have the baby in Hanoi just as easily as I can here. It will be born in December. A Christmas present."

Janvier snatched his hand away. His upper lip curled back from his teeth. "Are you mad? You will have to get rid of it at once. I know a woman in Cholon—all the men send their girls there. She is cheap and very clean."

"You can't mean—"

"You are as ignorant as a peasant from the countryside." He gripped her upper arms. His fingers drilled into her flesh. "Cut it out. Abort it. It is nothing. A little blob of jelly, a clot of blood, no more than that. It has no soul, no will, no feeling." Janvier shoved her aside. He picked up a pencil and found a scrap of paper. "Rue des Marins, number one-two-seven" He slashed the seven, European style. "Behind a bicycle-repair shop. The woman's name is Tiang."

Emma stared at the address. "How many other women have you sent there, I wonder? How many have gone to number one twenty-seven Rue des Marins, and other places like it, because they didn't want to lose you?"

"What do you care? My business is my own. If you're going to pester me with questions—"

"No, no," she said hastily. "No more questions."

She sat on the edge of her bed. She knew every detail of his face, every contour of his body: his tight black curls and small ears; his hands, weathered yet delicate; his sturdy, strong legs with their steely muscles. But did she know the man underneath, the soul that lived behind the fierce black eyes? Sometimes he seemed more alien to her than the thousands of Vietnamese she saw every day.

"I have no time for stupid girls who can't look after themselves." Janvier grabbed his red beret from the chair near the door. "I can find a hundred girls in this town who are better in bed than you are. A thousand. Go ahead, have your brat. But don't expect me to pay for it. You'll never see me again."

"Robert, wait, please, I want to talk to you. Robert, don't leave me!"

The door slammed. He was gone. Emma lowered her head onto her pillow. Too stunned to cry, too numb to scream, she felt her sorrow harden and petrify into a stone that she knew she would carry for the rest of her life.

* * *

Rue des Marins, number one-two-seven. Rue des Marins, number one-two-seven. Emma had committed the address to memory, but she still carried Janvier's slip of paper in the pocket of her dress. The trishaw dropped her at one end of the street and she walked the four blocks to the bicycle shop. Ordinarily the streets of the Chinese city delighted her, but now she saw nothing. She did not notice the great copper and brass vats of soup and noodles ready to eat, the racks of flattened red-glazed ducks and pork ribs, the platters of pigs' snouts garnished with scarlet cocks' combs. Once in a letter home she had written that the urban Chinese and Vietnamese feasted twice, once when they shopped and again when they ate. But on this day the smell of food sickened her. Evil flowed from the sinister faces along her path. The enemy. Every breath she took was a gasp of fear.

The bicycle shop looked ordinary, a reassuring jumble of tires, wheel spokes, inner tubes, and grease guns. A young man crouched in a corner, hammering at a dented fender. Pieces of red glass from a broken reflector glittered on the cement floor. When Emma asked for Mrs. Tiang, he did not look up, but jerked his head slightly in the direction of the beaded curtain at the rear of the shop.

Stepping through the rattling strands, Emma found herself in what appeared to be an ordinary living room. Two small children were working at the table in the center of the room—one drawing characters with ink and brush and the other fingering an abacus—while an old woman nodded over her mending in the corner. Red votive candles flickered at a small altar against one wall. Before Emma could speak, a younger woman came through another doorway.

"Mrs. Tiang?" Emma said hesitantly. "*Je veux voir Madame Tiang, s'il vous plaît.*"

The woman shook her head. She wore navy blue trousers, and a white overblouse like a high-necked pajama jacket. Her black hair was shiny and straight, drawn tightly into a knob at the back of her neck. "No. No Mrs. Tiang here." She turned to leave.

"Oh, please!" The intensity of the anguish in her words startled

Emma. She had not realized how close she was to hysteria. "I will pay. Look!" She scrabbled in her purse. "Look, I have plenty of money. How much is it? A thousand piasters? Two thousand?" Her hands fumbled, and green bank notes fluttered to the floor. The woman watched impassively while Emma knelt and gathered them up. After a curious glance, the children once again bent their heads over their schoolwork. The old woman in the corner did not awaken, but sat with her head lolling, snoring gently. "Please don't send me away."

Mrs. Tiang hesitated, trying to decide whether Emma was genuinely in need. She might be an agent of the Sûreté. After a long, excruciating moment, she nodded and held open the curtain in the doorway through which she had come. Her heart pounding, Emma stepped inside. She was in a dark corridor, so narrow that when she stretched out her arms on either side, she could touch the walls without straightening her elbows. She felt the woman's hand on her waist, propelling her forward, guiding her through yet another curtained doorway into a room, this one lighted by a single naked light bulb hanging from a frayed wire. In the middle of the floor stood a table covered with a dirty sheet.

Emma groaned aloud and turned her face away. Mrs. Tiang tapped her elbow. "*Mille cinq-cent piastres.*" Emma did not understand her, and so held out her purse. The woman opened it, extracted the money, and handed it back. She gestured to the table. "*Asseyez.*" Emma seated herself on the edge of the table, on top of the sheet. The tabletop was metal, hard and cold against the backs of her legs. Mrs. Tiang, busying herself at a cabinet, looked over her shoulder. "*N'ayez pas peur.*"

Don't be afraid. Quick, easy, painless. Mrs. Tiang brought her a pill and a glass of water. Emma swallowed it. In a few minutes she felt herself becoming drowsy. Her terror mellowed into mild concern. Good, she thought. I'm getting braver. When Mrs. Tiang pushed her shoulders down, she cooperated willingly, arranging herself on the table, hiking her skirt up around her hips, wriggling out of her panties. Her garter belt and stockings remained in place. The pill was having a wonderfully calming effect. Perhaps it was opium. Lovely opium, the food of dreams.

Mrs. Tiang spread Emma's thighs and adjusted the sheet under her bottom. Emma closed her eyes and waited. This was a bit like going to the dentist, only nicer because the kindly lady dentist had banished fear as well as pain. She felt some pressure on her shoulders and looked up. The boy from the bicycle shop was standing over her, holding her firmly. Seen upside down, his face resembled a grinning gargoyle on a church, a demon on a pagoda. Mrs. Tiang was standing at the foot of the table, between the white V of her open legs. Two more women joined her, and each one grabbed one of Emma's knees.

The pain, when it came, was like a sword thrusting up through her entrails, straight through her heart, and into her brain. She tried to scream, but the old woman who had been dozing so peacefully in the other room clamped a strong hand over her mouth.

They were pulling her apart, each one taking a limb and wrenching and tearing for all they were worth. Then the pain and the pressure eased. Sobbing, Emma lifted her head. A crimson flower of blood blossomed on Mrs. Tiang's white blouse, right over her heart. The others had vanished, melted into the concrete walls.

Mrs. Tiang helped her to sit and handed her a cup of tea. Emma waved it away. "No, I'm all right." She just wanted to leave this place, to go back to the little room in Monsieur de Chesnay's house that held her notebooks and diaries, her type-writer, her little stack of letters from her mother and aunt, who seemed determined to love her no matter what craziness she got into. And to Robert, beautiful, adorable Robert, who loved her, whose strong arms waited to shelter her, whose sweet words waited to comfort her.

Out in the street, drops of rain caressed her face like loving fingers. The nightmare was over. The pain had been intense but brief, and she had survived it. She could still walk—a little stiffly, but the pain had receded to a dull ache. The opium still held her in its cloudlike embrace, giving her a sense of well-being and

and accomplishment. She realized she felt hungry, and bought a bowl of soup from a sidewalk vendor. The hot salty broth and noodles restored her. She glanced at her watch. Only thirty-five minutes had passed since she had entered the bicycle shop.

A trishaw dropped her at the top of Rue Catinat, in front of the cathedral. She preferred to walk the rest of the way since the trishaw drivers had trouble finding Monsieur de Chesnay's villa even when she directed them. The rain had no effect on the traffic in Saigon. Bicycles and taxis and private cars swirled around the well-manicured park that faced the cathedral, their tires sending up fan-shaped sheets of spray. Emma, startled by an angry blare of horns, discovered that she was standing in the middle of an intersection. Traffic had come to a halt all around her, and the policeman in his shaded kiosk was shouting at her. Someone guided her toward the curb, maybe the policeman, but she couldn't remember seeing anyone.

Her room felt damp, as dreary as midwinter but stiflingly hot. Emma sat in her armchair and waited for the afternoon to finish plodding its long course to evening. Time seemed to have collapsed, a phenomenon she remembered from the few occasions when she and Janvier had smoked opium. She dozed, and wakened, and discovered that only a few minutes had passed.

Old familiar objects in the room assumed attitudes of menace. The armoire loomed over her, huge and hungry, ready to open its doors and draw her into its moldy depths. Murderer. On the desk, her lamp glowed dimly, creating more shadows than light. Murderer. The bed, that frothy, oversized cradle of delirious excitement and pleasure, exuded an unpleasant odor, at once musky and acrid, like the inside of a casket where the corpse had begun to rot. Murderer. Murderer. Murderer.

Terror-stricken, Emma shrank into herself. The room vibrated with condemnation. Murderer. You murderer. When she had left that morning, her body had contained another life. Now she was empty, more hollow and lifeless than the furnishings that surrounded her.

"No, no," she gasped, "you don't understand. I had to do it. I had to do it for us. Our love is more important than all the babies in the world. I had to make him stay." Tears flowed down her cheeks.

Why didn't he come? Why didn't he come to celebrate their union? Their perfect, unchangeable union. She heard Monsieur Varigny, the human time clock, return from his evening meal. Still Janvier did not appear.

Murderer. The room turned as cold as a graveyard. She had to get outside, to a warm world full of living, breathing creatures, or she would turn to frozen stone. When he came, Robert would find her grown as stiff and hard as the sink or the bedstead. Emma tried to stand, but her legs had softened so that she could hardly move. Slowly she made her way out of the room, snatching at walls and banisters and railings for support.

Out in the street, the night breathed with her, sighing, panting, moaning softly with the sheer exertion of existing. She headed for the waterfront, where Janvier had found her on another night long ago. He always knew where to find her. He loved her.

At the corner of Avenue Boddard, she was wracked by a spasm of pain that brought her to her knees. She clung to the trunk of a tamarind tree, frightened and confused. The hurt was supposed to be over. What was happening to her?

She got up and forced herself to go on. The thought came to her: Perhaps I'm dying. No, not yet. I must pay, but not yet. Let me see Robert once more. I want to tell him how much I love him.

An umbrella hovered over her like a flying saucer, blocking the darts of rain that had been striking her head and shoulders. Someone touched her arm. A man, wearing a light summerweight suit.

"Emma? What are you doing? Are you all right? It's raining very hard. Are you drunk?"

At last. Emma turned and tried to hold him, but her hands

were too weak. Her knees buckled and she fell. "Thank God," she whispered. "I knew you would find me."

Quickly, Hazen reached down with one strong arm and pulled her up under the umbrella. "Emma? I'm Alan Hazen. Don't you know me?"

"Oh." She slumped against him. Her head lolled back but she was unable to focus. "I'm all right. Just leave me here. I'm waiting for Robert. Have you seen him? I know he will come. I waited, but the room was so dark and cold. I didn't want to die there. I've got to find him. Maybe I should go back. He's waiting for me, I know he is."

"What is it, the fever again?" Hazen bent over her and pressed his cheek against her burning forehead. "You may be having a bout of malaria. Come on, my car's right over here. I'll take you to a doctor."

"No." She stiffened her arms and tried to push him away. "No, I'm not sick. I'm dying. I have to pay. I'm a murderer. I'm a murderer. I have to pay."

"Emma, you're very ill. You're feverish. Come on, let me—"

"No!" she screamed. "You don't understand! I'm a murderer! I had an abortion today."

The umbrella wavered. Water sluiced over Hazen's shoulders. The sidewalk, the street, the cars all disappeared. They were standing on the bank of a sizzling river filled with fast-paced roaring water serpents with pairs of flaming eyes. "Was it mine?" he asked hoarsely.

"Yours? Yours?" Emma began to laugh, and the laughs changed to sobs. Hazen lowered the umbrella to let the rain cool her face, and he held her tightly until her sobbing subsided. "My baby," she wailed. "My baby. Mine and Robert's. I love him so. I killed my baby. I killed my baby. Robert, I've got to see Robert." She clutched the lapels of Hazen's jacket. "Will you find him for me? Please! I must see him, tell him—he must know that I love him. Find him for me—"

Pain struck with a viciousness that doubled her over. Hazen

caught her before she went down and held her until she stopped heaving. His umbrella whirled away down the sidewalk, a single spoked wheel with an axle but no vehicle.

Hazen lowered his head. Blood was running down Emma's legs and splashing on their shoes before it merged with the swift current of black rainwater in the gutter.

13

JULY 14, 1953 (Postcard)

Dear Mom,

Usually Bastille Day is a big deal here, but this year
the high command banned fireworks because they
might encourage grenade or bomb attacks. Sorry
I've been such a lax correspondent lately, but that
fever I told you about lingered for weeks. I'm fine
now—will write a real juicy letter soon.

Love, Emma

Eliane de Mornay opened the door to the private hospital room
and beckoned to Hazen, who was sitting in an armchair near
the bed. He set aside the book of poetry he had been reading and
left the room after a quick glance at Emma, who was still under
heavy sedation and sleeping soundly.

"How is she?" Eliane whispered.

"Out of danger, I think. They gave her seven pints of blood.
She was in surgery for three hours." Hazen himself was almost
staggering with weariness as they walked toward the end of the
green and white corridor. His voice trembled with emotion and
exhaustion. "The minute she wakes up, she'll start asking for him
again. Did you have any luck?"

"Yes. A telephone call, about five minutes ago. Janvier just
went into a little bar near the waterfront. You probably don't

know the place. It is owned by a Corsican named Martinelli. If you want to talk to him, I'll drive you there."

Eliane launched her little Renault into the traffic on Boulevard Charner and accelerated with a few deft twitches of the gearshift. Two minutes later, she pulled into a narrow side street two blocks away from the Saigon River.

"That's the place, on the corner. I'll wait here."

The bar was a hangout for sailors, syphilitic whores, backstreet punks, and small-time gangsters. Hazen looked them over, but Janvier was not among them. A burly Italian with a patch over one eye dragged a filthy rag over the zinc countertop. Faded posters on the walls advertised boxing matches that had taken place in Marseilles twenty years ago. The stains and cracks in the tile floor looked like the scars on a face that had gone too many rounds.

Hazen stepped up to the bar and asked for Captain Robert Janvier. The bartender shrugged. Hazen propped his elbows on the bar and waited. Five minutes passed; then he felt the sharp prick of a knife under his left ear. A hand gripped his elbow. He looked around, into the face of an obese Japanese who might have been an ex–Sumo wrestler. The man pushed Hazen through the silent crowd, opened a door at the back of the room, and shoved him through.

Janvier was seated at a table with a burly tough who was probably Martinelli. A sleek Vietnamese prostitute sat on Janvier's lap, one arm slung around his neck. A couple of thugs lounged against the wall. Bodyguards. One of them hefted a switchblade in the palm of his hand.

"I want to talk to you, Janvier," Hazen said in French. "In private."

"Private?" Janvier grinned. "I have no secrets from my friends. What do you want to say to Robert Janvier?"

"Mademoiselle Vaughan is very sick, maybe dying. She has been asking for you."

"Ah, yes, the pretty American. What a pity. Still, women are such fragile creatures—"

"She nearly died from an abortion," Hazen said in a cutting voice. "I hold you responsible for that, Janvier. You forced her to go through with it."

"I?" Janvier looked the very picture of wounded innocence. He appealed to his friends. "How could I force any woman to do anything she did not want to do? An abortion, he says. Why, I don't even know what that means."

"It means they cut out her pussy," one of the toughs suggested.

"No, no," Martinelli said, "an abortion is when a sow starts getting big in the belly, and so you stick a knife up her cunt and give it a few twists, and pretty soon she explodes like a balloon and you have piglets sticking to the walls." He roared with laughter. The other men joined him. Only Hazen remained stony-faced.

"I found the address in her pocket," he said. "I went there with the police, but it's gone. Nothing there now but a little grocery store with a family of twenty-six living in back. Everybody in the neighborhood swears the store has been there for years. Nobody's ever heard of Madame Tiang."

"Madame Tiang?" Janvier looked puzzled. "I have never heard of her either. Why should I?"

"Because you sent Emma to her." Hazen gazed at him through narrowed eyes. "You don't feel anything for her, do you, Janvier? She did it for you, you bastard. She loves you. Doesn't that mean anything? But you let that woman carve her up as if she were an animal ready for slaughter. You stink, Janvier. You're so rotten you've started to putrefy in the heat."

Janvier shoved the girl off his lap and told her to get lost. Grinning, he leaned back in his chair. "You are just angry because I got into her pants first. I don't blame you. She was a good-looking piece of ass, and a great fuck. Too bad she was so stupid. Smart girls don't get themselves knocked up." He laughed.

With a snarl, Hazen hurled himself across the table at Janvier and caught him around the throat. Janvier broke his grip and twisted him around while Martinelli grabbed Hazen's ankles. Hazen fell so hard that his skull cracked on the tile floor. Nevertheless, he jumped up again and aimed a couple of punches at Janvier's jaw. One of them connected, and Janvier reeled backward, into the wall. Then one of the thugs grabbed Hazen's arms and another a handful of hair, and they held him while Janvier righted himself.

"No," Janvier panted, "let him go. I can take care of him. Come on, big American hero. Are you ready to test my courage one to one, face to face?"

As Hazen wiped the blood out of his eyes, he could see Janvier's shadowy bulk weaving in front of him. Enraged, he lowered his head and charged at his adversary, who sidestepped him neatly, laughing. The thugs began to crowd in, scenting the kill. One of them tripped Hazen, and kicked him viciously when he fell. Hazen tried to rise and received more kicks in the chest and groin. Above the shouts and cheers of the mob he could hear Janvier taunting him.

"Come on, hero, come on. I am still waiting to show you how brave I am."

Hazen was on his knees, retching and spitting blood. The Sumo aimed a hard kick at his rump, and he sprawled on his face. The vultures gathered, their toes twitching. A kick in the side. A kick to his head. Laughter. Jeers. And then a loud blast like a gunshot, blood spurting from Martinelli's ear, and Eliane's shrill voice:

"I will shoot anyone else who touches him. Come on, back up, and leave him alone." Eliane knelt beside Hazen's head. "Oh, you are such an idiot, charging in here like some crazy Galahad. And where is that monster Janvier? Damn him, he's run out, the coward. Let's go. Can you stand? You, Martinelli, help me get him up. Come on, damn you, or I'll shoot your face off. Alan, you can lean on me. You, fat man, hold the door. What a stinking cesspool. Somebody ought to throw a bomb into this place."

Outside, Hazen doubled over the fender of the Renault and groaned.

"Do you need to throw up?"

"Don't know."

"Well, make up your mind. I don't want you being sick in my car. All right now? Let's go. I'll take you home."

"No. Hospital. Take me to the hospital. I need to see Emma."

"Are you crazy? Do you want that girl to wake up and see you looking like you've just been through a meat grinder? You'll scare her to death. I'll take you home first and clean you up. Sit down, get your legs in. Look at those morons staring at me." She shook her fist at a group of onlookers from the bar. "That's right, you idiots, I'm a woman. What did you think? Now get away from this car before I run you all down."

She backed the car up, tires squealing, and roared away from the waterfront.

Hazen said through swollen lips, "Poor Emma. That guy is even worse than I thought. God, what a fool I've been."

"A real dope," Eliane agreed. "Next time you decide to do battle with someone, make sure you both follow the same rules. No hitting below the belt, and each one brings plenty of reinforcements."

In the early hours of the morning, Hazen tiptoed into Emma's room and pulled the door closed. He sat in the armchair and watched the shallow rise and fall of Emma's breasts in the pale light that seeped in from the corridor. Hour after hour he sat and watched. In the darkest hours before dawn he shed soundless tears. Tears for her, for himself, for her baby. Tears for his own child and the wife he had lost.

Later that morning, when Emma finally roused from her sleep, he was still there, sitting in his accustomed armchair near her bed. A broad piece of adhesive tape covered the bridge of his nose. The cuts on his cheeks were painted with iodine and crisscrossed with gauze and adhesive. His lips were swollen and crusty with scabs.

"Who's that?" She stirred sleepily. "Is someone there?"

"Only me. Alan. Go back to sleep."

"What time is it?" Emma sat up. The venetian blinds admitted the gloomy light from the rain-drenched sky. "Did you bring me here? Where is Robert?"

"He couldn't make it."

"Oh." She twisted the coverlet that lay over her lap. "I wish he would come. I just want to see him, to tell him what happened. Why doesn't he come?" She turned her head on her pillow and looked at Hazen. "You—you're hurt!"

"Street accident." Hazen got out of his chair. He stood with the light from the window behind him. "Got run over by a trishaw. Two or three times."

"I don't believe you. You look like somebody tried to kill you. Did you see Robert? Did you talk to him?" Hazen did not answer, but the curve of his spine and the sag of his shoulders gave him away. Emma's hand flew to her mouth. "Oh, no. Robert! Robert did this to you. Because of me."

"That's not true," he said gruffly. "I told you, I got tangled up with—"

"Don't lie to me, Alan. I don't want to hear any more lies." She began to weep. "It was my fault. I shouldn't have involved you in this."

"I am involved, Emma."

"No, no, it was wrong, so wrong. He had no right to do that to you. You're a good man, the finest man I've ever known, and he beat you—he beat you the way he beat me! I never meant it to happen, I swear, Alan. I only wanted to see him."

Hazen knelt by the side of her bed and held her hands. "Hush, Emma, hush. You're not to blame. You didn't know what he was like—"

"But I did! I did know." Her fingertips fluttered over his cheeks. He closed his eyes. Her touch warmed him, healed him, made him whole again. "Your poor face," she whispered. "Oh, why couldn't I have fallen in love with you instead of him? I'll never forgive myself for what's happened. Never. Oh, God, why didn't I die?"

Hazen put his arms around her and held her as she wept.

"Don't, Emma, don't cry. I'm as much to blame as you are. I should have been smarter. I should have saved you from him. But it's over now. Forget him, Emma. Forget Robert Janvier ever existed."

Emma turned her face away from him. "I heard the doctors talking—I'm not sure when it was. You were here, too. I couldn't understand what they were saying. Am I going to be all right?"

"You'll be fine," Hazen said too quickly. "You just need rest and a little time off from work."

"You're lying to me again." Emma turned her face back to Hazen. "What did they really tell you, Alan? I have a right to know the truth. I have a right!"

Hazen hesitated for a moment; then he said, "Your uterus was punctured in three places. You had a serious infection that poisoned your system. They spent a lot of time sewing you up, giving you blood and antibiotics. Because of the scar tissue, you probably won't be able to bear children."

Silently, Emma stared at the ceiling over her bed.

Hazen went on, "They may be wrong. I've heard of some specialists in the States, really excellent doctors who might be able to—"

"It doesn't matter. I was a fool to think he could ever love me. A man like that. I thought I was in love. But it wasn't love. Infatuation. Madness, more likely. I'm twenty-four years old, twenty-five next month, and my life is over."

"No." Hazen took her hand and squeezed it firmly. "Your life is not over. It's going to be different from now on, that's all. I'll take care of you, Emma. I'll give you everything I have. Just tell me what I can do to make you happy and I'll do it."

"Nothing," she said bitterly. "Nobody can make me happy."

"I can." His tone was confident. "As soon as you're well enough to leave this place, I'll take you home with me. You'll be your old self in no time, I promise. Now go back to sleep. You don't need to worry about a thing. You'll be all right. Everything will be all right."

Emma nodded listlessly, but her nod was a gesture of politeness from someone who didn't really care.

The villa that Chrome Petroleum provided for Hazen was in Dakow, on the northern edge of the city. It was small but elegant, a polished *Petit Trianon* enclosed by a high cement wall. Inside, the rooms were clean, bright, and uncluttered, furnished only with those items essential to a petroleum company executive who lived alone and who entertained his guests in restaurants and nightclubs. Pham headed a small staff of servants that included a cook, a part-time laundress, two housemaids, and a gardener. So well-trained and quiet were the servants that most days the only sounds Emma heard from her room were birdsong and the rustling of branches as monkeys swung through the trees. Except for the occasional distant wail of a siren or the hoot of a foghorn on the river, the nights were blessedly silent.

Emma opened her eyes and glanced at the clock by her bedside. Seven twenty-eight. Alan would have been up for three hours already. In two minutes a maidservant would bring her morning coffee. Breakfast would be ready on the dot of eight. She could either take it in her room or with Hazen in the dining room. The routine was unvarying. Almost like being in prison.

She shook her head to rid herself of the thought. She had been a guest in Alan Hazen's house for six weeks, and no one could have been kinder or more generous to her. Six weeks of unflagging courtesy, unfailing good humor, and complete devotion to her needs.

Her coffee arrived. With the first sip, Emma felt her brain clearing. At least Hazen's cook knew how to brew decent coffee.

Hearing a metallic clatter outside, Emma threw off her covers and walked to the window that overlooked the garden at the rear of the house, an undisciplined canvas of vivid flowers and trailing vines, small iron benches, and a murky pool in which goldfish glided beneath bronze lily pads. Hazen was working in the six-by-eight plot he called his vegetable patch. His lanky figure was stooped over a tomato plant whose leaves were the color of weathered khaki. Nearby a cucumber vine rampaged over a trellis, producing a host of yellow blossoms but no fruit. Hazen was strangely unscientific in his gardening. He expected his vegetables to grow as lustily as they had in his garden in Illinois, and he seemed genuinely surprised when humidity, a host of fungal diseases, and battalions of insects defeated them.

Emma looked at the clock again. Seven fifty-five. Time to get dressed and present herself at the breakfast table.

Her skirt fit loosely at the waist. She noticed when she looked in the mirror that her collarbones jutted out and that her cheeks were pasty and sunken. The past few weeks had transformed her from a plump-cheeked, corn-fed ingenue into a withered hag. No man would love her now.

Emma poked at the rubbery fried egg and desiccated slice of ham on her plate. Her toast was dry, the color of chocolate, as hard as a wooden shingle. She wondered if Hazen's Vietnamese cook had been trained in the Nebraska state prison system. All his meat dishes, be they poultry, beef, or pork, tasted the same, like boiled cardboard. Vegetables were boiled to death and then shrouded in white sauce. Applesauce, shipped in from the United States in institutional-sized cans at great expense, accompanied every meal.

When Emma first joined Hazen at the breakfast table, she had to remind herself that she was no longer in Lincoln, Nebraska. Pham had brought an assortment of cereals on a silver tray: Rice Chex, Wheaties, and Cheerios. Every morning Hazen filled his bowl with tiny waffles, flakes, or O's and drowned them with milk.

Now Hazen unfurled the morning paper. "I love the way the press in Saigon always relegates items like this to the middle of the paper, next to the advertisements for girdles." He read, "'The rebels waited to blow up the bridge until the train had gone halfway. Over one hundred people were killed and many more injured. This is the second time that the Hue-Tourane Bridge has been vandalized in the past year.' Vandalized! They make the

Viet Minh sound like a bunch of juvenile delinquents. What do you think, do you want to fly up to Hue and take a look? It's a nice spot—palaces, moats, lakes. No side trips to the floor of the jungle this time."

"No, thanks." Emma poked at her grapefruit.

Hazen said, "It will be a short trip. Sometime this summer I need to go up to Hanoi and talk to the minister of the interior. He hasn't answered my letters. I think it's time I started negotiating with Ho Chi Minh if I really want to do some mineral studies up there. You've never been to Hanoi, have you? You'll find some good stories. I know a few officers at the Citadel—"

"No, thanks. I'm not interested."

"That's up to you," Hazen said. "I just thought you might feel more like working if you got out of Saigon for a while."

"Damn it!" Emma slammed her palms down on the table. The coffee cups rattled. "I do not feel like working. I don't feel like doing anything. Just leave me alone!"

"Excuse me." Hazen was shocked by her outburst. "I didn't mean to nag."

"Nag? I wish you would nag. I wish you'd yell and scream and curse—anything but this everlasting niceness. Why don't you just come right out and say what's on your mind, Alan? What I did was selfish and despicable and horrible. I hate myself for it. I can hardly stand being alone with myself. But here you sit, pretending that everything is normal when you know very well that I've got blood on my hands. I killed something that would have been a human being. Walking, laughing, breathing, trying to communicate with other human beings—and I killed it. Don't baby me anymore, Alan Hazen. Don't treat me like an honored guest in your house and don't fight battles for me and don't come over all sweet and kind when you're with me, because I can't stand it anymore. Call me names—bitch, whore, sinner, murderess—I'm sure you can think of plenty that would suit. Believe me, they're a lot nicer than the names I've called myself." Emma pushed her chair back and ran out of the room.

Hazen found her upstairs, flopped facedown on her bed. "I think it's time we had a little talk, Emma."

"I don't want to talk."

He sat on the side of the bed. "You've had six weeks to recover from your surgery. Physically, you're as healthy as you've ever been. But you'll be an invalid forever if you don't make a serious effort to recover your spirit. Do you know what I'm saying?"

"Yes." Sitting up, she wiped her eyes with her fist. "You want me to shape up or ship out. Don't worry, I know when it's time to push off. I'll leave this afternoon."

"Leave?" Hazen looked astonished. "Who said anything about your leaving? I want you to be happy, Emma, but I can only do so much. The decision has to come from you. To live in the past or to look to the future. You decide. I will never blame you for what happened. I've done too many things in my life that I would rather forget. But I try not to agonize over them. Life is too short. I leave the final judgment to the Lord and do my best to be happy today."

A tiny tear like a diamond rolled down Emma's cheek. "I'm sorry," she said. "I know I'm not much fun to be with right now."

Hazen grasped her hand. "Emma, I want to marry you."

"Marry?" She sat bolt upright, as if she had been stung. "No, no, I won't! I don't want to marry anybody!"

"But I love you, Emma."

"No, you don't. You want to redeem the poor young sinner and save your own soul in the bargain. I wonder how many points heaven gives you for lifting a fallen woman out of the muck? Not only fallen, but sterile as well. You couldn't have made a better choice, Reverend Hazen. Mine is the blackest soul in Saigon. The only problem is, I'm not about to cooperate with your little scheme. You can find yourself another Mary Magdalene." She bounced off the bed and wrenched open a bureau drawer. "I'm getting out of here."

"You're free to go. I won't stop you. We all make our choices and we have to live with the results, Emma. We can't go back, we can't change history, and we can't erase the past. I don't despise anyone who makes mistakes. God knows, I've made enough myself. I love you. I can't think of any better way to put it than that. I love being with you. I love hearing you talk. Whenever I put my arms around you, I never want to let you go. I didn't realize any of this until we made that trip down the river. If I had known what would happen, I would have ditched that plane a little sooner."

She had been emptying her drawer, tossing underwear on a chair. She stopped, a lacy slip in her hands. "But I'm not worthy of you, Alan."

"Listen to me, Emma. The fact that we may never have children of our own doesn't matter to me at all. I don't want to marry the spirits of possible children. I want to marry you."

Emma shook her head. "I think you'd be a terrific husband, and I don't know why some smart woman hasn't snapped you up by now, but I'm not the right woman—"

"You are the only woman." Reaching out, Hazen grasped Emma's hand and gently drew her toward him. He pulled her down on his knee. "We'll have fun together," he promised. "I'll show you parts of the Far East that few white persons have ever seen. Why, in two months I'll have you piloting your own plane."

Emma shuddered. "I doubt that."

"Marry me," he urged. "Today. Now. Right away. You won't be sorry. I'll make you happy, Emma, I swear it. I won't neglect you. I won't scold you. And I will love you until I die. Say yes, Emma. Yes. Yes."

The power of his yearning melted the coldness and filled the empty space inside her. Placing her hands alongside his face, Emma kissed him tenderly. The kiss tasted good, like a rich food she had denied herself for too long. She wanted still more.

She lay in his arms. For the first time in weeks, she felt calm and at peace with herself. "Why can't life be this simple all the time?"

"Because we're human beings and not amoebas."

"We'll be happy." She said the words as if they were a solemn vow. "I'll be a good wife. The best. I'll bring you your pipe and warm your slippers and bake as many apple pies as you can eat. I'll take care of you, too, Alan. And I won't look back. What happened with Robert Janvier was like a disease, but I'm cured now, I know I am. I'm immune. The past can't touch me."

They were married in the American embassy. The service was performed by a visiting Presbyterian minister, a friend of Ambassador Bunning's. Among the handful of guests were Madame de Mornay and Monsieur de Chesnay. Afterward the wedding party dined at the Arc-en-Ciel, Cholon's famed Rainbow restaurant. In honor of the occasion, Hazen permitted himself a single glass of champagne.

"I hope this doesn't mean you're becoming an alcoholic," Emma teased him.

"Would you divorce me?" he asked.

"Not at all. I would rehabilitate you."

He laughed. "You already have. I've never felt happier in my life."

Emma raised her glass to him in a toast. "To us."

"To us. And to you. You've never looked more beautiful."

Emma's hairdresser had pulled her hair into a sleek twist but had left two soft curls in front of her ears. She wore a fitted suit of powder blue linen with a matching veiled hat, and she carried a bouquet of white roses and lilies. A hired photographer snapped plenty of pictures so that Emma's mother and aunt would have a full record of the proceedings. Before the wedding, Hazen had sent a telegram asking Mrs. Vaughan for permission to marry her daughter. He received an answer the next day: "MAY GOD BLESS YOU BOTH AND KEEP YOU HAPPY ALWAYS LOVE MOM."

They spent a week in the mountain city of Da Lat, enjoying the fragrant pines, riding horses, making love. In mid-August, business took Hazen to Hong Kong. Emma gamely traveled with him, but she clung to his hand from the moment they took their seats in the airplane until it landed.

In Hong Kong, a Chrome executive lent them his sailboat. Emma was not surprised when her husband proved to be an expert sailor.

"I'll never understand why you can't grow tomatoes," she said. "You can do everything else."

They made a good team, with Hazen as expert navigator and Emma as cook. He taught her how to handle the boat in all weathers, and with her love of the water she soon overtook him as a helmsman. He called her a natural sailor and praised himself for marrying her.

Their week sailing in the South China Sea ended too quickly.

"Someday we'll have a boat of our own," Hazen promised. "And we'll call her *Emmy Lou*."

"We will not! I hate that name."

"But I love it. Sometimes I lull myself to sleep by saying it over and over: Emmy Lou, Emmy Lou, Emmy Lou. At least if we name our boat *Emmy Lou*, I can say the name out loud and you won't be able to scold me."

Back home in Saigon, Emma undertook the redecoration of their house and the rehabilitation of their chef. She bought a couple of French cookbooks and asked Pham to translate the recipes into Vietnamese. Hazen, still reeling from his good fortune, never complained about the disappearance of applesauce from the menu and the strange dishes that began to emerge from the kitchen. Emma started to write again.

One morning after Hazen had left for his office, Emma took her coffee out to the garden. She still had an hour or so before a morning press briefing. After weeks of persistent rainfall, the clouds had finally broken and the sun peaked through. Emma sat on one of the benches near the fishpond and watched a small lizard trying to blend with a banana leaf.

Pham came out of the house. "A gentleman wants to see you, madame."

"To see me? Oh, maybe that wallpaper I ordered has finally come in. Send him out here."

Pham disappeared. After a moment, Janvier stepped out of the house. He was carrying a bouquet of roses. "Hello, Emma."

"Oh, my God." Frantic, she looked around for someplace to run, but the walls were too high to climb and Janvier's bulk was blocking the way into the house. If she tried to bolt down the path toward the front gate, he would stop her.

"I hear you have been ill. I am sorry. I brought these for you." Emma stared at the flowers in horror, as if they were tainted with some deadly bacteria. "Take them away! I don't want them!"

"No? Perhaps you are right." He tossed the bouquet aside. "They looked better in the shop. So, you are living here now." His gaze swung around the garden. "Very nice. Nicer than any house I could give you."

"Mr. Hazen and I are married," she announced in a ringing voice. "You can't hurt me now. You can't touch me. He'll protect me—"

Janvier's laughter was harsh. "Oh, yes, I have seen how well your new husband can fight. I saw him after he was beaten by a pack of waterfront bullies, crawling along the floor through pools of beer and blood and piss. Yes, he is a magnificent fighter, your husband. We might even take him into the Legion, he is so good."

"You monster!" Emma cried. "You let them do that to him! Why didn't you stop them?"

"Why should I?" Janvier said with a languid shrug. "I didn't care if they killed him. One life means nothing to me. 'Hundreds of thousands of people die every day. The death of one is not important.' Those are not my words. Our enemy General Giap said them. That is why he will win and we will lose. Because he is willing to pay the highest price for victory." He leered at Emma. "I, too, am willing to pay well for my victories."

"I hate you," Emma said through clenched teeth. "I can't believe I ever loved you."

"Really? Are you so sure you no longer love me?" Janvier's

brows arched. "Why don't we try a little experiment? I will kiss you, and if you feel nothing, then I will go away and bother you no more. Just one kiss, Emma." He advanced on her. "A kiss for the bride, eh?"

"No, no." She retreated until the backs of her legs struck an iron bench. "No, get away from me!" she cried. "Pham! Pham, help me!"

Pham came rushing out of the house, a kitchen knife in his fist. Janvier swung around to face him, his hand on his pistol. Emma ran to Pham's side. "Get away from here," she shouted to Janvier. "Go away and don't come here again. I'm through with you, understand? Through!"

Janvier shrugged, then raised his hands in a pacifying gesture. "I am a reasonable man. I have no wish to intrude on this happy household. But do not forget, Emma, you still belong to me. I have not yet given you up. In time, perhaps. But not yet."

He strolled down the path along the side of the house. Emma and Pham could hear him whistling the *"Marseillaise."* Finally the whistling stopped. Emma's knees gave out and she slumped onto the back step. Looking concerned, Pham disappeared into the house and returned with a glass of water.

As she gulped the water, Emma's gaze fell on the wilting bouquet. "Throw those away," she ordered. "Burn them. And don't tell Monsieur Hazen that that man was here. *Comprenez?* If he comes again, don't let him in."

Up in the bright new study Hazen had outfitted for her, Emma sat in front of her typewriter and tapped out, "I am happy." Then she returned the carriage to the left margin and typed the three words again. She typed down the length of the page until she came to the bottom; then she reset the tab at the middle of the page and typed another column. When she was finished, the paper was filled with the words "I am happy" typed in three neat columns with not a single error.

"I'm happy!" she cried. "Damn him, I am happy." Furious, she ripped the paper to shreds. Then she lowered her head onto her arms and sobbed. "What am I going to do? Oh, God, what am I going to do?"

Hazen was working in his library when he heard the imperious ring of the doorbell and Eliane de Mornay's shrill soprano.

"Get out of my way, you moron. Vietnamese savage. I don't care if he's writing *Hamlet*. He'll see me. Won't you, my darling?" She sailed into the room and, embracing Hazen from behind, kissed him on both cheeks. "You'd better tell that servant of yours to show me more respect. If he were in my employ, I would fire him. But only after I boxed his ears. Really, how do you tolerate such insolence?"

"I'm used to rude behavior," Hazen said blandly.

Eliane made a face. "I will box your ears if you're not careful. How are your ears, by the way? And the rest of you? I did a pretty nice job patching you up that night. A regular Florence Nightingale, eh?" She looked around the room. "I don't see your charming bride. What happened, have you two quarreled already?"

"She's not feeling well tonight. She went up to bed right after dinner."

"I am sorry to hear it. But this heat would make a saint crazy. Did you ever experience such an abominable climate? Ah, to be in Paris again—"

"Care for a drink?" Hazen offered.

"No, I cannot stay. You have been so neglectful of me since your marriage that I just came by to see if you were still alive. My new lover is waiting for me in the car. Well, don't you want to know who he is? You will be horribly jealous when you find out. He is an American, just like you."

"I rather doubt that he's just like me," Hazen said dryly.

"That is what I find most offensive about you, Alan. I know very well that you don't give a damn who I sleep with, but you might at least pretend. Very well, I will leave you. At least walk me to the gate."

Her Renault was parked in the street. From the gateway Hazen saw a young man leap out and run around to the driver's side to open the door for her. W. Powers Brewster, the chief of communications at the American embassy.

"You see, I told you I wouldn't be long," Eliane trilled to her escort. "Well, where shall we go next? How about the Grand Monde? I feel lucky tonight."

"Great." Brewster sounded as enthusiastic as a college freshman at his first varsity football game. "You know I'd go anywhere with you, Eliane."

"Even down the road to perdition?" Laughing, she waved to Hazen, standing in the shadows, and she said loudly, "I rather doubt that. On the other hand, you won't know what road you're on until we're almost there, will you?"

A few days after Janvier's visit, Hazen announced that he needed to fly up to Hanoi for a vital meeting with the French minister he had been courting. He told Emma that he would be gone for two days, perhaps three. Emma, who had finally obtained permission to interview General Navarre privately, would stay home.

She drove him to the airport in the Buick. Before he boarded the plane, Hazen teased her, calling her his child bride and his little Nebraska farm wife. Seeing the love in his eyes, Emma felt herself die a little behind her smile. She had not told him about Janvier, and the incident weighed on her like a secret sin.

After a few days of sunshine, the monsoon winds had begun to blow again from the southeast. Emma typed up a list of interview questions in her study. By midmorning, she suddenly felt overwhelmed by the heat and the closeness and the rain. The house felt like a tomb. She craved noise and life and bright colors. She decided to visit Monsieur de Chesnay. His house was always full of activity, music and talk and the happy laughter of children.

Monsieur de Chesnay welcomed her warmly. As they sipped coffee, he inquired about Monsieur Hazen.

"He is a good husband to you, eh? I can see that you are very happy with him. And he loves you so very much. You are fortunate."

Emma agreed that she was indeed lucky.

"Take it from me," de Chesnay said, "you don't want to marry a Frenchman. They make fine lovers but terrible husbands." He grinned. "I said that I would paint a portrait of you as a wedding present, yes? Would you like to begin today? Let me make a few quick sketches, and we will decide what pose we like best. We will surprise your husband with a beautiful picture of you."

After an hour, Emma became restless. She and de Chesnay ended their session. "Have you rented my old room yet?" she asked as she was leaving.

"Oh, no. Where could I ever find a roomer as charming and beautiful as you, madame? Some people have come to inquire, but I have sent them away. Do you wish to visit it? Feel perfectly free. Perhaps I will never rent it, but keep it for you as a secret hiding place, eh?"

Emma climbed the outside stairs to the balcony. After weeks of being closed up and shuttered against the rain, the room had a musty smell. Sadness overwhelmed her. The price of folly was a high one, almost too high to bear. She lay on the bed and pressed her face into the pillow.

She may have dozed off, or perhaps her thoughts simply merged with the shadows. Hearing a sound, she sat up. Someone was in the room.

As he moved into a shaft of light, she recognized Janvier. "I told one of de Chesnay's girls to call me when you came back," he said. "I have missed you, Emma. How are you enjoying married life? I would have expected you to look happier."

"Alan is very good to me," she said stoutly.

"Oh, yes? Perhaps you were right to marry him," Janvier said with a wise nod. "I will never be good to you, you know. How could I? I don't know how to love." Seeing Emma flinch, he laughed. "You think I am asking for your sympathy? Perhaps I am. You are a sympathetic person, Emma. I have not been fair to you, I think. I should have warned you. I should have told you that you were wasting yourself on a man like me, a man who cannot return your love."

Emma huddled against the headboard, her knees drawn up and her arms pressed tightly against her waist.

"We were Jews, living in Lyons." Janvier made himself comfortable in the old armchair in the corner. He spoke in a reminiscent tone. "My father was a doctor, very prosperous, very stubborn. Before the Nazis came, I begged him to let us leave France, but he refused. Finally, when he heard about the arrests and the trains taking Jews to Germany, he agreed to let his friends help him. Our family went into hiding, in a crumbling chateau in the Loire Valley. It was a nightmare; four of us living in a small cellar under the barn. My father and stepmother, my half brother and me. My own mother had died when I was born. My stepmother was a spoiled bitch, a rich man's daughter who did nothing but whine and complain. My little brother cried because he could not go to school. My father took incredible risks just to get him the books he wanted so that he could keep up with his studies. Nothing was too good for his precious Theo. Food was scarce, and I could feel myself growing weaker every day. I did not want to spend the war in that stupid barn. And so one night I ran away. If the Gestapo had caught me, they would have tortured me, forced me to reveal our hiding place. Fortunately, I got away. I heard later that they were arrested, as well as the people who had sheltered us."

Somewhere in the house, a baby cried, a woman scolded, a radio blared a lament by a French chanteuse. Edith Piaf, most likely, the little sparrow from the streets of Paris. The French in Saigon were crazy about Piaf.

Emma felt cold. Janvier had dragged the shadowy past into the room like a black beast on a tether. He had released it, and now it was roaming freely, devouring everything in sight.

Janvier left his chair and lounged on the bed beside Emma. He seemed confident that she would not run away. "I never regretted

what I had done," he said. "I had to get out. I would have died
there, even if the Gestapo never came. I needed air, food. And
fighting. I needed the Legion, and I found it."

Emma turned her face away from him.

"So now, my Emma"—his fingers closed around her wrist—
"you know the worst about me. I have not reformed. I still think
about myself first, and to hell with everyone else. I know nothing
about love. I take. I don't give because I don't know how. I am
not asking for your pity, Emma. I merely want you to see me as I
am, without lies, without pretense. Help me, Emma." He spoke
into her ear. "You love me, Emma. You have never stopped loving me."

"No," she said helplessly. "I have a husband. He's a wonderful
person, a fine man. I respect him—"

"But you do not love him. Come with me to Hanoi." His lips
brushed her cheek. "I am leaving tonight. There is room for you
on the plane—I have already checked. Just show them your press
credentials. Like old times, yes? Emma and her captain."

He kissed her throat. She closed her eyes and imagined that
she was underwater, swimming in the ocean, pulling herself
down, down with every sure stroke until she came to rest in the
soft sand at the bottom. On the floor of the sea, far away from the
light and air, the tide combed your hair and stroked your limbs
gently. The water wasn't heavy, because it was part of you. Down
there, the darkness was more gentle than the night because it was
so silent.

Janvier straddled her and unfastened his trousers. She took
him into her mouth. He stroked her cheek, his fingers as gentle
as strands of seaweed. When he felt her excitement rising, he
covered her and entered her fiercely. The lethargy that had possessed her since the abortion dissolved under the onslaught, like a
castle made of sand. She was alive again, a whole person.

"You belong to me, Emma. You will never be separated from
me. Never, never, never."

* * *

The Air France plane from Bangkok skidded on the wet runway after touching down. It was two hours late, having been blown off course during a raging thunderstorm. When it finally halted in front of the terminal, the passengers, many of whom had become ill during the flight, breathed a collective sigh of relief. Hazen, the first one off the plane, commandeered a taxi and told the driver to take him to Dakow.

The windows of his villa were dark and the house was quiet. He knew that Emma would be sleeping at this hour. He crept up the stairs and opened the door of their bedroom. In the glow from the streetlamp outside, he could see that the bed was empty.

He switched on the light and noticed right away that something was terribly wrong. The bed had not been slept in. Her closet and bureau drawers were empty.

"Pham! Pham!"

The servant appeared in the doorway.

"Where is Madame Hazen?" Hazen demanded in French.

"Gone, monsieur. Two days ago. She took everything and went away in a taxicab."

"Did she leave a note?"

"Yes, monsieur. In the dining room."

Hazen found an envelope propped against a tureen on the sideboard. He ripped it open.

Dear Alan,

I'm trying to think of the hardest news story I ever had to write. It didn't compare with this. I like and respect you more than any man I have ever known. To be your wife has been the greatest privilege I can imagine, and I know I'm a fool for leaving you. But I don't love you the way a wife should love a husband. Marrying you was a terrible mistake. I wish I could think of the right words to thank you for all that you have done for me in the past two months. Your friendship was a wonderful gift that I shall cherish for the rest of my life.

Yours most sincerely,
Emma

*　*　*

The next morning, Hazen went to Monsieur de Chesnay's villa, hoping to confront her. But her old landlord told him that she had gone away with Captain Janvier.

"I saw them leave together, two hours after she said good-bye to me. One of those women must have told him she was here. If I had only known what they were up to." The old man tugged at his long gray mustache. "He is a bad man. Very bad. Ah, I am so sorry. You do not need to tell me about women. I have loved so many of them. Look, I have made some sketches of her. I was going to paint her portrait as a wedding gift. Would you like them?"

Hazen spent the rest of the day at his desk at home, studying the sketches while he nursed a bottle of bourbon. After the first few drinks, he decided that he hated Emma. Marrying her had been sheer folly. She was still Janvier's whore. Marriage hadn't changed that.

He drank some more, and decided that he would find her and bring her back. After all, he loved her, didn't he? And she loved him. They had been happy together, deliriously happy. He would keep her locked up if necessary until she came to her senses.

When the bottle was nearly empty, he decided he was an idiot for thinking he could tackle the entire First BEP. Did he really want to humiliate himself in front of Janvier again? Was Emma worth it? No, no, she was a whore. A Jezebel.

He held a match to the corner of one of the sketches de Chesnay had given him. But as soon as the paper started to burn, he slapped at the flames with the palm of his hand and snuffed them out. With a moan more like a sob than a sigh, he put his head down on his arms and closed his eyes.

Eliane de Mornay found him in this position when she called at his house at nine-thirty that evening.

"What is all this?" She shook him. "I heard from a friend of mine who is a pilot that he flew an American girl, a journalist, to Hanoi yesterday. Was it Emma?" Then she saw de Chesnay's drawing. "So she has left you. I am not surprised. Men like Janvier are like malaria parasites: Once they are in your blood, you cannot get rid of them. Every once in a while you burn with fever. Then it goes away. But you are never really cured."

"I don't understand," Hazen said in a dazed, whisky-roughened voice. "She loves me. I know she does. Why? Why did she go with him?"

"Robert Janvier has put a spell on your Emma. He has a tremendous power over most women. Not me. I have always known he was trouble. Come, Alan, I will put you to bed. I have never seen you like this before. I rather like it. You are much more human."

"Don't leave me tonight, Eliane." Hazen stumbled and fell on the stairs. Eliane hauled him to his feet. "Stay with me."

"Stay with you? Certainly not. You don't want me."

"Yes, I do. Please, Eliane. I need you."

"Oh, all right. Really, men are such babies."

Hazen fell back onto his bed. Eliane deftly removed his shoes and trousers. "Shouldn't have left her," he moaned as she pulled the covers over him. "Told her I was going to Hanoi, but from there I went to Bangkok. Stayed away too long. Shouldn't have gone. Mistake."

"You are right, that was very stupid." She stripped off her clothes and lay down beside him. "What did you have to do in Bangkok that was so important?"

"Special emissary from the White House—wanted a firsthand report on the war. The president thinks it might heat up since the Korean truce. All very secret. Couldn't be seen talking to him here or in Hanoi."

"Oh, naturally not. These politicians do love secrecy. I hope you persuaded him to tell his government not to throw good money after bad?"

"No. Said we needed more arms, planes. Vital we support the French. Worked, too. Did you see this morning's paper? Eisenhower's speech? Got to block the commies here before they infect the rest of Asia. Just what I told his man. Oh, God, Eliane, I feel so awful. Hold me."

"Poor Alan." Eliane smoothed the hair away from his forehead. "You are so afraid of your feelings. When they begin to control you and you don't know what else to do, you drink. I would not be here in your bed right now if you were the least bit sober. I know that. But I don't mind. No, I don't mind at all."

14

AUGUST 31, 1953 (Postcard)

Dear Mom and Aunt Louise—

Here I am in Hanoi covering the escalating war in
the north. Alan had to stay in Saigon, but he'll join
me soon. The Little Lake in the picture is just a
few blocks from the Hotel Metropole, my new
address. It's a step up from the Caravelle in Luang
Prabang, but still pretty tired. Good thing I'm an
old, experienced hand at Rat Control now! Honest,
I'll write a long, newsy letter real soon.

Best love, Emma

The green light flashed. The dispatcher slid open the door and
signaled to the men to get ready. Janvier took his place in the
first stick of twelve parachutists and clipped his static line to the
guide wire that was strung along the ceiling of the Dakota's fuselage. Folding his hands over the emergency pack on his chest, he
turned and faced the open door. His concentration was complete.
He did not look at Emma.

A buzzer sounded, telling them that they were over their target. One by one, the dozen paratroopers dropped out of the
plane.

In her notebook, Emma jotted down the order in which the
men jumped: Jazzi, Max, Spanish John, Pepi, Ahmed, Helmut,
Adolph, Fido. Janvier. Lucky Pierre gave her the thumbs-up and
a wide grin. Rocco, Gustave. One by one she went down the list.
She knew them well, and she concentrated fiercely, matching

face to name and story to face. If she concentrated hard enough, maybe the face and name of Alan Hazen would vanish from her memory.

The day after she arrived in Hanoi, Emma had visited the headquarters of the First Legion Parachute Battalion near the military airbase at Bach-Mai. Except for Constance Burton, who turned on her heel and marched away when she saw Emma, the men welcomed her warmly. They remembered that she had brought them luck in Cambodia, and they were eager to show off their skills as soldiers and paratroopers to the pretty lady journalist.

Her month-long sojourn with them had been Janvier's idea: "You want to write about the war? Make our war your war. Live with us, fight with us."

Emma embraced the tension, the grim humor, the intensity of life in a war zone. She ate the Legionnaires' food, admired pictures of their wives and girlfriends, even played poker with them during the nightly mortar attacks when sleep was impossible.

In October, Captain Janvier and Lucky Pierre were temporarily assigned to a special commando training school as instructors. Emma joined the class of fresh-faced soldiers newly attached to the First BEP, and accompanied them to an island in the Bay of Along. Although Hazen had told her about the numerous small islands dotting the bay, nothing had prepared her for the feeling that she was sailing among bones, exploring the exposed parts of the earth's skeleton. The launch that carried the soldiers out to the campsite glided under stone arches thirty feet high, slid through rocky tunnels, and circled spindles and columns that over the centuries had either been sculpted by the action of wind and water into fantastic shapes or whittled to an impossible thinness.

Emma was given one of the few houses on the island, a miserable shack made of rotting boards and roofed with corrugated iron. Lacking all the amenities, even a bed, offering only privacy and the company of some very large spiders, it served as a trysting place for her and Janvier.

During the two-week training course, Emma learned to handle rocket launchers and automatic rifles. She clambered up nets made of rope, crossed ravines hand over hand along bridges of fraying vines, and crawled beneath deadly tangles of barbed wire. But she never conquered her old terror of high places, and neither Lucky Pierre's gentle coaxing nor Janvier's sneering taunts would induce her to strap on a parachute and make her first jump. The idea of dropping like a stone, through strands of cloud toward the hard, spinning earth, gave her cold sweats and screaming nightmares. When the time came for her classmates to practice their skills in the air, she stayed behind, preferably on the ground or at least strapped into the plane.

Emma asked Lucky Pierre if he was frightened when he jumped out of a plane. He shrugged. "Sure. It feels good to be scared. At least you know you are alive, right?" Then he laughed loudly and clapped her on the shoulder.

Through it all, Janvier acted as her guide and mentor. He joined the other men in poking fun at her American accent and laughing at her vain attempts to maintain her composure during mortar practice, when the exploding shells shook the ground on which they stood. Like the rest of the First BEP, Janvier's new recruits accepted Emma's relationship with their captain in good humor. His leadership was not based on reciprocal love between him and his men, but on his phenomenal power over them, a power that seemed to serve him as well in the army as it did with women. Perhaps the soldiers felt a kinship with Emma, for whatever resentment they felt toward Janvier's flaunting of regulations with her, they did not let it interfere with their performance of duty. For his part, only on rare occasions did Janvier leer or swagger to show his men that his physical and emotional mastery of Emma was complete. And although he made few pretensions to discretion, frequently coming to her even before his men were all bedded down for the night, never once while she lived with the First BEP did Janvier strike her in anger.

Through the window of the Dakota, Emma saw the bodies hurtling down toward the patchwork green of the Red River delta. When their static lines had played out and jerked their parachutes open, the men were eclipsed by blossoming flowers of white silk.

"What if his parachute doesn't open?"

The thought crept into Emma's mind like a whispered message from Satan. She recoiled from it, tried to ignore it, and then she began to wonder if she had finally acknowledged her most secret desire. If Janvier died, she would at last be free of him.

"Oh, God." She lowered her head onto her knees. One of the men from the second stick, assuming she felt airsick, offered her a piece of chewing gum.

The plane made another pass over the drop zone and released the second group of jumpers. Then it rose higher before swinging around to head back to the Bach-Mai airfield near Hanoi. Janvier and the First BEP had dropped into the village of Lac Sam in the delta, a vital pocket that the Viet Minh had refused to yield. Down on the ground, the men were unbuckling their parachutes and wadding up the silk, gathering their weapons and locating supplies, coming together into a single fighting unit. Two men from the second stick, struck by enemy fire, would be dead before they even landed.

Back in Hanoi for the first time in two weeks, Emma began to type a rough draft of her story: "Hanoi lacks the sunburned brightness of Saigon, and some of that city's Parisian flair, but lately this staid northern capital has been charged with a new vigor and vitality. Since the war in Korea ended with a truce three months ago, the Chinese have increased their supply of arms to the Viet Minh. The focus of the war has shifted markedly from south to north, as the Viet Minh attempt to push the French out of the all-important Red River delta region. Crucial to the success of the high command's plans for the area are the men of the French Foreign Legion's First Parachute Bat—"

She looked at her manuscript. It was wordy, dull, guaranteed to make the reader turn the page to the funnies. She ripped the page out of her typewriter and discarded it. Pulling on a sweater, she set out for the Grand Lac on the eastern side of the city, a body of water so large that one could not see the opposite shore, only a smudged gray horizon scored by a couple of sailboats.

Emma decided that when she returned to America—if she ever did—she wanted to live beside the water. A stream, a lake, an ocean—anywhere, so long as she could gaze into shimmering depths and absorb the calm world that existed there, airless and rather colorless but never devoid of life. A child of the parched, windswept prairie, she found Hanoi's two lakes and numerous waterfront pagodas irresistible. She reached an arched bridge over a lagoon of the Grand Lac. For two hours she watched the ducks gliding past beneath her, dabbing with their beaks at floating bits of flotsam.

Waiting. Waiting for Janvier to come striding through the lobby of the Metropole in his camouflage fatigues, a cigar clamped between his teeth, a mysterious parcel tucked under his arm. After a mission, he always brought her something extravagant and expensive, spoils of war, as he called his gifts—bottles of perfume whose heady fragrance made her feel faint, silk stockings so sheer that they seemed to vanish when she put them on, elegant gowns, bits of lingerie so delicate that they fell apart in his rough soldier's hands. By surviving another mission, Janvier had earned his pleasures, and he took them greedily.

"My God, can't I go anywhere without falling over you?"

Constance Burton stood a few feet away. Her red beret was perched precariously on the side of her head.

"I noticed you didn't jump into Lac Sam today," Emma said. "Have you transferred out of Captain Janvier's unit?"

"Wouldn't you just love that? No, I had a go-around with malaria last week and those fool doctors wouldn't give me permission to jump. I'm surprised you didn't make the jump yourself so you could be closer to your lover. No, I forgot, you're too scared."

"I'm not here to participate in this war," Emma said, "only to observe and write about it."

"Oh, yes," Burton drawled, "I heard how you observed the

students at the commando school. Those boys had to sleep with you in order to graduate, isn't that right? They deserve a lot of credit. I'm surprised you haven't given the whole First BEP syphilis by now."

"I know why you're spreading rumors about me," Emma said. "You're jealous."

"Jealous? Why should I be jealous of a pig—" Seeing Emma take a step toward her, Burton whipped her pistol out of its holster and aimed it at Emma's chest. Her eyes were hard and gray like pebbles. "I would advise you not to. I would love nothing better than to drill a neat little hole right through your heart. I'm warning you, stay away from me. If we ever find ourselves in a place where there's no one else around and I can make it look like an accident, I'll kill you. I'll shoot you or knife you, and then I'll leave you to the crows and the buzzards."

"You won't get the chance," Emma said. "Robert will protect me."

"Robert!" Lieutenant Burton guffawed. "That's a good joke. But you're right. Perhaps I should be patient. If I don't kill you, he'll do it for me. It will just take a little longer, that's all. You're losing your looks already. Your health will go next. In a few months you'll be dead anyway, either from one beating too many at his hands or from those nice little cuts you'll put in your wrists some dark night when you can't escape the fact that you've thrown your life away on a lunatic and a monster. Think about it." Her tone changed, becoming smooth and silken. "An honorable way of getting yourself out of a messy situation. You won't feel any pain. I hear it's best done in a tub of warm water. You can bleed to death without making a mess on the floor."

"Shut up!" Emma shouted. "I have no intention of killing myself to suit you."

"I have nothing to do with it. When Janvier's finished with you, you'll be as good as dead." Burton holstered her pistol and walked away down the path.

Emma watched darkness descending over the water. She knew that the lakeside pagodas and pavilions were dangerous places after dark. Every so often a young couple seeking a private place to make love would be found massacred by the Viet Minh. But tonight, Emma was not concerned about her safety. She was too aware of the dangers she could see to fear those she could not see.

Not wishing to stay alone in her hotel room that night, she decided to attend a reception for some visiting congressmen from America. She would collect their impressions of the country and of the way the French were fighting the war and send them back to F. X., who might give them an inch or two.

She put on a strapless green brocade sheath with a matching stole. Her hair was loose, brushed back from her forehead and hanging in rippling waves to her shoulders. A small notebook and gold mechanical pencil fit neatly into a black beaded purse Janvier had given her.

Her press card and an engraved invitation admitted her to the Citadel, the building from which the officers of the high command conducted the war. A guard directed her to the ballroom on the second floor. As usual, the other reporters were doing their work at the bar at one end of the room. Catching sight of Ambassador Bunning and his wife, Emma started toward them. Mrs. Bunning saw her coming, and her face froze into an expression of horror and distaste, much like a Methodist churchwoman discovering that mice had built a nest in the cupboard under the sink in the church kitchen. Taking her husband's arm, Mrs. Bunning spun him around and marched him away to the far corner of the room.

Emma stopped in her tracks. Of course. Like everyone else in Saigon and Hanoi, the Bunnings must have heard that she had abandoned her husband of just a few weeks and had run off with her old lover, Captain Robert Janvier. She wondered if Alan Hazen was receiving sympathy in equal amounts to the scorn and loathing she had just reaped.

Her cheeks burning from the rebuff, she made her way to the bar. As she approached, Walter Ashbourne, who had lost his enthusiasm for the war on his second day in Saigon when he found out that the bar at the Majestic did not stock his favorite brand of bourbon, was talking to a newcomer to their ranks, a boy whose freckled nose and blonde crewcut branded him as an American even before one noticed his synthetic shirt and clip-on bow tie.

"Now you may not believe this, Duncan," Ashbourne said loudly as he caught sight of Emma, "but this magnificent creature is a reporter. Yessir, a real live reporter just like you and me. Makes you wonder if you've died and gone to heaven, doesn't it, when the competition looks like that? Emma Vaughan, come on over here and meet Duncan Ramsey. He's just out from St. Louis. His first trip abroad."

"How do you do, Miss Vaughan?"

Emma could tell that Ramsey's enthusiasm was still high; he was even being polite to a fellow journalist. She greeted the two men coolly and asked the barman for a daiquiri. Ramsey began to burble about how excited he was to find himself covering a war in Southeast Asia after only two years in the city room at the *Dispatch*. In ringing tones, Ashbourne reminded him to be sure and take his quinine pills every day and always to wear a rubber whenever he slept with a whore. Ramsey blushed to the roots of his fair hair. The other men at the bar laughed.

"If you want to learn how to find the news in this country, you'll take some tips from Miss Vaughan," Ashbourne counseled his protégé. "Of course, she has some advantages that you and I don't have. While you and I are out pounding the pavements in the heat or sweating in briefing rooms or picking up leeches in rice paddies, she does her work flat on her back in her hotel room. You'll have a hard time scooping our Emma, unless you want to bare your bum to the Moroccans."

Smiling, Emma took a sip of her daiquiri. It tasted tart and astringent, like vinegar. Ashbourne was still doubled up with laughter, and Duncan Ramsey was deciding where to look. She sidled up to Ashbourne and dashed her drink in his face. His laughter died, and he coughed and sputtered.

"And now you know, Mr. Ramsey, why Mr. Ashbourne has soared to the very top of his profession," she said icily. "He always knows just who to bare his bum to." She rode the tide of her colleagues' laughter out the door.

She was still rigid with anger when she walked into the lobby of the Metropole ten minutes later. The night clerk called to her as she passed the desk.

"Someone left this for you, madame."

It was a small leather case. Inside, nestled on a bed of white satin, lay a pair of straight razors with handles made of horn. Their steel blades glinted with wicked sharpness. With a horrified gasp, Emma closed the case and tossed it on the desk.

"Get rid of those," she told the clerk. "I don't care what you do with them—keep them or sell them or give them away. But get rid of them. I don't want to see them again."

In November, Janvier returned to Hanoi, having spent a month fighting in the delta paddy fields around Lac Sam. Jazzi was dead, he told her. And Spanish John. And a few others whose faces she remembered well. For them, the story had come to an end.

He was bearded, exhausted, disgusted by conventional combat methods that had so little effect against an enemy that would not stand and fight but who simply melted away into the irrigation ditches and paddy fields.

"They hide under the water and breathe through reeds." He threw himself down on the sagging love seat in the sitting room of their suite at the Metropole and stretched out his legs. Emma poured him a Pernod, then knelt in front of him and unlaced his boots. "They can stay that way for hours. We go along, poking around with our bayonets in the water, but do you think we find anything? Like fishing without bait. We did manage to catch one trying to sneak into our camp with a couple of grenades hung on his belt. A kid, thirteen years old. Wouldn't talk, no matter what we did to him. Finally I got disgusted and skewered him through the liver."

Emma uttered a cry of dismay. Janvier looked surprised.
"What's the matter? Do you think the Viets don't treat our spies
the same way? This is war, not a child's game of cops and robbers.
Come, kiss me, *chérie.* I have missed you, Emma. This is the
moment I look forward to the most, when I open your blouse and
kiss your lovely breasts."

He drew her close to him. The magic of his kisses and caresses
banished everything else from her mind. They slid to the floor,
the war forgotten.

"Now, open your present," he commanded.

"You've already given me my present."

"No, that was just the preview." He sat behind her on the carpet, his arms clamped around her waist. "Wait until later, my
darling. You shall have the full performance with colored lights
and music, firecrackers and cheering crowds—"

Laughing, Emma wrestled with the ribbon and the silver wrap-
ping paper. When she saw the contents of the box, her smile
faded into astonishment.

Janvier had brought her a blue silk *ao dai* and a pair of white
silk trousers. The dress was tightly fitted, with a high neck and
long sleeves and a skirt slashed to the waist on both sides.

"I miss the whores of Saigon," he said dreamily. "The most
beautiful whores in the world. Come, Emma, put on your new
costume and we will go have a drink down at the Taverne Royale
with the brave officers and their ugly wives."

"I can't wear this in public." Emma stood and held the blue
silk fabric against her body.

"Ah, but you can." Janvier smiled.

"I won't do it! I don't want to look like your—*congai!*" she
blurted, throwing the garment down on his lap.

"Put it on." Behind his unwavering smile, Janvier's teeth were
clenched. Slowly, he picked up the *ao dai* and handed it to her.

"I won't, Robert. Please don't ask me—"

"Listen, you stupid little slut." He jumped up and slapped her
face. "Don't you ever refuse me when I give you an order." She

gazed at him steadily, without moving or speaking. He slapped her again and again. Then he grabbed her breasts and dug his strong fingers into them until he drew blood and she thought she would pass out from the pain.

"Robert," she gasped. "Please. Stop." She tried to fend him off but he kneed her hard in the groin and she fell back on the floor, doubled over with agony.

Janvier hauled her to her feet and pushed her toward the bedroom. "Get dressed. And do something with your hair. You look like a witch."

Half an hour later, they left their suite at the Metropole. Emma's eyes were dry and her pale features were set in a neutral expression. Janvier was cheerful and garrulous. They walked to the Taverne Royale near the Petit Lac and sat sipping their drinks, Emma a double scotch instead of her usual daiquiri, Janvier his Pernod. She felt self-conscious about the turquoise blue silk that outlined her figure. The other occupants of the café, French and Vietnamese alike, were whispering and watching her with unmitigated scorn.

"Something's up in Saigon," Janvier was saying. "The high command is preparing to stage a big operation, but I'm not sure where. I have heard whispers about the Laotian border, perhaps the valley around Dien Bien Phu. Do you know where that is?"

Emma shook her head.

With his fingernail, Janvier made a wavy sketch on the tablecloth. "About eight miles from the border, in the highlands. It is a big opium-processing center. The Meo tribes in the area grow a lot of the stuff, and the Thais sell it."

"But that's solid Viet Minh territory."

"Of course. But it would be simple to take, easy to secure, and it would give General Navarre a strong defensive position in the northwest, as well as a base from which to stage guerrilla operations of his own." He stubbed out his cigarette. "I understand the airfield is a good one, the best in that part of the country. Supplies would have to be flown in, of course. The hills all around are covered with thick jungle. Like Nasan: If the enemy gets too close, we can pound them to bits from the air."

"But I don't understand. The French had to abandon Nasan."

"That is true. So what can our fearless leaders be thinking of? As I say, it is only rumor. Anyway, we don't have much time to spend together. I must report back to Bach-Mai in three days. But you and I, Emma, we can live a lifetime in three days, no?" He reached across the table and touched her cheek.

Emma felt her heart begin to race and skip. She must be crazy, she thought, but when he looked at her and caressed her, she melted inside. And yet only an hour earlier, he had come close to killing her.

Very lightly, Janvier stroked the back of Emma's hand, and then he took her hand in his. As their fingers meshed, Emma looked into Janvier's eyes. Their combined desire rose and was recognized and welcomed. They finished their drinks in silence, their heads almost touching.

As Emma rose from the table, the blue silk *ao dai* clung to her breasts and hips. I feel like such a parasite, she thought. I came to this country to watch their war and to spy on their grief. I eat their food, and I let them scrub my floors and iron my blouses and serve me in restaurants. Her hand tightened on Janvier's. Now I'm even wearing their clothes. I've left them nothing of their own. If I were a Vietnamese, I would want to kill me.

She moved toward the door, then halted sharply, paralyzed. She felt the room begin to spin, and she grabbed a chair for support. A middle-aged redheaded woman wearing some kind of government badge had just been seated at a table near the entrance. Her escort was Alan Hazen.

Janvier pushed Emma toward the door and rested his hands on her shoulders. "Ah, Monsieur Hazen. I haven't had a chance to thank you for your extraordinary kindness to my beloved Miss Vaughan."

Emma did not wait to hear Hazen's response. She bolted through the door and ran down the street, the skirts of her blue *ao dai* flapping like wings. She ran until her legs would take her no further and the pain in her side crippled her. She slowed to a walk. A taxi halted in front of her at the next intersection. The rear door opened and Janvier stepped out. Gently, he pulled Emma into the taxi beside him.

"We are going to smoke some opium. Driver," he barked, "take us to Rue de Soie." Janvier put his arms around Emma and kissed her eyes and her cheeks. "Your muscles feel quite tense, *ma chère*. The opium will relax you. You will see how small your problems really are, if they can melt away with a few puffs of smoke."

"Really, if I smoke enough pipes of opium, will I forget what a fool I've made of myself? Will I forget my husband, that man back there who loves me more than you ever could? Will I forget that I am a soldier's whore, scorned and spat upon by so-called civilized women, the joke of the Press Club? My mother would die of shame if she saw me now."

Janvier laughed. "You have had more pleasure in the past year than your mother has experienced in her entire lifetime."

Entering the Chinese quarter, the taxi wound through crowded narrow streets that bore the names of the crafts that had been practiced there since ancient times: Silk Street, Copper Street, Coffin Street, the Street of Veils, the Street of Metal Forgers.

They pulled up in front of a shuttered shop whose faded shingle advertised Ho Luk & Cie. *Soie Pure.* Emma shivered. Its bland innocence reminded her of the bicycle shop in Cholon. Yet somewhere in the bowels of this building was a *fumerie*, a room furnished with hard cots on which lay the inert and withered bodies of men who lived only to breathe the sweet stink of opium.

The proprietor welcomed them with a low bow and showed them to a private corner behind a carved screen. Two low couches lay end to end in the form of an **L**. Emma and Janvier lay down with their heads touching, her gold against his black, and their bodies angled away from each other.

A young boy came in with a tray bearing the pipes, the lamp, and other paraphernalia. He was twelve or thirteen, as beautiful as a boy could be, with long dark lashes and straight black hair. Emma watched his slender hands tending the warm opium, kneading a bit of the paste between two needles until it spun a fine thread, shaping it into a tiny ball. He prepared the first pipe and handed it to Emma.

Seconds expanded into days. Outside, unseen, the moon rose high over the city and called them forth, sated. Emma and her lover walked slowly through the winding streets.

They reached the edge of the Grand Lac. In the moonlight, the water was a great pewter platter, hard and smooth. On an island at the far end of a causeway, the golden pillars of a pagoda glittered like the portals of a fairy-tale dwelling. The world trembled.

Emma pressed her body against Janvier's. "I love you, Robert. Promise me you'll never leave me. Never, never, never. Hold me. Hold me."

Winter came to Hanoi, the season of the *crachin*, dense morning fog followed by a steady cheerless drizzle. On the lakes, the lotus flowers died, and their leathery blue-gray leaves yellowed and shriveled on high taut stems.

By mid-December, the city's cafés and hotels overflowed with diplomats, journalists, observers, and soldiers of every rank. With the occupation of Dien Bien Phu, the war entered a critical phase. Janvier's unit of the First Legion Parachutists had landed in the valley at the end of November, along with divisions of Vietnamese, Algerian, and French soldiers. Throughout December, fighting men continued to pour into Dien Bien Phu, along with tons of supplies. Army engineers built bunkers and shelters, laid down a perforated metal airstrip, and helped secure defensive positions on the perimeter.

"It's not fair for you to have a lover at the front," Walter Ashbourne grumbled. "That's something the rest of us have not been able to achieve, desirable females being in short supply out there."

"I don't depend on Captain Janvier to give me news," Emma said sharply. They were sitting at a table in Chez Betty, the bar currently favored by newsmen.

"Shit. I wish I'd written that piece you did on the First BEP's commando training school. Are you sure your boyfriend can't sneak us into Dien Bien Phu? So far the high command has given all the plums to Frenchmen."

Just then a French soldier wearing a pilot's wings came up to them. "Mademoiselle Vaughan? I am François Delaporte. May I speak with you a moment?"

"Of course." Her heart pounding, Emma led him to a quiet corner away from the bar. "Is it Captain Janvier? Is he all right?"

"I imagine so. I just saw him yesterday. He is on a search-and-destroy mission about twenty miles from Dien Bien Phu. He gave me this package for you. You're supposed to deliver it for him and pick up something in return." Delaporte withdrew a small parcel from his jacket and handed it to Emma. She glanced at the address: a Chinese name on Coffin Street. "If you want to send him anything, I will be flying a helicopter out there tomorrow morning to pick up some of their wounded. I will be leaving Bach-Mai at five hundred hours."

"Thanks." After the pilot had gone, Emma returned to her table and picked up her notebook and umbrella. "Sorry, Ashbourne, but we'll have to postpone our talk for a few days."

As she left the bar, he called after her, "Where are you going now?"

"I have to pack up some stuff to send to my lover at Dien Bien Phu."

"What are you sending him?" Ashbourne asked.

"Me."

15

DECEMBER 19, 1953

Dear Mom and Aunt Louise,

Merry Christmas! This card is coming to you
straight from the front at Dien Bien Phu, thanks to
a French army nurse who flies in regularly by
helicopter to pick up the men who have been
wounded and to drop off necessities like shampoo
and emery boards. Quartermasters and supply
sergeants don't cater to the female element here.
No battles have been fought yet, but the crews
building fortifications and bridges are under
constant attack, mostly by sniper and mortar fire
from the hills. This probably sounds terrifying, but
in reality my greatest danger is falling into a ditch
or getting hung up on barbed wire. . . .

The throb of the helicopter rotors marked the pulse of Emma's
fear. She felt a nudge in her side and looked around. Marie-
Claire Barrault, one of the flight nurses who would be attending
the wounded on the return journey, pointed to the window.
Emma gritted her teeth and looked down. They were flying over
gray-green crests of jungle whose regularity was broken occasionally by paddy fields, drained and dry and yellow with rice stubble
after the harvest.

Emma had outfitted herself in a camouflage shirt and trousers,
stout boots for hiking, a lined jacket to ward off the chill of the
nights at high altitudes, dark glasses, and a floppy canvas hat. In
her knapsack she had stashed several notebooks and pencils,
water purification tablets and tubes of insect repellent, a supply of
medicines and bandages, and a few tins of food. Her bedroll included a plastic groundsheet, a square of mosquito netting, and a

warm blanket. She also carried two pairs of quick-drying nylon underwear, a comb and a lipstick, as well as six bottles of cognac for Janvier and his men, of which they would relieve her at the earliest opportunity. She had decided against weighing herself down with a camera and film; F. X. would have to be satisfied with verbal pictures.

The helicopter, a huge French F-19 with space for a dozen wounded passengers, had lifted off from the Bach-Mai field at six o'clock that morning, an hour late. Emma had spent that hour persuading the pilot, François Delaporte, to take her along. He had finally yielded, despite Emma's not having a travel permit, and had quickly sketched their route for her on a map. They would bypass Dien Bien Phu to the north by at least thirty miles on their way to a rendezvous with the First Battalion parachutists in a place called Muong Muon.

As they lifted off, Marie-Claire, who was Delaporte's fiancée, had spoken directly into Emma's ear: "Do not be frightened. I have made hundreds of flights in helicopters like these. All the pilots are very good, and François is the best." Emma nodded, but did not relax her grip on her knapsack.

Now, as they neared their destination, she gazed south in the direction of Dien Bien Phu and tried to imagine what the days ahead would bring: war-hardened troops, haggard faces, dead faces, booby traps and guerrilla attacks, foxholes and gunfire. Anything was preferable to this deafening mechanical, impossible suspension hundreds of feet above the ground.

Marie-Claire poked her again and pointed downward. They were losing altitude, circling as Delaporte searched for the rendezvous zone. Emma wondered how the French could possibly carry out aerial reconnaissance missions over terrain like this even with constant radio contact. She could see nothing in the unending ocean of greenery below them: no campfires, no troops, no signs of any but vegetative life. What if the Viet Minh were listening in on their radio frequency? They could wipe out Janvier's unit on the ground and then destroy the helicopter as it landed.

Then a bare patch appeared below them in which a crude cross had been scratched in the pale green turf of a spent poppy field. As the helicopter alighted, Marie-Claire opened the doors and jumped down. Emma, desperate to find herself once again on hard ground, grabbed her gear and followed. From the fringe of jungle around the clearing, men ran forward carrying their wounded comrades in slings made of saplings and vines. The beating rotors created a wind as powerful as the relentless prairie gales that flattened the corn and whipped the dry topsoil into dusty columns. Bending double to avoid the whirling blades, one hand clamped on her hat, Emma ran toward the edge of the clearing. The first person she saw was Fido, a Basque from the Pyrenees who spoke his French with a thick Spanish accent.

"Where is Janvier?" she asked, grinning breathlessly. Fido, welcoming her with a flash of white teeth, jerked his thumb over his shoulder. Emma found Janvier assisting with the evacuation of the wounded on the other side of the clearing. When he saw her he dropped his end of a makeshift stretcher. The wounded man groaned, but Janvier paid no attention. Another soldier ran over to help.

"What in hell do you think you're doing here?" Janvier demanded.

"I wanted to surpri—"

Without even waiting to hear her explanation, he grabbed her arm and dragged her back to the helicopter.

"Have you gone crazy?" he shouted at Delaporte, who was just climbing down from his cockpit. "What do you think you're doing, bringing her out here? I'll have you demoted for this. I promise you, you'll never fly again. I suppose she doesn't even have proper clearance."

"She said that in your letter you asked her to come out," Delaporte replied with a shrug. "How was I to know she was a liar?"

"I had to get to Dien Bien Phu," Emma said. "I'm trying to cover this war as a reporter, remember?"

Janvier turned on her. "What do you think this is, a Boy Scout camping trip? This whole area is crawling with Viets. It is the

WILD NIGHTS • 262

same all around Dien Bien Phu. We are surrounded by at least three divisions of Giap's soldiers, and you say you want to report on the war. Get back in this helicopter, damn you. You're not staying here."

Just then Marie-Claire screamed at them that one of the wounded men they had just loaded on board had died.

"Dump him out and make room for someone else," Delaporte ordered. "I'm not taking any corpses back to Saigon. Janvier can bury him here."

"You'll take this woman back," Janvier said threateningly, "or I'll—"

"Got no room for her, either. I brought her out expecting to use her space for the wounded on the way home. Damn it." Frustrated by having to shout at the top of his lungs, Delaporte moved away from the helicopter. After ordering Emma to stay with the chopper, Janvier went with him. As soon as their backs were turned, Emma gave Marie-Claire a wave and sprinted off to join the men watching the action from the edge of the clearing.

"Hide me," she said. Rocco, a scrawny Neapolitan, pulled her over to a stand of palmettos and told her to keep her head down. The other men were grinning.

By the time Janvier and Delaporte returned to the helicopter, all the wounded were loaded and Marie-Claire was insisting that they must take off at once. From behind the screen of palmetto fronds, Emma saw the two men arguing and gesticulating. Janvier waved his arms; Delaporte shrugged. Then the pilot climbed into the cockpit and Marie-Claire closed the doors. The machine reared straight up, flattening young saplings with its wind. The whole operation had taken less than ten minutes.

Janvier waited until the roar of the machine had faded to a low hum; then from the middle of the clearing he yelled, "Emma! Emma, come here at once!"

"Might as well," Rocco said. "We can't hide you forever."

Her confident smile and easy walk concealing her terror, Emma approached him. "You want to see me, Captain?"

When they were alone together in the middle of the clearing, Janvier grabbed her arm. "That package. Did you deliver it?"

"Yes, of course I delivered it."

"And the money he gave you, what did you do with it?"

"He just handed me an envelope. I didn't know there was any money in it. I didn't have time to do anything else with it, so I posted it to myself at the hotel. They'll hold it until I get back."

"Are you crazy? Do you know how much was there? Fifty thousand francs. And you left it at the hotel! I ought to—" Janvier drew his fist back. Emma stood her ground, daring him to strike her with his men looking on. He thought better of it and contented himself with bellowing. "I am in the middle of a search-and-destroy mission and I have already lost half my men, and you tell me you left—Listen to me, Madame Reporter. I don't want to hear a whisper out of you until we get to Dien Bien Phu, is that clear? Stay out of my sight. If I see you, if I hear so much as a word out of you, I swear I will shoot you myself. All right," he shouted to his men, who were watching from the edges of the forest, "what the hell are you looking at? Get moving. Bury that man and be quick about it. We're getting out of here." He spun on his heel and stalked off.

"Whew." A plucky corporal named Gustave ran forward with Emma's knapsack and bedroll. "Never saw the captain that het up before. Don't worry, miss, you can march with me. The boys will look after you."

Emma spotted Lucky Pierre's unmistakable bulk near a thicket of palmetto. He was lying flat on his back, with his helmet covering his face and his rifle clutched in his two hands like a dead man with a lily, as one of the men said. She nudged him with her toe. With lightning quickness, he sprang into a crouch and pointed his bayonet at her belly. Then he recognized her, and his face split into a wide grin.

"Ah, so it is you, Madame Journalist! I almost cut you in two, you know that? The boss didn't tell me you were coming."

"He didn't know. He's furious with me."

"No matter. You are here now. Come to get a good story about the First BEP, eh?" He picked up his backpack. "Looks like we're getting ready to push off. See that native over there? That's our guide. A Meo." Emma had already identified the man from his black turban and weighty silver necklaces. "They're friendlier than the local Thais, and best of all they hate the Viets. This place was a real rathole. Two of those men the chopper took away just now were shot by snipers last night while they stood guard. You'd better march with me in the middle of the column. Don't stray off the trail, and don't touch anything—not a vine or a leaf—nothing. It might spring a booby trap. If shooting starts, fall flat on your face and roll into the underbrush at the side of the path, okay?"

"Where are we going?"

"We're heading for the Pavie Track, which leads straight into Dien Bien Phu. The Viets are everywhere, but you'll be all right if you follow my instructions. Let's go."

The Meo guide, a small barefooted man wearing the distinctive black clothing and silver necklaces of his tribe, moved to the front of the column, with Janvier right behind. Among the twenty or so soldiers, Emma saw Constance Burton. Her spirits sank. It was bad enough to have earned Janvier's enmity, but now she would have to endure this woman's sneers and threats.

Emma walked straight up to the lieutenant, who was tightening a strap on her pack. "Thanks for the razors," she said. "I don't think I'll have a chance to use them."

Burton bared her teeth in an approximation of a grin. "By the end of this march, you'll wish you had."

The men moved silently along the trail, which was no wider than a bicycle path in most places. They were alert to every sound and movement in the trees around them. Although the terrain was rough and steep and the pace relentless, Emma was determined not to slow the march. Damn Janvier anyway. She was going to cover this war whether he liked it or not. And neither he nor that hatchet-faced Burton nor a whole squad of Viets would stop her.

Under the cutting straps of her knapsack, Emma's shoulders grew sore, then numb. Although this was supposedly the dry season, the path underfoot was treacherous, slick with the moisture of heavy evening dew and early-morning fog, scored by heaving tree roots and deep gullies left by the torrents of the previous summer's monsoon.

In the middle of the afternoon, they stopped for a light meal of canned rations and cigarettes.

"You'll see for yourself what shit we're up against here." Pepi, another Spaniard, swallowed a bit of beef stew, then passed the can over to Emma, who finished it. Apprehensive about her helicopter journey, she had skipped breakfast that morning. "Those donkey-brained, mother-loving generals dumped us into a turd-filled basin in the heart of enemy territory, nearly two hundred miles from our closest source of supplies. Not only are we supposed to defend that stinking pesthole, but they want us to take up offensive positions all around it as well. I shit in the milk of those turd-licking cretins."

"Right now, we are supposed to be cleaning up the perimeter." Lucky Pierre had finished his ration and was enjoying a hand-rolled cigarette. "You can see what it's like: jungle so thick that a Viet could be hiding two feet away from you and you would never see him. We are supposed to be able to defend the Laotian border from Dien Bien Phu, but it is inaccessible. Eight miles away, but it might as well be eight hundred for all the good we can do."

Fifteen minutes later, Emma found herself wrestling against the hip-deep current of a swiftly flowing creek. The members of the platoon linked arms to form a chain and pulled each other across. Even so, Emma lost her footing and thrashed around so violently in her panic that the man in front of her lost his grip on her arm. But Lucky Pierre was behind her, and the icy waters had scarcely closed over her head when she felt him jerk her up into the air again. Spitting and coughing, Emma opened her eyes to find herself clasped tightly against Lucky Pierre's ample form. With the line broken, the two of them were being forced downstream by the current, but after some careful maneuvering over slippery rocks they rejoined the line and completed the crossing without further incident.

The water had hardly drained out of Emma's boots before they came to another stream, wider but shallow and much less treacherous than the first. Half the men had already waded across when suddenly Lucky Pierre scooped Emma up. Throwing her over his shoulder, pack and all, he pranced out into the stream. Halfway across, he stumbled over a submerged branch and fell face forward into the shallow water, dumping Emma on her rear. As soon as Lucky Pierre's head came up out of the water, Emma pushed it back under, much to the delight of the other men. Wide grins greeted Lucky Pierre as he and Emma clambered out of the creek. Only their fear of being heard by the Viet Minh kept the men from shouting with laughter.

For the rest of the day they climbed, winding up the side of the mountain that loomed above them, a blue-green citadel that could not be breached. The path disappeared in a welter of vines and tree roots. On near-vertical slopes, roots and jutting rocks offered precarious toeholds.

"I can't climb this," Emma gasped as she confronted yet another steep precipice where floods had washed out the path.

"I'll give you a boost," Lucky Pierre said. "You can stand on my shoulders and Gustave will grab you. Ready?" He spanned her waist with his huge hands and lifted her. Emma dug her fingernails into the face of the hill and clawed her way up for a few inches until she felt the solid strength of Lucky Pierre's shoulders under her feet. Gustave was waiting for her. He took her wrist and hauled her upward while Pierre shoved from behind. Emma surmounted the ledge and fell on her face. When she looked up, she saw Constance Burton smiling down at her.

"And this is only the beginning," the lieutenant said.

The next obstacle was even worse, a sheer limestone cliff that overhung a ravine; at the bottom a stream surged over knife-sharp rocks. An Austrian named Helmut made the climb first and tossed down a rope to the others.

"Hand over hand," Lucky Pierre instructed. "Keep your eyes on the top. If you look down, you'll get dizzy."

Emma felt her arms being pulled from their sockets. The rope burned her hands, so that she could see traces of her own blood on the fiber as she struggled upward inch by inch. Above her, Helmut and the men who had preceded her shouted encouragement. She tried to ignore the beckoning hiss of the creek below: "Look at me—yes. I am beautiful—yes. Just a quick look. Look." Emma gritted her teeth. Keep going, she commanded herself. Don't look back. Her grip loosened and she began to slide backward. She couldn't do it—couldn't make it. Then she heard an encouraging shout and felt Lucky Pierre's broad hand under her bottom.

"Come on, get up there," he barked. "We can't wait all day."

A final boost and she was over the edge. The men at the top clapped her on the back and offered her cigarettes and sips from their canteens.

Finally, they reached the mountain's summit. Darkness was already spilling into the valleys like ink filling green china cups. The guide promised a village just one kilometer further. They pushed on through the thickening gloom. The village did not materialize. Two kilometers, the Meo said. Or perhaps three. But no more. Janvier called a halt to survey their position, using a compass and a map.

"We are going northwest instead of south," he said to the guide. "Where are you taking us?"

The man told him that the trail twisted around like a snake. But he swore they would reach the Pavie Track at noon on the following day.

"You are lying. You're taking us into a trap. Ahmed, search him."

Adolph and Max held the man fast while Ahmed, who was half-French and half-Algerian, stripped off the guide's clothes and examined them along with Janvier. Inside the turban they found a wad of piasters, a small map, a message handwritten in Vietnamese, and a pocketknife of Chinese manufacture.

"No Meo knows how to read or write." Janvier walked over to the naked prisoner and grabbed him by his throat with his left hand. He thrust the map under the man's nose. "You said that you were born in this area, that you knew every mountain and trail." Janvier tightened his grip. Beads of sweat popped out on the guide's forehead. Fear glistened in his dark eyes. "You're no Meo, you're a filthy Viet Minh spy."

Without another word, Janvier pulled out his knife and jammed it between the false guide's ribs. The fear vanished from the man's eyes as his blood gushed out of the wound and spilled on the ground.

"Hide him in the bushes," Janvier said to Adolph and Max.

Emma watched the execution in shocked disbelief. Suddenly she found her voice. "Robert, you had no proof! Couldn't you have found someone to translate that note? It might be harmless. And Chinese knives like that turn up in village markets all the time."

With a fistful of dried grass, Janvier wiped the dead man's blood from his knife and returned it to the sheath on his belt. As he did so, he gave Emma a look that froze her to her marrow. When Ahmed presented her with the fake Meo's silver necklaces, she accepted them mutely, sick in her soul.

They drew back to the summit of the mountain and made camp under a deep limestone cleft. The dew had already fallen. Emma huddled in the deepest recesses of the slimy, dripping rock, as far from Janvier as possible. The men near her shared their rations, but she ate sparingly before smoking a few cigarettes and accepting a swig of cognac.

After their quick supper, a third of the men dispersed to take up guard duty while the others slept. Emma wrapped herself in her jacket and blanket and lay down on her groundsheet. She was soaked to her skin and she thought she would never be warm again. A heavy blanket of fog descended at ten o'clock, muffling sounds, soaking their cigarettes, insinuating its dampness into every fold and crease and corner. Emma, wedged against the wet stone wall behind half a dozen snoring Legionnaires, dozed fit-fully.

"*Cette guerre est atroce*," one of the soldiers grumbled wearily as he lowered his body to the ground after being relieved from guard duty. "This war is atrocious."

They awoke to a gray world saturated with fog. The men said that it would not lift until noon, if then. A plane passed over-head, invisible, the roar of its engines a muffled purr. A Morane, they said, taking a load of big shots to Dien Bien Phu.

They spent the morning retracing their steps down the moun-tainside. Janvier kept them on a strict southwesterly course, hop-ing that they would eventually intersect the Pavie Track. Halfway down the slope, Pinot, the radioman, who was marching in front of Emma, slipped as he was lowering himself by rope over the face of a rock. He fell ten feet and landed on his radio. Pinot was unhurt, but the radio was crushed, useless.

With that mishap, they lost their only contact with the rest of the world. Unable to ask air patrols for guidance, Janvier had to depend on his own wits to lead them out of the jungle. After a quick glance at the mangled radio, he set off at a brisk pace, and the men followed. Although their confidence in Janvier re-mained strong, they told Emma during halts that they had never experienced such a difficult march. Forced to choose between the valleys and higher ground, Janvier always took the steeper trails, hoping that the Viet Minh would stick to the easier lowland tracks.

By midafternoon on the second day, rain began to fall. The trails filled with mud, like pig wallows. Emma watched herself decaying, moldering, growing green with fungus. Inside her boots, her feet were blistered and bloody. The sores quickly be-came ulcerated and infected. Every time they stopped, she changed her bandages and reapplied antiseptic salve.

That night she felt chills and cramps in her lower abdomen. The first signs of dysentery. Lucky Pierre came down with the symptoms at the same time. From their swim in the creek, he said.

"All the rivers and creeks in Indochina are contaminated with the amoebas."

The medical officer gave them each a couple of tablets to swallow, but he warned that these would only alleviate the worst cramps. If they didn't want to experience cramping in their muscles, they needed to consume as much fluid as possible to keep their bodies from becoming dehydrated. A few of the other men were already suffering, but the march never slowed while the sufferers left the column to relieve themselves in the bushes. One of them, a pox-scarred Parisian who called himself Jimmy, was so badly afflicted that he cut out the back of his trousers with his knife so that he wouldn't have to pull them down every time he needed to squat.

Emma, buckling her belt for the twentieth time on the second day after she came down with the disease, saw Constance Burton watching her.

"I told you you would wish you'd slit your wrists," Burton said smugly. "This march will finish you."

"Not on your life," Emma said. Her face contorted as she experienced another crippling spasm, and she plunged into the brush again.

Then on the morning of the fifth day, the rain stopped. As the sun rose higher, they emerged from the jungle to find a wider path littered with cases of spent cartridges, cigarette butts, and empty Vinogel cartons. The men cheered. Janvier motioned them to keep silent, but Emma saw an expression of profound relief cross his face.

"Fighting has taken place here this morning." Janvier crouched down. "These cigarette butts are still dry. Let's move." The platoon marched on with quickened steps, quietly but with their spirits raised.

Then, as they crossed a small poppy field, its flowers spent and the opium-rich gum secreted by their seed pods long since harvested and processed, they were fired on from the trees. The shots were coming from all sides. They were surrounded.

Rocco grabbed Emma and pushed her facedown in the reddish brown loam. "Stay there," he ordered.

Despite her terror, Emma raised her head and peered through the shafts of weeds and grasses. Through the smoke and dust she could see very little. The occasional dull explosion of a grenade punctuated the steady crackle of gunfire.

"Over here!" she heard someone shout. "A ditch."

They took cover in a mud-choked drainage canal that traversed the field. "Good," one of the men said. "Now we can hold them off for days."

An hour passed with no letup of firing. Emma wondered what would happen if they were still trapped in the ditch at nightfall, up to their waists in mud. The enemy seemed to be creeping closer. A grenade fell short, sending up a shower of sod and grass. Pepi, who was known to be reckless and somewhat crazy, leaped out of the ditch and aimed a barrage of machine-gun fire in the direction from which the grenade had been hurled. They heard a yelp, and then silence. Satisfied, he jumped back into the ditch.

"Good work, Pepi," Janvier said. "I'll take the next one." But even as he lifted his head above the edge of the ditch, a bullet whipped past his ear and buried itself in the mud of the bank behind him. "They're getting close. We'll be fighting hand to hand soon."

They were pinned down, helpless, unable to move. The men lobbed grenades and raked the grass in all directions with machine-gun fire. Enemy fire slowed, then resumed.

"There must be a thousand of 'em," Max grunted as he reloaded his rifle. "Still, I'd rather be out here in the open than back in those damned trees. Let them come and get me. I'll take fifty of them with me."

Then they heard the distinctive flub-flub of helicopter rotors. Several of the men raised their red berets on their bayonets and waved them high above the ditch. The helicopter hovered overhead, surveying the situation; then it lifted higher, out of reach of enemy fire. Half an hour later, a plane circled the area. Emma, seeing black canisters falling from its belly, wondered if they were bombs. The canisters landed and exploded in towers of flame.

"Napalm," the men told Emma gleefully. "Jellied gasoline. Now those bastards are in for it. Fried sausages for supper tonight, madame."

A breeze wafted the heat and stink of the napalm across the field. Emma detected the tang of roasting flesh. At a signal from Janvier, the paratroopers left the ditch and headed for a break in the circle of flame. As she ran, Emma glanced at the trees. The jungle was burning.

"How far are we from Dien Bien Phu now?" Panting, Emma halted beside Lucky Pierre.

"What do you mean? We're here. That ditch we just left flows into an upper arm of the Nam Yum River. See that hill straight ahead? That's Gabrielle. Wow! They've done a lot of work on the fortifications since I was here last."

Totally denuded of vegetation, the stark hill looked like a beached warship. On its summit and sides, the muzzles of artillery pieces pierced through thickets of barbed wire. Mortars had been dug in and were protected behind walls of sandbags. The riflemen who would man the strongpoint had fortified lines of trenches for themselves.

A patrol met them and escorted them down the Pavie Track, past Gabrielle and then past Anne-Marie, actually a cluster of four strongpoints that guarded the airstrip, which was a 6,600-foot-long stretch of American-made interlocking steel plates. When Emma stumbled, one of the escort soldiers hauled her to her feet, saying, "What's the matter, old man? Had a hard day in the jungle?"

She removed her sodden canvas hat and grinned at him. "*Bon jour, monsieur*. Which way are the hotels and restaurants?"

The men—her men—laughed as the soldier first gaped, then blushed scarlet clear up to his cap.

Emma had expected to remain with the First BEP, but she found her entrance to their quarters on strongpoint Huguette blocked.

"This is where we part company, *chérie.*" Janvier came up to her. "The press bunker is down there next to general headquarters." He pulled her out of the group of men and turned her back over to the escort patrol. Emma passed along the column. The men grinned at her and gave her the thumbs-up. Behind a mask of grime and mud, Constance Burton's face wore a smirk.

Stumbling into the press bunker, Emma found some of her cronies from Hanoi huddled around a packing case. They were playing cards.

"Hello, everybody."

They looked up, their faces registering surprise and dismay. Walter Ashbourne said, "Jesus, Vaughan, we expected to find you all dug in when we got here. What happened to you?"

"I took a slight detour." Oblivious of the men, Emma stripped down to her bra and panties, unfurled her bedroll, and flopped down in the nearest corner. She was aware of nothing for the rest of the night, but when she awoke the next morning, she found that her colleagues had covered her with three extra blankets.

"You were shivering," Ashbourne said. "We couldn't concentrate on our damned cards with your teeth chattering like that."

Later that day, wearing clean fatigues and sandals on her bandaged feet, and with the symptoms of dysentery finally in abeyance, thanks to doses of powerful drugs, Emma and the other reporters toured the encampment with the latest contingent of foreign dignitaries, this time including Major General Thomas Trapnell, chief of the United States Military Advisory Group, as well as the British military attaché and General Navarre, the French commander in chief.

Engineers had built bridges over the Nam Yum River, joining the two banks. Earthworks were being dug, rolls of barbed wire unfurled, bunkers and dugouts reinforced and roofed over with logs, dirt, and sandbags. Radio antennae bristled from the headquarters of every strongpoint like metallic whiskers over the denuded, distorted landscape. The lush grass that had covered most of the plain west of the river was worn away, as were the trees on the hills to the east. A coating of thick reddish dust gave everything the look of having been sculpted out of the same dull material as the earth. After four weeks of French occupation, no traces remained of the quaint raised villages that had once dotted the plain of Dien Bien Phu. They had been leveled and their bamboo beams used to shore up the walls and roofs of the French fortifications.

Emma met the new commander of Dien Bien Phu, Colonel Christian Marie Ferdinand de la Croix de Castries. One of her colleagues, a Frenchman who was reporting the war for *Le Figaro*, told her that de Castries was an expert horseman and a gambler who liked to play for high stakes. He warned her that the colonel's attractiveness to women was legendary. The strongpoints around the camp were rumored to have been named for his mistresses. These strongpoints had been cleared of trees and brush and fortified against attack: Gabrielle and Anne-Marie on the north; Isabelle in the swamps to the south; Claudine, Françoise, and Huguette on the plains to the west; and Beatrice, Dominique, Marcelle, and Eliane on the series of peaks east of the river.

"You can guess who those twin peaks of Eliane One and Eliane Two were named for," one of the other reporters whispered to Emma with a lewd chuckle. "The wife of General de Mornay and Colonel de Castries were quite intimate back in Saigon. That woman changes her lovers as frequently as some women change their underwear. I would be willing to wager that half the senior officers at the Citadel in Hanoi have enjoyed her favors, and a good many junior officers as well. I wonder why that husband of hers doesn't just lock her up?"

Emma walked over to Colonel de Castries. "When do you expect the Viet Minh to attack?" she asked.

"When they are ready," he replied with a smile. Above his monumental aristocratic nose, his dark eyes gleamed appreciatively.

"Will you be ready for them?"

"We are ready for them anytime, madame. They have one

mortar company nearby, but they cannot move heavy artillery up those mountains, whereas we have several big guns of our own which can be trained in any direction. If they attack tomorrow, we will have no trouble holding them off."

The morning fog lifted, and the daily traffic of transport planes and helicopters began. A French reporter who had arrived in Dien Bien Phu during the invasion pointed out a huge crater in the earth near the perforated steel sheets of the main runway. "I saw a bulldozer land here. The biggest Roman candle ever—its chutes failed to open. Too bad if anyone was standing under it: He was drilled fifty feet into the ground."

Emma was astonished by the international complexion of the forces fighting in Indochina: dark-skinned Moroccan and Algerian riflemen manned strongpoint Gabrielle; battalions of Thai tribesmen were at Anne-Marie; soldiers from all parts of France were everywhere, fair-haired northerners and swarthy southerners; German and Austrian soldiers were scattered liberally throughout all the divisions of the Foreign Legion. Over half the men present were Vietnamese who had been trained by the French. They served with almost every company as well as having their own elite group of parachutists.

On the bank of the river, near a wooden bridge, Emma saw rows and rows of small stones marking the graves of the men who had already died during the invasion and subsequent sorties into enemy territory.

Near Colonel de Castries' headquarters stood the hospital, a compact unit with forty-four beds and well-equipped dugouts for the operating room, the X-ray machine, and a recovery room.

"But it's so small!" Emma exclaimed. "Surely there will be more wounded than that if the Viet Minh attack."

"We will find places to put them." Major Paul Grauwin, the bald chief medical officer, looked like a Roman emperor. His tone was grim. "We always do."

Emma returned to the press bunker, where she joined a poker game and immediately won the prized sleeping corner nearest the entrance, where the air was least fetid. The French photographer who had lost it protested that he would have yielded the corner to her anyway.

"Really? I've been here nearly two days and you haven't offered it to me yet." Emma shuffled the cards.

"You're in a sour mood today," Walter Ashbourne observed. "Lovers' quarrel with your handsome captain?"

"You talk so much about my handsome captain, Ashbourne"—Emma dealt five cards all around—"I wonder if you're not madly in love with him yourself. Is anyone going to open?"

Emma's winning streak continued. After an hour of play, the others tired of the game. They started making bets on when the Viet Minh attack would commence. Christmas Day was a heavy favorite. Ashbourne cited the Battle of Trenton, when Washington's soldiers surprised the British, who were sleeping off their Christmas feast.

"Lulled by C rations and Vinogel, our troops will be easy targets," he assured his listeners. "Things will heat up here real soon. I wouldn't leave now if Madame de Mornay herself showed up in her pretty little Renault to give me a lift back to Hanoi."

"I think it's disgusting," Emma said. "The sooner the Viets attack, the sooner those men out there will start to die. Don't you care about them?"

A French photographer hummed a maudlin tune while he played an invisible violin.

"Do you think we came all this way to play cards?" the man from the *Herald Tribune* demanded. "We're here to get a story, the biggest one this war has produced so far. You're no different from the rest of us, Emma. I've seen you when you're going after news. But I guess we can afford to be casual about Dien Bien Phu because we don't have an emotional involvement with these guys. We haven't screwed half of them."

"Watch it," Ashbourne warned. "If she had a drink in her hand, you'd be half-drowned by now."

"No, but she has the cards!" the French photographer cried.

Too late. Emma tore into the pack—the only one they had. Colorful confetti flew everywhere within the small bunker. By the time the men wrested the cards from her hands, she had destroyed half the deck.

"Why is it," Emma raged, "that nobody keeps a scorecard on you guys, but let a woman succumb to her natural urges once, just once, and you're all set to brand her with the scarlet A?"

Loud jeers greeted this remark.

"If it really were just once, nobody would get excited." Ashbourne was eager to avenge himself on her for the way she had humiliated him publicly at the Hanoi reception. "But lust rather than love conquers all in your case, kid. Seems to me you have a husband back in Saigon, isn't that so? Poor guy, he'll probably never get over the shock of being deserted before the honeymoon was quite over."

Sick of their razzing and nauseated by the close air in the press bunker, Emma went to sit in the little cemetery. There she found the peace and the solitude she craved: The living soldiers avoided the place, and the dead could not make her hear them.

Emma decided to stay at Dien Bien Phu until Christmas, one week away. If nothing had happened by then, she would return to Hanoi for a few days. She had not seen Janvier, but since he was only one man among ten thousand in an area twelve miles long by four miles wide, that wasn't too surprising. She knew that she could find him on strongpoint Huguette, but she held herself back. He knew where to find her, too.

By Christmas Eve, she had interviewed most of the senior officers present at Dien Bien Phu, including Colonel de Castries. With no exceptions, de Castries and his staff seemed optimistic, confident, and hopeful of an imminent attack and a quick victory.

"Giap can't possibly win here," one lieutenant-colonel told her. "He's never taken a course at the Staff College."

She experienced firsthand the legendary charm of Colonel de

Castries. He invited her to his headquarters for an interview. When she arrived, she saw that the interview was to be exclusive, with no aides or secretaries or other journalists present.

"We are indeed fortunate to have such a beautiful and charming writer in our midst," the colonel began after inviting her to be seated on a canvas camp chair. "I hear you withstood incredible hardships in the jungle in order to report on the activities of the First BEP."

Emma admitted that was so.

"You have the courage of a soldier," de Castries said approvingly. "I will suggest to the officers of the First BEP that they make you an honorary member, perhaps award you the red beret."

Emma shook her head. "The only way I would wear that beret is if I earned it by making a parachute jump. And believe me, Colonel, I would face any number of dangers on the ground rather than do that."

"You are too modest, madame. Before we go further, this morning's plane brought some cases of champagne to help us celebrate the holiday. I asked my valet to chill some for us. Would you do me the honor of sharing a glass with me?"

"No, thank you. I never touch champagne while I'm working," Emma said. "I find that it dulls my concentration."

"Then put work and concentration aside for the moment." The colonel hitched his chair closer and placed his hand over hers. "Allow yourself to feel rather than to think. In the end, I find, feelings always triumph over reason. Don't you agree?"

"In this case, I have feelings that no amount of reasoning will control." Emma stood up. "Excuse me, Colonel, but I feel a bout of dysentery coming on. Perhaps we can continue this interview another time, when I am completely cured?"

In a fury, Emma walked the length of the valley, all the way up to strongpoint Gabrielle and back again. She knew she made an easy target for a sniper, but she didn't care. Her anger blighted her enjoyment of her joke on de Castries, particularly the expression of revulsion and dismay that had crossed his face as he contemplated making love to a woman in the throes of an attack of diarrhea. She knew what stories the colonel had heard about her. Dien Bien Phu was like a small town in which rumor and gossip were as persistent as the red dust that insinuated itself into every crack and corner. And rumor had her sleeping with half the men in the First BEP, and more.

She raised her hands to her burning cheeks. What had happened to her? What had she become?

General Navarre flew in again to spend Christmas with his troops. The camp sported a few signs of the season: Emma saw a Christmas tree made of barbed wire and decorated with an enemy helmet, some empty food tins, and a condom or two. That afternoon the troops assembled on the airstrip to hear mass said by the chaplain. They sang "Adeste Fideles," their rich, sonorous voices ringing off the naked hillsides. Emma stood close to the altar and listened to the Latin responses of the soldiers who were assisting the priest. She felt someone standing very close to her. Looking around, she saw Janvier at her side.

"Come with me," he whispered.

"No. I want to hear the mass."

"That hocus-pocus? What for? I stopped believing in God when I was five years old." Janvier's fingers closed around her upper arm. "Come with me. Now."

She permitted him to lead her to the immense dugout that sheltered the aircraft. They halted under the wing of a Bearcat fighter and Emma shook off his hand.

"I see you've finally decided to break your long silence. Don't tell me you've caught the Christmas spirit, Robert. I don't believe it."

"We are in love." He flashed his dimple at her. "Do I need any better reason than that to want to see you?"

"Love? Is that what you call it? You didn't say one word to me while we were in the jungle, not even when you saw how I was suffering. You abandoned me! If it weren't for Lucky Pierre and the others, I would have died out there, and you wouldn't have shed a tear."

"Emma, Emma," Janvier sighed. "I would have credited you with more intelligence. Surely you could see that my behavior toward you was necessary? You were furious with me, no? And that was good, because your anger kept you going. You wanted to prove that you could survive on the trail, and you did. Besides, my men would have mutinied if they thought I had brought you there as my *congai*, to keep me company on the march. Instead, they accepted you as one of them. They sheltered you and protected you. I could not have done so well myself and still retained my command of the situation. Surely you can understand that?"

With her fingernail, Emma picked at a rivet on the Bearcat's fuselage. "I don't know. I don't understand anything anymore."

"I know very few women who could have kept up with us on the march as you did, without complaining and without slowing us down." Coming up behind her, Janvier slid his arms around her waist. "I said nothing at the time, but I was very proud of you. The other men were proud of you, too. Once again you brought us luck."

"I don't have anything left," Emma said wearily. "I've lost my integrity, my reputation, my youth. Even my enthusiasm for my work. Writing is just a job. I do it, but I don't enjoy it. I had a husband, a really good man. But I threw him away, too. Discarded him like an old newspaper. I used to care about so many things, but I don't care about any of them now. I feel empty inside. I spent everything I had on you, Robert. And now I'm broke. It all happened so fast. I've been in this country a little more than a year, and I don't know myself anymore."

"You are tired," Janvier suggested. "The war and the waiting are making you ill. You should go back to Hanoi for a rest."

"I suppose so. I hate this place, this valley. It used to be beautiful once, didn't it? Like me. Now it's the ugliest place on the face of the earth. A prison with barbed wire and trenches. What you have done to me, the army has done to Dien Bien Phu."

"You should be glad. You will both go down in history." Janvier nuzzled her throat.

"You're all I have now, Robert. I squandered everything else. If anything happened to you, I would be finished, as good as dead. The only time I feel happy is when we're making love. Love helps me to forget what I've become. My soul has scars like trenches, and it's wrapped around and around with barbed wire."

"Hush." Janvier kissed her gently. "I stayed away too long, I can see that now. You are so sad. But I will make you smile again, my Emma."

He took her to a dark place behind some crates of spare parts, to a bed made of dried grass and gunnysacks.

On the other side of the dugout, two thousand voices sang "Silent Night."

16

FEBRUARY 28, 1954

Dear Mom and Aunt Louise,

I can't call myself a war correspondent because I
haven't seen an honest-to-God battle yet, but with
any luck at all, I will be here at Dien Bien Phu
when the Viet Minh attack. Everyone says it should
be a classic confrontation, whatever that
means. . . . Thanks for the package! I picked it up
on my last trip to Hanoi. Riding back and forth in
those ambulance helicopters is more terrifying than
a descent into hell, but if I don't wash off the dust
and grime and recharge my batteries every so often,
I start going crazy. I never stay in Hanoi very long
because I don't want to miss the action. . . . The
cookie crumbs were delicious! A real taste of home!
I'm glad you liked the lengths of silk I sent. I'll
expect to see you both wearing beautiful new
dresses when I get back.

Steaming brown water gushed out of the faucet. In the walls of
the Metropole, pipes clanked and groaned. The flow lasted a
full twenty seconds before turning cold and dwindling to a
muddy trickle. Muttering, Emma turned off the tap. Out in the
jungle, she had been forced to bathe in a helmet full of contaminated river water. But here in Hanoi she would not be satisfied until she could slip into a tub brimming with hot water.
More often than not the Metropole's boilers refused to cooperate.

Hearing a knock, she drew the sash of her bathrobe tighter
around her waist and hurried through the bedroom and sitting
room. When she opened the door, a cry of horror stuck in her

throat. A barely recognizable Alan Hazen slumped against the doorframe. His hair was long, matted, falling in damp strands over his forehead. He hadn't shaved in weeks, and his full beard looked grubby and almost green, like moss on a stump. He wore shredded, filthy khakis. In his trembling hands he clutched his old battered knapsack.

Emma had known that they would meet again someday. But she had expected that encounter to take place in the quiet confines of a Saigon lawyer's office, where they would shake hands and talk stiffly about annulment or divorce. She never expected to see him like this, a walking corpse.

"Thank goodness you're here." Even his voice sounded coarse and roughened. "That idiot down at the desk—" His eyes glazed over and he started to fall.

"My God!" Emma clasped her arms around his waist and helped him into the sitting room. "Where have you been? What's happened to you?"

"Will you help me?" he rasped, collapsing into a sagging armchair. "Got to send a wire to Saigon. And then—I've got a story for you, Emma. A story like you've never heard before."

Emma wondered if his brilliant mind had finally snapped. Then she scolded herself for her lack of faith. Of course she would cooperate with him. She owed him that much.

"What do you want me to do, Alan?"

"Bring paper. And a pencil. Got to write—"

Hazen worked feverishly, printing two pages of coded information from the real message stored in his brain. Finally he looked up. "It's ready. Do you have money?"

Emma nodded. While Hazen was working, she had put on a dress and high heels. Downstairs, she hailed a trishaw and took it to the Post and Telegraph office on Rue Paul Bert. She sent the telegram to W. Powers Brewster at the American embassy in Saigon. The only uncoded words were a request that he forward an acknowledgment immediately in care of E. Vaughan at the Hotel Metropole.

When she returned to the hotel forty-five minutes later, she found Hazen slumped to the floor. He was barely conscious, and burning with fever.

"Malaria," he said when she roused him. "It'll pass. I have some pills somewhere. Did you send—"

"Yes, I did everything just as you asked. Come and lie down, Alan. We should have an answer from Saigon within the hour."

She got him into the other room and persuaded him to stretch out on the bed. He was restless and fretful, sitting up every ten minutes to ask if Saigon had sent his answer yet. After two hours, he sent Emma back to the telegraph office with another message for W. Powers Brewster. She waited two more hours for Brewster's reply: "REGRET WASHINGTON DOES NOT ACKNOWL-EDGE MESSAGE."

Hazen had fallen asleep in her absence, but he awakened the moment she entered the suite, and he called out to her. Emma handed him the flimsy yellow paper.

"Don't you think it's time you told me what this is all about?"

The telegram slipped from his hands. He stared so long at the ceiling that Emma feared he had fallen into a trance. Then he turned his head and looked at her. "Have you been to Dien Bien Phu?"

"Three times since Christmas. I'm a regular commuter."

"Well, what did you think?" Hazen continued to gaze at her without blinking. She wondered if he was seeing the young girl at Ta Prouhm, or the bride who had betrayed him, or simply a shopworn press correspondent who reminded him of a woman he had once loved.

Emma's gaze slid away from his face. "Morale is starting to crack a little, I guess. They've been waiting three months for an attack that doesn't seem like it will ever come off."

"Oh, it will come off, all right. I'm not talking about morale. I'm talking about preparation, fortification. I suppose de Castries and the others told you it was adequate. And you believed them."

"Why shouldn't I? What does this have to do with you and Chrome Petroleum, Alan? You know as well as I do just how many artillery pieces the French have at Dien Bien Phu. For once the stories in the press and the releases from the Citadel have been fairly accurate. They are extremely well prepared. The fortifications there are incredible, really impressive."

"Emma, it's going to be a massacre." Hazen dragged a shaking hand through his hair. "A massacre! General Giap has been biding his time, building up incredible strength. When the rains come—that's when he'll strike. He's following Mao Tse-tung's dictum: Never attack unless you hold the advantage and are certain of victory. Dien Bien Phu may be a dust bowl now, but between March and August it gets an average of five feet of rain. Do you know the expression 'shooting fish in a barrel'? That's what it's going to be like if the French don't pull out at once."

"Pull out!" Emma looked amazed, and then she laughed. "They can't pull out. They've put ten thousand men into that valley. Do you know how long it would take to get them out of there, not to mention all those tons of equipment? They can't just abandon that stuff to the Viet Minh. Besides, Dien Bien Phu is General Navarre's baby, his pride and joy. He's pinning his last best hopes on a smashing victory there."

"His last lost hopes." Hazen's glance drifted around the little bedroom. Emma waited, wondering if he would mention Janvier. "Do you have anything to drink?" he asked. "I'd really like a Coke."

Emma rang room service, and they promised to send someone up. In the meantime, Hazen accepted a glass of mineral water. After taking a long swallow, he said, "Can you get a story past the censors?"

"I think so." Emma spoke cautiously. "If it's really important. My standing as a press correspondent here will be nil if the French catch me sending out uncensored reports of their war."

"What if they do? Didn't you hear what I said? It's going to be a massacre. You might save lives. Thousands of lives. Listen." His grip tightened around the glass he was holding. Emma feared it would shatter in his hands. "Who's been supplying the French with arms and money for the past five years? The American government. Washington has a huge investment to protect out here.

If they know they're going to lose it all, they'll intercede with the French high command and demand immediate changes in the way that valley is being used. We've got to get this information to the president and the Congress. If I can't do it through the embassy, you'll have to do it in the newspapers. It's absolutely imperative that the French government call off this madness before it starts."

"What are you talking about, Alan?" Emma perched on the edge of the dressing table. Her doubts about his sanity returned. "What madness? You're not making very much sense. American military advisers have been flying in and out of Dien Bien Phu for the past three months. They've all declared themselves satisfied with the preparations. General Giap can't possibly mount an attack that the French can't overpower."

Hazen set down his glass. "Where's my knapsack?" Panic registered in his eyes until Emma retrieved the bag from the sitting room floor and handed it to him. Hazen raised himself up in the bed and opened the flap.

"The Viet Minh are bringing in heavy artillery pieces over the mountains. Everyone said it was impossible, didn't they? But the Viets have dismantled cannon, loaded them onto bicycles. Right now thousands of coolies are pushing the stuff over the most God-awful terrain—you know what that jungle's like. Someday very soon, maybe even next week, Giap is going to turn those guns on Dien Bien Phu, and then he'll unleash three divisions of his best troops. That's thirty thousand men against ten thousand. Three to one. Rotten odds in any fight."

Emma frowned. "I don't believe it. Loading mortars onto bicycles? It sounds so farfetched."

"You want proof? I'm an eyewitness, probably the most credible witness you'll ever meet. You may not care about me, Emma, but at least you know I'm honest. I am not lying. I even took a few pictures. Here." He handed her a couple of rolls of film. "If these films were developed, you would see dozens of coolies pushing modified bicycles along a sloping road."

"Alan, pictures like that could be taken anywhere," Emma said patiently. "On a road-building project in the south. You know Vietnam: Why use four wheels when two plus some cheap man-power will do the job?"

"But I saw them." Hazen swung his long legs over the side of the bed. "They walked right past where I was hiding, little men wheeling bikes that were so loaded down the tires were flat. Thousands of them, moving all day and all night. Picture it, Emma: They have stations where they stop to rest and pick up enough food to last them a week; then they push on. They've set up a ring of mortars all around the valley of Dien Bien Phu. Oh, yes. My camera was useless by that time, so I didn't get pictures of those. But I saw them. I saw them!"

"You were there? At Dien Bien Phu?" Emma doubted that Hazen could have paid a visit to the encampment without her knowledge. The gossipmongers would have let her know at once. "When?"

"I've never been inside the fortified area. I could see it only too well from the hills above Gabrielle. A Viet Minh's–eye view. I'm telling you, Emma, it's a disaster waiting to happen. Poorly con-ceived, inadequately guarded—a pond full of sitting ducks. Look at this." Hazen extracted a sheet of paper from a manila envelope that he had pulled from the knapsack. "A copy of a French intel-ligence report confirming what I've just said. Can you read it?" His forefinger slid along a typewritten line. "'Enemy troops con-verging on DBP in massive numbers.'"

"Where did you get that?"

Hazen handed Emma the sheet and pulled out another page from the envelope.

"Never mind that now. Here's another, a report from the chief of engineers at Dien Bien Phu, the man responsible for building all the fortifications there, the dugouts for the artillery, the planes. And for the men. Listen to this:

Impossible to obtain sufficient material to fortify locations in the event of an artillery attack. We have dismantled every building in the town and all the outlying villages, and despite continued ambushing of our woodcutting parties in the forests, we have amassed twenty-two hundred tons of wood for construction. But we are thirty-four thousand tons short of the minimum engineering requirements for fortifications. At least twelve thousand C–47 air transport missions are needed to deliver the necessary building materials alone, irrespective of manpower and weapon needs.

"Do you know what happened when this report reached headquarters?" Hazen said with a crazy laugh. "They hooted it down, and then they forgot it! General Navarre and General Cogny don't expect the battle to last long enough to justify stronger fortifications."

"Maybe they're right," Emma ventured.

"They're not! It's frightening, Emma. They've been told what they're up against, and yet they're going ahead with it and hoping that a few fighter planes circling overhead will take out the enemy's guns." He slumped down on the bed again and closed his eyes. "God, I'm tired. Got into town tonight and found these reports waiting for me. More confirmation of what I've been saying since November. After everything I've seen—and then this. If you think our little trip down the Black River was rough, it was a picnic compared to what I've been through. Pham was with me. He has double pneumonia and an infected arm. Maybe some gangrene. It looked pretty bad. I was glad to get him to the hospital."

Emma studied the engineer's statement. "So you've been sending reports like this to Washington all along?" She was certain now that Hazen was no geologist for Chrome Petroleum. "What do they say?"

To her surprise, Hazen exploded. "I can't understand it! They acknowledge my reports with as much interest as a comment on the weather. I don't think those bastards can read! Or else their brains have turned to mush. Something's wrong. I wish I knew—"

Emma felt a thrill of vindication. She had been right about him all along. "So you're with the CIA?"

Hazen nodded. "Special liaison officer for the White House. I report directly to the president."

"What's your assignment?"

"To assist the French in any way possible, from intelligence gathering to offering them discreet and private communications with the president, when necessary."

"Then you're not working directly with the CIA?"

"The White House passes my reports along to them, but I take my orders directly from the president. Their agents here have instructions to cooperate fully with me. That's what worries me. I don't trust some of those guys. They want France to lose this war in a big way. They see themselves moving in to fill the gap, Galahads in crew cuts and dark glasses. I've told the president that an all-out French defeat will leave this country torn apart and shaky, ripe for a communist takeover. We have to do everything we can to shore up the French while we work toward a peaceful settlement. Everything short of sending in troops of our own. The president would never agree to that. All-out aerial bombing of the whole perimeter around Dien Bien Phu might save it—but it's so late. I think—I think it's too late." Hazen's face was ashen. His eyes stared, as if he were already seeing the ghosts of the martyred men of Dien Bien Phu.

Emma stood over him. "Why have you come to me? Of all people, why me?"

Hazen looked up. "Do I need to enumerate the reasons? You're a fine journalist. I trust your professional integrity—you'll never betray a source. Besides, after all that's happened, I still believe in you."

"You didn't trust me enough to tell me what you were really doing here," she said. "Even after we were married."

"I was just waiting for the right time. That's typical Hazen: I act with enormous energy and conviction, but often too late to do any good. People get the wrong idea. They think I don't care."

"I always knew you cared."

There was a knock on the door. The room service waiter had

brought a bottle of warm Coke and a few melting ice cubes in a cracked bowl. Emma and Hazen were both grateful for the interruption.

When Emma got back to the bedroom with his drink, Hazen said briskly, "This information needs to reach Washington immediately, and I can't trust anyone else in this country to send my messages. I think the embassy in Saigon is under CIA orders to whitewash my reports before they hit the wires. If you put all this into a story, the *Chicago Tribune* will publish it and everybody will read it, including the people who count. I'm sorry you can't mention me by name. As far as this country is concerned, I'm still a geologist for Chrome Petroleum."

Emma paced the floor as she examined the intelligence reports Hazen had given her. Finally she said, "All right, Alan. The French may remand my visa, but I'll do it. I'll write your story for you, and I won't give you away."

She carried the reports to her desk and sat down in front of her typewriter. Her fingers began to fly:

"A source close to both French and American governments today called the defense of the fortress at Dien Bien Phu a disaster waiting to happen. The French high command, he said, has been advised that the place they have chosen for a showdown with the Viet Minh is now surrounded, and that the enemy has enough arms and men to wipe out the entire French encampment. Eyewitness reports confirmed the movement of three divisions of Viet Minh soldiers, plus a vast quantity of heavy artillery, into the area surrounding the valley, which is located about two hundred miles west of Hanoi, the capital of Vietnam's northern province of Tonkin."

Emma paused and glanced at the bedroom door. She could hear Hazen's breathing, slow and deep. She had never seen him so exhausted, and so close to despair. As she wrote, she thought about Janvier and his men, who had been waiting for nearly three months for a chance to fight. Did they know that their leaders had led them into a trap? Did they realize that their defenses were too feeble to withstand an enemy attack, and that they were grossly outnumbered? Did the high command, in its arrogance and pride, truly believe that the skills of their soldiers could compensate for their exposed position and lack of protection?

In Dien Bien Phu, she had been oblivious to the surrounding mountains, whose dark crevices concealed an enemy. An enemy who fought not for pay or for glory, but to win back its nationhood and its sense of pride. Alan Hazen's story was ghastly, terrifying. Unbelievable. Yet she believed him. She had to get Janvier out of there. Janvier and all his men. They must be warned.

It was three o'clock in the morning when she finished. She went in and awakened Hazen with a gentle tap on the shoulder. "You might want to read this over, to see if I've left anything out."

He pulled himself up. The short nap had refreshed him and he seemed more alert. He scanned the pages quickly, then looked over at her. A smile lurked behind his matted beard.

"You write a good story."

Emma said, "I'm going out. I don't suppose you came here by car?"

"As a matter of fact, I did. It's downstairs. One of the Buicks Chrome keeps in Hanoi for its executives. Funny, I don't even remember driving here." He started to get up. "I'll come with you."

"No. You stay here. You can take a bath while I'm gone."

Emma guided the car through the darkened city toward the suburbs. François Delaporte, the helicopter pilot who had been ferrying her out to Dien Bien Phu, shared a small villa with another pilot, who worked for Air France. She remembered that Pierre Longereau's weekly flight for Paris was leaving at eight o'clock in the morning. Once before he had taken a sensitive story to the *Tribune*'s Paris office. They had sent it on to Chicago without the French censors' ever seeing it.

The little house was dark. Emma pounded and rang the bell for a full five minutes before François Delaporte unfastened the locks and let her in.

"Sorry to wake you, but it's urgent, François. The most important story I've ever written. Is Pierre here?"

"Holy God, all this for a newspaper story?" François scratched his armpits. "Don't you newspaper people ever sleep?"

He shuffled toward the bedrooms and appeared a few minutes later with Pierre Longereau. The Air France pilot had deep circles under his eyes and looked scarcely awake. He wore gray silk pajama bottoms and was just struggling into the jacket. Emma pressed an envelope into his hands and told him what to do with it. He nodded.

"I've brought a couple of bottles of cognac as a bribe, and some money as well. Here." She handed him another package and turned back to François.

"Listen, can you give me a lift out to Dien Bien Phu tomorrow?"

"You're becoming a regular flying fool, Emma. I thought you hated my helicopter."

"I do, but the man I love is inaccessible except by air, as you very well know. Good night, François. You can go back to sleep now."

Her hotel suite was dark. She expected to find Hazen asleep in her bed, but it was empty. He had gone, leaving only a terse note instructing her to give his car keys to the desk clerk. Were it not for the rumpled bedspread and the half-empty bottle of Coca-Cola on the nightstand, Emma might have dreamed the whole thing.

Hazen's plane landed at Saigon's Tan Son Nhut Airport at noon. The hot delta sun beat down on his newly shorn head as he strode across the tarmac. He still looked haggard, but a hot bath, an early visit to a barber shop, and a suit of clean clothes had erased the most drastic effects of jungle living. The hospital had refused to release Pham yet, although his condition had improved. Hazen had already arranged for him to return to Saigon later in the week.

W. Powers Brewster was sitting at his desk, his sleeves rolled up above freckled forearms, his feet resting on an open drawer. He greeted Hazen with an insouciant grin. "Ah, Alan, old man.

Welcome to my little seat of wisdom. How was the frozen north? Take a seat."

Hazen kicked the door shut behind him. Reaching the desk in two strides, he leaned over, grabbed Brewster by the shirtfront, and hauled him to his feet.

"You've been editing my messages to Washington, Brewster. Tampering with them. You haven't even sent them all, have you, you lardy little turd? I risk my neck getting the facts for the president, and you sit your fat can on them. Your time is up, Brewster. I'm going to fix you so you'll never work in government again."

Brewster wriggled out of Hazen's grasp. He looked both amazed and affronted by the accusation. "I most certainly have not been tampering with your cables. I encode them exactly as they are given to me, and then I send them on. Unfortunately, I can no longer show you the originals and my coded copies; they have to be destroyed. I have my orders, you know. Too many Vietnamese around, secretaries and janitors and Gawd knows who else."

"Then why haven't I gotten an answer to the telegram I sent you from Hanoi last night?" Hazen demanded. "They always acknowledge receiving my messages, even when they're not thrilled with the contents. What's going on?"

"I haven't the faintest." Brewster tucked in his shirttails around his onion-shaped torso and smoothed his rumpled collar. "You know the White House, old man. Simply inundated with messages from people like you all over the world. Or perhaps the president forwards them to Mr. Dulles for top-level consideration. Give them a few more days, why don't you?"

Hazen walked to the window and looked out. His cables from home were received by a clerk in the embassy, transcribed by Brewster, who had the key to the various codes Washington used, and delivered to Hazen either in person, at a drop they had arranged, or by telephone in a verbal code. But Hazen could not even verify that Brewster had sent a cable to Washington without alerting numerous staff members to his interest and blowing his cover.

"I wonder if you can appreciate the damage you've done, Brewster?" he said. "You've handed this war over to the Viet Minh. You know that, don't you? You're not that stupid. Somewhere, the enemies of France—the enemies of an ally we have promised to support—are rubbing their hands and congratulating themselves on having a friend like you inside the embassy. The French effort in Indochina is going down the drain, and it's taking American prestige and a lot of lives with it. It was bad enough that the French had to be stupid about Dien Bien Phu, but for us to be stupid as well—that was totally unnecessary."

"You're so cynical, Alan," Brewster clucked. "Too many years as a spy, I suppose. You should think about retiring. You're getting too old for this game."

Hazen's eyes narrowed. He made his way out of the embassy and stood watching the nervous flow of cars and bicycles along Boulevard Charner. Maybe I am too old for this game, he thought. Maybe it's time for me to get out. But not without squashing that fat reptile.

"I have some bad news for you, Eliane. Your side's going to lose this war."

Hazen and Madame de Mornay were dining at a chic new restaurant in Dakow. "What?" she said, "and the big battle not yet begun? You are a pessimist, my old friend. I tell you what, I will bet you that you are wrong. My side will not lose. That should show you how confident I am."

"You've been listening to your husband the general again. Don't believe him. The thinking of generals is as distorted as the thinking of politicians."

"Not at all. Come now, do you want to bet or not? I think I would like a new Paris gown, a Dior or a Givenchy. That is fifteen hundred American dollars. But I will let you off easy, as they say. One thousand dollars U.S. You can afford it. Just submit it to your boss as a business expense."

"Sorry, I'm not a gambling man. And I'm too honest to steal your money."

"Ah, no, Alan, you would not steal my money." Eliane de Mornay's brows arched in amusement. "My side is going to win."

Earlier that same day, the twenty-sixth of February, Emma had flown to Dien Bien Phu with François Delaporte. Marie-Claire was taking a load of medical supplies to the fortress's chief medical officer, Major Grauwin. Not much had changed since Emma's last visit. The dugouts were a little deeper and the mounds of earth piled on top of them correspondingly higher. A few more tons of barbed wire had been unfurled around the strongpoints Gabrielle and Eliane, Isabelle and Claudine.

Emma gazed at the hills that loomed over the valley of Dien Bien Phu. In the past, she had hardly noticed them. Now her imagination stripped them of their cover of vegetation, and she saw the Viet Minh cannon and mortars lined up like the sacred idols of a new order, served by legions of small, yellow priests. She knew. And knowing, she was afraid and sick at heart.

Everywhere Emma went, the men were hollow-cheeked and restive. They were feeling the strain, eager for the battle to commence. She found Janvier supervising the digging of a new series of graves. A patrol from Huguette had suffered heavy casualties that morning.

"My God, who is that?"

A nun was weaving back and forth among the graves, sprinkling the fresh mounds with ash.

Janvier made a face. "Don't you recognize him? That's little Corporal LaLande, the Mad Breton. He found some blackout fabric and some white bandages and turned himself into Sister Marie-Jolie of the Little Sisters of Dien Bien Phu. I would put a stop to it, but the men get a kick out of him and so far he seems to be sane enough—for a complete lunatic. Maybe you will get to see the rest of his act. He flips up his habit and exposes his cock. But not in the cemetery, of course. He's lucky the men haven't raped him by now."

"But why?" Emma sounded bewildered. "Why is he behaving like that?"

"You need to ask?" Janvier's laughter had a desperate quality. "Like all the rest, he is crazy with boredom, with waiting. We sit here day after day in this stinking heat, cleaning our rifles, re-cleaning them, drilling in the hot sun, finding ways of busying ourselves so that we don't go mad. One fellow over on Beatrice made himself a pet—a dog, he called it. Beni. It was really just a piece of shingle and a tuft of grass. He spent hours grooming it, talking to it, walking it on a string. He even got up in the middle of the night to take it out for a pee. His C.O. decided the business had gone too far, and so he confiscated the dog and destroyed it. The man was as shattered as if he had lost a child. His friends almost mutinied. The next day, they all had dogs, a whole invisible kennel. You'll have to go over there and interview them."

Emma gazed at the little nun. Her face was troubled. "The folks back home will love the Hounds of Dien Bien Phu, but I don't think they'll care for Sister Marie-Jolie."

That afternoon Emma and Janvier found a quiet spot under the wooden bridge that spanned the riverbed near the hospital. Emma told him everything she had heard from Hazen, without revealing that Hazen was her source. She said that a man named Ritter had approached her with information and copies of top-secret documents from the Citadel.

Janvier grunted. "Do you think you are telling me anything I did not know already? Of course the Viets are closing in, beefing up their fortifications, moving in artillery and shells. What else would they have been doing for the past three months, sitting up there waiting for the proper signs from their necromancers? The soldiers of Dien Bien Phu know full well what will happen once the fighting starts. Most of us will die."

Emma was stunned. "You mean you don't believe you can win? Then all that claptrap the generals have been feeding the press was false!"

"Win?" Janvier looked amazed. "No, we won't win. The un-lucky ones will be the survivors, those who go to Viet prison camps. Surely you have heard about them: rotten food, no medi-cal care, constant lectures and indoctrination sessions. I would stand in front of a Viet Minh bayonet with my arms wide open if I thought I would have to endure that. I will never go to prison. Never."

"Robert! You're expecting to die!" Emma pressed her face against his shoulder.

"Me? No. Every soldier thinks that he will be spared even if death harvests all the rest, eh? I have been lucky so far. Janvier is indestructible, invincible. But luck runs out sometimes." He shrugged. "Almost all of us here have seen the Viet Minh in action before. The generals at the top attribute Giap's successes to a few lucky breaks. They have never fought one of those yellow bastards hand to hand in a rice paddy. They have never had a leg full of punji sticks, or a gut full of metal from a homemade nail bomb. Even if Giap's men had nothing but their teeth and their knives, they would attack us. But now they have Chinese and Russian guns, even some howitzers they have captured from us, cases of grenades, seventy-five-millimeter shells. Enough firepower to turn this valley into a charnel house."

"But how can you stay here, knowing what's ahead?" Emma gazed at him, appalled. "You've got to make them see, Robert! Talk to your officers, persuade them to pull out—"

"Are you out of your mind? Do you think they will take orders from a mere captain who rose from the ranks? I have been sent here by my commanding officers, and I will stay here until I am ordered to retreat."

"Then I'll talk to them myself." Emma jumped up and dusted herself off. Grabbing her arm, Janvier pulled her down again.

"You will say nothing!" he ordered. "I forbid you to speak of this to anyone. What the men know by rumor is one thing. But if they hear what you are saying, they will lose heart. You are spreading poison, Emma. Doubt is like a plague germ. It will spread until every soldier in the whole valley suffers from it. When the attack comes, I want my men to be ready. I do not want them to think about death until it happens. If you say one word about what your spy saw in the mountains—just one—I will kill you, I swear it."

"You men. Killing is the only thing you understand," she said bitterly. "It's the only solution you know, isn't it? The answer to everything. Kill and kill again."

"You think I am joking?" Smiling, Janvier put his arm around her and ran his forefinger across her throat. "Try it. Mention your intelligence reports and your Viets on bicycles. You will never see Hanoi or Saigon or the United States again."

Emma tried to break away from him, but he held her close. "Sometimes I hate you, Robert."

"An enemy comes in many disguises, Emma. He is a Viet Minh in black pajamas and a cone-shaped straw hat. He is the commander of a French artillery unit that fires on its own men by mistake. Or he might even be a pretty American girl with green eyes and blushing red cheeks, a girl who works her way into your heart and destroys you slowly, so that when you face the guns you find yourself loving life so much that you are afraid of dying." Janvier's hands moved down to Emma's belt buckle. "I am going to fuck you one more time. Then you are going back to Hanoi. Today. I do not want to see you here anymore. I am tired of you."

He left her lying on the bare earth under the bridge, twin tears carving deep furrows in the dust on her cheeks.

But she did not go back to Hanoi. Determined to let neither her fear nor Robert Janvier chase her away, Emma stayed at the camp for another two weeks, playing cards with the other journalists, examining the fortifications, interviewing one soldier after another, writing letters for those who could not write themselves. After just a few days, the strange pall of monotony and tension in the fortress began to have its effect on her, too. She snapped at her colleagues, and then retreated into dark corners to weep and sulk, to dream of exotic foods—corn on the cob and hot dogs cooked on an outdoor grill.

Late in the afternoon on March 12, Janvier found Emma alone in the press bunker.

"You are still here."

"I have a job to do, just like you."

"Why don't you go back to Hanoi today? Delaporte flew in this morning. He will take you out. You could use a bath and a visit to the beauty shop. You look as bad as some of my men."

"Really? I haven't heard any complaints."

"*Merde*. I cannot play games." Janvier seated himself on a packing case and braced his hands on his knees. "The Viet Minh cadres have asked the villagers to leave the valley by noon tomorrow. The attack is imminent. I have no doubt of it this time. We are getting ready for them."

Excitement renewed the faded brightness in Emma's eyes. "That means I'll be here to witness it! You can't ask for any better luck as a reporter than that. Almost everyone else has gotten tired of waiting." Only two other journalists were in Dien Bien Phu at present, a French reporter and a French photographer. The rest were monitoring developments in the valley from the bars in Hanoi.

"I want you to leave, too, Emma. It is not safe."

"No. It's not safe for me. It's not safe for you. It's not safe for anyone." Emma thrust out her chin. "This is where I want to be. I came to report on a war. I want to be here when the attack comes."

Janvier stood up. "You will have to go. It is all arranged."

"All right, Robert, I'll go." Emma stepped up to him and rested her hands on his shoulders. "Only if you come with me."

"You know I can't do that."

"Then I'm staying." She wrapped her arms around his neck and whispered in his ear, "Don't you understand? I love you. I want to be with you, in Hanoi or Saigon or Paris or Dien Bien Phu. I'll do whatever I can to help—carry water or ammunition or bandage wounds. If you're going to die, I'm going to die with you."

Janvier put his arms around her and kissed her, a long, timeless kiss. They kissed again, and then Janvier pulled away. Emma did not see his fist crashing out of nowhere to land on her jaw. She reeled backward, and he caught her.

"Pierre," he shouted, "give me a hand with her."

Lucky Pierre entered the bunker. When he saw Emma lying unconscious in Janvier's arms, he scowled. "You didn't have to hurt her."

"She wouldn't listen to reason. We're going to be busy enough around here without more women underfoot. If she stays, she'll die." Janvier carried Emma to the door. Over his shoulder, he said, "Pack up her stuff—in that corner over there. Delaporte isn't going to wait forever."

They took Emma to the helicopter and loaded her aboard. Marie-Claire Barrault strapped her into a seat and placed a cold cloth on her head.

"Oh, my poor little friend. But what happened? You mean she just fainted, with no warning? Perhaps she is pregnant?"

"I doubt it. Good-bye, Emma." Janvier saluted Delaporte and kissed Marie-Claire's hand. "See you after the battle."

Captain Janvier and Lucky Pierre trotted away from the whirling helicopter blades. Marie-Claire closed and fastened the doors and made sure her patients were comfortable. In the bunks and on the floor of the cabin, soldiers who had been wounded by sniper fire from the hills while on patrol listened to the throb of the rotors and felt the helicopter lift off. Most of them knew that the attack was imminent. But this battle was not for them.

Emma was still nursing a sore jaw and a bad temper the next afternoon when she heard that the fortress at Dien Bien Phu had been attacked. The battle had begun.

17

MAY 1, 1954

> . . . After a year and a half, you might think I
> would stop being homesick, but lately I miss you
> both more and more. I would love to spend just
> one night in my own bed, and sit downstairs in the
> kitchen the next morning in my old red bathrobe
> eating bacon and eggs and drinking Aunt Louise's
> coffee. . . . War is more devastating than I ever
> imagined, not only to those who fight but also to
> those who watch and wait.

"Tell me again what it will be like."

"Emma, please, I beg you, do not go. It is madness. You cannot do any good there, and you will be hurt or killed, one more casualty that we cannot take care of—"

"You promised you would help me, Marie-Claire. Please, we've gone too far to turn back now. Now tell me. When I jump, I push myself far out so that I can't get caught in the slipstream. Then the chute opens—"

The two girls sat in a corner of Chez Betty, sipping coffee and smoking cigarettes. Emma would have liked a double whisky to calm her nerves, but she needed to awaken early the following morning, and she had to be fully alert.

"All right." Marie-Claire sighed. "When the chute opens, it really gives you a jolt. Make sure your helmet is fastened on good and tight, otherwise it will slip down over your nose and give you a nasty blow. I know. My profile is much lumpier than it was before I started jumping. If you find yourself twisting from side to side, just reach up and grab the tapes of the parachute. That will steady you right away. Remember, keep your chin down and your legs together. Don't worry about the parachute not opening properly. I will pack it myself—I am an expert, believe me. When you land, try and be limp, very relaxed, but do not spread your legs. Just bend your knees and roll." Marie-Claire lit another cigarette. "I am the crazy one. If anyone finds out about this, I could be court-martialed or even shipped home."

"No one will find out. I've worked in a hospital before. I'll make the best nurse you ever saw. Now, what about sniper fire from the ground?"

Marie-Claire lifted her shoulders. She was small, as delicate as a Vietnamese girl, with frizzy brown hair, slightly protruding teeth, and keen brown eyes. "What can you do? Worrying will not help. If you are hit, you are hit. Chances are you won't be."

Twenty-four people would jump from their plane in two sticks, or groups, of twelve, just as Emma remembered from her training with the First BEP six months earlier. A few of them were likely to be killed. Marie-Claire was right: Worrying about the odds ahead of time wouldn't help.

"Weren't you scared the first time?" Emma asked.

"Not at all." A smile transformed Marie-Claire's plain face. "I could hardly wait. Ever since I was a child and saw the heroes of the Resistance parachuting down into France to save us, I wanted to float through the air like them. I knew what it would be like, and I was right. You are so free. The one thing I did not expect— the best thing—was the silence. For a few moments after the chute opens, and the sounds of the airplane engines go away and the rushing of the air stops, you feel like a feather in the wind, just floating, floating. Even tomorrow: I cannot wait to jump. I know there is danger from the Viets. I know that down on the ground I will find a hell on earth. But the idea of jumping makes everything else seem unimportant."

"I believe you love parachuting even more than you love François," Emma suggested.

"Perhaps I do. If he could make me feel like that—la, la, la! I would never want to leave the bedroom."

Out on Rue Paul Bert, they separated. Emma promised that she would be at Bach-Mai no later than five in the morning. Marie-Claire would have her jump suit, pack, and parachute ready. A nurse named LeBlanc, who was scheduled to make the jump, had become ill that afternoon, and Emma would take her place. At that hour of the morning, when the world was dark and the other parachutists were tense and preoccupied with the ordeal to come, no one would notice her. Marie-Claire had drilled her in the routine over and over again. She had learned it before from Janvier and Lucky Pierre. Now all she had to do was jump.

A single leap into the void, a few minutes in the air, and it would all be over. Down on the ground, inside the fortress area of Dien Bien Phu, she could easily make herself useful as a nurse. From what she had heard, the medical officers were unlikely to refuse her help. She had to know for sure if Janvier was still alive. She no longer cared whether she lived or died. Odd, to be so unafraid of dying yet so terrified of jumping out of a plane with a bundle of silk.

Although the reports that the French censors permitted Emma and the other journalists to cable home sounded optimistic about French chances of holding the fortress, everyone in Hanoi and Saigon knew that the odds overwhelmingly favored General Vo Nguyen Giap's hordes. Six to one—those were the figures by mid-April, a month after the attack began. Emma pictured thousands of lean Vietnamese coolies trudging along the narrow jungle trails, bringing ammunition and supplies to their men at the front. The few French air strikes from Hanoi had been totally ineffective in curtailing the flow. As Hazen had predicted, Viet Minh artillery had been astonishingly well placed, and just a few days after the attack began, they had rendered the airstrip unusable. The only way the French could replenish men and supplies was by parachute, a procedure made twice as risky by heavy fire from the ground, as well as by the arrival of the monsoon season.

As Emma entered the Metropole's cavernous lobby, she saw Alan Hazen sitting in a wicker chair, an open copy of the French daily *Le Figaro* in his lap. He was waiting for her.

"Hello, Emma." He stood up and waited for her to approach. "Have you heard the news? The president has promised to consider offering air support to the men at Dien Bien Phu. But he won't involve ground troops without congressional approval."

"Are you giving me another Alan Hazen exclusive?" Emma asked.

"No, the *New York Times* printed it yesterday morning. Other than granting a few civilian pilots permission to fly transport planes, I suspect American support won't amount to much. It's far too late."

"Yes." Standing near him, Emma felt the tension in his tall body. He was rigid with resentment and frustration. Two weeks before the attack on Dien Bien Phu, they had tried together to stop the carnage, but forces stronger than they had prevailed. "You did your best."

"Yes, and so did you. Your story created quite a ripple in Washington. There are a few red faces at the Pentagon, and Congress is asking pointed questions about the wisdom of giving the French eighty percent of their military budget without attaching any strings."

"It was a pretty small ripple. Not a big enough wave to lift the men out of Dien Bien Phu before disaster struck. You and I seem to be the only people in the world who think the massacre of ten thousand Frenchmen could have been averted." That was another thing she shared with Hazen: a profound bitterness at the obtuseness of the political and military minds that had created Dien Bien Phu. "General Navarre is blaming the Viet Minh. He said yesterday that this wouldn't have happened if the Viets hadn't changed their strategy. It would be funny if it weren't so tragic."

Hazen offered to buy her a drink, but she declined. "I need to go up and get some rest. I have a hard day coming up tomorrow."

"Really? Are you jumping into Dien Bien Phu?" Hazen's lame attempt to be humorous fell flat. He saw rather than heard Emma's reply. The blood drained out of his face. "Emma! No!" His hands fastened around her upper arms. She felt hard and cold, but as fragile as porcelain. "Emma, you can't. My God—"

When Emma spoke, her voice was flat, devoid of any emotion. "I can't sit here in this stinking hotel waiting for word that he has been killed. It's making me crazy. I want to be with him, and even though he doesn't want me there, that doesn't matter. I have to do what's right for myself, and if that means jumping out of a plane and falling on my head or getting a Viet Minh bullet through my gut, then so be it. I don't expect you to understand."

"No, you're wrong," Hazen said aloud as Emma disappeared up the stairs. "I understand very well."

The plane hit a downdraft and dropped sharply and swiftly. A few of the parachutists sitting on the sides laughed or made joking remarks to each other. Others remained taut and silent, trying to control their fear and muster their courage.

Marie-Claire glanced over at Emma. Her mouth formed the question: "Are you all right?"

Emma nodded. So far their plan had proceeded without a hitch. Outfitted in the uniform of a French army nurse, complete with lieutenant's bars and a nameplate over her left breast that read LeBlanc, she had attracted no unusual attention that morning when she presented herself for boarding. The dispatcher had ticked her name off against his roster without hesitation.

Loose images flitted through Emma's brain: her mother's sunny yellow kitchen, the chocolate cakes Aunt Louise had always baked for her birthday, a puppy she had dressed in a bonnet and diaper and wheeled around in her doll carriage. Robert Janvier grinning at her and Hazen before he ran toward the temple at Ta Prouhm. Alan Hazen, his expression forlorn and bereft. College nights spent jitterbugging with men in uniform, sipping Coke, standing on her own front porch under the wide Nebraska sky, trying to follow the slow march of the moon. Wild Nights, Wild Nights. Alan Hazen crouching over the smoking hearth of a Laotian hut, then looking up at her with a special shared knowledge.

Marie-Claire jostled her arm. Up in the cockpit, the pilot had flicked on the green light to signal that they were approaching the target. The dispatcher opened the doors. Emma and Marie-Claire were scheduled to jump with the first stick, numbers five and six. Marie-Claire had agreed to go behind, to give Emma a push if necessary.

"All right, on your feet, let's go, hook 'em up." The dispatcher moved down the line, tugging at their static lines, checking their equipment, adjusting their positions. "You people in the second stick, get ready to move into place. Look sharp."

While she waited for the buzzer, Emma stood with her chin down and her hands folded over the pack on her chest. Her mind was empty. She felt the weight of her gear, the tightness in her legs, the quickened pulse in her neck. Fear possessed her totally. If they didn't jump soon, she would drown in it.

Through the thick, mottled mass of clouds outside, she searched in vain for a patch of green.

"They're not going to make us jump in this," the man in front of her said. He was a medical officer, twenty-three years old. Having recovered recently from a serious chest wound, he had demanded to be sent back into action. "The clouds are thicker than blood out there. He'll land us right on top of the Viets."

As if responding to his statement, the signal light went out. The pilot had missed his target and was circling around for another pass at the drop zone. Emma could picture the men in the fortress below, listening to the drone of invisible planes, scanning the clotted sky for a break in the clouds that would mean the arrival of reinforcements and supplies.

Emma heard no joking now; the next few minutes would decide whether or not they could make the jump today. The signal light flashed on again. Her heart strained inside her chest, and her legs turned to water. Seeing her start to sag, Marie-Claire put a hand on her shoulder.

"Courage, you're doing fine."

They circled the drop zone again. Suddenly the plane rocked violently. They had been hit by flak, antiaircraft fire. Word came back from the cockpit that one of the engines was sputtering. But the green light stayed on.

With each passing second, Emma's terror grew. She reached for her static line and slid her hand upward toward the hook at the top. She couldn't go through with it. She would release the catch and step aside out of formation. Marie-Claire would understand; so would the dispatcher and the rest of the parachutists, many of them first-time volunteers. No one would blame her.

Then the light went out, and they felt the plane begin to lift. "That's it," said the medic with disgust. "I knew it. They've called it off."

After a minute, the dispatcher confirmed the statement. "Everybody unhook and relax, we're heading home. No jumping today. Cloud cover is too thick."

Emma heard a few disappointed groans. She slumped to the floor and began to vomit.

"Tough luck." Marie-Claire grabbed a bucket and squatted down to support Emma's shoulders. "It's rough, getting your courage up and then having to quit at the last minute."

Emma closed her eyes against a flood of tears.

They rode a troop truck back to Hanoi with the other parachutists. "Another time," Marie-Claire consoled her. Emma kept silent. For her, there would be no other time.

Her room at the Metropole was the same jumble of clothes, notebooks, cosmetics, and papers that she had left that morning. She glanced at her watch: only eleven-thirty. In the past seven hours, she had aged a hundred years. She stripped off her fatigues and threw herself facedown on her bed. Alone in her room, she gave herself up to her grief until exhaustion overtook her. She slept.

A knock on the door awakened her. Outside her window, the world was dark. Emma moaned and pulled a pillow over her head. The pounding stopped, then resumed again. Emma tried to ignore the sound. She did not want to see anyone, ever again.

The pounding continued steadily. Someone was calling her name. In a raging fury, Emma sprang out of bed and pulled on her silk wrapper. She stumbled across the floor and, hurling herself at the door, yanked it open.

"You!"

"Hello, Emma." Alan Hazen's forehead was creased with concern. Clean-shaven and immaculate, wearing a beige suit and blue tie, he looked like a different man from the one who had staggered into this room some weeks ago to ask her help. "Are you okay?"

"Yes, I'm just fine. Go away. No, I'm not. I'm terrible. I don't know how I am. Oh, damn."

Emma whirled away from him and threw herself down on the faded love seat. Hazen stepped into the room and closed the door.

"I'm sorry you weren't able to make that drop today."

"You damned liar!" She lashed out at him, making him the target for her pent-up sorrow and rage. "Don't tell me that. You're not a bit sorry. You're delighted that I couldn't run off and join my lover again."

Hazen winced, but said calmly, "Of course I want you to be safe, Emma. I love you. But loving you means that I want for you what you want for yourself." He lowered himself into the wicker armchair near her desk. "You won't get another chance to make that jump. Orders came through from the high command this morning, about an hour before your plane touched down. No more women allowed in the battle zone, not even volunteer nurses. They already have one French nurse and a dozen Algerian whores trapped in there, as well as Lieutenant Burton. I suppose they figure that's enough."

"Is that why you came here? To gloat?" Emma launched herself out of the love seat. She snatched a bottle of scotch from a small table and tipped it over her bathroom tumbler.

"You know better than that. I knew how disappointed you would be."

"Disappointed?" Scotch dribbled down her elbow. "Are you kidding? I'm delighted. Delirious. Relieved." The last word exploded on a sob. "Oh, Alan, I'm such a goddamned miserable failure." She set her glass down and swiped at her eyes with her sleeve. "At the last minute, I couldn't go through with the jump. I was terrified. I guess I don't love him enough."

"I don't blame you for being scared." Hazen's voice was sympathetic. "When I was dropped into Berlin near the end of the war, I was so scared I soiled my pants. I didn't care. I thought I would die of fright before I hit the ground. I'd already made two practice jumps back in England, but sometimes the second or third jump is even worse than the first."

"I lost my nerve." Emma's face was hidden behind her hands. "If they had gone ahead with that drop, I would have stayed behind in the plane. I know it."

"You can't be sure of that."

"Oh, yes, I can. I know how I felt." She dropped her hands. Her face was distorted with anguish, awash with tears. "I thought I loved him. I didn't care what he did to me—that's love, isn't it? Whenever he hit me, I knew it was because he was angry at someone else, or maybe himself, but since I was there he could take it out on me. And I didn't stop loving him. And the abortion. I made my choice to go through with it because I didn't want to lose him. Do you know what? I'd do it again if I had to. He means that much to me. It was hard sometimes. He would be so tender, so wonderful, and everything would be fine. And then something would happen and he would act like he wanted to kill me. I didn't even mind that. If he wanted to kill me, then I wanted to die. But today was the test, the real test. And I failed it."

Hazen said earnestly, "No one could love Janvier more than you. I think God tries to teach us something by having us love people who cannot return our love. I thought I was the loser, but perhaps Janvier is. I have my love for you, you have your love for him, but he is cursed by an inability to love anyone."

Emma opened her arms to him. "Hold me, Alan. Just hold me. I'm so tired. I feel cold and dead inside."

Hazen went to her and enfolded her in his arms. He closed his eyes. For months he had lived for just such a moment. But he knew it could not last.

He held her away from him. "Emma, I have to tell you something." He led her back to the love seat. They sat down together and he took both her hands in his. "I would give anything to be able to forget what I've learned, but you have a right to know it too. One reason I have to get out of this business is because it's making me sick in my soul. Spying is a dirty business. But I'm good at it, and I couldn't stop myself this time. I had to do some checking on Janvier. He has too much money to be earning it legally."

Emma, staring down at their interwoven hands, shook her head.

"He owns a couple of brothels in Cholon as a sideline. Cheap and dirty, for the enlisted-man trade. He makes out all right with them. His real source of income, though, is opium. But the kind of opium he sells has nothing to do with the old men you've seen lying on wooden couches in *fumeries*. Janvier is a small-time partner of some Corsicans who refine the stuff and turn it into heroin. Distilled death. They have a factory in Cholon, and all his factory workers are Chinese. Every plane and ship that leaves Saigon carries some of their merchandise, small packages of pure heroin. Robert Janvier is raking in a small fortune."

Emma snatched her hands away. "You're lying! You're making all this up. He's not like that—he couldn't be. I'd know. I know everything about him. But you—you're just jealous of him. You've always been jealous. You think you can win me back by slandering the man I love. Get out of here, Alan. I don't want to hear any more of your outrageous lies. Get out!"

With a weary sigh, Hazen stood up. "I would sell my soul if I could stop loving you, Emma. God knows I've tried. But it doesn't work. You're still my wife. The time we spent together was precious to me. I will keep those memories until I die."

She refused to meet his gaze. "Go away. And don't come back, do you hear me? I never want to see you again."

Hazen left the room without saying another word. The door closed firmly behind him.

Two days later, Emma received a message asking her to meet Marie-Claire Barrault at Chez Betty at six o'clock that evening. She went straight to the café from the daily press conference at the Citadel, the offices of the high command in Hanoi. As the siege of Dien Bien Phu ground on, the official tone at the daily press briefings became less optimistic and more somber. The Americans, as Hazen had predicted, had lent only minimal aid. The fortress would be overrun by the communists any day. Nothing could stop them.

The only hope of ending the hostilities and saving the lives of the remaining men at Dien Bien Phu lay with an international peace conference that had just convened in Geneva. The Viet Minh had agreed to negotiate an end to the fighting. The French, no longer able to deny that they were losing the conflict, were ready to bargain, eager to find a solution to a war that had become abhorrent to their citizens at home. The Chinese and Russians were sending high-level diplomatic representatives to lend support to their communist brothers in northern Vietnam. Even the United States was participating, albeit reluctantly.

Marie-Claire was waiting at a table on the sidewalk. "François made a trip to Dien Bien Phu last night," she said. "It is a miracle that he was able to get out. The airfield is completely useless; the Viets have their guns trained with incredible accuracy to blow up any plane or helicopter that tries to land, and the French have been totally unable to pinpoint the Viet Minh artillery. François landed the helicopter right in front of general headquarters near the hospital. He brought out a load of wounded soldiers for the military hospital at Lanessan. And one of them is asking for you. He calls himself Fido, although that can't be his real name."

"Yes, I know him! He's in Robert's unit. Can I go see him right away?"

"He's in pretty bad shape. Both legs blown off. I'll go with you."

They finished their sodas and took a taxi to the military hospital in the suburb of Lanessan. Following Marie-Claire into the ward, Emma caught her breath. The beds were filled with wounded soldiers, some horribly maimed, many of them groaning wordlessly from pain so severe that morphine could not dull it. The man nearest the door wore a flat mask of bandages with tubes running into the places where his nose and mouth had been.

Marie-Claire led Emma to a bed in a corner near the far wall and left her. Fido greeted her with his same flash of white teeth. "Hullo. I think I must have died and gone to heaven. Your face is so damned pretty. You see what being a lazy soldier gets you? I was standing at the cook's tent having a cup of that piss he calls coffee and minding my own business, and a mortar shell landed right on top of me."

"I wish I'd been there." Emma held his hand.

"Jesus, Mary, and Joseph, be glad you weren't. It was atrocious. That place is a cesspool. Mud and blood everywhere. Bodies? You have to step over them, they're lying so thick on the ground. I was real lucky to get out. After they bandaged me up they left me right by the door of the hospital. They just loaded up the first ones they came to. A lot of guys won't make it."

"Captain Janvier? Is he all right?"

"He was two days ago. Like the rest of us, he hasn't had any sleep for the last month. Beard down to here. You learn to recognize people by their eyes, because you can't see anything else."

Fido told her about the initial attack on Huguette, where the First BEP had taken command. First the Viet Minh had pounded the strongpoint with artillery; then they sent in a horde of infantrymen.

"You never saw so many. We held them off, but we had no place to pull back to, understand? And we didn't get no support from the air or the ground, neither. Stinking high command put us out there and left us to die."

"What about Lucky Pierre? Is he okay?"

"He carried me to the hospital. He's too dumb to be afraid, that one."

Fido recited a list of the dead, men of the First BEP with whom she had marched and joked and battled fatigue and bugs and enemy gunfire. Gustave. Rocco. Ahmed. Helmut. Max. Emma wrote down the names in her notebook. Readers of the *Chicago Tribune* had come to know them well. For the past six months, they had followed Emma's adventures with the Legion paratroopers in their red berets. Emma had looted the soldiers' lives for her stories, and now most of them were gone. She would write one more account of their heroism at Dien Bien Phu. Their obituary.

In the valley of Dien Bien Phu, General Giap was tightening his net. One after another, the strongpoints were falling. Giap had sacrificed thousands of Viet Minh soldiers in the first human-wave attacks that had overwhelmed the guardians of the fortress. Now he was adopting a slower and more persistent approach. Viet Minh soldiers were tunneling toward the heart of the fortress, until they were within just a few feet of the barbed wire perimeter.

According to Fido, casualties were so heavy that the French were unable to bury their dead. They were left rotting in piles or shoved into trenches. Even by the end of the first day, the wounded had overflowed the small field hospital. And the rains fell relentlessly. Everywhere, bunkers and dugouts collapsed on the men, burying them with mud. Disease was rampant, discomfort a fact of life. Dien Bien Phu had become a hell with no escape.

"Thanks, Fido." Emma patted his hand, but avoided looking at the truncated body under the rough blanket. "I'll come back again tomorrow. Can I bring you anything special? Some cognac? Cigars?"

"You can bring me a new pair of legs," Fido said. "I don't want nothing else."

Back in her hotel room, Emma sat for a long time staring at the sheet of blank paper in her typewriter. Finally she began to write. After she finished, she went downstairs and called a taxi. Half an hour later, it pulled up in front of the little villa where François Delaporte and the Air France pilot Pierre Longereau lived. Government censors were not going to make her memorial to the First BEP another casualty of the war.

Under spring rains, Hanoi became dreary and tear-streaked, a mourner waiting for a corpse. Emma's spirits sagged and time hung heavily on her hands, but she avoided going back to see Fido. Ten days passed before she returned to the hospital ward. Fido had died the day before. A large blood clot had broken loose and traveled to his brain. Dien Bien Phu had claimed another victim.

Riding back to her hotel in a trishaw, Emma noticed that almost every white person she saw was wearing a uniform of some kind. Far from the battle zone, they looked serene and cheerful. Their complacent arrogance infuriated her. What right did they have to come here, to make a war in a country thousands of miles from home, to subdue a people and violate their traditions and customs, to deny them the liberty for which they hungered? What right did they have to die here, to spill their blood on this soil?

Seething, she went to Chez Betty and ordered a double whisky. Before she had taken even one sip, she looked around and saw a group of senior French officers entertaining themselves at a nearby table with their mistresses, Vietnamese *congais*.

"I congratulate you, gentlemen." Lifting her glass to them, Emma spoke in a loud voice. The men looked at her with mingled surprise and disapproval. They thought she must be drunk, and so she was: drunk on rage and frustration. Emma Vaughan, disgracing her sex and her profession and her country once again. And she didn't give a goddamn. She approached them. "While your comrades in Dien Bien Phu are dying in a cesspool of blood and mud, you sit here wallowing in the delights of civilization." Emma hurled the words at them like stones. "How can you do it? How can you send ten thousand men to die, and feel nothing? How can you sleep at night, and not be haunted by their screams? Do you know what I say? To hell with France. To hell with the army and to hell with all of you!" With a sweeping gesture, she dashed her untouched double whisky in their faces. The girls squealed.

One of the younger officers, a lieutenant-colonel with the patch of the Fourth Colonial Artillery Regiment on his sleeve, jumped up. "You are wrong, mademoiselle," he said in an angry voice. "At this moment, every Frenchman in Indochina is grieving for his brothers in Dien Bien Phu. Every man at this table has volunteered several times to be parachuted in, even those of us who have never made a jump before. We officers are not the villains you think us. Every year more of us die in this country than graduate from the military academy at St. Cyr. We did not choose this war, but we will fight until it is won, or until our country calls us home."

Emma blinked at him. The room was revolving around her, a kaleidoscope of shocked and sneering faces. Her knees buckled, and the floor rose up to meet her. But in a second, a strong arm lifted her up again.

"You are ill, mademoiselle." The lieutenant-colonel spoke more gently. "Permit me to take you home."

The café was silent as he guided her through the maze of tables toward the door. Outside on Rue Paul Bert, Emma shook off the officer's supporting arm and inhaled deep lungfuls of air.

"Thank you, I'll be all right now." She started to walk. The young officer stayed with her. "I don't know what's the matter with me. A man died—all the men have died—I hardly even knew them, but they—I—"

"Don't worry about it. I understand."

Emma halted and turned to face her companion. "Listen, do you know Captain Janvier of the First Legion Paratroop Battalion? He is there, at Dien Bien Phu."

"I regret I do not know him," the officer said.

"Please, will you tell me something?" They stood under a streetlight. "What will happen to him and his men if the fortress falls? Will the Viet Minh kill them all?"

"Oh, I doubt they will do that. They will be captured, taken to prison camps, kept there until our government arranges for the release of our soldiers. It will not be pleasant. But prisoners are useful currency in war, mademoiselle. They can be traded for concessions, peace terms, anything the enemy wants. Do not worry about your captain. If he survives the battle, he will come back to you someday. The men of the Legion are tough, everyone knows that."

They walked on until they reached the doors of the Metropole. Emma thanked the officer for his concern. "I'm sorry I made a scene back there. Please apologize to the others for me."

"They understand. Your captain is a lucky man. By the way, my name is Siméon. Claude Josephe Siméon. I am on General Cogny's staff at the Citadel, if you ever wish to speak to me. Perhaps I can be of service to you again. Good night, mademoiselle." He saluted, then turned away.

When Emma arrived at the Citadel on the morning of May 7, every reporter in Hanoi was there. The heavy silence that pervaded the atmosphere in the briefing room told the story as it was unfolding, long before any official announcements were made.

All day, the journalists waited, speaking occasionally in whispers. No one left. In midafternoon they sent out for sandwiches and coffee. Every hour an officer entered the briefing room and announced that no announcement would be made until later.

Finally, at five minutes before six, a senior officer appeared. In subdued tones, he announced that the center of the camp, codenamed Castor, had been overrun by Viet Minh.

With the others, Emma pressed him for details. So far as anyone knew, the men who were holding strongpoint Isabelle were still hanging on, but no one expected them to persevere for more than a few hours. The battle was over. All remaining ammunition had been destroyed. The soldiers had systematically sabotaged their weapons. Rifles and machine guns were fired with their barrels stuck into the ground to burst them. Truck and tank engines were drained of oil and raced until they seized and burned themselves out. Optical equipment was smashed. White-phosphorus hand grenades were thrown into the barrels of the big guns to melt the inner linings beyond repair. At 1730, twenty-five minutes before the press briefing, de Castries, who had received a battlefield promotion to general, had destroyed his radio transmitter.

But no white flags were flown over the valley. Dien Bien Phu had fallen but not surrendered.

After the briefing, the journalists scattered to track down their favorite sources, hoping to ferret out more information. Emma found Siméon, the lieutenant-colonel who had befriended her at Chez Betty.

"Have you heard anything about the men of the First Legion Paratroop Battalion?" she asked him. "Please, I must know."

He sighed. "Mademoiselle, since Castor fell, we have lost all radio contact with the men of Dien Bien Phu. Conditions are chaotic, and no one knows how many of our men are left alive. All I can tell you is that the name of Captain Janvier was not on the list of casualties that came through yesterday. More than that, we do not know."

After she wired the news to Chicago, Emma walked the streets of Hanoi late into the night. All the next day she walked, without destination, shedding tears with men, with women, with soldiers and civilians. Some were mourning. The fall of Dien Bien Phu marked the fall of France's colonial empire. The outcome was as inevitable as rainfall during monsoon season.

18

JULY 14, 1954

. . . canceled the usual festivities for Bastille Day.
Instead the atmosphere in Hanoi is more like a
funeral. By the way, F. X. McGraw has asked me to
go to Egypt to cover events there, but I want to stay
here until I'm ready to come home. I would love to
see you both, but I can't leave yet. I care too deeply
about this country and the people who have fought
and died here.

"**W**hat's the matter with you, Vaughan? You're looking a little
green around the gills."

"Being forced to travel in these oversized coffins is bad enough
without some thoughtless oaf breathing whisky and cigar fumes
into my face." Emma fanned her notebook at Howard Corrigan,
a reporter from the *New York Times*.

"What, are you still complaining?" Corrigan laughed. "We're
getting a free ride out to Haithuon, and there's a decent story
waiting at the other end: 'Bastille Day Exchange of Dien Bien
Phu POWs.' The French may have lost the war, but they haven't
lost their knack for making news."

"Corrigan, if you don't put that cigar out, I will vomit all over
you."

The man complied, squashing out the offending cigar in a
coffee can. "Some people have no sense of adventure."

A French military plane filled with Viet Minh prisoners had already flown ahead to Sam Son, near the point where the exchange would take place. Emma and a few other reporters, as well as a party of observers from the International Red Cross, followed a day later.

For days after this first exchange had been announced, Emma had been unable to sleep. She had to find Janvier, or at least someone who knew about him. In the weeks following their victory at Dien Bien Phu, the Viet Minh had allowed the French to evacuate some of the wounded that had been left behind. Emma had visited these men in the Lanessan Military Hospital, but none of them had fought with the First BEP, or knew anything about Janvier and his men.

In the Red River delta, southeast of Hanoi, the war ground on. The armies of France fought a few more battles, but their victories were hollow. In Geneva, the loss of Dien Bien Phu had given the negotiations new impetus. With the help of Russian and Chinese mediators, the ministers of France and northern Vietnam were working toward an agreement to end the war. But no matter how peace was eventually achieved, it would come too late to save the tens of thousands of French and Viet Minh soldiers who had died at Dien Bien Phu.

The plane landed on a muddy airstrip in the middle of the jungle, about three hundred miles north of Hanoi. Two parties of diplomats, French and Viet Minh, were meeting at a bridge that crossed the Red River, where the actual exchange would take place. To their disgust, the reporters found themselves herded into a corner of the airfield, well out of sight and hearing range of the bridge. Armed guards kept them at bay while the Red Cross representatives joined the members of the French delegation.

Grumbling at their cavalier treatment, huddling under oilskins and umbrellas to ward off the persistent drizzle, the journalists waited to see the first French prisoners of war.

"Here they come!" someone shouted. Binoculars were raised. In the distance, they could make out a ragged group of men moving toward a large tent that had been pitched near the bridge.

"Debriefing first," one of the French guards said. "Then maybe the brass will let you see them. Poor bastards."

Poor bastards. Emma repeated his words silently five hours later, when she and her colleagues were finally permitted to interview a select group of released prisoners. These brave soldiers of France looked as skeletal and emaciated as the survivors of Nazi concentration camps. She listened and wrote as the men described their death march.

The handful of prisoners, who had been chosen to speak to the press because they were in better health than any of their companions, told a story of captivity that was a testament to human courage and human brutality. After the defeat at Dien Bien Phu, they had been forced to march westward over four hundred miles, into Laos. Some men tried to escape and were shot. Any who had sustained severe wounds of the abdomen, chest, or head died along the way or in prison camps. No medical care was given to them. The Viet Minh had no antibiotics. Survivors were subjected to courses of indoctrination in Vietnamese history and communist ideology. Daily they received long lectures on the crimes their country had perpetrated against Vietnam. Some men went insane; a few committed suicide.

"The sickest ones were left along the wayside," an eighty-pound corporal told them. "They could never have survived the camps. We tried to help each other, but the Viets wouldn't let us slow the column. One man I will never forget, a Legionnaire who had lost both his legs. He dragged himself along on his hands and the stumps of his thighs."

Emma wanted to ask him, "Was that man Captain Janvier?" But she bit her tongue. It couldn't have been he. Or could it?

In fact, none of the 250 men released was a Legionnaire, nor had any of them fought anywhere near the First BEP on Huguette. But thousands of Frenchmen, Algerians, Moroccans, Senegalese, and Vietnamese troops still languished in Viet Minh prison camps. Janvier was among them. He must be.

* * *

Two days later, Emma flew to Saigon. Unlike Hanoi, which twitched at the sounds of artillery from the delta and hummed with rumors of vicious communist reprisals against the peasants who had supported the French, in the southern capital the war seemed as remote as ever. And thousands of miles away, diplomats in Geneva were deciding the fate of those two cities, while the residents did their best to carry on with their lives in the face of enormous impending changes.

Emma took a taxi from Tan Son Nhut Airport to Hazen's villa in Dakow. It, too, looked the same, stately and secure behind its high walls. Within, its small gardens overflowed with hibiscus and bougainvillea, and the heat of the late afternoon felt a little less intense. Hazen was not at home, but Pham expected him to return shortly. Emma decided to wait, and sat sipping a cold lemonade in the stiffly furnished drawing room.

She had planned to redecorate that room. A cheerful flowered chintz on the sofa and armchairs, some new prints on the walls. She had even chosen the wallpaper, a green toile with a charming scene of eighteenth-century lads and lasses disporting themselves on swings in a shaded grove.

Oppressed by memory and remorse as well as by the stifling heat, Emma stepped out into the walled garden behind the house and walked around toward the fishpond. Bright orange and yellow koi carp glided under bronze water lily leaves, as silent and serene as spies. As Emma watched them, lost in the contemplation of the secret world under the water, she gradually became aware that a man and woman were arguing inside the dining room, just a few feet from where she stood.

They spoke rapid Vietnamese in hushed tones. Emma recognized Pham's voice. The woman's voice also sounded familiar: shrill, high-pitched, peevish even at low volume. Emma realized that they were whispering so she would not hear them in the drawing room. Now the woman was calling Pham a stupid pig-brained peasant—one of the phrases Emma had learned from the Vietnamese paratroopers in Janvier's battalion. Those men had crippled themselves laughing when she had tried to pronounce the words. Most of them were dead now. Even if they had survived Dien Bien Phu, the Viet Minh had probably killed them afterward. They were notoriously harsh with Vietnamese who fought for the French.

After a moment, the voices ceased and muffled footsteps echoed through large rooms. Emma followed the gravel path around the side of the house. She reached the corner just in time to see a petite blonde swirling out through a small side gate, Pham scurrying at her heels. Emma slipped back into the drawing room before Pham could see her. She heard the distant roar and screeching tires of an automobile. Eliane de Mornay drove a Renault, Emma recalled. And drove it wildly.

Hazen returned half an hour later to find Emma flipping through a year-old copy of the *Saturday Evening Post* in the drawing room. His heart stopped. She had come back to him.

"Emma!"

Her smile reflected her real pleasure at seeing him, but he saw no glimmer of love in her eyes. "Alan. I'm so glad you're here."

"Have you been waiting long?"

"I can't remember. I think I must have dozed off. This heat makes me so sleepy. Maybe I've just been working too hard. You won't believe this, but lately I've been spending almost as much time in the air as I do on the ground. And I don't like it one bit better." Her smile faded. She tossed the magazine aside. "Oh, what am I babbling about? I've been going crazy. Every time the Viets release some prisoners, I have to check to see if Robert is among them. But he hasn't come back yet."

"I see." Hazen leaned against the mantelpiece and pulled out his old pipe. After scraping the bowl with the small blade attached to his pipe tool, he packed it with tobacco from the pouch in his pocket. "He's probably sweating it out in a POW camp."

"I wish I could be sure." Emma went to his side. "I have no right to ask any favors of you, Alan, but I will anyway. You told me back in Hanoi that you still loved me, and that you wanted for me what I wanted for myself. I believed you. Despite everything that's happened, you're still my friend. My only friend. Will you at least listen to me?"

Hazen held a match over the tobacco in his pipe and drew in a few puffs of smoke. "I'm always willing to listen, Emma."

"The communists have lists of all the men they have taken prisoner. I know. Right after Dien Bien Phu fell, they started to read the names on their underground radio. But the French jammed the broadcasts. They said they were bad for morale, civilian as well as military. I have to know if Robert's name is on that list."

"I see. How do you intend to find out?"

"That's just it. I've explored every avenue, exhausted every possibility. I don't know anyone else to ask. Only you, Alan. You've been in this country so long and you know so many people. I thought you could help me."

Hazen knocked the smoldering tobacco into the cold fireplace. Then he went out through the open French doors into the garden. Emma followed him. He was sitting on an iron bench, his head in his hands. She sat beside him. Five minutes passed before she spoke.

"Did I ever tell you about my father? He was one of life's amiable losers. Good old Tommy Vaughan. He worked at a variety of jobs but never seemed to make any money. Most of them lasted no more than six months. The record was the two years he spent driving a truck for Trumble's Bakery. But then he wrecked the truck and banged up his legs. He never worked again. I was nine years old when that happened.

"For as long as I can remember, my mother worked as a secretary during the day and a clerk at the supermarket nights and weekends. She took in sewing and mending. When we couldn't pay the mortgage on our house, she moved us into an apartment. She decided I was going to be a beauty queen and make us all rich. I didn't lack for much when I was growing up, even though my father never lifted a finger. 'I'd love to help you, Lizzie, but I can't. My back's hurtin' something terrible this mornin'.' 'Aw, Emmy, I wish I could see that contest you're in, but my legs just won't carry me that far.' His legs carried him to the bar on the corner, and to a little building he called 'the club,' where he played cards with a bunch of others guys. Most of the time he just lay on the couch in the living room, drinking and studying the racing forms. Eventually his liver stopped working and he died. I hardly noticed he was gone. In the eyes of the world, he was a loser and a bum. I'm afraid I shared that view.

"But do you know something? My mother thought the sun rose and set with that man. 'Oh, your poor father is in such pain.' 'Don't nag your dad, Emmy, he's feeling bad this morning.' 'No woman ever had a finer husband than your father. Imagine, that terrible accident, and he's still able to smile and tell a joke. And that awful Mr. Trumble, saying it was Tommy's fault and that he was drinking on the job—it just goes to show that some people don't appreciate a good worker when they have one.'"

Emma rose and walked to the edge of the little pool. A dark mud-colored fish that she had not noticed before swam a little apart from the others.

"Like mother, like daughter, isn't that what they say? We Vaughan women just can't admit that we've made fools of ourselves over the wrong man." She turned and looked back at Hazen, but his face was still hidden. "Don't you think I would stop loving Robert Janvier if I could?" she went on in a softer voice. "I know what he is. Those terrible scenes, the times when I've been beaten up so badly that I couldn't look at myself in the mirror. They play over and over in my mind like a reel of film. But they don't stop my wanting him. Nothing does. At this moment, I would sell my soul if I could see him and touch him and be close to him just once more."

Emma returned to the bench where Hazen was sitting. "Help me, Alan. I've got to find him. I swear, I'll never ask you for anything again."

Hazen lifted his head. His eyes were dark pools of anguish, his mouth a shapeless gash. "I don't know what to do with you, Emma. I swear, I don't know what to do."

"Alan, I—"

"Every day since I saw you last I've tried to persuade myself that the pain of loving you is fading a little. And now you want me to help you find a man who is as loathsome and vile as any creature God ever created. If I loved you, I would do as you ask, isn't that right? But if I really loved you, I would do everything in my power to keep you and that man apart, because I know he'll destroy you. Oh, the tests we devise for ourselves and each other, the so-called proofs of our love." He pressed his hand over his eyes. "I can't take much more, Emma. Love and hate are tearing me apart. This is killing me."

"Oh, God, I'm sorry, Alan. I should have known better than to ask for your help."

Hazen expelled his breath in one long sigh. "Aside from the fact that I don't want to help you, I can't. Someone, I don't know who, possibly Mr. W. Powers Brewster at the embassy, has informed both the French and the Viet Minh that I'm working for the CIA. All my sources of information have dried up. Everyone in Hanoi and Saigon knows I was behind that story you wrote about Dien Bien Phu before the attack. The French have rescinded my visa. I'm being deported, thrown out. They've given me three days to settle my financial and personal affairs. I'm booked on a flight to Hong Kong tomorrow night. I will arrange for a divorce as soon as I get back to the States. I'm sorry, Emma. I'm useless to you. You'd better go. Ask Pham to call a taxi."

Emma rested her hand on his shoulder. He took it and pressed his lips into her palm. Then, releasing her, he turned away. His whole body shuddered. He was weeping without making a sound.

"Alan, please don't." Emma watched helplessly, wishing she could relieve his torment.

She reentered the house, where she found Pham straightening the cushions in the drawing room. He promised to telephone for a taxi at once. She would spend the night at Monsieur de Chesnay's villa before flying back to Hanoi in the morning.

Pham's hooded cheerfulness reminded her. She stepped out into the garden again. Hazen was still sitting on the bench. He had composed himself, and a neutral expression masked his pain.

"I don't know if this makes any difference now, but Eliane de Mornay was here this afternoon." Emma described the encounter between Eliane and Pham. "I always thought there was something phony about that woman. I'll bet you she's not French at all. She's Vietnamese! If it's any consolation, your betrayal may have come from closer to home than the embassy." Out in the street, a car horn blasted. "There's my cab. I really am sorry, Alan. For everything." She squeezed his hand. "Try and forget me."

The corner of the yard that Hazen had once devoted to his vegetables had grown up in weeds. He had forbidden his gardener to pull them or even to shear them off. As the afternoon sun slipped behind the trees, a cloud of mosquitoes rose above the weed patch. Hazen stood it as long as he could; then he went back inside.

Pham met him in the entrance hall. "Oh, Pham." Hazen kept his voice casual. "Ambassador Bunning said he might drop in this afternoon. Did anyone stop by?"

"No, monsieur. Only Madame Hazen—I mean, Mademoiselle Vaughan." The young man's smile was as open and honest as it had always been.

Hazen found Brewster dining alone at the Arc-en-Ciel, the famed restaurant in Cholon that offered the cuisines of three countries, China, France, and Vietnam. He was finishing a masterfully prepared dish of roast Peking duck when Hazen pulled out a chair and sat at his right elbow.

"Alan, old man." Brewster was surprised but not displeased by this unexpected visit. "You picked a good time to join me. Care for a piece of duck?"

"No, thanks, I don't want to take the edge off my thirst. Waiter, a double bourbon."

Brewster said, "I assume you've heard the news. The truce was signed at Geneva today. Premier Mendes-France brought it off just as he promised. Divides the country in two along the seventeenth parallel. France agrees to withdraw all her troops from the northern half by October, and to assure that countrywide elections will be held in two years so that the people can decide if they want to be slave or free. I suppose I should say communist or capitalist." Smirking, Brewster applied a dab of plum jam to a thin crêpe, added a scallion and a square of crisp duck skin, and folded the crêpe into a neat package. "We have a lot of work to do between now and then."

"You're feeling pretty pleased with yourself, aren't you, Mr. W. Powers Brewster?" Hazen sipped his bourbon, delivered a moment earlier by a silent waiter. "Thanks to you, I am being deported. And I am no longer in the employ of the United States government. I tendered my resignation two days ago. You are looking at Alan Hazen, private citizen. And since we have no more official business to conduct—"

"Congratulations, old man." Brewster swallowed his last bite of crêpe. A smear of duck fat glistened on his plump chin. One waiter removed the soiled plates as another set down a huge square of chocolate cake. "I must say, we'll be sorry to lose you. You're a credit to your country—and your profession." Brewster reached for his cake only to find he had no fork. "Oh, darn. Boy! Boy! Fork, please."

"Tell me the truth just this once. You watered down my cables to Washington, didn't you, Brewster? Until I gave my story to Miss Vaughan, nobody there had any idea that the situation in the north was as serious as it was. Isn't that right? Please don't lie. I want a simple yes or no. A single word of truth." Hazen's speech was clear. Only his glazed eyes betrayed the fact that he had been knocking back double bourbons steadily since early evening.

"I had to, old man," Brewster said with an apologetic shrug. "We couldn't let this appalling conflict drag itself out forever, could we? The outcome was as inevitable as a Greek tragedy.

Better to end it quickly, and put the Frenchies out of their misery." His eyes flickered away from Hazen. "Where is that waiter? They're never around when you want them."

"Yes, Dien Bien Phu was pretty miserable. Too bad you weren't there. It wouldn't have happened if the U.S. military advisers had had a clearer picture of just how well armed and well prepared the Viet Minh were. You didn't send that cable at all, did you? The one describing the movement of all those weapons along the trails from the Chinese border?"

Brewster licked his lips as he eyed the cake. "How could I, without confirmation of the facts from other sources? Even French intelligence didn't have information like that. I couldn't let you embarrass yourself by sending in an unfounded report."

"It wasn't unfounded. I was there. I saw it with my own eyes." In a gesture of comradeship unusual for Hazen, he shifted his chair closer to Brewster's and threw his left arm around the fat man's shoulders. "By the way, are you still sleeping with Madame de Mornay, or have you lost your usefulness to her?" he said in a locker-room whisper.

Brewster reddened. "Really, you can't expect me to answer a question like that."

"You don't have to. Have a piece of cake." Hazen picked up the large chunk of gooey chocolate cake and shoved it into Brewster's mouth. "It's too late to warn you about consorting with beautiful foreign women. How much did you tell her?"

"Nothing!" the man sputtered as he tried to swallow.

"You're a fool, Brewster. An egotistical, narrow-minded, ignorant fool. With credentials like that, you should go far in the diplomatic service. All I can say is, heaven help democracy." Hazen stood. From a passing tray, he picked up a bowl of ice cream covered with butterscotch sauce and whipped cream. He inverted the bowl over Brewster's head.

"Aah—hey, what—"

Hazen's fist connected with Brewster's jaw. Brewster's chair overturned and he fell backward into a pastry cart. A pink strawberry bombe slid off its stand and joined the whipped cream on

Brewster's head. Hazen wiped his hands on Brewster's napkin, then took a long, bitter swallow of bourbon. As he stood there admiring his handiwork, two youthful Vietnamese in business suits entered the restaurant and came over to him. Each took an arm and they dragged him toward the door.

"Don't worry," Hazen called over his shoulder to the waiters and the maître d'hôtel, "he'll pay for the damage. He's one of those rich Americans you always hear about."

Eliane de Mornay, reclining on a chaise lounge, poured champagne from a bottle chilling in a silver bucket at her elbow. She wore a jade green silk *ao dai* over white trousers.

Hazen sat on the floor just inside the door, where the thugs had dumped him. He gazed at her, bleary-eyed. He had never seen her in the national costume before. A picture of Emma wearing a blue *ao dai* shimmered before his eyes. Both women, the real and the visionary, struck a wrong note, but Eliane, with her hard face and tight bleached curls, looked downright obscene.

She greeted him with a cheery smile and brought him a glass of champagne. "Ah, my dear friend. Do you think you can handle one of these? For a man who drinks so seldom, you certainly can put it down. Thank God my spies found you before you ended up in an alley in Cholon with a knife in your back."

Hazen toasted her with the champagne and took a small sip. "Sorry to horn in on your celebration, Eliane."

"Oh, Alan, to think that I am so old that I have to kidnap someone to party with me! I am delighted to see you. Tell me, what shall we celebrate?"

"The end of the war." He shrugged. "Peace. Your new wardrobe. Victory. I'll send you a check tomorrow to cover our bet." He raised his glass to her and said in Vietnamese, "I congratulate you for your fine work, Comrade Eliane. Uncle Ho could not have succeeded without you." Even in Vietnamese, Hazen's words sounded bitter.

A smile spread over Eliane's face. "Thank you. He has already sent a message of appreciation. Surely a mere change in costume did not give me away. How did you guess?"

"Victory must have made you careless. A visitor overheard you and Pham arguing at my house. I must say, I never realized. I never even suspected. You were very good."

"I was extraordinary." Her eyes flashed.

"Pham." Hazen sighed. "Pham has been working for you all along, hasn't he?"

"You were important to us, Alan. A vital source of information. His orders were to protect you at any cost."

"I thought my luck was too good to be true sometimes. All those surveys of enemy territory—that trip down the Black River, the hills around Dien Bien Phu. I never would have survived without him. He took care of the local cadres, minimized the danger, made it look real."

"He is a good man, one of the best. But we all make mistakes. We are expendable. When you return home, he will be gone."

"And Brewster, too. Is he in your employ? He's done a lot more to lose this war for the French than you have."

"Oh, no. He was just a pawn. Like you."

"And you?" Hazen raised his glass and peered at her through the crystal and the golden bubbling liquid. "What are you, Eliane?"

"Me? I am just another piece in the game. But on the winning side, as I told you I would be. My people have been at war for centuries, first against the Khmers, then the Chinese, the Japanese, and finally against the French. The Vietnamese are a patient people. We have had to be."

"You talk as if you were Vietnamese yourself, instead of a traitor to your own country."

"My dear Alan, I have had blonde curls for so long that I can't remember what I look like with straight black hair." Eliane's white teeth gleamed. "Do you like stories, Alan? Come." She patted the cushioned seat beside her. "Sit beside me and I will tell you one, about a little girl named Annette. She was born here in Saigon forty-one years ago. Her mother, whose name was Li, was

Vietnamese, the *congai* of a French army officer, a major general. The general must have felt some affection for his concubine and their bastard daughter, because when he was transferred back to France, he made arrangements for them to go, too. In a separate ship, naturally. Tourist class, so that no one would know of their connection with him."

During World War I, while the general fought the Germans, the woman and child lived in Nice, far from the front lines. After the war, the general moved his illegitimate family to Paris and installed them in a small apartment near the Clignancourt Gate. The general, who already had a wife, two grown sons, and four grandchildren, nevertheless managed to visit them once a week, bringing gifts for little Annette and enough money to keep the household going. Then one winter the visits ceased abruptly. Li and Annette never saw him again.

Li sold off their possessions one by one and finally moved with the child to a furnished room in a cheaper neighborhood, where she found work as a laundress.

Eliane de Mornay draped her arm over the back of the chaise lounge. "Li did not want her daughter to be an ignorant woman like herself. Li's parents had sold her to a brothel when she was only ten years old because they could not afford to feed her. But she was quick and clever and learned to ape other people's fine talk and good manners. Still, she never learned to read and write, and she did not want her little daughter to grow up without those skills. Every spare sou went to buy clothes and schoolbooks for Annette and to pay for special lessons in music and art."

But Li was small and frail, a tropical flower that could not thrive in Paris's chill, damp winters. In the winter of 1925 she contracted pneumonia and died. At twelve, Annette found herself orphaned, penniless, and homeless. She slept under the Seine River bridges, and raided garbage cans behind restaurants for food. One day she saw a woman who resembled her mother:

delicate, brown-skinned, with long black hair and huge almond-shaped eyes. She followed the woman home, to a neighborhood in which several Vietnamese families lived. They had been imported after the war to help the country rebuild in a time of labor shortages. Now most of them had lost their jobs, and they lived marginal existences as laundresses, cooks, tutors, and shop assistants.

After watching the woman closely for several days, Annette knocked on her door. "Please, can you help me?" she asked. "I want to go home."

As the woman tried to push her out, a man appeared. He was as slender as his wife, with unusually pale skin and fine features. He recognized immediately that Annette was a child of mixed parentage.

"Home?" he sneered. "People like you have no homes. Do you think you would be any more welcome in Vietnam than you are here? Get out. Go and ask your father for help."

"My father is dead. So is my mother. I have no one."

"I have four children myself, and we can hardly feed them. Go away."

"But I will work for you!" Annette promised. "I am strong, and I am good at my studies. I can read and write French, and I can recite pages and pages from Racine. I swear, I don't eat much. I only want to be with my own people again. Please don't send me away."

They allowed her to stay. Le Duan worked as a clerk in the Indochina section of the Foreign Ministry, but he was also a member of the International Communist Party. He told Annette about a man, an Annamese like himself, who had gone to the League of Nations after the war with a petition asking that the peoples of Indochina be allowed to govern themselves. But his was only one voice among many representatives of small nations crying out for independence. Nguyen Ai Quoc, later to be known as Ho Chi Minh, failed in his first peaceful attempt to liberate his countrymen from their colonial oppressors, but he did not give up.

For the first time, Annette learned how the French had plundered and exploited her mother's people, how they had imposed their traditions and values on a culture more ancient than their own. They had raped the countryside, removing coal, tin, minerals, rubber, cotton, and rice and leaving the peasantry ill-housed, badly fed, and uneducated. Only a few members of the mandarin class were able to send their children to schools, and these grew up to be more like Frenchmen than Vietnamese.

Le Duan taught Annette to speak and read Vietnamese. After two years, his eyes began to fail, and by the time she was fifteen, she became his secretary, writing minutes of cell meetings, drafting resolutions, learning about Party policy and politics. One day he told her that the Party had work for her to do.

A plastic surgeon operated on her face. By narrowing her nose and removing the small epicanthic fold over her eyes, he made her look more European than Eurasian. On her nineteenth birthday, she was admitted to the Communist Party. Two weeks later, she received a new name and a new history. The daughter of an army colonel, she had been born in Algiers, orphaned, then raised by an uncle and aunt in Touraine. She was the widow of another military man, a soldier who had been killed at Normandy soon after the Allied invasion.

Under her new persona, she took a job as a companion to an elderly Parisian woman. Her employer's middle-aged son was a colonel in the French army. Two months later, he and Annette were married in a small ceremony in his parish church. When the colonel was posted to Indochina in 1947, she went with him, saying that her duty was to follow him anywhere, even to a stinking tropical outpost beset by savage Viet Minh.

Eliane laughed her shrill, brittle laugh. "And so our little Annette returned to Saigon, the place of her birth. Her husband the colonel was a kind man and a complacent cuckold. He had mistresses of his own, and he quickly learned that his wife's intercession with his superiors was very helpful to his career. The rest you know."

"Did you ever feel any affection for any of us?" Hazen asked. "For General de Mornay? For Brewster? For poor old Morton, who hanged himself?" He twirled the stem of the empty champagne glass between his fingers. "For me?"

"For you, perhaps a little pity. I admired your intelligence, but I will never understand how you could continue to believe your false, imperialistic ideas. Alan, listen. We have been good enemies, yes? We can be allies as well. Stay in Saigon. Work with me. Help our cause."

"No, thanks." Hazen stood up. His legs felt wobbly and about twice as long as they should have been. "I don't want to enlist my brain in the service of the Party machine."

"We are all parts of the same cosmic machine. None of us is that important, or that necessary."

"The illusion counts. I like to think I'm a free man. *Au revoir*, Annette. I'm leaving for Hong Kong tomorrow."

"No, no, my name is Eliane. I was born in Algiers. My parents were both French." She fitted a cigarette into a long holder. "The story I told you a few minutes ago was an entertainment, a fiction, a fairy tale spun by a whore who has drunk too much champagne, smoked too much opium, loved too many men."

Hazen glanced around the room. The furnishings were luxurious and expensive, purchased with the profits she made playing the currency market. Perhaps the surplus went into the coffers of the Viet Minh. "Will you do something for me, Eliane? For old time's sake? Find out if Captain Janvier was taken prisoner after Dien Bien Phu. Is he alive or dead? Send the information to Miss Vaughan at the Metropole in Hanoi."

"You have helped me, so now I will help you, yes?" Eliane looked amused. "Very well, I will see what I can learn about the evil Captain Janvier. Your Miss Vaughan is rather presumptuous, asking so much of the husband she scorned. Perhaps I should make up a good story for her. If she thinks he is dead, maybe she will turn to you for comfort."

"No, it's all over between us. I want her to know the truth. I've never been a very good liar."

"Only because you are not a woman. Good night, Alan. And farewell."

19

OCTOBER 22, 1954

Dear Mom and Aunt Louise,

Hanoi is like one big train station these days, people arriving and departing, hurrying to get out before their tickets expire. Marie-Claire Barrault stopped in to say good-bye this morning. She and Captain Delaporte were married last week. The journalists are leaving in droves, along with French civilians and thousands of Vietnamese refugees. I don't much like being left behind, but I'll be leaving for Saigon myself as soon as the French evacuate the north. . . . Lately I've had a powerful longing to see some autumn leaves. Do you think you could send me a few? That's probably a silly idea. By the time they got here, they'd be brown dust. How about a snapshot of those big maples out near the lake?

"Good morning, mademoiselle."

Emma looked up from her breakfast. Lieutenant-Colonel Claude Josephe Siméon seated himself opposite her and ordered coffee from a passing waiter.

"You have some news?" Emma leaned across the table. Her blonde hair sparkled in the morning sunshine.

"The most promising development so far. Over one hundred Legionnaires are arriving this afternoon from a prison camp in the north. I checked. A few are from the First BEP."

"Is Janvier with them?"

"I did not see his name on the list."

"You have a list! Did you bring it with you?"

"No, it was not possible. I will have my secretary make a copy. I can give it to you later today."

"The men. When can I see them?"

"They will be taken to the military hospital at Lanessan first, of course. After our intelligence officers have debriefed them, you will be able to talk to them, perhaps as early as this evening. If you like, I will take you there in my jeep."

They agreed to meet at Chez Betty at seven o'clock. Siméon promised to bring her the names of all the prisoners who had been released thus far.

Over the rim of her coffee cup, Emma watched the traffic moving along Rue Paul Bert. "Have you noticed how much Hanoi has changed? I've been talking to some of the French women I've met in the shops. The older ones have lived here for more than thirty years. Through the Depression and the Japanese occupation. Liberation. They know they must leave soon, and they're terrified. They'll have to get used to being French in France again."

"We soldiers must make similar adjustments. I have been away from my home for three years."

"Are you married?"

"Oh, yes. I have one child, a daughter. She was only six months old when I shipped out. Would you like to see her picture?" He opened his wallet and displayed a small color photograph of a smiling, fair-haired child. "I could have brought her mother to Indochina with me, but she did not want to leave Lyons—her parents, her sisters. You know. I am glad they are not here now."

"What about you, Colonel? Do you hate Vietnam?"

Siméon looked surprised. "Not at all. I have been quite content here. I only wish the war had been a better one, with an enemy who would stand and fight. But I must go. I will see you at seven."

Emma arrived at Chez Betty at six. A couple of reporters hailed her and offered to buy her a drink. It sat untouched while she listened distractedly to their conversation and watched the

door for Siméon. Finally, at seven-fifteen, a jeep pulled up outside the café.

"Sorry I'm late," Siméon said as she jumped in. "The paper-
work at headquarters these days is ridiculous. Here are the names
I promised you."

Eagerly, Emma scanned the list he gave her. Janvier's name
was not on it. She did not recognize any of the other names.

Siméon told her that most of the returning prisoners were being
treated for dysentery, infections, unattended wounds, malnutrition,
and gangrene. "It is a miracle that more of them did not die. Here
we are." He pulled up in front of the main door of the hospital. "I
hope you will learn something about your friend. I will wait for you
here. Perhaps we can dine together this evening?"

The wounded overflowed the wards. The new arrivals lay on
cots and stretchers in the corridors. Emma greeted them with a
cheerfulness she did not feel. Their eyes, which had witnessed
too many horrors, seemed unable to focus on a single face. She
felt invisible, nonexistent. Their minds were in Dien Bien Phu,
or with their friends who were still being held in Viet Minh POW
camps.

Then she heard a loud bellow from the far end of the corridor.
A gaunt, hairy giant limped toward her, leaning on a cane.
Lucky Pierre. They fell into each other's arms.

"You're safe, you're safe," she kept repeating. "I saw a list, but
your name wasn't on it."

"What! You didn't see Corporal Jean Louis Christian Lévêque?
Those idiots, I'll tell them—"

"Jean Louis Christian— But your name is Pierre!"

"No, they just called me that when I enlisted. *Pierre* means
'rock' in French, see. They called me that because I am as solid
as a rock."

"But you're hurt. What happened?"

"You won't believe this, but I sprained my ankle jumping out
of the chopper this morning. Nothing the matter with me that a
bottle of cognac won't cure."

"I'll see that you get one," Emma promised. "Tell me about Robert. Where is he? Is he alive?"

Pierre's smile faded. "I will tell you the truth, mademoiselle. I do not know. He disappeared a few days before the final assault and I never saw him again. Maybe he got pounded into the ground by an enemy shell. If he received a direct hit, you see, there wouldn't be anything left of him."

"Do you believe that?"

"No." Pierre looked solemn. "Come in here, where we can talk." He led her to the solarium at the end of the corridor, where the more able-bodied patients were playing cards or reading magazines. They chose a quiet corner away from the windows. Even in these days of cease-fire, the Legionnaire was wary of grenade attacks. "I will tell you what happened. We were holding down Huguette, right? Have you heard what it was like? Under fire day and night, no time to sleep, no decent food, no place even to take a shit—excuse me, but that's how it was. But we were hanging on, defending that shithole because we couldn't do anything else, waiting for someone to bomb those hills so that we could break out. We knew we were finished. The Englishwoman, Lieutenant Burton, was with us the whole time. As tough a soldier as any of the men, I'll say that much for her. And she could shoot the eye out of a sparrow hawk."

"What about Robert?"

"Hold on, I'm getting to that. Say, do you have any cigarettes? I just smoked my last one. Thanks." Lucky Pierre waited until the match he had struck had burned down nearly to his fingertips before blowing it out. "Anyway, a few nights before the Viets ran all over us, we had been ordered to organize a breakout operation. The shelling had slowed down a little because it was raining buckets. Suddenly we heard a scream and then a shout. One of the new replacements told us he had just seen the captain and Lieutenant Burton standing outside the barbed wire fence. Outside, mind. But then the shelling and the gunfire started up again, harder than ever. We all rushed for the dugouts. Lieutenant Burton was still out there, plastered against the wire, drawing Viet Minh fire."

"But what about Robert? Where was he?"

Lucky Pierre shook his massive head. He wanted to tell the story in his own way. "Later that night I made my way over to the new fellow who had raised the alarm. He swore he had seen Lieutenant Burton crawl under the wire, and that she and the captain were having an argument on the other side. Some of the men thought Burton was going to desert, you know, to save her own skin while leaving the rest of us behind. But I don't think so. She was as loyal as any of them. And she wasn't scared. Not her."

Emma leaned forward. "But Robert. Wouldn't he have tried to stop her from leaving?"

Pierre looked grim. "I think it was the other way around. I think he slipped out first, and she was trying to stop him."

"You mean he deserted? No, I don't believe it! He never would have done that. You—you don't think he killed her!"

"He was my *copain*," Pierre said sadly, "but I didn't trust him anymore. The man who saw them said he heard a shot just before Lieutenant Burton screamed, and before the Viets started firing again." Lucky Pierre stared at a spot on the floor. "I guess the place had gotten to the captain. He looked like he was keeping secrets. And he got mean. He wouldn't talk to me—or anybody else. And he wouldn't lend a hand when somebody needed it. Not even to the wounded. He sneered at them. He never helped carry the guys to the hospital, and he never visited anybody. I think he had decided he was going to escape, and that the rest of us were all going to die, so there was no point bothering with us."

Emma felt dazed. "Do you think he made it? Do you think he got through?"

"Him? Sure, if anyone could. He had maps and he knew the terrain. He could take care of himself in the jungle, living like a Viet, traveling at night, stealing food from the villages. I think he's still alive. Don't ask me why. Just a feeling I have. Even if he was a bad man, he was my buddy, right? My *copain*. What I don't understand is why he didn't tell me what he was planning. He left me behind. All of us. Left us behind to be killed."

They sat in silence for a few minutes, listening to the muted talk of the card players. "What will you do now?" Emma asked.

"They're letting me out of here tomorrow. I'll find myself a girl and a bottle of cognac and then—but never mind. When the Legion has work for me to do, they'll tell me. What about you?"

Emma said, "I'm going to stay in Hanoi until the last Frenchman leaves. That way I'll know he's never coming back."

In the next two months, under the protection of the cease-fire, an awesome tide of humanity surged southward. Thousands of peasants, many of them devout Catholics whose clerics had ranted against the communists for years and who feared for their lives under the new regime, thronged to the port city of Haiphong, where they lived in refugee camps until they could board French or American ships that would take them to Saigon.

Emma heard that Dr. Jack McGraw was assisting in the removal and relocation effort. Catching a ride with a photographer from one of the wire services, she traveled down to Haiphong, only fifty-five miles downriver from Hanoi. She found the doctor working in a makeshift clinic that had been set up in an old warehouse near the docks. He and a U.S. Navy corpsman were inoculating a large group of passengers who were preparing to board the U.S.S. *Kentucky.*

"Have you forsaken Laos, Dr. McGraw?"

He glanced up. His eyes were bloodshot and glazed with fatigue. "Hello, Miss Vaughan. I heard the navy was here helping the refugees. As an old army man myself, I thought I'd give them a hand."

"Where's Tran?"

"Tran is gone. Dead."

"Oh, no! Was she killed by the Viets?"

"No. She died in childbirth. I couldn't save her, or the child. That was another reason for leaving Muong Cham."

"You'll never go back to Laos, will you?" Emma asked softly.

"I might, if I can persuade some of these young guys to give me some help after their time with the navy is up."

The navy corpsman spoke up. "The doc here is worse than any navy recruiter. He makes that little country sound like the lower forty of paradise."

"It is." Emma pulled out her notebook. "And what are you telling your new recruits, Doctor? About getting along in a country like Laos?"

"I tell them that I'm only a guest in this part of the world. I don't go marching into some little village and start giving orders. I find the headman, ask his permission to set up a clinic to help his people. As long as I live there, I obey the rules of the community and abide by their taboos as much as possible. I eat their food, learn their language, attend their festivals, and celebrate their holidays. I don't proselytize about Catholicism or democracy or anything else. If they want me to leave, I leave. I'm there to serve, not to bully. And not to spy."

"I'm glad I ran into you." Emma scribbled down his words. "You're good copy."

"Tell F. X. I said hello. For a newspaperman, he's a lousy correspondent."

"It's an occupational failing. Letter writing is too much like—"

Through the open door of the warehouse, Emma glimpsed a man wearing a beige summer suit and a brown fedora. Even in civilian clothes, his figure was unmistakable: broad-shouldered, slim-hipped, compact, and muscular. Robert Janvier. Leaving Dr. McGraw in midsentence, she rushed out of the warehouse in time to see the man vanishing into the crowd of refugees waiting to board the ship after their inoculations.

"Robert! Robert, wait!"

Emma shouldered her way through the press of bodies. Ahead of her, the brown fedora bobbed along on the sea of humanity. She stumbled over crying children and hurdled bundles of possessions, some with holy pictures and crucifixes pinned to them. The crowd was quiet, numb. Terrified of life under the anti-Catholic communist regime, they had left their homes, put themselves in the hands of fate and the Christian God and the French government, from whom they expected a reward for their loyalty.

Finally the crush thinned and Emma breathed a sigh of relief. But where the mob ended, a new obstacle course began. Breaking into a run as she followed the man through a pair of wire gates, Emma found herself in one of the new refugee camps, a village composed of cardboard huts and shelters made of packing crates. Scrawny dogs sniffed smears of feces. Piles of refuse burned, filling the humid air with acrid, stinking smoke. Women cooked rice over the flaming garbage. Emma threaded her way through humanity at its lowest ebb: dispossessed, hungry, victimized by filth and disease and poverty. Straining to keep the brown fedora in sight, she dodged down an alley, a conduit for liquid waste. She wondered which would overcome her first: the overpowering stink or her own physical exhaustion.

As the horde of people on the docks had merged with the refugee camp, the refugee camp merged with the city of Haiphong, no beauty spot even in peacetime, but a rough-and-tumble port whose red-light district was bigger than most large Vietnamese towns. The man in the brown fedora moved swiftly here, across tramcar tracks and along cement sidewalks, past the offices of the Post and Telegraph and the Waterfront Commission. Too breathless now to call out to him, Emma needed all her energy just to keep him in sight.

Finally, on the other side of a small park dominated by an equestrian statue of Napoleon III, the man turned down a narrow side street. Panting, Emma ran to catch up with him before he disappeared in the maze of whorehouses and opium dens. The street curved sharply about thirty yards along, but Emma reached the mouth of the artery just in time to see her man disappear into a small *bar-tabac* with a pink neon sign on the window that said "René's." Gasping, almost weeping with fatigue, she plunged through the beaded doorway.

The room was empty. Chairs were upturned on the scarred tabletops, but the floor was still littered with crumpled papers, cigarette butts, and bits of food. Yellow fly specks coated the mirror behind the zinc bar.

"Hello!" Emma called. "*Bon jour, patron. Personne ici? S'il vous plaît?*"

A short round Frenchman wearing a stained apron stepped out of a curtained doorway behind the bar. He blinked at Emma but said nothing.

In stuttering phrases—Emma's command of the language faltered whenever she was fatigued or excited—she described the man she had seen and repeated his name three or four times: "Robert Janvier, he calls himself. Janvier. He is a soldier, a Legionnaire. Please, can't you tell him I'm here? I am Emma Vaughan. He knows me. I am a friend, a good friend." The man remained mute, stolidly impassive. "Look, can't you at least call him? Robert!" she shouted. Her voice echoed off the tiled walls and the display of bottles behind the bar. "Robert, I know you're here. I want to talk to you. It's me, Emma." She stepped behind the bar and started toward the curtain. "I'll just take a look back here, if you don't mind." The proprietor did mind. He lifted his arm, as stout and sturdy as a tree trunk, and blocked her path. Abashed, Emma retreated. "All right, I'll leave a note. You'll give it to him, won't you?"

On a page torn from her notebook, she asked Janvier to meet her between nine and midnight at a tearoom called Irene's that she had seen across from Haiphong's central railroad station. Handing the note to the proprietor along with fifty francs, she again stressed her need to see the man in the beige suit.

"Please, just give it to him. It's very important. I beg you."

Back at the docks, she found the wire service photographer still wandering around taking pictures. She told him to go back to Hanoi without her, that she had met some friends and was going to stay in Haiphong for a couple of days.

In the warehouse, Jack McGraw was still inoculating passengers. Emma glanced at her watch: only an hour and fifteen minutes had passed since she had dashed out of that door. McGraw glanced up at her.

"Just like F. X.," he said. "No manners."

"Do you know a place in town called René's?" Emma asked. "It's up past the post office and Waterfront Commission. A *bar-tabac*—I can't remember the name of the street—"

The navy corpsman, who was still helping McGraw, looked up, astonished. "Wow, you really are a reporter! You've been in town only two hours and you've found that place already?" He swabbed a thin brown arm and held it firmly while he stuck a hypodermic needle into it. His patient, a scared-looking ten-year-old, whimpered but did not cry out. "René's is the worst spot in Haiphong. Probably on the whole China coast. Sailors don't go there alone and they don't go in pairs. They go in packs, and they go armed. I went in there once, and I never went back. You been in there, ma'am?"

"I just poked my nose in, out of curiosity." Emma's head throbbed. She wished she could sit down. "Is it just drinks and gambling, that sort of thing?"

"No, ma'am. Stabbings, shootings, murders. And a lot of drugs. Hash, cocaine, heroin. The hard stuff."

"Heroin!"

"Miss Vaughan," Dr. McGraw growled, "pick up a syringe and get to work or stop bothering my assistants and push off."

"Sorry, Dr. McGraw. I have to find—I'm just trying to do my job."

"I've heard about that place. It's a festering boil on Haiphong's bottom which a lot of people would love to lance. I hope Ho Chi Minh will have better luck cleaning it up than the bishop did. Now scram."

The train station and the surrounding area were almost deserted now. Nine years of war had destroyed most of Tonkin's rail lines and rolling stock. Emma waited in the dreary tearoom until it closed, and then she fell asleep on a bench under a streetlamp outside. She was awakened by a Vietnamese policeman.

"It wasn't Robert," she muttered as she stumbled along the street toward a hotel. "It couldn't have been. It wasn't Robert."

* * *

The soldiers of the French Expeditionary Forces marched through the streets of Hanoi on their way to the planes and ships that would carry them to Saigon and from there back to their homes. Emma watched the parade from the window of her room at the Metropole. In the past few weeks, the town had been emptying itself of the foreign invaders. Only a few journalists and photographers were left to cover the story of the French retreat.

"In a couple of hours you will be going with them," she said to Colonel Siméon, who had joined her at the window to watch the French exodus. He had come to bid her good-bye.

After Emma came back from Haiphong, Siméon had invited her to attend a reception at the Officers' Club in honor of those who had returned from prison camps and Dien Bien Phu. The affair had been disappointing, even depressing. Too many old friends were missing, and the wasted bodies of the Dien Bien Phu veterans mocked the ruddy good health of those who had remained in Hanoi. Afterward in Emma's room, she had allowed Siméon to make love to her, but they were both distracted, more than a little drunk on too much wine and too many sad memories. Siméon had taken her out to dinner a couple of times since, but Emma had not encouraged him.

"One of the maids told me this morning that the communists have already moved into the suburbs." Emma twisted the lace curtain at the window. "She's terrified."

"Just listen to them: brass bands, company songs. Just like a victory parade. That's the kind of spirit and pride that kept us fighting here in this dismal country for eight years."

Emma watched a Legion paratroop battalion march past, their arms swinging, their red berets flashing in the sun. Their voices drifted up to her through the leaves of the dusty acacia trees that lined the street: "Let us jump, jump together. Legionnaires, we will never return. The enemy is waiting for us down on the ground. Be tough. We are going into combat." She wondered if Lucky Pierre was down there marching with the rest. "Let us jump, jump together."

She turned away from the window. The armoire and drawers

were empty, her suitcases packed. As an American, she had been ordered to leave Hanoi when the new rulers took over. But F. X. had agreed to let her stay in Saigon long enough to cover the arrival of the new prime minister, Ngo Dinh Diem.

"What will you do when you get back to France?" she asked Siméon.

"Get acquainted with my wife and baby daughter again while I wait for a war to erupt someplace else. Otherwise I will sit at my desk and try to keep my nose clean for the next ten years. I'm bound to make general before I retire."

"You will. You're a good soldier."

"You are quite right. A good soldier. The army rewards loyalty and luck. At least I am going back in one piece, which is more than I can say for some of those poor bastards down there. This war was atrocious." He turned away from the window. "You are looking at the end of an era, my dear Emma. Never again will a foreign army try to decide the fate of this poor little country."

"No, I suppose not."

"Oh, well. I had better get back to the office and make sure my secretary has unscrewed all the light bulbs and picked up all the paper clips. We are not leaving those savages anything, not even a single roll of toilet paper."

The French soldiers had systematically dismantled Quonset huts, barracks buildings, guardhouses, fences, and watchtowers all around Hanoi. Their orders had been to strip Tonkin and the Red River delta of everything that might conceivably be useful to the enemy. At the end of War War II, the departing Japanese had left behind weapons and tons of ammunition that the Viet Minh had later used to fight the French. The French would not make the same mistake.

"Farewell then, dear Emma." Siméon set his officer's cap squarely on his head, tucked his swagger stick under his arm, and kissed Emma on both cheeks. "Perhaps we shall meet again in Paris."

"*Au revoir*, Claude."

After the parade had passed, a peculiar hush descended over

the city. Houses and office buildings were shuttered and silent as the remaining inhabitants awaited the arrival of the communists. Emma, watching from her window, saw the first of them coming down Rue Paul Bert pushing bicycles loaded with supplies. They were small men, as tough and brown and stringy as tree roots. Their uniforms were laughable, shorts and tattered shirts, with straw coolie hats on their heads and sandals made of old rubber tires on their feet, and no bars, stripes, or insignias to distinguish officers from enlisted men. They carried rifles, some of French or Chinese or Russian manufacture, some made from pipes in jungle factories. From each man's waist hung a small sack containing his weekly rice ration.

Emma rang the front desk and asked them to send up a bell-hop. After waiting half an hour, she gave up and carried her own suitcases down to the lobby, then made a second trip for her typewriter. The elevator was not working, the operator having fled to Saigon with his family.

In the lobby, Emma came face-to-face with a Viet Minh soldier, but whether he was an officer or an enlisted man, she could not tell. In fluent and idiomatic French, he asked to see her papers. She handed over her press card, travel permits, and her passport and told him that she would be leaving Hanoi at once. He nodded and returned her documents. As he turned away, she called him back.

"Monsieur, I want to offer my felicitations," she said. "You have won a great victory. I wish you and your countrymen every success."

His face remained impassive. He had no need of her congratulations. Nevertheless, he said politely, "Thank you, madame."

Saigon was as hot and sunny as ever, and bloated with refugees. Vehicles of all types vied for space on the stately tree-shaded boulevards. Emma saw more Americans than she remembered, smiling men with crew cuts and colorful sports shirts, and cameras slung around their necks. They were everywhere these days, sitting at the best tables on the terrace of the Hotel Continental, standing at the bar in the Majestic, waiting on line for cinema tickets, taking pictures, making notes, talking in loud, ringing voices that cut through the hum of native conversation like motorboats roaring across a placid lake.

"What are they doing here?" Emma, sipping a daiquiri, addressed her question to an acerbic middle-aged reporter for *Newsweek* who had just arrived in the country. "What do they want?"

"They're advisers, honey. Ngo Dinh Diem is Washington's boy, the way Bao Dai was Paris's. I've met him. He's earnest as hell and duller than Sunday, but he's clean. You couldn't find a more lily-white character. Studied for the priesthood, lived in Catholic seminaries in New Jersey and New York. Practically Cardinal Spellman's altar boy."

Emma missed Ashbourne, Corrigan, and the other reporters with whom she had shared close quarters in Saigon, Hanoi, and Dien Bien Phu. She resented the way this new man spoke of North Vietnam as a stepchild of Red China, and the way he seemed to regard Ho Chi Minh as a dime-store version of Mao Tse-tung. To this newcomer, the battle of Dien Bien Phu already belonged to the myth-laden past, along with Carthage and Verdun and Omaha Beach. He was seeing a Vietnam different from the one Emma had known: a country newly divided into North and South; a country split along clear ideological lines; a country that after a decade of war had won only a fragile peace.

That afternoon Emma took a taxi out to Hazen's villa in Dakow. Someone else was living there now. She stood on the sidewalk and peered in through the gate. Hazen had announced his intention of divorcing her, but three months had passed since his departure and she had heard nothing. Did he still love her? Or had he forgotten her? She couldn't believe she had actually married him, or that they had been happy together for that short time. She wished she could remember what it felt like, being happy. Perhaps if Janvier had disappeared sooner, her marriage to Alan Hazen would have lasted and grown stronger. They might be living in the United States now, adjusting to supermarkets and home appliances and the miracle of television.

Later she sat in the Café de la Paix and watched the daylight turn to darkness. Maybe she should start thinking about going home. Except for her landlord, Monsieur de Chesnay, who had vowed to stay in Indochina until he died, everybody she had known in Saigon had left. As for Janvier, she would never see him again, never taste his kiss, never feel his touch, never hear him whisper her name. That era, too, was finished.

The next day, she received an invitation to the traditional Christmas Eve cocktail party at the American embassy. She wore a blue silk gown Janvier had bought her in Hanoi, along with a string of pearls he had given her on her birthday. A few other journalists were there, newcomers like the *Newsweek* man whose experience in Indochina was brief and whose knowledge of the country was limited. Emma entertained herself by composing scathing remarks about the new ambassador and his serious-looking young aides, the ambassador's wife, the marine guards, the rookie reporters, and the Vietnamese officials who seemed so eager to impress the Americans.

Emma munched hors d'oeuvres and tried to stifle her yawns while she pretended to drink a glass of cheap champagne. Then at ten o'clock, a wave of excitement rippled through the room. She saw Eliane de Mornay's brassy head mingling with the crew cuts and permanents on the receiving line. Emma moved closer. Eliane was wearing a skin-tight black sheath studded with rhinestones and jet beads, cut high in front and daringly low in back. A diamond collar encircled her slender throat.

"The Merry Widow," Emma said half-aloud.

Indeed, Eliane hardly seemed to be mourning the loss of her husband, who had died of a heart attack on the day the French marched out of Hanoi. At the funeral, General Navarre had blamed their country's failure in Tonkin for breaking his colleague's heart. He did not mention that General de Mornay had made this patriotic gesture in the arms of a Vietnamese whore.

Eliane bestowed her kisses freely on both men and women. Her ringing tones made the crystal pendants on the ambassador's chandelier quiver.

The two women encountered each other over the buffet table. Emma was munching a small square of melba toast decorated with caviar when Eliane swooped down on her.

"Ah, I am delighted to see you, my dear. I was beginning to think that everyone interesting had left Saigon. Tell me, have you heard from that rascal, Alan Hazen? He promised to write to me, but I have not had one word from him, not one."

"I'm surprised to see you're still here, Madame de Mornay. I always thought you loathed Vietnam." Emma wondered if Hazen had told Eliane that she and Pham had been overheard talking in Vietnamese.

"Ah, my child, the sad truth is that I know I can shine here," Eliane confided. "I am not a young woman anymore. In Paris I would be just one of many military widows. Here, everyone knows me. And the Americans—how they adore me! They call me the Queen of Saigon. How can I disappoint them by leaving? Tell me, have you seen this remarkable vase? It was a gift to Bunny from the emperor." Taking Emma's elbow, Eliane steered her toward an uncrowded corner. "It is Ming, quite charming, but a reproduction. They turn them out by the thousands in Hong Kong." Emma squirmed, but Eliane did not release her hold on her arm. "A moment more, madame," she purred. "I understand you are still interested in the whereabouts of a certain French soldier."

Emma's heart lurched. "Janvier! Where is he?"

"Here in Saigon. I do not know anything more than that. He was seen in Cholon. But do not look for him. Wait for him to find you."

"I don't believe it. You say he's here? But why wouldn't he come and see me?"

"Don't you know what the Legion does to deserters? They hang them. Your soldier is a wanted man now, a fugitive. They may even be watching your home."

"But I could help him! Doesn't he know that?"

"He has other friends in this city, powerful ones. If they cannot help him, how could you? Be patient."

"Thank you," Emma whispered. "Oh, thank you."

Eliane shrugged her narrow shoulders. "Alan asked me to help you. He thinks so highly of you. Excuse me, my dear, the ambassador seems to be searching for me. Perhaps I should give his wife a few lessons in feminine comportment. He would look happier and live longer." She walked away, swinging her hips, a bewitching smile planted on her face.

Emma left the party soon after. She walked back to Monsieur de Chesnay's villa. A thousand questions sprang into her mind: Where was he? Why didn't he come to her? What was he doing? Was he safe? Had she really seen him that day in Haiphong? At every moment, she expected Robert Janvier to step out of the shadows and take her in his arms. It would happen, and soon. Until then, she must be patient.

Her heart soared. He was alive. He was alive!

20

MARCH 18, 1955

. . . know the world isn't very interested in
Vietnam anymore, but even though F. X. stopped
paying me two months ago, Saigon is still my
favorite city in the whole world and I don't want to
leave yet. I had a job interview with the editors of
the new English-language <u>South Vietnam Weekly</u>,
and I may take some courses in Vietnamese so I
can get work translating or interpreting. It would
probably be a waste of time—my French is still
pretty lousy. If I can just last until . . .

"I can hardly believe that one year ago I was sitting in a foxhole in
Dien Bien Phu, waiting for the Viets to attack." Emma picked
idly at a splinter of rattan on the arm of the fanback chair in
which she was sitting. "Time passes so quickly in this part of the
world."

Monsieur de Chesnay dipped the point of a small brush into a
smear of paint on his palette. "Time is a river," he declared.
"Some of us float along and follow the current wherever it takes
us, others swim through it, still others ride over it in powerful
motorboats. Keep your head very still, madame. I must put a
little dot of white on your nose. There."

"But rivers flow at different speeds, depending on the season."
The heat of the morning was making Emma sleepy. She swallowed a yawn.

"Ah, but when you are in the river, you know how swiftly it

moves by watching stationary objects on the bank. If you cannot see them, you cannot judge, is that not so? Such was Einstein's theory as I understood it twenty years ago—but then, I am only an artist and not a scientist. The River Time is so wide that you cannot observe the banks, only the other swimmers and boaters in the water." He stood back from his work, wrinkled his nose and furrowed his brow, then added a dab to the lower right-hand corner of the canvas.

"If everyone else in the water is floating like you, you think you are standing still, or moving slowly. But if some are trying to swim upstream against the current, you see how they struggle and you decide that the river must be moving swiftly. Twenty years ago, everyone in Saigon floated with the current. Today, everyone wants to go upstream. I thank the good God that within the walls of this house, my life has not changed." He glanced at Emma, sinking ever lower in her chair. "You have changed, madame. When you came here, you were a pretty child, an innocent. Now you have greater wisdom in your eyes." De Chesnay sighed. "You have paid dearly for that, I know. But you are a woman now. Do not regret your lost innocence. Wisdom is always a good investment, a lasting one."

"Can you recall the exact moment in your life when you lost your innocence?" Emma asked. De Chesnay had shut himself off from the world years ago, but not from the pleasures of art and friendship and the companionship of women. "I don't mean your virginity, exactly. Your illusions about life."

De Chesnay understood her meaning instantly. "Oh, yes, I remember it quite well. I was in Tonkin, in the far northeastern corner near the Baie d'Along—you are familiar with that part of the country, are you not? The district commissioner had taken me to see a coal mine. Up until that time, my tour had been like a dream of beautiful women and fragrant jungles, pagodas and temples and peasants laboring peacefully in the paddy fields. The Indochina that every French boy learned about in his textbooks. That coal mine was the first ugly thing I saw in this country. It was an open pit, a great running sore in the side of the mountain.

Workers were crawling all over it like maggots. The day before we got there, one of them had been caught stealing food from the company larder. The foreman dragged him up before the commissioner, who agreed he must be taught a lesson. They assembled the entire work force, an army of men and women and, yes, even children, all of them so starved and exhausted that they were more like beasts than humans. In front of all the other workers, the thief was stripped naked and lashed between two posts. Then the foreman whipped him with a short riding crop, whipped him until the earth under his feet was soaked with blood. That man made not one sound, not even a whimper. Nor did any of the workers. Unable to look at the poor victim, I watched them, and in their eyes I saw a look that I will never forget: a hatred so deep and cold that it existed as a thing apart from those people. A hatred with a life of its own. When the scourging was over, they took the man down and dragged him away, and the workers were told that their rice ration would be cut in half for the next three days as punishment for harboring a thief in their midst. The foreman and the district commissioner congratulated themselves on a good day's work, and then we all went down to the mine offices and had our lunch, a fine meal with three different wines, an excellent soup, a fish course, a meat course, and fruit and cheese at the end. I could not eat one bite. I was twenty-five years old, and I had already known many women. But on that day I became a man."

"And is that when you decided to stay in Indochina?"

"I never actually made that decision. I just kept postponing my return to France, and after a while I stopped thinking about it altogether." De Chesnay wiped his paintbrush with a stained rag. "We have done enough for today. It is nearly lunchtime. Yes, I think your mother will be very pleased when she sees this."

He had posed Emma on a rattan chair near the open French doors that led to the terrace. On the wall behind her, just over her right shoulder, hung a painting of a pagoda framed in gold. In the garden outside, scarlet bougainvillea cascaded over the fence. The leathery trunk of a palm tree strained to break out of the background like some monstrous beast trying to escape a net of twisting liana vines. Emma had wanted to buy a de Chesnay landscape as a gift for her mother, but the artist had insisted on incorporating her portrait into the picture.

"In years to come, you can show this to people as proof that you were really here, in Vietnam. And everyone will say, 'Really? Vietnam? Where is that? What kind of place is it?'"

Emma walked around to the front of the easel to examine the painting. The woman in the chair—she could not think of that figure as herself—seemed pensive and preoccupied, and very tense. "She looks like she's expecting someone to walk through the door."

"Your destiny. Your Legion captain. Or that tall American, perhaps." De Chesnay swished his brushes in a can of turpentine. "Do you ever hear from them?"

"No. That is—he—when the— I think they've forgotten all about me."

"I doubt that."

Emma had a lunch date at the Hotel Majestic with a French newspaperman she had met the week before. He told her that with new troubles flaring up in Algeria, his countrymen might well abandon their responsibilities in Indochina before the plebiscite that would determine the political fate of South Vietnam. Those elections were scheduled to be held one year hence, in 1956.

"A war nearer to home is always more popular than one six thousand miles away. Besides, our ties to Algeria have always been close. Some people even call the Mediterranean the river that runs through France." He paused, his wineglass halfway to his lips. "Ah, look at that."

They gazed out at the Saigon River. A steel gray U.S. Navy cargo ship was nosing its way into the harbor, assisted by tenders and tugboats.

"More refugees?" Emma plunged her spoon into a mound of raspberry ice. Such sights were common on the Saigon River.

"More American aid, I would say. Your government is a generous friend. I am not one of those who think the Americans should have given us more assistance in fighting the Viet Minh. If you want my opinion—which my newspaper does not share—no amount of money would have been enough to defeat them."

"Well, it's all over now," Emma said with a philosophic shrug.

"Yes, it is all over."

They parted after lunch, the Frenchman returning to his office, while Emma wandered down to the docks to watch the coolies who were unloading the American ship. A mountain of bales and crates began to rise on the wharf like a birthing volcano. Stenciled in black on the containers were the words "A GIFT FROM THE USA." The sight failed to impress Emma, who had seen the contents of many such crates and bales displayed in black-market shops and stalls all over the city: food, clothing, toiletries, insecticides and tools, fertilizers, medicines. The people for whom these gifts were intended did not receive them unless they paid inflated black-market prices. Emma doubted they felt much gratitude to the United States.

The bells in the cathedral towers were chiming one o'clock, and on the streets and sidewalks traffic had thinned miraculously as the citizens of Saigon headed to their homes for their siestas. After two and a half years in Vietnam, Emma had learned to follow their example. The oppressive heat made hard physical and mental effort impossible.

Emma strolled up Rue Catinat, avoiding the sleeping bodies sprawled under the tamarind and plane trees. After the heat of the day had waned a little, those bodies would stir, stretch, and become vertical again, taking up their soup ladles or shoeshine boxes, their bundles of newspapers or their little trays of pencils, lighters, or black-market cigarettes. With the arrival of a million refugees in the south, the number of vendors and customers in Saigon had risen dramatically. It seemed to Emma that anyone not buying something was selling it.

The shabby old villa was quiet. Even the smaller children napped readily after lunch, and were sometimes found sleeping in odd, out-of-the-way places—under tables or shrubs in the yard, inside closets, on staircases. Emma climbed the stairs to the balcony. She missed her neighbor's gentle snoring. Monsieur Varigny had left Saigon in December to take up a new position with the Ministry of Culture in Paris, and Monsieur de Chesnay had not yet rented his room.

As she opened her door, she heard a faint scuffling noise and then a voice: "Emma."

Although he had spoken in a harsh whisper, uttering only one word, she knew him. If emotions were colors, she thought, at this moment her portrait would be a rainbow of dazzling pigments, her face stippled with dots of fear and dread and longing and relief—and love.

"Robert."

He had been standing in a shadowy corner beside the armoire. As he moved into the light, she saw that the months he had spent either on the battlefield or in hiding had not ruined his health or marred his beauty. He was clean-shaven and well manicured, and as sleek and muscular as a panther. His clothes were rumpled but clean, a beige tropical suit over a pale blue shirt. On her desk sat a dark fedora hat and a pair of dark glasses. In such a disguise, he would have been indistinguishable from the hundreds of clerks who still serviced the shrinking French government agencies in Saigon.

She flew into his arms. "Robert! Robert! So it was you I saw in Haiphong!"

Janvier kissed her fiercely and held her so tightly that she could scarcely breathe. Their bodies feasted on each other.

"How I wanted to hold you, to kiss you that day in Haiphong, but I could not even speak to you," Janvier whispered. "It was impossible. I will explain."

"That doesn't matter now. I knew you would come back to me eventually, when you were ready." Her words, although whispered, were exultant. He still loved her. "I knew you weren't dead."

"How did you know that?"

The molecules between them were so charged with energy that

Emma could feel the words as he spoke them. Her afternoon torpor was gone. His appearance had revived her like a stimulant.

"Pierre told me you had escaped from Huguette. He was sure you had survived, and so was I. Oh, Robert, why didn't you come to me sooner? Where have you been? Were you hurt?"

"A bullet wound in my back. It slowed me down for a few weeks but it didn't stop me. At least I didn't die in that hellhole."

"And so you left your men to die instead."

"I had to. Once I was outside the wire, it was too late to get back in. Anyway, we were under orders to organize a breakout operation from Huguette that night. It didn't make any sense to break in and break out again."

"But your orders from headquarters—"

"My orders? Do you think I was still listening to orders? The Viets were so close I could hear them breathing, like hungry wolves circling around a deer, waiting for just the right moment to close in for the kill. But I knew I could get past them in the rain and the darkness. It was almost a perfect escape." He sat down in her creaking wicker armchair and took a cigarette from a pack he carried in an outside jacket pocket.

Emma stood over him as he struck a match. "But I don't understand. What about Lieutenant Burton? She went with you, didn't she?"

"That crazy bitch." Janvier laughed. "That's how I got out: I was trying to bring her back. For weeks she had been following me around like a dog—I could hardly take a piss without her standing over my shoulder, watching me. I don't think she ever slept. But that is not so surprising. None of the rest of us slept either. The Viets kept their artillery blasting away day and night. You just moved away from the firing line and hoped they wouldn't follow you before you had a chance to rest a little in your new patch of mud and filth. They didn't care if they hit us or not. They knew that after a week of that kind of punishment, we would all be half-dead anyway."

"Lieutenant Burton," Emma said. "What do you mean, you were trying to bring her back?"

"She went nuts. She had been right beside me; then all of a sudden she was gone. I looked over and saw her crawling through the rain and the mud and scooping out a hole under the barbed wire. When she reached the other side, I was right behind her. I ordered her to come back, but she refused, and we lay there in the slime, arguing. Her mind had completely snapped. She said we belonged together, and she had some notion that if we escaped together, our love would be some kind of shield so the Viet Minh bullets couldn't touch us. I grabbed her under the arms and started to drag her back under the wire, but she stood up and started to scream at the top of her lungs. 'Kill us, kill us, we want to die together!' I shook her off and ran like hell."

Emma remembered Pierre's description of the lieutenant's body lying just outside the perimeter of the barbed wire fence. "Did your men hear her?"

"Of course they heard her. Everyone heard her. Especially the enemy. But I didn't care. Let the silly cow draw their fire, I thought. They can't see me, but they can see her. Then that crazy bitch shot me in the back. I know it was her. She used to pick off Viet snipers in the dark. She always knew just where to find them, by the sounds they made."

Emma swallowed. "Did you kill her?"

"Me?" Janvier laughed again. "Are you crazy? If I had fired a shot, I would have given away my position. But the Viets opened up on her. I fell facedown in the mud at the bottom of the slope and lay there until things were quiet, and then I started to crawl. I crawled right through Giap's lines, so close to some of their big guns that I could smell the oil and the smoke and the stink of their dead. When dawn came, I found a hole, a crater from one of our bombs. I pulled some branches over myself and stayed there until darkness came again. I didn't move a muscle. I just lay there, feeling the blood seeping out of my back as I listened to their heavy artillery making blood sausage out of my men still trapped at Dien Bien Phu."

"Some of them survived." Emma knelt beside him and stroked his muscular arm. "You could have made it back. You didn't have

to go crawling through enemy lines on your hands and knees."
His story erased her uneasiness. She could hardly believe that
Lucky Pierre had gotten things so twisted up. Emma had always
known that Constance Burton was verging on insanity.

"I was not going to be a prisoner." The set of Janvier's mouth
was grim. "I saw the newspaper photographs of those men after
they got out of the Viet camps. Walking skeletons. But that's not
the worst part. You have never been in prison, Emma. You don't
know what it's like being caged up like an animal, at the mercy of
keepers who don't care if you live or die. I remember hiding from
the Nazis, in that barn in France. That was my first experience
with prison. And my father was my first jailer."

"Your father?"

"The confinement—I couldn't stand it. I got out and joined
the Legion. They took my father's place." He mashed the butt of
his cigarette into the ashtray. "They told me when to fight, when
to jump from a plane, when to blow up a bridge. But I have quit
the Legion. Nobody tells me when to die. I will decide that for
myself when the time comes." Janvier grinned at her. "Do you
still love me?"

"Oh, Robert, I love you so."

Janvier stood up and lifted Emma into his embrace. "Yes, I
believe you do. I need your help, Emma. I have to get out of this
country. If any Legionnaire recognizes me, he will kill me. That
is how they deal with deserters, with people who have minds of
their own. Will you help me?"

"Oh, yes, yes!" The heat from his body poured over her like
hot lava. Her longing to be part of him was stronger than ever.
"That's why I stayed in Saigon, because I knew I would see you
again, when you were ready for me."

"We will go away together," Janvier breathed. "Tonight. A
Greek freighter in port is leaving for Hong Kong at midnight. I
know the captain. We have done business before. But now I have
nothing to sell him. We need money, Emma. He won't take us
without money."

Emma was stunned, but a warm glow came over her. In the

past, Janvier had always had so much money, and he had always been so generous to her. Now she could help him. "What about your—your business?" She hesitated, not wanting to reveal that Hazen had been spying on him. "Don't you have friends here?"

Janvier let out a guffaw. "My Corsican partners are worse than the Legionnaires. We had a disagreement in Haiphong, soon after you were there. They decided that since I was a fugitive from the Legion, I was less useful to them and they could cheat me out of my share. I took what was mine, but I had to fight for it. A couple of Corsican sons paid for their fathers' greediness. So now my old business partners are searching for me, too. They even killed the madames in my brothels and kidnapped the girls. What villains, what blackguards they are!" Janvier led Emma over to the bed. They sat down, clinging to each other. His eyes filled with tears. "I could not come to you sooner. They are more skilled than the Viet Minh in extracting information from their victims. I could not expose you to that kind of danger. You are all I have, Emma."

He pressed her back on the bed and kissed her passionately. His hands moved over her body. Emma returned his kisses eagerly, giving affirmation and assent. Whatever his love demanded, she would give. Even the last drop of her blood.

"Good." Janvier pulled himself away from her lips. "How much money do you have?"

Emma struggled to regain her senses. "All I have in my purse is a few piasters for meals and taxi fares. The rest is in the bank, at Crédit Fourcier. They open again at three o'clock."

"Very well, present yourself at the bank at three, *ma chère*. Take everything out of your account and change the money into French francs. American dollars will be even better if you can get them. If anyone gets nosy, tell them that you have to return home at once. Stress that it is an urgent matter. The death of your mother, perhaps. Then come back here to me." He leaned over her and kissed the hollow of her throat. "It won't be safe for me to leave this room until after dark. I have too many enemies in this city."

Emma sat up and gripped him fiercely. "Thank God you're safe. Thank God you escaped from Dien Bien Phu."

"I was lucky," he said. "I have always been lucky, especially when I met you, Emma. We have had some fine times in the past, haven't we? And so we shall again, away from this stinking city, this stinking country. I will change my name for the last time. Perhaps you would like to choose a new one for me? How about Monsieur and Madame Adam, in honor of the first man? Or would you like to be Mrs. Barrett Browning? Or Lady Waterloo Station? We can be anything we like from now on. What is the matter, Emma? You don't look very happy."

"Oh, I am." But her radiant smile faded and she began to sob as she recalled the agony of waiting for him. Months of pent-up tensions came pouring forth. "A—a whole ye-year has passed since you disappeared, Robert. A year of—of not knowing where you were, if you would ever come back to me. You could have sent word that you were all right. When—but—I would never have betrayed you."

"*Ma chère* Emma, don't you think I would have done that if I could? Oh, Emma, I spent two months in a Thai village in Laos, burning with fever, not knowing if my wound would heal or if I would die in a bamboo hut above a pig yard. When I could finally walk again, I made my way south by night, trying to avoid both the Viets and the French. Only my thoughts of you gave me the strength to continue. I had to be careful, *chérie*, very careful. After I got to Saigon, I tried to collect on old debts, but the people who owed me favors either were gone or would not help me. And you know what happened in Haiphong. You are the only one left, the only one who still cares about Robert Janvier. Do not look so sad. Do not weep. Let me kiss away your tears."

Their lips lingered together while he unfastened the buttons on her blouse and pulled it back over her shoulders.

Emma trembled so violently that she thought she would explode into a million shining particles, each one a star, each one a glittering witness to the power of this man to sunder reality into nothingness, and to transform nothingness into a love so real it was a living, breathing thing. His spell, his magic, his heat, his touch filled her with complete, universal knowledge. She responded to his fine, fierce lovemaking with matching ferocity. Their bodies rose and fell in perfect, fluid harmony, reaffirming their faith, proving their love, reestablishing the purpose of their creation.

But the moment the last tremors of his passion had released their bounty, he pushed her away. "You must go now. Do not rush. If someone stops you and wants to talk, make some excuse to get away, but don't act nervous. Be natural. Do you understand?"

"Yes, of course. Oh, Robert, are we really leaving tonight? Where are we going?"

"To Hong Kong first, then who knows? Get dressed. You must be waiting at the bank when it opens. When you have finished there, go to the Galerie d'Eden and buy me a few things. A suitcase, some shirts, another suit. I have written it all down for you."

Emma obeyed him. When she left the room, he was still lying on the bed, his hard nakedness gleaming under the wands of sunlight that shone through the slats of the shutters. As he smiled at her, a flush of happiness rushed to her cheeks. She had never loved him more.

The elderly clerk at the Crédit Fourcier called the manager over to look at Emma's identification. Once they had approved the withdrawal and the closing of her account, they discussed methods of payment. Could they give her a check? No. American dollars were out of the question, but they could give her French francs since she was leaving the country. Would she like half in piasters to purchase her fare home? No? The old man took his time counting out the bank notes. He moistened his fingers frequently and complained about the humidity and the wretched ceiling fans that served no purpose but to disarrange the papers in his cubicle. Emma was writhing impatiently by the time they had completed the transaction.

At five minutes to four, she walked quickly out of the bank. As she cleared the first set of doors she broke into a trot, but forced herself to slow down, remembering Janvier's orders not to run.

"Bah, the French government is no more efficient than their ridiculous army." Eliane de Mornay closed her fingers around Emma's upper arm, jerking her to a standstill on the steps right outside the bank. The shrill voice buzzed in Emma's ear like an angry bee. "I know that everyone in this stupid city thinks that I am growing fat on my pension as the widow of a general, but they should see what I have to go through to collect it. Fortunately, the president of this bank is a dear friend, and I know he will intercede for me. And you, dear Emma, you nearly collided with me a moment ago. Where are you going in such a hurry?"

"Away. I mean, my news has given me a new assignment back in the States, closer to my mother. She's very sick."

"Poor little one! I am sorry to hear that. When are you leaving?"

"Tonight." Emma cast a longing glance over her shoulder at the trishaw waiting by the curb. "That is, I'm not sure, but as soon as I can get away."

"Would you like me to talk to those idiots at Air France for you? If they told you they had no room on the evening plane to Hong Kong, they are lying. They always keep a few seats for diplomats and military people. Leave it to me, I will arrange everything."

"No, no, thank you, Madame de Mornay. It's not necessary, really. I'm sure I'll get a seat, if not tonight then on Wednesday. It's not that urgent."

"But with your mother so ill—"

"She's not that ill. Just a little. Will you excuse me? I have a lot to do—shopping and packing. *Au revoir.*"

The clerks at the Galerie d'Eden were even slower than the old man at the bank. They seemed to have on their shelves none of the items Emma wanted and kept ducking into their storerooms to check. It was past five-thirty when Emma got back to her room. She half-expected Janvier to be gone, but he was there, pacing furiously.

"Where have you been?" Emma started to explain, but he cut her off. "Never mind, just give me your purse." He snatched it and removed the envelope containing the money she had just withdrawn from the bank. He counted it swiftly. "Not as much as I had hoped, but it will take us part of the way. Now you must do one more thing for me before we can leave tonight, Emma. Go to Cholon, to Rue des Tous Saints behind the Grand Monde. That's a right turn off Rue des Marins, and then stop about half-way along. The house is on the right-hand side, the pink one with green shutters, number forty-two and a half. Here is the key. Your driver must wait for you. Upstairs in the front room, you will find two parcels. Bring them back here."

"But what do they look like, these parcels?"

"I cannot take time to describe them. You will see them at once. They are small and not very heavy. They will fit in the trishaw with you. But they are very important. Promise me that you will take good care of them. You will know what to do. Do you promise?"

"Yes, of course." Emma swallowed. "Are they—what if—what if the police are watching?"

"Police? Why should the police be interested in that house? Don't worry, you will be quite safe. Once again, do not hurry, do not act suspicious. But go at once. I will pack your things for you while you are away. Do not look so frightened, little Emma." He kissed her cheeks. "Nothing terrible will happen to you. My enemies are looking for a Frenchman, not a pretty blonde American girl." He pushed her toward the door.

"Oh, Robert, please hold me before I go."

"Plenty of time for all that later, when we are away from Saigon. Hurry now."

Emma did not find a trishaw until she was nearly in sight of the cathedral. Traffic on Avenue Gallieni was heavy for most of its two-mile length, and on the fringes of Cholon it backed up behind an overturned trailer that had been loaded with bales of old rags.

"*Maulen!*" Emma shouted. "*Maulen!* Faster! Faster!"

Her driver took it into his head to detour around the obstruction, but he quickly became lost in the maze of warehouses and shops in the side streets. An hour later, they pulled up at number 42½ Rue des Tous Saints. Shaking with anxiety, Emma instructed the man to wait.

Using Janvier's key, she unlocked the door and stepped into a cool entrance hall. After pausing for a moment until her eyes adjusted themselves to the dim light, she moved toward the stairs. The house was eerily silent. What were these parcels waiting for her in the room above her head? Opium? Forged currency? Gold or silver? They were small, Janvier had said, and not too heavy. Heroin? Why hadn't he taken them when he left the house?

Then she heard a high-pitched whining noise, like a bat squeaking. Frightened, she pressed herself against the wall and waited. The sound persisted. Carefully, her heart thumping wildly in her chest, Emma proceeded upward toward the landing at the top of the stairs.

The door to the front room was ajar. Emma approached it slowly, feeling her way along the wall. The sound grew louder. It was irregular, distressed. A caged animal, perhaps? A cat or a bird? Glancing down over the banister to reassure herself that the way to the street was still clear, Emma pushed the door open. She pressed her hands over her mouth to stifle a scream. As she did so, the noise that had so unnerved her changed from a whimper into a wail.

Two corpses lay in the middle of the floor, a Vietnamese woman and a man so large that he dwarfed her and made her seem like a child. Stepping closer, Emma gasped with horror when she recognized Lucky Pierre's profile. A trickle of blood had dried on his chin, like a jagged crayon mark. A broader stain spread over the back of his shirt. The fingers of his left hand were clenched around his red paratrooper's beret. He wore a gunbelt, but the weapon itself was still holstered.

The woman lay on her back. Her face was obscured by a veil of long black hair. She was wearing white silk trousers and a pink *ao dai*. A crimson flower blossomed in the center of her chest.

A small boy sat clutching her right hand, which was flung out to the side. He gazed up at Emma with dark, grave Western eyes that reminded her of Janvier. A few feet away, an infant thrashed in a cradle and screamed for attention.

Janvier's parcels.

21

APRIL 8, 1955

Dear Mom and Aunt Louise,

I'm on my way home. Hang on to your hats: I'm
bringing two children, war orphans. I don't know
yet how I'm going to take care of them, but I do
know that I can't abandon them. They're
Eurasian—French and Vietnamese—and because of
their mixed blood won't be accepted here. I know
this is all very sudden, and you're probably
wondering if I've lost my mind, but I have to do
what my heart tells me is right.

Giving the two bloody corpses a wide berth, Emma approached the cradle. Somewhat awkwardly, she slid her
hands under the child's back and bottom and picked it up. With
its eyes screwed up and its mouth gaping wide, it looked more
bestial than human. She had never held a baby before, and she
had no idea how to stop its crying. Even after she shook it gently
up and down, it continued to wail.

"Oh, please don't cry," she begged. "Hush, baby. Hush."

Holding it against her shoulder, she went over to the small boy,
who was crouching near the dead woman. He was no longer
a toddler; probably somewhere between four and five years of
age.

"Your mother is sleeping," Emma said in slow, careful French.
"Why don't we leave her while she sleeps? Will you come with
me?" She held out her hand. The boy hesitated; then he looked

down at the dead woman and released his grip on her stiffening fingers. "Come," Emma repeated, "let her sleep. I will bring you back later, after she wakes up." She walked to the door. After a moment he followed. Still refusing to take her hand, he crept down the stairs after her, one step at a time.

During the long jolting ride back to the villa, the baby continued to wail, and the little boy gripped the side of the vehicle. His eyes were wide, and Emma wondered if he had even ridden in a trishaw before.

The police would have to be told, of course. As well as the representatives of the new Diem government, the French government, and the French Allied Forces. She would be blamed for leaving the scene of the crime, and perhaps even suspected of complicity. But she needed to talk to Janvier first. Perhaps he could explain what had happened.

By the time they reached the villa, the exhausted baby had fallen asleep. Telling the boy to stay close to her, Emma climbed the steps to her room.

"Robert?"

She opened the door. Almost at once her eyes flashed to her desk. Her typewriter, the faithful Olivetti, was gone. So was the new suitcase she had bought for Janvier that afternoon. Her jewel box lay open on the bed, its contents emptied. The drawers of both desk and dresser gaped and the door of her armoire swung wide. Janvier had gone, taking with him everything that he could sell, including her wallet, her passport, and every cent she possessed.

Astounded by the magnitude of his betrayal, Emma could only stand and stare. Two minutes passed in sticky silence, after which the baby awakened with a volcanic eruption of noise. Only the small boy, standing in the doorway, remained stony-faced and calm, a miniature Buddha who seemed to accept every human failing as typical of the species.

Janvier. The dashing young paratrooper who had cut such a romantic figure in the boudoir and on the battlefield.

Janvier. The man who had inflamed Emma's passions to such

a degree that she wondered why she had never spontaneously combusted from the intense heat of her desire for him.

Janvier. To whom she had given her heart. In the past two years, he had stripped her of everything: her innocence, her dignity, her fresh and unspoiled beauty, and now all her salable possessions and even her limited savings. He had disappeared, leaving her with the offspring of his lissome Vietnamese *congai*. She sat down and the tears poured from her soul, but her eyes remained dry. He had permitted his native mistress to bear his bastards while denying Emma the same chance.

Hazen had been right. Janvier really was a murderer, a pimp, a criminal without a conscience, a seller of drugs, and a deserter from the battlefield. If only she had listened, and believed. No, Janvier had never loved her. Even his lovemaking that afternoon had been calculated to quell her suspicions and to lull her into a trancelike state of obedience. He had repaid her loyalty with perfidy, her love with treachery. After all she had given him, all she had sacrificed for him, he had left her with nothing. No, not nothing. His children. Had he loved their mother? Did he love them? She would never know.

"I hate you, Robert Janvier! I hate you!"

She cried aloud to the empty room in which the memory of the last hour they had spent together was as sharp as pain and as real as blood.

When she had recovered her composure, Emma took the children downstairs to Monsieur de Chesnay's studio. She found him sitting in the rattan armchair, sipping a Pernod while a young girl trimmed the gray hairs that bristled from his ears and his nostrils.

"I do not know what ails the women in this house," he growled when he saw the baby in her arms and the little boy slinking into the room behind her, "letting their brats crawl around unsupervised. I am sorry if those two bothered you."

"They're not yours, monsieur." Emma raised her voice so she could be heard over the baby's squalls. "They're mine."

"What did you say?"

"Monsieur, will you please call the police? I want to report a murder. In Cholon. They will have to act quickly if they want to catch the killer."

Emma gazed blearily at her three interrogators, a sharply uniformed senior Vietnamese policeman, a rumpled French officer from the Sûreté, and an orange-haired junior consul from the American embassy. She had told her story at least six times, in two different languages. Armed with her description of Janvier, detectives had already been dispatched to the airport and the docks to apprehend him. But no Greek freighters were anchored in the harbor. Emma was sure the police would not find him. Janvier knew this city and its escape routes too well. By now he was probably on his way to Phnom Penh. From there to Bangkok was only a short hop by plane. By tomorrow he could be on his way to India, and from there to Europe.

The investigators had pieced together a rough scenario of the shootings on Rue des Tous Saints. Corporal Lévêque, acting either on his own or on behalf of the Foreign Legion, had traced Janvier to his house. He may have urged Janvier to give himself up. Perhaps the two men had quarreled. In the end, Janvier had shot his old friend, his *copain*. The woman had tried to interfere, perhaps to protect her children, and he had shot her, too. They all agreed that he was an animal, a madman.

They might have been discussing a stranger, the subject of a sensational news story. At this moment, Emma felt nothing toward Janvier. She did not even know his real name. The remnants of her love for him had vanished the moment she entered her own room and discovered his final, absolute betrayal.

The American was concerned with the loss of Emma's passport. After a skilled forger had made a few changes, Janvier could easily use the document to admit himself to the United States. The younger consular official promised to inform the Immigration and Naturalization Service, the customs authorities, and the FBI, but he doubted they would find the man. In any case, an

American passport could be traded for hard currency in almost any country in the world.

"It will take a while for us to replace it," he warned Emma. "You could be stuck here for months."

The Vietnamese demanded to know how much she knew about the packet of heroin his men had found under a floorboard in the house on Rue des Tous Saints.

"Did you never suspect that this man was producing drugs to sell on the black market?" He seemed not to believe Emma's denial. "We could have arrested him and his friends, put them out of business. You are in serious trouble, mademoiselle."

The Frenchman seemed more interested in Janvier's personal history.

"If he hid from the Nazis, he must have been a Jew. And later he became a Legionnaire," he mused. "In any case, he appears to have been utterly without moral scruples. I am surprised that you did not see that."

"I saw what I wanted to see," Emma replied woodenly.

The Vietnamese interrupted. "He fell out with his Corsican and Chinese partners after Dien Bien Phu and, as a way of protecting himself after his return to Saigon, took up with the Binh Xuyen. You know about them, Mademoiselle Vaughan?"

"I know who they are. The gangsters who run this city."

The officer bridled. "Our prime minister is waging all-out war against those corrupt elements of our society—"

"You didn't know anything about that, did you, Miss Vaughan?" The American's freckled forehead was drawn into a worried frown. "A Binh Xuyen connection could look very bad for you at this point."

"I don't have any Binh Xuyen connections! I think these children should be in bed."

Janvier's son lay curled up in a fetal position in the corner of the sofa on which Emma was sitting. The baby, a girl child who the women in the de Chesnay household had decided was about nine months old, sprawled contentedly across Emma's lap, her bottom dry and diapered, and her belly stretched with the soft rice cereal that the de Chesnay kitchen seemed to be able to provide at a moment's notice. Her mouth was open and she snored softly.

"The French have left us thousands of these little mongrels to feed," the Vietnamese remarked. "I suppose our orphanages can make room for two more."

"No!" The three men looked at Emma in surprise. "These children are mine now. You are not putting them in an institution, do you hear me? Captain Janvier asked me to take care of them, and I will."

The Frenchman tried to dissuade her. A promise made to such a monster was not binding. After the way he had treated her, she owed him no loyalty. The tragedy on Rue des Tous Saints was unfortunate, but she did not have to compromise her future happiness for the sake of the children of a woman she had never met.

"I have made up my mind," Emma said. "I am going to adopt these children and take them back home with me. You can either help me or you can throw obstacles in my path, but you cannot take them away from me. I have powerful friends in this city."

She tried to think of one person she could call a powerful friend. The French were lame ducks, their influence eroded and their capacity for getting things done diminished. So far the Americans were wary of showing too much muscle. Those Vietnamese who had wielded power during the Bao Dai years were fading into the woodwork as those loyal to the new prime minister, Ngo Dinh Diem, asserted themselves. If Alan Hazen had been here, he would have worked strenuously on her behalf. But she had spurned him. Now she had no one.

After they had gone, Monsieur de Chesnay sat in the chair vacated by the American. "You did not endear yourself to them, I fear. They could make trouble for you."

"They couldn't make any more trouble for me than I've already made for myself."

"Do not make any sudden, rash decisions. You feel nothing for these children. How can you? You never saw them before today. Think it over, madame. What man will want to marry a woman who has two little ones, not even her own?"

"Right now I need money more than I need a husband. I'll wire Chicago tomorrow, beg F. X. McGraw's forgiveness, and ask him for an emergency loan. And then I'll go and see Eliane de Mornay."

"Madame de Mornay? But what can she do?"

"If she can't help me, no one can."

"I?" Eliane dropped two lumps of sugar into a cup of café au lait. "But what can I do? I am a poor widow, a woman without influence—"

"You know everyone in Saigon, you're close to the Americans, and you've always had every Frenchman here eating out of your hand." Emma, who had refused coffee, sat on the end of the chaise lounge in Eliane's boudoir while the lady of the house breakfasted in bed from a white wicker tray. "The question is, will you help me? I know we've never been friendly. You tried to warn me about Robert Janvier years ago, and I didn't listen. You don't owe me anything. All we have in common is a mutual friend."

"Ah, yes, dear Alan." Eliane smiled over the rim of her cup. "Where is he now, I wonder? He would certainly want me to assist you in a crisis. But I am not sure he would approve of this. What you are considering is madness, my dear girl. Why should a single lady with your youth and ambition want to saddle herself with a couple of brats, the children of a man she no longer loves? Or perhaps you do love him?"

"The man I loved never existed." Emma gazed down at her hands. "I never knew Robert Janvier. I'm glad. I would have killed him."

"You have grown to hate him," Eliane observed. "You might turn that hatred against his children."

"I wouldn't. Please, madame, you know they won't have a chance if they stay here. They're outcasts already. The Vietnamese don't want them; the French won't acknowledge them. They'll end up on the streets, as beggars or lepers or whores. As much as I hate Robert Janvier now, I don't want that to happen to his children."

Having finished her coffee, Eliane inserted a cigarette in a long holder and snapped a gold lighter. "Yes, I know of many such cases. Children who are neither wholly Vietnamese nor wholly French, discarded by one race, not welcomed by the other. They have to make their own way in the world, those poor little ones, and the world is a cruel and vicious place."

"They will be my children. Mine." Emma pressed her fists against her chest. "The only ones I'm ever likely to have. I will tell them the truth about their mother and the country they were born in. If they want to come back, to be Vietnamese, I won't stop them."

"You could not stop them if that is what they wanted." Eliane flicked ash into a saucer. "Listen to me, Miss Vaughan. Thousands of children have been orphaned and abandoned in this country, and they have grown up without the assistance of well-meaning Americans like yourself. How much time did that Frenchman Janvier ever spend with his children? None. Their mother was Vietnamese, and so are they. Take my advice. Turn them over to a foundling home and forget about them. And now you will have to excuse me." She moved the tray and swung her legs over the side of the bed. "I am meeting the wife of your ambassador at the Cercle Sportif. We are playing in a bridge tournament together."

"I don't know why I came here." Emma stood up. "I guess I didn't want to believe that all the horrible things people said about you were true. You really are the most self-centered, cold-hearted bitch in all of Southeast Asia. What I can't understand is how Alan Hazen, whom I credit with a fair amount of intelligence, could have fallen for your phony charm." She marched to the door and paused with her hand on the latch. "This may slow me down, but it won't stop me. I am not leaving this country without those kids. I don't care if it takes me five weeks or five years. They're mine now."

Eliane cocked an eyebrow but said nothing. As the door slammed, her crooked smile widened into a grin. Stretching her arms out in front of her, she waggled her fingers like a puppeteer jerking the strings of dancing marionettes.

"How very amusing," she said aloud.

She rang for her maid and demanded a paper and pencil. Ten minutes later, the servant was hurrying toward the nearest Post and Telegraph office with a wire to the headquarters of Chrome Petroleum in Fort Worth, Texas.

The plane taxied down the runway. Emma was alone with her children for the first time since she had found them. Monsieur de Chesnay's women had taken charge of them right up until the moment of their departure, which was accompanied by much blowing of noses and wiping of eyes. But now Emma was on her own. She felt more frightened than when she had walked along booby-trapped paths in the jungle.

The members of the de Chesnay household had adored tiny Lydia, who charmed everyone with her ready smile and the way she chirped to herself when she was content. James, her brother, maintained his reserve. He disliked being mauled by adults, and he preserved a careful distance between himself and the other children.

Emma had named the two after her maternal grandparents. She had been unable to learn their real names, or even the name of their mother. The boy, when questioned in French or Vietnamese, refused to speak. He was watchful and obedient, but silent. Emma wondered if the shock of his mother's death had rendered him permanently mute.

Janvier's neighbors on Rue des Tous Saints had seen little of the children's mother. The police had located one old woman who had been a servant in the house. According to her, Janvier and his wife had lived peacefully and privately, with no thought for the outside world. She had understood that the children's mother was from the north, probably Hanoi, and that she had no friends or family in Saigon.

Emma was still astonished at the ease with which her problems with Saigon's various bureaucracies had been solved. Papers that might have lain for weeks at the bottom of a stack rose to the top with magical swiftness and received prompt attention. Those Vietnamese social service agencies that might have blocked her plans to adopt Janvier's children placed no obstacles in her path. Indeed, Prime Minister Ngo Dinh Diem himself had signed the final papers. Even the Americans cooperated. Within three weeks of the double murder, she had a new passport for herself and the children. If Emma hadn't known better, she might have credited Madame de Mornay with exerting her influence on their behalf. As it was, she attributed such untypical Asian efficiency to incredible luck.

As the plane lifted off, Lydia whimpered a little. James, slumped in a seat by the window, showed no interest in the tilting landscape outside. Emma looked over his head. For once, she had been too preoccupied with other problems to feel afraid of flying. Below them, the city looked flat and colorless in the heat, a sprawling and ragged refugee trying to cover its nakedness with a few trees. On all sides, the arms of the Mekong River stretched to the sea, embracing swamps and grasslands, paddy fields and scrubland, small villages and the busy capital. For the first time in decades, the countryside was at peace. Emma hoped the peace would last forever.

An Air France stewardess hovered over them. "Your kids are adorable. Will their father be joining you in Hong Kong?"

"No." Emma shook her head. I certainly hope not, she thought.

The plane hit some rough pockets. Lydia vomited all over Emma's skirt. James spilled a container of orange juice onto her shoes. When the stewardess handed him a coloring book, he laid it carefully aside and stared blankly at the back of the seat ahead of him. Lydia started to howl and would not be calmed. The other passengers regarded Emma and her brood with loathing.

By the time the plane landed in Hong Kong, Emma's nerves were frayed and her patience was exhausted. So this was motherhood. She should have taken Eliane's advice and left Janvier's brats in Saigon. Instructing James to hold tight to her skirt, she crossed the macadam to the terminal. No friendly faces waited to greet her, only crowds of rushing strangers. Emma grabbed James's hand and held him tightly, ignoring his struggles and his dragging feet.

In the middle of the terminal building, James rebelled and refused to take another step. His eyes were wide and his face was very pale. He seemed tense and clearly terrified. Emma tried to reason with him. When she attempted to pick him up, he kicked and threw himself convulsing on the floor. Emma was mortified. She had lost control of both of her children, and she had not the slightest notion of how to get it back.

"James, stop it at once. Stop it or I'll spank you."

He began banging his head against the floor. Of course, he did not understand English, and very little French. Frantic, Emma looked around. She hoped to see a Vietnamese face, to find someone who could explain to the child that he had no reason to be afraid. But the other travelers streamed past without even looking at them.

"James, I beg you, please stop." She knelt down and tried to protect his head from the hard floor. "I promise you, no one will hurt you. Please, calm yourself. Calm yourself."

Lydia's wails joined her brother's convulsions. One of her tiny flailing fists struck Emma's nose. Tears of pain and frustration rushed to the new mother's eyes. She had never felt so helpless, and so desperate.

"Emma. May I help?"

She looked up. Alan Hazen was striding toward her, a briefcase in his hand and a raincoat slung over his arm. She was so amazed to see him that she nearly dropped Lydia.

"Alan! What—what are you doing here?"

"Meeting someone."

"Oh. I—uh—" Lydia's lusty wails drowned out Emma's words. She gestured helplessly at the still-convulsing little boy, whose forehead had begun to bleed. Without another word, Hazen dropped his briefcase and raincoat and lay down flat on the floor in his gray business suit so that his head was on a level with the child's. He spoke softly and persuasively, in fluent Vietnamese. Gradually the child stopped thrashing. He turned his head and watched Hazen with troubled eyes. And then he uttered a few choked words.

Hazen glanced up at Emma. "He wants to go home to his mother. He says you promised he could go back to her."

"Oh, God. He can't, Alan. She's dead. I've been wondering how to explain it to him—"

"Tell him the truth. He has a right to know, and he's old enough to understand." Rising, he lifted James gently and set him on his feet; then he took the child's hand and led him to a bench in a quiet corner. Meanwhile, Emma carried the squalling Lydia into the women's lavatory to change her. When she emerged ten minutes later, she saw James sitting in Hazen's lap. The tall man's arms nearly engulfed the small body. "He'll be all right now," Hazen said when Emma approached them. "He just didn't understand what was happening. Since when have you taken up babysitting?" His glance took in her untidy hair and stained skirt and the half-dozen items of hand luggage that lay scattered twenty feet away in the middle of the concourse. "From the looks of things, you could use some instruction."

"They're mine."

"Yours?" Hazen looked astonished. "I didn't know. I mean, Eliane never mentioned—"

"I adopted them. They were Robert's, but he—he abandoned them. Legally, I'm their mother now, but in their eyes I'm just the shrill foreigner who snatched them away from their home and took them to live with strangers and then put them inside a big airplane that made them feel sick." Emma, holding Lydia against her shoulder, felt the warm wetness of baby spittle seeping through the fabric of her blouse. She sat, and transferred the baby to a towel on her lap. She was learning. "I don't blame them for hating me. I don't know what I would have done if you hadn't come along."

"You'd have managed. You're a capable woman."

"But I can't even communicate with James."

Hazen tickled Lydia's foot. She smiled and shook her fists at him, then sang a phrase of her favorite tuneless song. Charmed, he smiled back.

"How would you like a father for both of them?" he said.

"Oh, Alan, no." Tears rushed to Emma's eyes. "It's too late for that—"

"I never filed for that divorce. Officially, you and I are still married. I'd like us to stay that way. For a long, long time."

Emma shook her head. "I don't need to remind you that these children are Robert Janvier's."

"I haven't forgotten that. They're God's children, too, aren't they? And they had a mother. She would have wanted this for them, parents who would love them, provide for them, bring them up in a country where their looks won't be a barrier to happiness. They deserve a future in spite of Janvier. And we can give it to them, Emma. The two of us, together."

The baby started to fuss. Emma dug in her purse for a rattle. Lydia grabbed it and hurled it away. Hazen retrieved the rattle, but instead of handing it back, he held it in front of the child's nose for a second or two, then made it vanish. Lydia looked astonished, and even James blinked his eyes rapidly to prove to himself that he wasn't dreaming. Hazen snapped his fingers and the rattle appeared again. Both children laughed.

"Where did you learn that?" Emma gasped.

"I've been taking lessons back in Chicago. I have to do something to keep myself awake between classes at the university. After Indochina, math is pretty dull business. But I'll stick with it until something more interesting turns up. F. X. tells me he's holding a job for you. That's nice. I'll be able to spend a lot of time with the children while you're working."

"But Alan," Emma said despairingly, "I'm such a rotten candidate for marriage. A man would have to be a fool to take on a crowd like this. And you're no fool."

"A man would have to love you very much."

Hazen removed a quarter from Lydia's ear. James was delighted, and laughed out loud. Hazen told him to look in the pockets of his shorts. He did so, and found a cat's-eye marble, five copper pennies, a baseball trading card, and a tiny jade horse, the best Hazen's pockets could produce on short notice.

"And I do love you, Emma." Hazen's tone was warm and confident. He was about to win his dearest hope, and he was trembling with excitement and elation. "That's no illusion. I am not in the business of telling lies anymore. I knew you'd come to your senses sooner or later, and so I waited. I would have waited twenty years. Forty. Until you were ready to give your love to the one man who will love you in spite of everything, forever and ever until death do us part."

Emma sat quietly with her head bowed. Tears rolled down her cheeks and fell on Lydia's bonnet.

"Don't cry. Beautiful Emma. Emma of the golden hair and the flashing green eyes. Don't cry. You have nothing to be ashamed of. You followed your heart in good faith until you realized the path was false. And now you've come back to the real world. Don't cry. Life is good, Emma. A triumph for people who know how to love." Leaning forward, Hazen lifted her chin and kissed her. "Wait a minute, what's this?"

Smiling, he plucked a wedding ring from her lips. Janvier had stolen the first gold band Hazen had given her, along with the rest of her jewels. "Ah, a sign from heaven. Be my wife again, Emma. Give me the gift of yourself. I don't need anything else to be a happy man."

"I will." Emma held out her hand and let him slip the ring on her finger. "We'll be happy, Alan. I know we will. Thank you for this."

"And thank you." Hazen opened his arms and enfolded them in a fierce, warm embrace. "Thank you one and all."

ABOUT THE AUTHOR

NATASHA PETERS is the author of *Savage Surrender*, *Dangerous Obsession*, *The Masquers*, *The Enticers*, *The Immortals*, and *Darkness into Light*. Under her real name, Anastasia Cleaver, she lives with her husband in a drafty old Victorian house on a hill near Philadelphia. The ideas for her books have taken her to many foreign lands in the East and the West, and through volumes of history and biography. She is also an actress, an artist, a singer, and a grower of old-fashioned roses.